LOVE'S RESCUE

KEYS
—OF—
PROMISE
1

LOVE'S RESCUE

A NOVEL

Christine Johnson

Revell

a division of Baker Publishing Group
Grand Rapids, Michigan

© 2015 by Christine Elizabeth Johnson

Published by Revell
a division of Baker Publishing Group
P.O. Box 6287, Grand Rapids, MI 49516-6287
www.revellbooks.com

Printed in the United States of America

Library of Congress Cataloging-in-Publication Data
Johnson, Christine (Christine Elizabeth)
    Love's rescue : a novel / Christine Johnson.
       pages cm. — (Keys of promise ; 1)
    ISBN 978-0-8007-2350-7 (pbk.)
       1. Teenage girls—Fiction. 2. Tomboys—Fiction. 3. Family life—Fiction.
    4. Family secrets—Fiction. 5. Ship captains—Fiction. I. Title.
    PS3610.O32395L68 2015
    813'.6—dc23   2015000434

Scripture quotations are from the King James Version of the Bible.

15 16 17 18 19 20 21   7 6 5 4 3 2 1

For my husband, my captain

Hope deferred maketh the heart sick:
but when the desire cometh, it is a tree of life.

Proverbs 13:12

Prologue

October 11, 1846

The gale nearly knocked Elizabeth Benjamin flat. In all of her sixteen years, she'd never experienced such terrible winds, and Key West enjoyed its share of storms. She held fast to her brother's hand. At eleven, Charlie usually rebelled at her mothering. Not today.

"Maybe we shouldn't be here." His words could barely be heard above the howling wind.

Elizabeth was beginning to think the same, but time had nearly run out. Within days, she must sail for Charleston, where she was expected to secure a prominent match. That meant leaving her beloved Key West and the man who had captured her affections. Today might be her only opportunity to change the course her parents had set out for her.

She and Charlie had nearly reached the harbor, where Rourke O'Malley's wrecking sloop was moored. Just thinking of him bolstered her courage. If he could endure such weather, so could she. Though the rain now pelted down, ruining the fine blue muslin gown she'd donned just for him, maybe he'd see her as courageous.

"Can we go home?" Charlie asked.

She yanked her brother toward the wharves. "We need to secure our skiff."

The twelve-foot boat belonged to Charlie, but he only went sailing when she bribed him. She adored the freedom of the turquoise seas and seized every chance to improve her seafaring skills. That secret love cost her many an evening helping Charlie complete his studies.

When she'd told her maid this morning why they must leave the house in such weather, Anabelle had shaken her head and proclaimed that Mother would tan both their hides when she found out.

"We will be home before Mother returns," Elizabeth had assured her. She could wriggle anything past the girl who giggled with her every night after the lamps were blown out. "She'll never know we were gone."

The striking, caramel-colored maid grinned. "You're a fool for him."

Elizabeth had pretended she didn't know who Anabelle meant, which was silly, considering their every conversation centered on him. Rourke O'Malley wasn't the richest wrecker in Key West, but he was by far the handsomest and most daring. He wore his sun-streaked dark hair pulled back at the nape in the fashion popular decades before. His bronzed skin and eyes the color of the emerald depths made her stomach flutter. His smile left her speechless. For the first time in her life she'd seen an advantage to being born female.

If only he would stop treating her like the barefoot child she'd once been. At the last dance, he'd chosen older girls for partners. With her, he talked of the voyage across the straits to his native Harbour Island, or Briland as he sometimes called it, of turtling and wrecking. He inquired after her fishing exploits and noted how she'd sailed Charlie's skiff past his sloop on a perfect beam reach. Her excellent seamanship ought to show him how perfectly matched they were, but instead he'd danced with empty-headed girls. He'd even bowed and kissed her friend Caroline's hand, but not hers. Never hers.

Well, today he'd see her as a woman.

Elizabeth stomped forward, pulling the reluctant Charlie with her. They turned off Caroline Street to take their usual route to the wharves, but the boardwalk across the tidal pond was flooded. Though Charlie begged to go back, Elizabeth refused. By the morrow, Rourke might have sailed or, even worse, begun to court one of those addle-brained girls who whispered behind their fans whenever he walked into a room. The ship to Charleston might arrive to whisk her away. Good things did not come to those who waited.

So she tugged Charlie another block to Whitehead Street, which had a small bridge over the narrow end of the pond. Even there, the water ran deeper than she'd ever seen, nearly to the planks. If this gale continued, the bridge would be underwater too, necessitating an even lengthier return.

After they rounded the corner onto Front Street, the wharves lay ahead, but the two-story warehouses blocked her view of the vessels except for a smattering of mastheads. Usually the harbor was so full of ships that the masts sprouted like grass. Some of the masters must have decided to haul anchor and ride out the gale at sea.

Not Rourke. Please, not Rourke.

Heart pounding, Elizabeth hurried her pace over the coral

gravel. One foot landed in a puddle, drenching her kid leather shoe. The closer they drew to the harbor, the more water pooled on the ground. Soon wet feet could not be avoided. The skies loosed again. Elizabeth squinted into the windblown rain, trying to make out the warehouses that had been so clear moments before.

The wind shoved each breath back into her chest, which was already aching from the stays she'd insisted Anabelle cinch particularly tight. Only when they reached the lee of Tift's warehouse could she take in enough air. Though this warehouse was built solidly, the old one nearby creaked and moaned. Charlie pointed fearfully at its roof, which had already lost a few shingles.

Elizabeth could not be deterred by a shaky old building.

She pulled Charlie around the corner and into the full force of the wind. The seas, whipped up by the northeast gale, crashed over the piers and sprayed high into the air. The water, ordinarily several feet below the docks at high tide, now overran them. Charlie's tiny skiff, once moored with the other dinghies at the base of the nearest pier, was gone. The few vessels left in the harbor strained against their anchor lines, barely visible in the howling mists. With the water so high, they looked as if they could sail straight onto Duval Street.

Charlie's hand gripped hers even more tightly. Perhaps he'd been right.

She couldn't see Rourke's sloop through the rain and sea spray. He must have left with those who chose to weather the storm at sea. All her preparations had been for naught. If he did not return once the storm passed, she had no choice but to sail for Charleston. He would return. He had to return.

"We'll go home," she shouted, but the wind carried her words away.

Charlie clung to her. Terror danced in his eyes.

She motioned back toward the way they'd come. This had been a bad idea. Best return while they could. But before she could move, a terrible blast of wind caught her voluminous skirts and shoved her to the ground. She lost hold of Charlie, and the slight boy fell to his knees.

She reached for him, but her fingers brushed just short of his hand. "Charlie!"

He could not hear.

She tried to rise, but the wind pressed her down. It suffocated like a blanket pressed over her face. Only by lowering her mouth to the crook of her elbow could she draw in a breath.

Her brother struggled to his feet only to tumble farther away.

She crawled toward him. The rough coral rock ripped at her lace and bows, and sand ground into the fine muslin gown.

Then she saw the waves. They'd crested the wharves and rolled toward her, turning the land into a shallow sea. The first wave dampened her hands and knees. The next rolled in deeper. She tried again to stand, to get to Charlie.

He stared at her, his eyes wide. He could not swim, had refused to learn.

Oh, that she had not donned six petticoats and a bustle. In the murky water, the garments tangled around her legs and weighed her down. Oh, that she'd listened to Anabelle and stayed home where she belonged. If anything happened . . .

Elizabeth could not allow doom to seize a toehold. This moment required courage.

She cupped her hands around her mouth and yelled, "I'm coming for you!"

Charlie showed no sign he'd heard her.

With all her strength she rose to her hands and knees and

inched toward her brother. He'd reached high ground near the old warehouse and was safely out of the water. If he could get into the lee of the building, he could stand. If he had the strength. If the water didn't rise higher.

Again she attempted to stand. The swirling water knocked her down. She cried out. Seawater filled her mouth. She gagged on the brine and coughed it out. When she'd regained her balance, she noticed the surging sea had carried her even farther from her brother.

Despair knocked, but she could not let it take hold. She must reach her brother, but how? Another wave rolled past, and she struggled to hold her ground.

The sea! Rather than fighting the waves, she could use them to her advantage. If she allowed each one to push her forward and angled toward the warehouse, she could reach her brother and bring him to safety.

Crack!

The sharp report came from above. Looking up, she saw with horror that the warehouse roof heaved up and down. Shingles swirled like a maddened flock of gulls. A piano-sized section tilted upward, a giant flap of heavy wood, and then a gust ripped it free. For one agonizing moment the chunk hung in midair. Then it began to spin. Down, down, down.

"Charlie!"

He did not hear.

She waved her arms.

He did not see. The section of roof struck him on the back of the legs. He flopped to the ground like a rag doll.

"Charlie!" This cry proved as useless as the first, for he did not move so much as a finger.

Fear drove her limbs through the churning waters. He could

not be dead. God would not let an innocent boy die. Charlie hadn't even wanted to come to the wharf. She'd talked him into it.

Please, God. Let him live.

She hoped her fervent plea would be enough to capture divine attention. Yet as she drew near and saw the pallor of her brother's face, she knew that her words had blown away on the wind.

1

Four Years Later
Off the Florida Keys

Crack!

The sharp report jolted Elizabeth from the muddle of dream and memory.

A quick survey of her surroundings confirmed she was indeed aboard the schooner *Victory*, not battling the hurricane that had devastated Key West. The dull light from the gimbaled oil lamp revealed little of the cabin's mahogany paneling, but it illuminated the worried faces of her maid and great-aunt. The lamp squeaked and tilted with each pitch and roll of the vessel. Aunt Virginia eyed it with the same suspicion she'd harbored since Charleston.

"This voyage will be my death." Aunt fluttered a plump hand before her pallid face.

Elizabeth gritted her teeth rather than point out that her great-aunt was the one who had insisted on joining them. Instead she forced a smile. "Soon we will reach home."

Home. Her stomach knotted at the thought of what awaited

her there. Charlie. The terrible void that Mother's death had left. She took as deep a breath as her stays would allow, but neither the pain nor the stale cabin air could remove the crushing numbness that had gripped her since they'd received the news.

She brushed at the wrinkles in the black crape skirt and then grabbed the bunk's frame when the ship pitched sharply forward. Her chair scraped an inch or two across the plank floor before the vessel righted.

"We're going to drown," wailed her great-aunt, who occupied the lower bunk. The sixty-five-year-old woman had kept company with a bucket from the moment they'd left Charleston harbor. Other than the stop in Saint Augustine and the brief pause at Fort Dallas to take on a pilot, she either moaned or complained for every one of the six hundred miles.

Elizabeth had lost patience five hundred and fifty miles ago.

"We're perfectly safe." She said the words automatically now. Her mother—Aunt Virginia's niece—had suffered the agonies of yellow fever. What was a little tossing about on rough seas?

"But those terrible noises. It sounds like the ship is going to break to bits."

Though the noise that had jolted Elizabeth out of troubled slumber *had* sounded unusual, admitting it would send Aunt Virginia into hysterics. So again, she consoled. "Those noises are normal aboard ship." Two sea voyages might not have made her an expert, but she had heard the creaks and groans of many a moored vessel when she was a girl. "A seafarer grows accustomed to such things."

"Perhaps sailors do, but not us poor women." Aunt launched into the next part of her endlessly repetitive argument. "I don't understand why the captain didn't offer us his quarters. We would have been much more comfortable there. If Jonathan knew, he would dispense with the man at once."

Elizabeth tried again to emulate her mother's patience. After all, that was the entire purpose of the voyage, to prove to Father that she had matured into a proper young woman. "We are fortunate the mates offered us their room."

"You make it sound as if they gave up fine accommodations." Aunt Virginia swept a plump arm to encompass every corner of the cabin. "Two bunks!" She sniffed. "Straw mattresses full of fleas."

"It's better than sleeping in hammocks with the crew."

"They wouldn't dare. My nephew owns this ship."

"I understand he owns a share of it," Elizabeth corrected, "along with other investors."

"Well, that's neither here nor there." Aunt Virginia heaved a petulant sigh and dabbed at her mouth with a lace-trimmed handkerchief. "I simply hope we arrive before I perish."

Elizabeth's maid, Anabelle, rolled her eyes, the whites stark against her caramel complexion. "Ain't no one be doin' no dyin'."

Anabelle spoke flawless English and could read and write, but Aunt Virginia looked suspiciously on any Negro who had learning. After the first whipping, Anabelle had chosen to play the role of a simpleton in front of Aunt Virginia. Elizabeth had been indignant at the rough treatment, but Anabelle begged her to let the matter rest. Raising a fuss would only make her life more difficult.

"When will this end?" Aunt moaned.

"It won't be much longer." Elizabeth offered her a sip of lukewarm tea.

"I don't want any of your tea. It's dreadful, probably moldy.

Heaven knows how they keep anything dry on this ship. Why, water is running down the wall."

Elizabeth's gaze shot to the wall behind the bunk. "Impossible."

"Don't you believe me?" Aunt harrumphed. "The bedding is positively damp."

"But that's an interior wall." She reached across her aunt and did indeed feel dampness. That wasn't good. She needed something to distract everyone from this disturbing discovery. "Let's read from the Bible. I'll fetch a lamp."

Aunt waved a hand. "Have your girl bring it."

While Elizabeth pulled her aunt's Bible from her trunk, Anabelle unfastened the lamp from its holder. With sure steps, she carried it to Elizabeth.

"Would you be wantin' me ta hold it for you, Miss Lizbeth?"

"I suppose you must." She was grateful her aunt didn't mention again the inconvenience of not having a lamp near the bunks. "Bring your stool near."

Once everyone was situated, Aunt Virginia suggested a passage. "Shall we have the parable of the prodigal son, Elizabeth dear?"

More like the prodigal daughter. No doubt her aunt had chosen that particular parable to point out Elizabeth's faults. After all, she was now returning home without having accomplished the one thing her parents had insisted upon—marriage. She regretted adding yet one more disappointment to her father's heavy burden.

"Perhaps the wedding feast at Cana would be better?" Aunt hinted with a gleam in her eye.

Even worse. Elizabeth had discouraged every suitor who'd called at her aunt's house. Aunt scolded that she was too particular, but none could compare to Rourke. Elizabeth had tried, truly she had, but the men of Charleston paled alongside a daring wrecker.

"Cana it shall be," Aunt decided. "A wedding always lifts one's spirits. Soon you'll be out of mourning and able to accept suitors, though with one exception I can't imagine there being a single respectable gentleman in such a godforsaken wilderness."

"It is not a wilderness, and there are plenty of respectable gentlemen."

Aunt lifted an imperious eyebrow. "That is not what your father wrote, and considering his . . . well, we shall leave it at that. Your father would know as well as anyone the quality of eligible suitors in Key West. That is why they insisted you come to Charleston. Poor Helen." She sniffed and dabbed at her nose. "She would be so disappointed."

The mention of Elizabeth's mother cast a pall over her spirits. She had indeed disappointed Mother, who had encouraged her to make a good match. Yet her parents had dismissed as frivolous the only match that mattered.

The wind howled and the seas battered the hull, but nature's tempests could not surpass the storm in Elizabeth's heart. For four years she'd tried unsuccessfully to forget Rourke O'Malley. Soon she would set foot in his home port. There she could not avoid him. He might appear on the wharves or any street. One look into those green eyes and all other suitors would fade into the background. Once again she would be at odds with Father.

He did not like wreckers as a rule. He opposed them in admiralty court. But he didn't truly know Rourke. He didn't know the strength of his character. He didn't know what Rourke had done for her.

Shame colored her cheeks.

The ship rolled violently, throwing Elizabeth out of the past. Anabelle fell off her stool. The lamp tipped and wobbled when her elbow hit the floor. Aunt Virginia clutched the counterpane to her throat, her eyes wide and cap askew. Elizabeth grabbed the teapot, ready to douse the flame, but Anabelle regained her balance and set the lamp on the desk.

Elizabeth took a shuddering breath and set down the teapot.

"Best get that lamp back in the holder before you drop it," Aunt Virginia commanded.

"Yes, Miz Virginia."

"A well-trained girl is sure of foot," Aunt said to Elizabeth. "Training and discipline are essential. Remember that. The mistress must take command."

"Mother always had the servants' respect without barking out orders."

"I'm sure she did, dear." Aunt patted her hand. "But you haven't had the benefit of her instruction. Follow my lead, and you will do well."

Elizabeth could not read in such poor light. She put Aunt's Bible back in her trunk. "But things are different in Key West."

"Nonsense." Aunt smoothed the counterpane. "Servants are the same everywhere. You must show your Mr. Finch that you can manage a household."

Elizabeth cringed. Aunt considered him the only eligible suitor in Key West, but she found the man insufferably dull. "He is not my Mr. Finch."

"He soon will be, if I'm not mistaken."

Percival Finch had paid numerous visits to Aunt Virginia's house last winter and spring. Though he was perfectly man-nered and possessing passable looks, Elizabeth had found him even more devoid of spirit than other callers—and utterly unlike Rourke. All eyes turned to Captain O'Malley when he entered a room. If not for Mr. Finch's gaudy waistcoats, a person could forget he was there. His departure had been a relief until she learned her father had hired him as clerk.

"I wish Mr. Finch hadn't left before you decided to return to Key West." Aunt Virginia sighed for what must be the hundredth time. "He is such pleasant company and so dedicated to your comfort. He would have made an excellent escort on this voyage. He will make a fine match for you. Your father agrees. I'm certain you will get reacquainted in no time."

"My father agrees?"

Aunt nodded. "Your mother did too."

Again the ship pitched forward, but that was not nearly as alarming as Aunt Virginia's news. If Mother and Father approved of Mr. Finch, she would never be rid of the man.

Aunt Virginia pressed her handkerchief to her mouth. "I do wish this were over."

"Mr. Buetsch indicated we might well arrive in Key West by morning."

"Morning! We'll be dead by morning thanks to this terrible storm."

Elizabeth rose, irritated at the thought of facing Mr. Finch again. "It's just an autumn squall."

"Like four years ago? That was no squall, was it?"

The painful memory of that day came back as vividly as if it had just occurred. Once she'd reached her brother, she'd tried to wake him, had held up his head as the waters rose, but she could neither rouse him nor pry his legs from under the heavy piece of roof. The water had risen higher and higher until it lapped against Charlie's shoulders. She'd given up hope. Then out of the mists Rourke had appeared, strong and valiant, like a knight of King Arthur's court.

"That wasn't a squall," she whispered. "It was a hurricane."

That hurricane had ripped apart the island and their lives. Only a handful of buildings had survived unscathed. Their house had lost its roof, and many of their belongings had washed away. But the greatest damage could not be measured in missing boards or rotted clothing.

After depositing Elizabeth on high ground, Rourke had gone back to get her brother. Though she clung to the mangrove trees through the night and into the next morning, neither one returned. Only when the clouds retreated and the full devastation could be seen did she learn he'd taken Charlie to the now-roofless Marine Hospital. There doctors saved his life but not the use of his legs.

The ship lurched again, this time with a grinding crunch, but Elizabeth barely felt it. Her aunt's mouth moved, but she didn't hear it. She heard only the sobbing of her mother as she'd held Charlie's motionless hand.

"Why would he have gone to the harbor in such weather?" Mother had cried.

Elizabeth had stood silent, unable to admit her guilt. The seconds had stretched on, broken only by the whistle of wind and muted sobs. She tried to confess but could not bring the words to her lips.

Then Rourke answered. "He came to see me."

Elizabeth squeezed her eyes shut. Rourke had taken the blame, and she'd let him. She drew in a ragged breath and blinked fast to keep back the tears.

At first she'd felt relief. Then the repercussions had begun. Father directed his anger at Rourke. Mother spent her days nursing her son back to life. Elizabeth sailed to Charleston as planned. She'd gone gladly rather than face the truth of her choices.

Now the truth waited for her, poised like an eel ready to strike.

Yet as she felt water soak through her cloth slippers and heard the hull creak ominously, she wondered if she'd ever have to face it.

⁓⁜⁓

"Fool," Rourke O'Malley muttered, spyglass to his eye. "They're heading straight for the reef."

Either the schooner's master hadn't hired a pilot, or he'd secured an incompetent one. Any seaman familiar with these waters knew better than to set that course in heavy weather. The schooner was large enough to carry both passengers and cargo. Against the backdrop of the last gasps of light along the western horizon, he could make out that her sails were tattered. The foremast had snapped off, and the vessel was sitting low. Either her holds were filled with heavy cargo, or she was taking on water.

He tensed with the familiar rush of fear and exhilaration. A wrecked vessel could bring riches to the wreck master—the first to reach the foundered ship—but it also brought danger. Many a wrecker had perished salvaging a ship. Some slipped overboard and were crushed between the two vessels. Divers drowned when the wreck shifted and pinned them in the submerged holds.

An active wrecker's career was short, and Rourke had already spent over a decade in the trade. He needed just one good award to set up as a merchant and ship owner, where the most profit

23

could be earned. One valuable wreck would give him enough to build his own warehouse. Then he would collect the fees, rather than hand them over to the men who currently controlled the wharves and commerce in Key West.

"She be sittin' low," called out John Malley, his longtime chief mate from back home in the Bahamas. Upon emancipation, John had taken a shortened form of Rourke's family name rather than that of the master who'd cruelly abused him. "Prob'ly holed."

Rourke wasn't willing to concede. "The hatch covers might be loose, making her take on water."

John grinned, his teeth white in the gleam of the lantern. No words needed to be exchanged for Rourke to know that his friend also dreamed of treasure. Few Negroes could ever hope to gain wealth. Even after emancipation, only the most menial jobs were open to them. Across the Caribbean, slavery and the lack of opportunity had driven many to piracy, including the infamous Black Caesar. Though Negroes were prized as divers, most wreckers paid them a pittance. Rourke paid each man according to his skill and effort, not the color of his skin.

Some in Key West, like Charles Benjamin, suggested a Negro hadn't the wits to serve as mate, but Rourke wouldn't have any other man. John knew these waters. He could read the skies, and he wasn't afraid to dive wrecks. Once Rourke stepped down from captaining his ship, John would make a fine master.

Rourke squinted into the wind. Though he'd anchored the *Windsprite* in a sheltered cove, the swirling tempest whipped even the shallows into peaks. This was shaping up to be the storm of the season.

"She be goin' down," John said. As if in answer, the schooner

24

lurched oddly. "She hit da reef." If she wasn't taking on water before, she would be now.

Rourke held his breath and watched. "I think she's still moving."

John shook his head.

Rourke couldn't give up hope. He peered through the glass. The schooner's deck and cabin lights still bobbed forward. Darkness would soon swallow all but those lights. If the reef got her, even the lights would vanish. "We'd best lend assistance. On that heading, she'll only get in worse trouble."

"All hands on deck!" John rubbed his hands together. "We be gettin' fed tonight."

Fed. The distasteful term had circulated aboard Rourke's ship for years. When a vessel foundered and broke up, Rourke and his men stripped the cargo and rigging from its bones and ferried off any survivors.

Please, Lord, let them all live.

Rourke swallowed the lump that had formed in his throat. With every passing year it got harder to witness the drownings, especially the children. No child should die before his time, and drowning was the worst death of all. To gasp for air and draw in only water. He shuddered as the pale form of a motionless boy flashed through his mind. Little Charlie Benjamin.

Rourke, you're getting soft. Maybe it was time to retire. Just one big salvage award and he would. Maybe this would be the one.

He scanned the charcoal-gray horizon for other wreckers.

"We be alone," John confirmed.

He was right. Rourke couldn't spot a single twinkle of light or splotch of black that marked a wrecker in pursuit. He lowered the spyglass. If the schooner wrecked, he'd be wreck master. He would garner the largest share of the prize in wreckers' court. He gripped the gunwale as his pulse pounded.

His crew prepared to haul anchor and set sail. The sloop rocked wildly despite its sheltered anchorage. After all these years afloat, Rourke barely noticed it, but the new man, Tom Worthington, clung to the gunwale as he inched his way aft.

"Lights out, Captain?" Tom called out with eager anticipation.

"No!" Rourke barked. "We don't do things that way on this ship."

Some masters and ship owners claimed wreckers used lights, or lack of them, to lure vessels into danger. That might have been true in the lawless era two decades ago. But times had changed, and every wrecker was now licensed and had to abide by the rules. Break them, and the judge would yank that license and leave a man to fishing and sponging to eke out an existence. Poor exchange for the chance at wealth.

"Flash the danger warning," he commanded. "We'll caution the schooner to change course and steer clear of the reef." It might be too late, but he had to try.

Tom shouted out, "Aye, aye, Captain," and proceeded to obey orders.

Rourke smiled at the young man's eagerness. Soon enough Tom would learn that a wrecked ship brought tragedy and heartache, not just adventure and riches.

"Repeat until they acknowledge the signal," he said before heading below deck.

If the schooner didn't heed his warning, he'd have a long night ahead of him. Best prepare for survivors.

Elizabeth took deep breaths to still her pounding heart. The cabin was situated topside aft. A wet cabin floor did not mean the ship was sinking, merely that the seams weren't well fitted or caulked. Yet the creaking and grinding of the hull did not sound normal. She knew too well the hazards of the Florida Straits. Wreckers patrolled these waters for a reason. Ships frequently ran aground on the reef. Sometimes people died. She leaned against the cabin door and braced herself as the vessel pitched again.

On the other side of the door, several crew members shouted frantically.

Prickles danced up and down Elizabeth's back. Ordinary seamen should not be outside her door. In addition to the mates' cabin that she and Aunt Virginia now occupied, the great cabin contained the captain's quarters and officers' dining saloon. Those shouts had not come from any of the officers. The presence of crewmen meant that the structure was badly compromised.

Her throat tightened. For the first time in six hundred miles of catastrophic predictions, Aunt Virginia might be right.

She ran her hand down the varnished mahogany door to the brass latch. If she could look out that door for just a moment, she could tell what was going on.

Anabelle slipped close enough to whisper, "Don't let Miss Virginia see what you're doing."

That only made Elizabeth's pulse pound faster. Anabelle had heard the shouts too. She also suspected disaster. If Aunt knew, she would go into hysterics. But Elizabeth had to risk it. She needed to know what they faced. She took a deep breath and drew the latch.

Anabelle put her hand on the door as Aunt Virginia bent over the bucket again. "Send me to fetch the first mate."

"Mr. Buetsch would be busy." Elizabeth pushed aside Anabelle's hand. She would never again risk anyone's life but her own.

Before Anabelle could react, she flung open the door. Water sprayed through the opening, beading onto her crape gown and dampening the curls Anabelle had so carefully pressed this morning. The cook had protested that the galley stove was not to be used for hair tongs, but Anabelle had insisted until the cook gave in. No one would scold them now, for at the end of the passageway the outer door was ripped off its hinges. Water rushed over the deck. Sailors lugged a canvas knotted with cord to starboard. It could have only one use: to plug a breach in the hull that could not be reached from inside the ship.

"Where are you going?" Aunt Virginia cried from behind. "Don't leave me."

Elizabeth closed the door and pressed her forehead to the smooth wood. "I'm not going anywhere."

Though Anabelle ran a comforting hand down her back, Elizabeth could not forget what she'd seen. Barring a miracle, the ship would not last the night. The crew was too busy to consider the plight of three women. Their lives depended on her.

What could she do? Until the captain gave orders to abandon ship, they were expected to stay in the cabin, but Elizabeth could not sit and wait. She knew how to sail and swim. She understood the workings of a vessel and what happened when a ship sank. She must act, but how?

She paced the length of the narrow room, pausing only to glance out the darkened window, through which the lamplight illuminated the spray of the waves.

Anabelle moved to close the shutters.

Elizabeth waved her off. "The air is too thick to close them."

"Why don't we play whist?" her great-aunt suggested. "It will take our minds off this dreadful tossing, and we can take turns playing the extra hand."

Games at such a time? If the worst happened, they needed to be ready. There would be no time then to gather their belongings. She faced her aunt. "We must prepare ourselves."

"I've already gotten out the cards." Aunt held up a deck. "Your trunk can serve as a table. Have your girl move it closer."

"I wasn't speaking of cards." Elizabeth didn't want to terrify her aunt, but ignorance could prove deadly. She could not lose one of the last female blood relations in her family. "We need to prepare in the event the ship founders."

"Founders?" Aunt Virginia paled, but no hysterics yet.

Elizabeth didn't give her time to gather steam. "We need to put our valuables into something small enough to carry."

"What are you talking about, dear? The stevedores will take care of our trunks."

Elizabeth choked back frustration. Her great-aunt thought she was talking about their arrival in Key West. She looked around for something small and light that would hold their most important possessions. "There are no stevedores aboard ship."

"Of course not. The crew will bring our trunks onto deck." Aunt Virginia rearranged the pillows behind her back.

Pillows. Of course. "A pillowcase would work beautifully. Hand me one of your pillows."

Aunt eyed her suspiciously. "What did you see out there?"

"I'm simply saying that we should prepare ourselves to walk calmly to the ship's boat if we are instructed to do so."

Aunt Virginia sucked in her breath. "The ship's going down?"

"Hopefully not, but in the event of trouble, we should be

ready." She threw out the one reason her aunt would accept. "You would not want to lose your pearls."

Aunt's eyes rounded, and her jowls shook. "Call for Captain Cross."

"We can't call for the captain. He is busy with . . . more pressing matters."

"I won't hear of anyone thieving about Jonathan's ship."

"I didn't say there were thieves aboard. I simply want us to prepare in case we must abandon ship." There, she'd said it.

Her aunt leaned back in disbelief. "You're exaggerating. Jonathan would never send us on any ship but the best."

Elizabeth growled with frustration. "All I want is a pillow-case." If only Aunt hadn't taken every pillow in the room to prop herself up on the bunk, Elizabeth could have gotten one herself.

At that moment the oil lamp sputtered and died, plunging them into darkness.

All three women gasped.

"Don't move." It took a moment for Elizabeth's eyes to adjust to the darkness. Nothing had changed. The sea still crashed against the hull, and the ship still plowed forward. Perhaps the crew had managed to plug the hole in the hull. Perhaps they would reach Key West as planned.

"What do we do now?" Aunt Virginia whispered.

"We wait."

Aunt apparently thought she meant wait for death, for her whimper was followed by a series of poorly suppressed sobs. "I don't want to die here, away from family. At least poor Helen had her husband and son at her side."

Her words tugged at Elizabeth. Aunt Virginia was terrified—not of what might happen to them but of being alone. That was how Elizabeth had felt from the moment she learned of her mother's death. Never again could she ask her dear mama for advice. Never again would her mama comfort her past a nightmare or disappointment.

"It's all right." Elizabeth navigated to her aunt's side. Sitting on the bunk, she embraced the elderly woman. "I won't leave you." She choked back a strangled sob of her own.

"Poor dear, I wasn't thinking. I should never have mentioned your mother's passing. Try to remember her beauty and grace."

Tears stung Elizabeth's eyes. "I've nearly forgotten her appearance." She fingered the tiny miniature she kept in her watch pocket. That image had been painted when the bloom of youth colored Mother's cheeks. She had aged over the years, losing that bright flush and adding lines of care around her eyes and mouth until she bore little resemblance to the girl on the miniature. "She was beautiful, wasn't she?"

"As pretty as they come." Aunt Virginia patted her back. "You remind me of her. I seem to recall that she had a handsome portrait painted upon her wedding day. Surely that still hangs in your father's house."

Elizabeth wiped her eyes on her sleeve. "It suffered damage in the storm, but I believe Father sent it for repair." Her attention was drawn to a light blinking outside the open window. Not only blinking, but in a very specific pattern, like a lighthouse. Had they reached the Key West light? Caroline had written that it was the only light that had been rebuilt thus far.

She rushed to the window. "Look! Lights. We're safe!"

At that moment the ship shuddered, pitched, and shuddered again before rolling severely to starboard. Aunt Virginia screamed. Wood splintered. Elizabeth went flying. Her hands smacked against solid wood, and the impact shivered all the way to her shoulders. Everything, including Elizabeth, slid toward the interior bulkhead. The teapot rolled over her hand and crashed against the wall. Something large scraped past her leg, landing with a thud.

Then all movement stopped.

The wind still howled. Rain and sea spray pelted the ship, but the creaking and scraping of the vessel took on an ominous tone.

"What happened?" Aunt cried.

Even as Elizabeth struggled to right herself, she had no doubt. They'd struck the reef.

2

How many times did you signal?" Rourke yelled at the new deckhand.

Tom stiffened. "At least ten times, Captain."

"Well, keep at it," Rourke growled, pacing the deck.

What was wrong with that master? Even an incompetent pilot or master should recognize trouble at first impact, yet the ship maintained the same course. His gut clenched. Most pilots were wreckers or former wreckers and wouldn't risk losing their license, but a few didn't know the waters on a sunny day, least of all in a storm.

If Rourke knew the pilot—and odds were he did—he'd flay him in court. A man who claimed knowledge he didn't possess was a liar and a cheat. One day such a man would cost someone his life, but not today—not if Rourke O'Malley had anything to do with it.

"Set the mainsail," he shouted. No jib in this wind. Too much sail and the northeast gale would drive his sloop into the shallows before he reached Hawk Channel.

Within minutes, the crew had set sail for the tough run into the wind. A gust heeled the *Windsprite* the moment they pulled away from the lee of their anchorage, pushing them back toward land.

Rourke stormed the deck, shouting orders to bring the ship onto a tack that angled toward the reef. Spray pelted his face and ran into his eyes. It soaked his clothes and reinforced his decision to shun shoes aboard ship. Many captains dressed like gentlemen, but Rourke stuck to his humble roots. He liked the throb of the waves beneath his feet. The ship was a living, breathing creature, like a whale or tortoise. He wanted to feel its every move.

Rourke surveyed his crew with pride. Despite the tempest, they hauled in the main sheet until the sail caught just enough of the wind, and soon the sloop flew across the water. The first run took them into Hawk Channel far short of the doomed schooner. Rourke followed the ship's lights with his spyglass. The hull appeared to list to starboard. Either it had taken on even more water or was heeled over in the gale.

On the next tack they headed back toward the string of islands with equal haste, but the maneuver had gained them little ground. At this rate, it would take hours to reach the foundered ship.

He barked out the order to come about again. "And keep that signal going. Maybe the fool will finally see it."

John shook his head. "She on da reef."

Despite the fact that the schooner's lights hadn't moved since before they set sail, Rourke wasn't willing to concede it had run aground. Perhaps the master had heeded his warning and put out anchor. Maybe the darkness played tricks with his eyes, and the vessel sailed in safe waters. If so, his arrival cost nothing. If not, the poor souls aboard that ship would need assistance.

He stormed from deckhand to deckhand, adding his strength

to the difficult tacks. In such a stiff wind, the swing of the boom on each jibe had to be controlled, or the wind and sea would send the sloop over on her side. Rourke knew the *Windsprite*'s temper, her tendency to hesitate before coming about. He knew she'd make the turn and skip across the waves like a flying fish. He'd worked this old sloop all his sailing life, as his father had before him. No more than a dozen planks in the hull were original, but he'd patched her up year after year, and she rewarded him by flying faster than any other wrecking vessel.

"You can do it, girl," he urged as they made the next turn.

Once again they faced the schooner, which was still in the same spot. As they raced along on this tack, the rains slowed to a drizzle, the storm clouds broke, and the waning three-quarter moon peeked out. Its silvery light sprinkled the inky water, revealing that John had been right. The schooner was fast aground and rolled onto its starboard side on the outer edge of the reef. Its tattered sails flapped wildly. With this sea, the ship would soon break up and sink beneath the waves.

Deep sadness swept over him, as it always did when he saw a ship founder. Nothing was more tragic than a wounded ship, its masts and booms holding out shreds of sail like a gull with broken wings. Too often lives were lost.

"Should I keep signaling, Cap'n?" Tom asked, his drawn face ghostly pale beneath his wind-whipped dark hair.

"No. No use now. Help trim the sail."

Tom sped off with an "Aye, aye, Cap'n."

"God save her crew," John said, as he always did before a sinking.

"Aye." That was what those poor souls would need.

"And may He bring good cargo." John's grin reflected the other part of this business.

A valuable cargo would make them rich men. That was something worth praying for, wasn't it?

⟡

Elizabeth fought to her feet on the wildly slanting floor. Or was it the wall? She felt around but could make no sense of her surroundings. Her aunt was screaming hysterically, and Anabelle was trying to calm her, without much success.

"We're going to die," Aunt Virginia shrieked.

"You be fine, Miz Virginia."

Yet the calmer Anabelle's voice, the louder grew Elizabeth's aunt.

"I knew we would drown." The woman barely stopped for breath. "Didn't I say so from the start? If not for my love and respect for your dear mother, Elizabeth, I would never have consented to come along on this foolish voyage. Business can be conducted by post. Why didn't your father fetch you if he wanted you home so badly?"

Because Father did not ask for me. Elizabeth had stretched the truth just a bit. Father *did* need her. He simply didn't realize it yet. A busy attorney couldn't hope to care for an invalid son. Servants could not possibly give Charlie the love and attention he required. That was the reason she'd formulated back in Charleston, but as they drew nearer to Key West, her resolve had faltered. Charlie had not once written her. He had signed Mother's notes at Christmastime and Easter, but never a word of his own. No doubt he blamed her.

It would have been easier for everyone else if she'd stayed in Charleston and settled into a proper marriage. But she could not get Key West from her mind. The smell of a lime or coconut could set her to remembering the desserts Cook concocted out of Cuban sugar, cream, and fruit from the trees planted beside the house. The ocean air, ripe with salt and fish, had fueled a hunger that could not be quenched at Charleston's wharves. She longed for the brilliant sun against her cheeks and the trade winds ruffling her hair. She longed to shed these shoes and sink her bare feet into the white coral sand.

To return home to the last of her family, she must survive this night. She sucked in a breath and ventured a step to the side. Her foot landed in a pool of water.

"What was that?" Naturally Aunt Virginia heard that tiny splash over the roar of the wind and the grinding of the ship against the reef.

"Just a little water."

"I know your tendency to paint a rosy hue on disaster, Elizabeth Marie. You can tell me the truth. We're sinking, aren't we?"

Elizabeth had lost patience with her aunt's hysterics. Perhaps a dash of truth would shock her into some semblance of calm. "Yes, we are."

Aunt gasped.

"Now is the time to act," Elizabeth stressed. "We are strong women. We will find our way out of here."

"Where is the door?" Aunt said.

"I'm looking for it. Is anyone hurt?"

"I struck my forehead," Aunt said, "and it aches terribly."

"I git you a compress, Miz Virginia," Anabelle offered.

"Where are you?" Aunt cried. "I can't see a thing."

"Right here by yor side, Miz Virginia. Try ta keep yor feet under ya. Da bunk is right der."

Elizabeth's eyes gradually adapted to the darkness, but she couldn't make out much in the room. "Hold on to the bunk, Aunt Virginia. The floor is slanted."

"Did you find my trunk? I won't leave without my pearls."

Elizabeth bit back a retort that she would have already gathered them if Aunt hadn't put up such a fuss. "We may need to leave them behind."

"Leave them? I can't lose my pearls." Aunt Virginia wore them to every social occasion. "You have to find them. The little trunk is unlocked. With all this tumbling about, it might have come open. Maybe they fell out. I can't lose them." Her volume rose with every statement.

"The wreckers will find them," Elizabeth assured her.

"They'll steal them. You read that article in *Godey's* about the pirates in Key West."

"It was a story, Aunt. Fiction. There aren't any pirates there anymore. In fact, some wreckers are fine, Christian men." Like Rourke.

The memory of his strong jaw and sea-green eyes warmed Elizabeth's damp toes. Four years ago he'd picked her up like she weighed no more than a feather bed. He'd held her close as he carried her through the howling storm to safety. She'd leaned her head against his shoulder and took comfort in the strong, steady beat of his heart. She'd breathed in that scent of the sea washed with courage and honor. Rourke O'Malley was no pirate. He put his faith in God and treated every man with respect.

But her aunt scoffed at the idea of a gentleman wrecker. "I'm not leaving a thing to chance. If you won't get my pearls, I'll get them myself."

"Now watch yer step, Miz Virginia," Anabelle said.

In the murky light, Elizabeth saw the bulky shape of her aunt rise beside the steadying Anabelle. They stood directly ahead of her and somewhat above, due to the sloping floor. She couldn't see any of the trunks. They must have slid down near her.

"Stay where you are, Aunt," Elizabeth said. With her aunt's unsteady legs, she could easily fall. "I'll look for the pearls."

She felt around. Nothing near. She recalled the room's layout. The door must be behind her. If she could open it, the light from the hallway lamp would help her find the trunks. She felt around for the latch. Wood. Everywhere wood and not a bit of metal.

Waves continued to smash against the hull. The scraping and splintering sounds worsened. At last she found the latch and pulled. The door didn't budge. She tried again, using her full weight. It would not open. Now what?

Water gurgled all around. Elizabeth stepped to her left and ran into something solid. She felt around in the darkness. The object came to just above her knees. Made of wood. Brass strapping.

"I found one of our trunks."

"Whose is it?" Aunt Virginia asked.

"I think it's your small one. It doesn't feel like mine."

"Open it." The woman sounded out of breath already. "That's the one with my pearls."

Elizabeth searched for the latches. "It's wedged against the wall, and, oh—" Her head struck something hard. She ran her hands around the object. "The chair is here too." She pushed the chair off and tried to open the trunk. The lid didn't budge. "Was your trunk latched?"

"Of course it's latched. I made sure to latch it when I put the cards back. As if any fool would leave her trunk open in such a place. Let the roaches and rats into my clothing? Never!"

"Rats?" Elizabeth scampered out of the pooling water. The mere thought of vermin made her skin crawl. "I couldn't get it open."

"But my pearls!"

"We'll ask the mate to help us open the trunk when he comes for us." Absently she looked up, where the cabin's window now blinked with stars. The sky must be clearing. In time the wind and waves would abate, but if the groaning of the hull was any indication, they wouldn't be here to witness it.

"Then we will have to abandon ship." Her great-aunt sounded resigned. "My James died like this."

"James?" Elizabeth had never heard her mention anyone named James.

"My first and only love."

Elizabeth's jaw dropped. Her aunt had once loved a man? She'd always been the spinster, happily ensconced in the family home. A lost love, especially in a shipwreck, made Aunt's hysterics more understandable. "What happened?"

"The ship went down. All hands lost." She sniffled. "That's all the shipping agent could tell me. For a long time I dreamed that he'd survived as a maroon, alone on some unknown island. Even after I accepted his death, I wondered how he'd perished. Did he suffer? Was anyone with him or did he die alone? I-I-I don't want to die alone."

Elizabeth embraced her trembling aunt. "I'm here. I won't leave you."

The way she'd left her brother. Never again would she turn away from family in need.

"We'll get out of here," she added, though with the door jammed shut she didn't know exactly how.

As if in answer, silvery moonlight streamed through the window overhead, revealing the extent of their difficulties. Aunt Virginia's small trunk was now partially underwater, as was the bottom portion of the door. At this rate, the cabin would fill within the hour. The passageway outside must be halfway submerged. If help didn't arrive soon, their only avenue of escape was the window overhead.

The slap of waves and scraping of the reef continued for long, agonizing seconds while Elizabeth considered the window. Aunt Virginia would never fit through it, but Anabelle could. Then she could send one of the crew with an ax to hack open the door. But first Anabelle needed something to stand on so she could climb out the window.

Elizabeth tugged on the desk. It must have been hammered into the wall, for it didn't budge. She considered the options. Perhaps a drawer would give enough of a boost. The bottom one opened easily. Elizabeth tested its soundness with first one foot and then the other. This would work.

She reached for the window.

At that instant, a large wave hit the hull, and the drawer slid from underfoot, spilling its contents all over the floor. Elizabeth grabbed the window frame and managed to hold on. Aunt Virginia screamed. Anabelle consoled her. With a shudder, the entire room tipped backward. Elizabeth lost her grip and fell onto her backside. She grabbed the desk.

Then everything stopped.

Elizabeth gulped in air. Her hands ached. Her limbs trembled. "Is everyone all right?"

Aunt Virginia and Anabelle gave quiet confirmations.

Slowly Elizabeth got to her knees. Then, in the flicker of moonlight, she saw something glitter inside the hole where the drawer had been. Elizabeth felt around until she could grab it. The object was cold and hard and round in shape. She opened her fingers. In the moonlight she could see the fire of gems and the warmth of gold shaped into a delicate filigreed brooch.

What was that doing inside the first mate's desk?

A knock sounded on the cabin door. The mate?

After several shuddering thuds, the door scraped open. "Ma'am? Miss? You all need to go topside right now." The lantern revealed the wild-eyed visage of a deckhand.

Not the first mate. Elizabeth slipped the brooch into her watch pocket. She'd get it to him later, once everyone reached safety.

❧

Guided by the moon, Rourke crossed Hawk Channel, safely traversed the reef, and neared the foundered schooner. The seas battered her larboard side, which rose high above the water. The starboard had clearly holed, for it was sunk. A goodly number of men clung to the bulwarks between the forecastle and the great cabin aft. A single lantern illuminated their plight. From what Rourke could see, they'd launched the ship's boat and were preparing to abandon ship. He counted quickly. Appeared to be a full complement.

The heaviness in his gut lightened.

"Glory be," John said, a smile easing onto his face. "Dey be safe."

Rourke could have echoed those words. He ordered the helmsman to keep the *Windsprite* well off the schooner. Usually he came alongside in the lee, but the schooner's position made that impossible. The reef jutted nearly to the surface alee of the wreck. He'd keep his distance and take his boat across to the wrecked vessel.

A large swell crashed over the *Windsprite*'s bow, and the helmsman lost her to starboard. The next wave drove her parallel to the wreck—and the reef. One more and they'd find themselves on top of the wrecked schooner.

"Bring her into the wind," Rourke yelled.

The wild-eyed helmsman struggled to bring the *Windsprite* about, but the force of the seas was too much for one man. Rourke joined the effort, and together they brought her into the wind and out of danger.

"Drop anchor," he ordered.

Only after his men had set anchor fore and aft could Rourke turn his attention to the schooner.

"Lower the boat!" Rourke fingered the license in his pocket, which he would produce as proof he could complete the job. Masters usually insisted they did not require assistance. This one could not, or he was a fool. He could, however, ask Rourke to tow the wreck off the reef in the hope it would float. The *Windsprite*'s boat was already equipped to bring the necessary lines for such an operation.

Rourke flung one leg over the bulwark and reached for the rope ladder to descend to his boat, but he paused when he noticed the schooner's boat heading for the *Windsprite*. Two oarsmen flanked the master and another officer, likely a mate or pilot. If the master was coming to him, the man must have accepted his need for assistance. That made Rourke's task easier.

After Rourke's crew secured the schooner's boat alongside, the white-haired master climbed aboard, followed by a fussy gentleman that Rourke instantly recognized as the most worthless pilot in Key West. The man—Poppinclerk by name—had the gall to brush at his wool coat as if the *Windsprite* had dirtied it. No wonder the ship had foundered. Rourke fisted his hands. If any lives were lost due to that dandy's incompetence, Rourke would pound the man so far out of Key West that he'd never set foot on the island again.

The master approached. "Captain Cross of the schooner *Victory* out of Charleston. Are you a wrecker?"

"I am." Rourke introduced himself and presented his license. His pulse accelerated. A ship out of Charleston could be hauling valuable tobacco.

John held up a lantern, and the master gave the wrecking license a cursory glance. Procedure dictated Rourke ask what services the master required. He scanned the horizon for any sign of other wrecking vessels. It wouldn't take long before the first arrived.

"Do you want us to haul your vessel off the reef?"

"Name your terms," Captain Cross said briskly.

"Flat fee if we can float her. Salvage rights if not." Standard procedure.

"She's fast aground and taking on water." Cross rubbed his whiskered jaw. "Try floating her first."

That was no surprise. Masters hated turning over their vessels to salvagers. "The cargo?"

"Mostly rice and raw muslin bound for Havana."

Rourke fought disappointment. If the vessel was bilged like he suspected, he didn't stand to make much of an award. This cargo and its destination pointed to goods intended for slave consumption. That meant poor quality. Even though the cloth could be salvaged, salt water would ruin the rice. He would make almost nothing off salvage.

"If you can't float her," the captain added, "we'll need passage for our crew and passengers."

"Passengers?" That snapped Rourke from his calculations. "How many?"

"Two. Both women."

Women! That would make the rescue more difficult, for women usually did not handle adversity well. Some swooned. Some succumbed to hysterics. Others appeared calm but slipped climbing into or out of the ship's boat. Women often had off-spring with them. "Any children?"

Poppinclerk, who'd stood near during the negotiations, absently polished a gilt button with his handkerchief. "Not unless you count the darkie wench."

Rourke held his tongue at the derogatory term. A tongue-lashing would be lost on Poppinclerk. Instead, he focused on the master. "Then there are three passengers."

"Two ladies and a Negro," Cross confirmed.

"From Charleston?"

Cross nodded.

John's eyes widened.

Rourke shook his head. A city the size of Charleston boasted thousands of women, any of whom might book passage on a schooner. Moreover, Miss Benjamin would not be bound for Havana, and Cross had not indicated a planned stop in Key West.

John would not let it go. "Dis Negro, what her name?"

The master shrugged. "How would I know? She belongs to Miss Benjamin."

Rourke choked.

They both knew what that meant.

John looked ready to leap over the side of the *Windsprite* regardless of the heaving seas. Rourke grabbed his arm, even though the same desire thundered in his ears.

Elizabeth was on that ship. He'd expected her to return after her mother's death, but when the months passed without so much as a rumor of her return, he'd given up hope. "Miss Elizabeth Benjamin?" He held his breath.

Cross looked surprised. "You know her?"

Rourke more than knew Elizabeth Benjamin. He'd spent the last four years dreaming of her soft skin, sun-kissed hair, and deep blue eyes. Whenever he smelled jasmine, he looked for her and was always disappointed. He painfully recalled the day she'd left Key West without a word. But most of all he remembered with absolute clarity the moment when he'd realized that the girl he'd teased for years had grown into a woman he would never forget.

3

*H*e'd appeared out of the mists, like a specter, but Elizabeth knew at once that it was Rourke. The breadth of
his shoulders, the cut of his waist, the commanding
presence. He'd come for her—for them.

She lifted her arm into the howling winds and called his
name.

That moment of incaution cost her. The tempest ripped her
from the fragment of roof. She reached for the jagged corner.
Missed. Tried again. Her fingertips grazed the edge before the
surging water pulled her away from her brother.

"Charlie!" Her cry flew away on the gale.

She clawed at the earth bumping along beneath her and
grasped only gravel.

The water was coming up too quickly. Soon it would cover
Charlie. Rourke was too far away. She alone could save him.

With her last ounce of strength, she fought the surging sea.
One foot found solid ground. The second followed. She tried to
stand, but the flood knocked her down and carried her farther
from the warehouse. Her next gasp for air brought only water.

She coughed and choked while the seas tumbled her farther and farther away.

Then strong arms caught her. She lifted salt-stung eyes. He would save her. He would save them. His hair whipped in the wind, lashing her cheek. He knelt beside her and cradled her to his chest. Then he lifted her from the waters and headed away from the waterfront and away from her brother.

"Charlie!" She pounded on his chest. She pointed. She had to make him return.

But he carried her in the opposite direction. Helpless, she watched her brother's prostrate form vanish in the mist.

⌘

"Bring my trunk," Aunt Virginia demanded, pulling Elizabeth from her past.

The harried seaman standing in the doorway made no move to obey.

"Over there," Aunt insisted. "The small one."

"Beggin' yer pardon, ma'am, but the wreckers'll get it."

"Wreckers are here?" Elizabeth asked.

"Yes'm."

Her spine tingled. Could it be Rourke? Like all wreckers, he patrolled the reef, but he was only one of dozens. Most likely it would be someone else, someone who didn't torment her thoughts and dreams. But it *was* possible. Caroline's letters had kept her informed of all the local news, including the fact that Captain O'Malley had not yet married. But her last communiqué had arrived over a month ago.

"Which wrecker?" she asked so breathlessly that her aunt gave her a sharp look.

The man shrugged. "How'm I ta know?"

How indeed. He was from Charleston, not Key West. He wouldn't know one wrecker from another.

"They're all a villainous lot," Aunt grumbled.

"Yer right about that, ma'am." In one small sentence the deckhand undid all of Elizabeth's work. "They'll pretty near strip us clean."

"Strip?" Aunt gasped.

"He's speaking figuratively," Elizabeth said quickly, before her aunt got hysterical again. "He means that the wreckers will claim everything of value, but it's not true. They are licensed under the admiralty court and must abide by the law or lose their license. You have nothing to fear. I've met many a woman saved by a wrecker. Not a one had a word of complaint."

She took her aunt's hand and guided her into the slanted passageway already knee-deep in water. Anabelle followed, with the seaman bringing up the rear. His lantern revealed the extent of the disaster. Beyond the missing outer door, strips of sail slapped against the sloping deck. A mast or spar hung at an odd angle. Elizabeth slogged ahead with great care. Bits of wood bobbed in the black water. Any misstep could twist an ankle.

"Step carefully now," she instructed, "and use the walls for support."

A sniffle was her only response.

At least Aunt still had her wits. Slowly they traversed the short distance to the gaping doorway. Only then did Elizabeth see the enormity of the challenge. Men clung to the rail, awaiting rescue. Between the doorway and them lay a steeply sloped, wet deck. Earlier in the voyage she'd learned how slippery a deck became when wet. Her incaution had landed her on her posterior. That experience had been humbling. This was impossible. None of them could manage the slope when there was nothing to hold on to.

"What will we do?" she muttered.

"Wait here, miss." The deckhand handed her the lantern. "We'll send someone ta haul ye off." He then scrambled up the deck, reaching the rail with a final leap.

"Oh dear," Aunt Virginia said. "We have to do that?"

"There must be another way. The men will rig something to assist us." But she spoke with greater confidence than she felt.

She'd seen the bodies of women whose skirts had dragged them to a watery grave. For all her assurances, many did perish.

The wrecked ship shuddered beneath her feet. If it gave way before help arrived, none of them would see Key West.

Help must be on its way.

She squeezed her eyes shut, knowing she ought to pray but unable to believe that it would do any good. It hadn't helped Charlie. Yes, Rourke had saved her brother, but Charlie had to live with the wages of her sin. So did Rourke. She had betrayed him, let him take the blame, and then left for Charleston without a word. He must despise her.

She hoped the wrecker wasn't him. Dozens of men wrecked. Surely it would be another.

Elizabeth peered into the moonlit night, but the slope of the deck hid the wrecking vessel from view. She could only make out its mast. One mast. More than likely a sloop, just like Rourke's ship.

Her stomach clenched. What if it was him?

⁂

Rourke beat John to the ship's boat, but he could not persuade the man to wait aboard the *Windsprite*. Under ordinary circumstances, Rourke trusted John with his life, but a man's inclinations changed when desperate. If the colored maid proved to be Anabelle, John might disappear with her into the night. Rourke would if he was in John's place.

Rourke pulled hard on his oar, but he couldn't match John's fervor. The man hadn't seen his wife in four long years. Elizabeth had left with her maid and without a word.

In short order they neared the wreck. The waves hammered it. The spray shot high in the air, silvery in the moonlight, before raining down on them. The three masts pointed away from him like trees toppling over a cliff. Each swell ground the hulk against the reef. The schooner wouldn't hold together long, and some twenty souls clung to the rail, wide-eyed and desperate.

The moment they reached the schooner, Rourke grabbed its ladder and scampered up the tilted hull. John followed.

"Get as many on board the boat as possible," he shouted to the mate who'd helped him onto the larboard bulwark. "Women first." He looked around but saw no feminine figures nearby. "Where are they?"

"Great cabin." The mate looked anxiously toward the larboard side of the sloping structure where a black doorway loomed. "Should be waiting in there."

Rourke peered into the darkness but could see no one. Hysterical women might have retreated or flung themselves overboard. Except for the hurricane, Elizabeth had displayed calm under pressure. Unfortunately, that exception had cost her brother the use of his legs.

The hulk shivered from the impact of a large wave. He had to get everyone off soon. The reef edge plummeted in this location. If the schooner broke free, it would sink to the depths. Anyone inside would perish. No wrecker received a penny for saving a person's life, only for salvaged cargo, but even the most villainous wreckers rescued stranded passengers and crew.

John started ahead of him, ropes slung over his shoulder, but Rourke held the man back. "Follow me. I want someone at my back in case I slip." In truth he wanted to keep his chief mate under control. A man in such heightened state of emotion was liable to take deadly risks.

The slick, tilted deck would prove difficult for a seasoned seaman to navigate. Women would find it impossible.

"The long rope," he shouted to John as another wave crashed over them. "String it between here and the poop deck."

John set about securing a line that would give the women something to hold on to while they traversed the deck. Once he secured their end, he held up three smaller lengths. "Ta put round 'em."

"Good thinking." Even if the women lost their footing, the line would keep them from sliding into the churning sea.

Rourke grabbed the coiled long line and worked his way along the sloping deck by climbing on capstans, winches, and other deck structures. At three spots on the way, he wound the rope around something solid. His pulse pounded, urging him to race toward the gaping entry, but his head kept that impulse in restraint. One wrong move and he'd slip into the sea. That wouldn't help anyone. It wouldn't save Elizabeth.

When a particularly large wave hit, he braced himself, always keeping his gaze on the entryway. Already water surged into it. If this hulk slipped any more, the women could drown.

As he drew near, a familiar face poked out of the doorway and into the moonlight.

"Anabelle!" John's whoop brought a flicker of a smile to

the stunning woman's face. In her native land, Anabelle would have been a queen. Tall and straight-backed, she carried herself with undeniable grace.

Though she could captivate a man's attention, Rourke peered past her into the black doorway, looking for the woman who'd danced through his thoughts every day for the past four years. She'd been lovely then. How much more beautiful she would be now. Why had she left without a word? Why hadn't she written? If not for her friend Caroline, he wouldn't even know where she had gone or that she was still unwed. That news had sustained him and given him hope.

Soon he would know if that hope had been misplaced.

He headed for the doorway, but John pushed past him to get to Anabelle. Instead of rushing into her husband's arms, the woman extended her hand, a signal that she dare not embrace. That meant her mistress was near. None but Rourke and the minister knew of their marriage.

"Elizabeth?" Rourke peered into the inky void.

Instead of the golden-haired object of his dreams, a plump elderly woman stuck her head out of the deckhouse. "Who are you to use my niece's Christian name?"

Rourke froze. The captain had said there were two women plus Anabelle, but in his eagerness to reach Elizabeth, he'd forgotten. "Forgive me. Is Miss Benjamin all right?"

A slender figure moved behind the matron. "I-I-I'm fine."

Though Rourke could not make out her features, the trembling voice was Elizabeth's.

John, meanwhile, had looped the safety rope around Anabelle's waist.

"Tell your man to stop helping that slave girl," the elderly woman demanded. "Ladies must be rescued first."

John looked like he would knock the portly woman to her backside.

Rourke pushed past him. "We'll bring all of you to safety."

"My niece and I first," the woman demanded. "Tell your darkie to take my niece and leave the slave until last."

"No, Aunt Virginia. I will wait." Elizabeth appeared, so lovely in the moonlight that for a second Rourke could not think or move.

Before the matron could protest, John whisked Anabelle away.

Rourke extended his hand. "Come with me, Miss Benjamin."

Her wide eyes shimmered in the moonlight. "Please escort my great-aunt."

The woman jutted out her chin. "The young should go first. Someone my age is expendable."

"No, Aunt Virginia." Elizabeth retreated into the darkness to affirm her decision.

With a creak, the hulk shifted a bit lower. The women cried out. Rourke steadied the matron and then reached for Elizabeth.

"I am all right," she said from deep within the passageway, each word firmer than the last. "Please bring my aunt to safety."

Rourke hated to leave Elizabeth behind. That settling of the wreck meant the hulk could break apart at any moment. Yet he couldn't ferry them both at once. He must make a choice. Four years ago he'd chosen the beauty over her brother, only to lose her.

This time he extended his hand to her aunt.

❦

The moment Elizabeth heard Rourke's voice, her resolve shattered. The feelings she'd had for him hadn't diminished over four years. If anything, they'd grown stronger. She'd begged him to rescue Aunt Virginia in the hope that another crewman would come for her. She couldn't trust herself in Rourke's arms.

She drew in a deep breath. Charlie needed her. Father needed her. That had to be her focus, not some childish infatuation. Once Rourke left with Aunt Virginia, Elizabeth blew out that breath and collapsed against the passage wall.

Relief soon gave way to fear. It gnawed at the pit of her stomach and weakened her knees. The ship was breaking apart. The spars now dipped into the ocean. The starboard rail was underwater. Each large wave shook the wreck. If it sank before someone came for her, she could perish. Though she knew how to swim, the weight of her clothing would drag her to the bottom.

She closed her eyes, knowing she ought to pray, but she had stepped away from unquestioning faith the day Charlie was hurt. Her prayers then had gone unanswered. What God let the innocent suffer? Cook had scolded her, saying that God wasn't to blame, but she'd still cast fault in His direction. It was easier than the truth.

"Hold on!"

Rourke's shout opened her eyes. He was inching Aunt Virginia forward, almost completely supporting her bulk. The memory of his strength only intensified the longing she was trying to quench. When he asked for her, she had wanted to run from the passage and take his hand. She wanted to feel again the beat of his heart against her cheek. In his arms, she would be safe. How she wanted that, but it could not be. Her father held wreckers in contempt. He would never approve of Rourke as a suitor.

Yet her gaze followed Rourke forward. Time had not changed him. His dark hair was still drawn back at the nape. He still cut an impressive figure, tall and strong. His rich baritone still reached deep into her soul. Four years had not changed him, but it had changed her.

Elizabeth clung to the door frame as a large wave doused the shipwreck. After wiping the seawater from her eyes, she looked for Rourke and her aunt. They had survived the deluge, Rourke balancing Aunt's weight like a cotton bale. After two more steps, he assisted her into the arms of two waiting seamen.

Now someone would come for her. Perhaps Rourke.

The thought sent a hum of conflicting emotion through her tired limbs. Father had made the marriage requirements clear. She must choose a husband from her own class or higher. Mother had seconded that. Rourke O'Malley did not qualify unless his fortunes had risen dramatically since she left.

Rourke made his way toward her, moving quickly along the rescue line.

Her pulse accelerated. Soon he would reach her. They would be alone together. No chaperone. No hovering relatives. Not even another crew member. Only the two of them were left on the wreck.

She drew in a shaky breath. He'd passed the midpoint of the rope. Soon he would take her in his arms. Soon she would feel his heartbeat and hear his whisper in her ear. Would he speak of love or blame? His emotional cry for her suggested it would be the former. She gripped the door frame until her fingers hurt. How dreadful to receive the one thing she wanted most, knowing that she must cast it away.

He slung an arm around a winch and yelled something in her direction.

The wind snatched his words away.

She shook her head.

He pointed to larboard.

A towering wave loomed above the wreck. She ducked into the passage and grabbed the railing just as the wave hit. It knocked her feet out from under her. She slammed into the wall but held on. With eyes squeezed shut, she dared not breathe as the water gushed around her, first in and then out. The force ripped her fingers from the railing. She grabbed for anything as the ocean sucked her down into its bowels.

Her knees hit solid wood when the wash of the wave subsided. Cloth slapped her hands, and she grabbed hold. With a yank, her downward progress came to a halt. She gulped for air and opened her eyes to the sting of salt water.

"Take my hand, Elizabeth."

Rourke's voice brought hope. Though her arms ached and a terrible weight was pulling her down, she might yet survive. After blinking away the tears, she spotted his hand far above her. He was hanging upside down, one leg hooked on the rescue line and the other braced against the great cabin. His hand was beyond reach. The distance between them was too great. He could never reach her. She must somehow get to him.

She was hanging on a remnant of the sail, her feet dangling into the sea. The heaving waves spun her around. Her arms ached. Her fingers slipped. The weight of her skirts dragged her down. If she let go with one hand, she would fall.

"Climb, Elizabeth!"

"I can't."

"Yes you can. I've seen you swim in pounding seas. You rowed around the island."

"That was years ago."

"You still have it in you." A trace of desperation colored his pleas. "You are strong, Elizabeth Benjamin. Hold on a little longer, and I'll come to you."

Help me, Lord. The prayer came from desperation and with little hope, yet when Elizabeth looked up, she saw Rourke moving down the line, a short rope between his teeth. He stopped and slung his legs over the rescue line. It bowed under his weight, but it held. He reached for the dangling spar. Then he began to lift. His face contorted with effort, but she felt herself move upward.

He was attempting to pull her up.

His effort opened a well of strength she didn't know she possessed. She inched upward, gaining some ground.

His fingertips brushed her hand. "A little more."

Her hands ached. She hadn't any more to give.

"Come to me, Elizabeth," he urged, his fingertips trying to coax her hands off the sail. "Let go with one hand, and I will lift you to safety."

Oh, his touch! It resurrected feelings and memories and hopes that couldn't be. The feel of his arms would shatter every vow. Elizabeth squeezed her eyes shut.

"I can't!" she cried.

"You must."

Rourke or death. The choice was simple, but in her fevered mind Elizabeth could not save her life simply to propel it into the risk of Rourke's embrace.

"Better to suffer with grace than to unequally yoke oneself," Mother had counseled before Elizabeth boarded the ship to Charleston. Her letters had expressed disappointment that Elizabeth had turned away every suitor, explaining that no man was perfect.

Mother hadn't understood. Rourke was perfect for her. No other suitor had ever come close.

"I'm sorry." She needed to say more, to explain what a coward she had been four years ago and beg his forgiveness, but even with death knocking she could not find the words.

"Hold on!"

A wave tossed her against the deck, and her burning fingers slipped. Something between a scream and a moan tore out of her. She couldn't hold on a moment longer.

Then she felt him grab her left hand. His grip hurt, but he pulled her out of the sea and onto the spar.

"Hold on," he said. "I need to let go a moment so I can get this rope around you."

Though his touch left her, she now knew she would be safe.

Then another wave slammed the wreck. The spar gave way. Elizabeth slid down, down. She squeezed her eyes shut, preparing for impact. Old memories flitted past. Rourke tenderly touching her bruised lip. Father scowling. Mother weeping at Charlie's bedside. Father demanding answers. The disappointment that flashed across Rourke's face when she let him take the blame. The sinking knowledge that all was lost.

Elizabeth cried out.

Something yanked her upward. God? Was she rising to heaven like a prophet of old?

Her eyelids flew open. Somehow Rourke had swung the spar so it deposited her right into his arms. He gathered her close and pressed his lips to the hollow below her ear. "I thought I lost you."

Elizabeth choked back a sob. He did not know it yet, but he had.

4

Dawn's orange glow revealed three wrecking ships approaching from the west-southwest. As wreck master, Rourke decided which of those vessels would ferry the passengers to Key West and which would help with the salvage. He must reach an agreement, or consortship, with them on the division of the spoils. Since the cargo lacked substantial value, most would leap at the chance for an equal share.

He strode toward the lookout, his boots clattering on the deck. Shoes pinched his toes and slipped on the damp planking, but he couldn't very well go barefoot in front of Miss Benjamin and her aunt. John had laughed when Rourke appeared with combed hair and dress coat. Rourke claimed he'd donned the fancy garb in order to convince Captain Cross and the other wreckers to accept his counsel, but John knew better.

Rourke shouted up at young Tom, "Can you spot whose ships they are?"

"Not yet, Cap'n!"

Rourke itched to know. He wouldn't trust some wreckers—such as the Littlejohn fleet—with his enemy, least of all Elizabeth. Oh, they all knew the repercussions of mistreating the only daughter of Charles Benjamin, but some crews were more genteel than others. The worst vessels culled crew members from the grogshops and alleyways. Those men required a strong hand and a sharp blade to prompt obedience. He couldn't place her in such hands.

"Let me know the instant you make them out," he called up to Tom.

"Aye, aye, Cap'n!"

He chuckled at the lad's exuberance. Soon enough Tom would offer the same muttered reply as any other seaman.

Rourke leaned on the gunwale and surveyed the task at hand. The gathering daylight revealed what he already knew. The seas were flattening. Swells still lifted the *Windsprite* above the remains of the foundered schooner, but they no longer had the force to tear the hulk to bits. Unfortunately, those waves had sunk the *Victory*'s boat overnight, leaving only his boat to run between vessels. The minute the master gave permission to proceed with salvage, Rourke would draw the *Windsprite* alongside and off-load cargo onto his vessel. To hurry that decision along, he had sent John down to examine the extent of damage to the schooner's hull.

He watched the heaving swells for John's reappearance.

The master ambled alongside. "I don't see why you had to send your man down. It's a waste of time. Just pull my ship off that blasted reef."

"If I do that without first examining how badly it's holed, you'll lose everything."

"I know my ship, and I know my rights under the law. Don't think you can steal my cargo."

Rourke gritted his teeth. No doubt Poppinclerk had planted

that idea in the master's mind. "If the hull can be patched, we'll haul her off."

"I know my vessel better than some profit-seeking salvager. I order you to haul her off the reef at once."

Rourke set his jaw lest angry words cross his lips. Too many masters saw wreckers as little better than pirates out to take their profit, thanks to unsavory wreckers of the past like Jacob Housman. Captain Cross was clearly one of those. These days, a few less scrupulous wreckers might attempt to negotiate a high salvage fee, but the deceptive dealing of the past was over. Unfortunately, few masters believed it.

"Send your own man down then," Rourke said.

"I can't risk one of my men. None of them know these waters."

Neither did the pilot he'd hired, but Rourke did not point that out. "Then we wait."

"Coward." The master stomped off when the insult didn't generate the response he wanted.

Rourke had heard worse. From bribery to threats, he'd faced them all down and survived. After last night's rescue, Cross couldn't say a thing to upset Rourke. Elizabeth had returned. For four long years he'd waited. Now she was here on his ship.

He eyed the women, who were huddled together under blankets amidships, sipping the coffee he'd had sent up earlier. After depositing Elizabeth on board earlier that morning, he'd had no opportunity to converse further with her. Now her aunt and Anabelle effectively buttressed her from any masculine attention.

Their wet gowns could not be comfortable, but with the sun rising and in the fresh breeze, their clothing would soon dry. Elizabeth cradled the rude tin cup like a porcelain teacup. Even though she was soaked to the bone with salt-stiffened locks, he'd never seen a more perfect example of femininity. Her coral pink lips nestled like a shell beneath sky-blue eyes. Since she didn't wear a bonnet or carry a parasol, the sun would soon grace her complexion with the freckles that he'd so teased her about when she was a girl. The memory brought a smile to his lips, but he also realized the discomfort the sun would bring.

He strode down the deck to stand before them. "I can rig a tarpaulin overhead to give you shade."

Elizabeth's eyes shimmered with what he hoped was gratitude.

Her aunt snapped, "A gentleman would give us a cabin."

He instinctively glanced at the low quarterdeck, well aware that the only cabin—one he shared with John—would not meet the woman's expectations. "As soon as another ship arrives, ma'am, you will board that vessel and sail for Key West."

"And when will that be?" The woman somehow managed to look down her nose even though she sat well below him. "We are horribly indisposed sitting on this filthy, rotted wooden structure."

"Hatch cover."

The woman glared at him. "I don't care what it's called. No lady should be forced to endure such discomfort."

As she railed on, Rourke watched Elizabeth, hoping for more than that single glance. She gave the cup to Anabelle and averted her gaze. How different she'd become! The Elizabeth he'd known ran about town hatless and barefoot. This one sat stiff-backed and silent. The modest mourning gown had been cut of the finest fabric. Her salt-stained skirts were carefully arranged to hide even the toes of her shoes. She had become a lady, too polite to complain. As soon as the sun blazed high, she would be overcome by heat.

63

"Rander," he said to the nearest crewman, "fetch a tarpaulin to shield the ladies."

Elizabeth lifted her gaze with gratitude, but the moment he smiled back, she again looked down at her folded hands.

"Well, that's something," her aunt sniffed. "This coffee is terrible. I don't suppose it would be possible to get a decent tea service."

"I will have the cook send tea and breakfast at once."

This time Elizabeth mouthed her thanks. In her eyes he saw something else. Embarrassment? Worry? She was not as calm as her expression would lead one to believe.

Her aunt dismissed him with a wave of her hand. "That will be all."

Rourke wasn't used to receiving orders, but he had the sense to ignore the insult. Clearly Elizabeth's aunt had taken it upon herself to guard her niece against men in general and him in particular. He stood no chance of speaking to Elizabeth unless he could get her away from the watchdogs.

Anabelle's gaze met his. Fierce, proud, strong. She exemplified every one of those qualities, yet he could see a hint of concern beneath the careful exterior. Her gaze darted to the rail. John!

Rourke hurried over and scanned the heaving sea from stem to stern. No sign of John. He should have finished by now. What if he'd ventured into the hulk and got pinned? Rourke stripped off his coat, ready to plunge into the warm waters.

John knew better than to take such a risk. Rourke would wait a few more seconds.

He gripped the gunwale, muscles tensed.

Anabelle drifted to a position beyond reach but not hearing. "He wants to take the boat."

"What?" But even as he asked, Rourke understood. John would be desperate to escape with his bride. Key West meant continued enslavement for Anabelle, but if John could get her to the British waters of his native Bahamas, she would be free.

Below them, John surfaced, drew a deep breath, and dove again.

Anabelle watched before turning to Rourke again. "All night they fret, and now they sleep." She glanced toward Elizabeth and her aunt, both of whom had indeed drifted into slumber. "Tell him to wait. Now it is not possible."

How bitterly John would take that news. All night, when the difficult escape might have been possible, Anabelle's mistress had stayed awake. Rourke eyed Elizabeth at rest against a cushion of blankets. How peacefully she slept, as if without a care. Of course that couldn't be true. She must mourn her mother's death bitterly. Rourke knew the pain of losing a parent. A year later, it still hurt.

The doomed schooner's master drew near. Upon spotting Anabelle, he sneered and strode away.

Anabelle stiffened. With a swish of her drying skirts, she returned to her mistress's side.

"Hull's breached bow to amidships," John shouted from the base of the rope ladder. "Another hole aft starboard."

Captain Cross, poised within hearing distance, scowled at the report.

"Then we salvage?" Rourke waited for the master's decision.

Cross gave no answer.

"It's the *Eva Marie*, the *Joseph M*, and the *Dinah Hale*," Tom called down from the lookout.

All Littlejohn boats. The bad news kept coming. Harold Littlejohn ran the most ragtag fleet in the Keys and manned them with the hungry and the derelict. Rourke hesitated to send any passenger on a Littlejohn boat, least of all Elizabeth Benjamin, but they could not stay here.

"Any others?" he called up.

"No, Captain."

Rourke made the decision in an instant. Only one man could ensure Elizabeth's safety. He crossed to the ladder and waited for John to climb aboard.

The moment his mate set foot on deck, Rourke barked out, "You're in charge of the salvage. I'm escorting the passengers to Key West."

John instantly looked to Anabelle. "On de *Windsprite*?"

"On the *Dinah Hale*." It was the best of the lot.

"But you de wreck massa."

"I'm turning that honor over to you."

John shook his head. "Massa not listen ta Negro."

Rourke hated the truth in that statement, so he ignored it. "I must guard the women's safety."

"I go."

"No." Rourke could not trust John to stay with Elizabeth until they reached Key West. If an opportunity arose, the temptation to steal Anabelle away would be too great.

The crew of the *Dinah Hale* slid into view as the ship came about. At least three of them had been kicked off every respectable vessel in the wrecking fleet. Rourke could not put Elizabeth on that vessel unprotected. Neither could he trust John with her safety.

"I go," John reiterated.

"No." Yet Rourke knew his commands weren't enough. "Anabelle told me that it's not the right time. You must wait."

Bitter disappointment twisted John's features before defiance set in. "If'n you don't mind, I ask meself."

"Ask."

But Anabelle now tended an awakened Elizabeth, and they both knew the question could not be posed or answered. Miss Benjamin would take Anabelle with her to Key West, and John would lose his wife mere hours after rejoining her.

Rourke could not bear John's pain. "I will get her to Bahamian waters." Since severe punishment had just become law for anyone caught assisting a fugitive slave, this vow could cost him dearly.

John's dark eyes glowed with feverish intensity. He knew the danger. If their marriage was discovered, Charles Benjamin wouldn't hesitate to claim John as property, and there wasn't a justice on the island who would question the legitimacy of that claim.

"Promise before God?" John demanded.

"Before God."

John seemed satisfied with that. "Who you send with dem?"

With a surge of disappointment, Rourke accepted he could not escort Elizabeth, just as John could not make the voyage with Anabelle.

He scanned his crew. They were all decent men. He demanded that of even the lowliest deckhand, but he needed every one of them for the salvage. His gaze settled on Tom Worthington, who was climbing down from the lookout. The lad was young and green but sufficiently adept with a blade if his last scrape was any indication. He also had little experience in salvage.

"Come here, lad." He motioned to Tom. "I have a job for you."

⌘

Elizabeth ought to be glad to leave the *Windsprite*, even for an inferior vessel, for it removed her from temptation, but she longed to stay. She wanted to converse with Rourke, to ask dozens of questions and plead her remorse, but her aunt watched every move. His solicitous care only made it worse. Despite her clinging to the impossible hope that time would change her feelings toward him, Rourke had lived up to every expectation she had woven in her daydreams over the years. If not for Aunt Virginia's firm grasp, she would have walked away from her vow and her duty.

Charlie must come first. She owed him the remainder of her days. With Mother's passing, the mantle fell firmly upon her shoulders.

By the time Tom Worthington helped her aboard the *Dinah Hale*, an aching emptiness had set in. Oh, people surrounded her. Anabelle and Aunt Virginia hovered within reach. Mr. Worthington followed a few steps behind. This ship's crew bustled fore and aft in preparation for departure. Orders rang out, followed by confirmation. Still, she felt so alone. Would this feeling saturate the rest of her life?

"Well, this is certainly no prize." Aunt Virginia looked around the new ship's accommodations. "I certainly hope the cabin is in better condition than this deck. What a derelict. My nephew would never allow such a vessel in his fleet." Within minutes, she'd managed to denounce every aspect of the vessel.

Elizabeth rather enjoyed telling her aunt that they would not enjoy the luxuries of a cabin. A vessel this small only afforded private quarters for the master, and on such a short voyage he would not relinquish his cabin to nonpaying passengers. "With the favorable winds, we should reach home before nightfall."

"Not my home," Aunt Virginia said. "If we aren't to have a cabin, where do we go?"

"Let's sit here, in the shade afforded by the sail." Elizabeth led her to the main hatch cover.

"You want me to sit on that?" Aunt drew back. "It's filthy. The splinters will tear holes in my gown."

Elizabeth did not point out that Aunt Virginia's dress would need extensive laundering and repair after its dousing in the sea. "I'll fetch a shawl to sit upon."

Tom Worthington removed his jacket. "Allow me." With a flourish, he settled it on the hatch cover.

Aunt Virginia gaped at the patched, sweat-stained garment. "That?"

"Thank you, Mr. Worthington," Elizabeth interjected. "It's very kind of you to offer your jacket, but we can make do."

"Indeed," Aunt said. "Even my niece's old shawl is better than that rag."

"If that's your trunk, I'm afraid the shawl is wet." Tom pointed to three trunks piled near the rail.

Elizabeth spotted a pool of water growing around the base of her trunk. "Nevertheless, we cannot accept your gesture, Mr. Worthington."

"Yes, we can." Aunt dropped onto the jacket.

He grinned and nodded toward the trunks. "Do you want anything from these before I stow them in the captain's quarters?"

Elizabeth shook her head. Though surprised the captain had agreed to house their trunks in his cabin, she appreciated the gesture. "Everything is wet anyway."

"I'm afraid you're correct."

His gentlemanly language brought a smile to her lips. The crew of the *Dinah Hale* was a rough lot. Elizabeth hadn't heard so many foul words since leaving the Charleston wharf. It was thoughtful of Rourke to send Mr. Worthington with Aunt and her.

The captain climbed aboard and shouted the order to raise anchor and set sail.

As the crew rushed to obey, Tom leaned close to Elizabeth. "I'd lock your trunk if I were you." He lowered his voice. "Some aboard might stoop to stealing."

"From the captain's cabin?" Most masters demanded obedience, and this one looked no different. "Surely no one would dare."

"Best to be certain," Tom said as the *Dinah Hale* inched away from the wreck site. "Do you have the key?"

Elizabeth reached into her watch pocket and discovered the brooch she'd found in the mate's desk on the *Victory*. "Oh dear, I forgot."

"Forgot your key?"

"No, no. That's not it. Something else I meant to do." Already the *Windsprite* was a sizable distance away. Even if she asked the master to turn around, he would not do so for a bauble. "It doesn't matter. I'll take care of it later." She'd return it to the mate when the *Victory*'s crew arrived in Key West.

"Take care of what?" Aunt Virginia called out.

"Nothing of note." She tucked the brooch back in her pocket and pulled the key from around her neck. "I suppose I should fetch my aunt's keys also."

"No, miss. Her trunks are already locked."

"They are?"

How could that be? Her aunt had insisted her trunks were latched but unlocked when the ship hit the reef. She'd wept when Elizabeth couldn't unlatch the smaller one to get her pearls. Had Aunt Virginia forgotten that she'd locked her trunks, or had someone gotten hold of her keys during the rescue?

But who?

Elizabeth sucked in her breath. Only one man had gotten near enough to Aunt Virginia to snatch the key—Rourke.

5

Rourke barely had time to offer a prayer for Elizabeth's safety when the master of the doomed schooner stomped across the deck with another demand. Unlike Poppinclerk, Captain Cross's boots were stained and scuffed. His coat was clean but threadbare. His cocked hat sagged atop white hair and a weather-beaten face whose lines indicated he never smiled.

He drew up before Rourke. "I'm sending my men over to patch the hull and pump the bilges. Once we get her afloat, you can haul her off the reef."

Hadn't the man heard John's report? "You can't patch that large a hole. My diver said it's breached from stem to amidships."

The master's gaze narrowed. "You expect me to take the word of a darkie?"

So that was what this came down to. Rourke glanced at John, who had pasted on the blank expression that effectively concealed his feelings before those who refused to see him as a man. John, who had experienced the bitter end of slavery under a cruel owner, showed greater restraint than Rourke would have.

Rourke squared his jaw. "I expect you to take the word of my chief mate. I trust this man with my life."

"That's your mistake," Cross snarled. "Not mine. Keep in mind, Captain, that the *Victory* is my ship, not yours. My word is law."

Rourke smothered his frustration. Cross was right. "Do what you need to do, Captain." He would have to wait a little longer to see Elizabeth.

The master leaned back on his heels, triumph curling his lips. "I will require the use of your boat, Captain."

"Of course."

The master nodded curtly and headed for his crew, who ranged along the rail waiting for orders. This attempt served no purpose but delay. By the time Rourke finished the salvage and returned to Key West, Elizabeth's family would have had ample time to turn her against him.

He chased down the master. "Let my men assist. Together we can patch the hull twice as fast."

The master waved his hand as if swatting a fly. "Extra men would only get in the way. We know the old girl better than you. You stay here and prepare your chains and winches. Mr. Buetsch, come with me." He glanced at Poppinclerk, who yawned like a cat. "You stay here."

Rourke chafed at the arrangements, even though they made sense. Poppinclerk could lend no assistance worth having, but Rourke didn't relish having the man underfoot. He had little choice, though.

He watched Cross muster his men and board the ship's boat. The master's insistence on floating a bilged ship meant the cargo must be infinitely more valuable than he was letting on. A little poor-grade muslin and ruined rice would not induce a man to take such desperate measures. Rourke's spine tingled in warning. He glanced at John, whose nod indicated he'd come to the same conclusion.

Something valuable was on that vessel.

⌁

The idea that someone might have tampered with their trunks bothered Elizabeth. Who and why? It made no sense. Other than Aunt Virginia's pearls, they carried nothing of value. More than once she almost blurted out what Tom had shared, but Aunt would blame Rourke. He would never steal. Never. If he locked Aunt's trunks, he'd done so at her bidding. She must have given Rourke the key when he rescued her. It was the only explanation.

While considering the possibilities, Elizabeth watched Tom whittle what appeared to be a child's whistle. He stood at the starboard rail with the uninhabited islands, called keys, passing by in the distance. Other than a large gap midway, the keys followed one upon another like a string of pearls.

Perhaps she ought to ask Aunt to check her trunk for the pearls, but that would entail getting permission to enter the captain's cabin. Moreover, Aunt had drifted off to sleep and was snoring softly. Anabelle had moved to the stern soon after departure, where she gazed at the ship's wake and the disaster they'd left behind.

After ensuring her aunt was comfortable, Elizabeth joined Tom. Perhaps he could calm her fears over the matter of the trunks.

"Everything all right, Miss Benjamin?"

This was her chance to ask the question. "You said my aunt's trunks were already locked. Do you know who locked them?"

"No," he said slowly. "Should I? Is there a problem?"

Embarrassed, she focused on his whittling. "Are you making that for a nephew?"

He cast the wood shavings into the sea and pocketed both knife and whistle. "Little brother."

"Do you miss him?"

Tom shrugged. "Sometimes."

"You could go back."

"Not yet. Need to earn enough for passage."

That embarrassed her even more. She seldom thought about finances. Every shop in Key West had extended her credit. Even in Charleston, Aunt Virginia spared no expense. Elizabeth must appear wealthy to Tom, who wore patched trousers.

"This wreck ought to help," she offered.

"I'm not helping with the salvage. I won't earn a share."

"That doesn't matter. Captain O'Malley rewards each man equally, regardless of his task."

"He does?" Tom brightened. "I've only been on the *Windsprite* a month. How do you know the captain?"

"I knew him when I was much younger, before I went to Charleston."

"I see." He began whittling again.

Elizabeth wouldn't let this opportunity to learn about Rourke slip away, so she turned the conversation to a more personal topic. "Did you leave a sweetheart back home?"

Tom laughed. "I was only sixteen then. Signed on to a Yankee clipper and traveled up and down the seaboard a couple years before ending up here. Haven't been ashore more than a day or two between ships. That's not much time to court a lady."

"I suppose not. Does Captain O'Malley ever talk about a sweetheart?" Her cheeks instantly heated, so she looked forward.

Tom didn't seem to notice. "He doesn't much talk about himself."

"That sounds like him."

"That it does. Always thinking of others first."

A lump caught in her throat. Wasn't that the way Rourke had always been? In all those years of teasing, he'd never spoken about difficulties or his family on Harbour Island. He'd let her rattle on about every silly thing. She knew he had parents and seven younger siblings, but he'd always directed the conversation to her dream of sailing the high seas. Though he pointed out the less savory aspects of the occupation, he hadn't attempted to dissuade her. If anything, he encouraged her silly ideas. But he'd still treated her like a child until the day of the storm, when he looked into her eyes as if for the first time.

"Are you all right, miss?"

"Yes. Oh yes." She again looked forward and spotted a white tower gleaming in the distance. "Is that the lighthouse?"

"Key West light. Would you like to see?" He handed her a spyglass.

"Is it in a different location?" The moment she asked, she realized Tom wouldn't know that the hurricane had washed the old lighthouse away, along with everyone inside. "Forgive me. That was a silly question." She lifted the brass instrument warmed by the sun and gazed at her future. "Home."

Visions of the place she once knew mixed with memories of the roofless houses and streets filled with debris. The wind had stripped the leaves from the mangroves and mahogany trees. Coconuts had flown like cannonballs. Mud and seaweed caked everything. She would never forget the stench.

"What is it like now?"

"Pardon, miss?"

"The town. Do many people live there? Has the custom house been rebuilt? Are the wharves busy? Are there any flowers?"

"Aye, miss. All of that."

Elizabeth returned the glass and closed her eyes, letting the breeze toss her salt-stiffened locks. The sun felt the same. The islands looked green again. The sea smelled as it always had, but time had passed. A town had been rebuilt. Would her beloved Key West be a stranger to her now? Surely she would recognize some things. Some buildings, like the Marine Hospital, had only needed repair. Her home had been devastated, though. They had slept on the floor of the dining room in the days after the storm. Mother spent every day at the hospital. Father assisted the other men with keeping order and returning valuables to their rightful owners. At Father's insistence, she set sail for Charleston as planned.

She glanced toward the wheel, where an unfamiliar captain patrolled the quarterdeck. Even the wreckers were new. Except Rourke.

"At least he's still there," she breathed.

"Who?" Tom asked.

She'd forgotten she wasn't alone. "No one in particular. I'm simply looking forward to seeing my family again."

"It won't be long now."

The lighthouse loomed ever closer. On the fresh northerly wind, the *Dinah Hale* was making excellent time. They might enter the harbor before sunset. Rourke, on the other hand, wouldn't arrive for days or even weeks, depending on the extent of the salvage.

No one would greet them at the pier. Father didn't know she was coming. No one in Key West knew of her arrival. Yet. The minute they landed, word would race through town. Father, Charlie, her friend Caroline. Everyone would hear of the wreck, that she had been on the *Victory*, and that Rourke was salvaging it.

Did someone wait on the docks for him? Even if Rourke had no particular sweetheart, the girls had always flocked to him. He might even have someone back home in the Bahamas. Though the thought pained her, what did it matter? The moment she set foot in Key West, she would give her life to caring for her brother.

The crew sprang to life as the ship rounded Key West. Tom left, and her regrets faded as the island she loved came into view. The seas calmed, and Aunt Virginia joined her at the rail.

"This is it?" her aunt sniffed.

"It's beautiful, isn't it?" They glided past the huge brick walls of the fort rising from the sea. A narrow strip of earth connected the fortress to the island. Piles of brick stood beside temporary barracks for the workers. Men, many of them servants hired out by their masters, swarmed over the worksite in the late afternoon sun.

To the west of the fort lay the most beautiful sight of all. Building after building, silvered gray by the weather, lined the streets. Palm trees poked up between them, as did wild tamarind, gumbo-limbo, and the beautiful Geiger tree with its orange blooms. Railings lined verandas. People dotted the wharves.

Elizabeth ought to tell her aunt that she had neglected to inform her father of their pending arrival, but six hundred miles had not made that omission easier to admit. "I doubt Father will be there."

"Why not?"

She sought and found a ready excuse. "He could not have heard of the wreck nor have known that we would arrive on the *Dinah Hale*."

"Nonsense. If Captain Littlejohn knew to bring three ships to our aid, your father will know of our dire circumstances. He is, after all, greatly involved in the trade."

Father would doubtless represent his brother-in-law in admiralty court, but he could not have known of the wreck.

"Captain Littlejohn must have been patrolling the reef," Elizabeth pointed out. "Word could not have gotten all the way to Key West so quickly."

"Trust me. Your father will greet us. If nothing else, Charles Benjamin possesses prescience."

Elizabeth must have misunderstood. Aunt Virginia took great delight in pointing out Father's flaws. In her mind, Mother had married beneath herself in settling for an attorney when she could have married a plantation owner or statesman. A compliment, even a backhanded one, from Aunt Virginia was rare.

"Despite his grief," her aunt continued, "he will welcome us. I expect he will be overjoyed to have a woman manage the household again."

Aunt patted her hand, and the sight of their black sleeves yanked Elizabeth away from the fantasy of childhood. Mother was gone. Elizabeth would step into a home much different from the one she had left, and her mother would not be there to guide her.

"I'm not sure I can."

"Courage, dear," Aunt Virginia said. "I will instruct you and get the servants"—she glanced at Anabelle—"under control."

Thoughts of Rourke were whisked away on the same wind that carried the ship into the harbor. Instead of joy, this homecoming would bring sorrow. She could no longer avoid the memories of the past. In short order, she must face a father who did not know she was coming and take on the burden of caring for an invalid brother. She would have few precious minutes between disembarking and hiring a porter to determine a course of action.

What would she tell Father when she showed up with her great-aunt and luggage in tow? She hoped he would be pleased, but the displeasure over her continued refusal of suitors portended a difficult meeting.

She pressed a hand to her abdomen in a vain attempt to quell the nerves. Mother could no longer mediate their disputes. Now Elizabeth fell solely under her father's direction. All fanciful dreams must be forgotten. She squared her shoulders, prepared to face whatever storm arose.

As the ship came about to ease alongside one of the wharves, a solitary figure emerged from the crowd of sailors, stevedores, chandlers, and curious onlookers. His dark suit and top hat befit a man of serious pursuits. Though he was somewhat thinner than she remembered, Elizabeth would recognize that figure anywhere.

Father.

⌀

Slaves, munitions, or stolen gold. Rourke's mind hopped from one potential cargo to another and dismissed them all. No owner would load volatile or illicit goods into a ship carrying his female relations. No, there must be some other explanation.

One look into the holds would tell him what Captain Cross was hiding. Unfortunately, Rourke couldn't do a thing with his boat tied off to the *Victory* ten yards distant.

He paced back and forth, waiting for some sign of activity on the wreck. The last of Cross's men had disappeared almost an hour ago. Littlejohn's remaining two ships waited at a distance, but they'd soon tire of this charade. Rourke had seen no attempt to patch the hull and no water flowing from the pumps, futile though it would be. Whatever the crew was doing, it did not appear to involve raising the hulk.

"I can't stand this," he complained to John, who stood midway between the fore and aft extent of his pacing. "Tom had better keep Elizabeth—Miss Benjamin—safe."

John lifted an eyebrow. "Anabelle strong."

True. Years ago, Rourke had seen her shinny up a rope to rendezvous with John. "She's been living in the city for four years."

"Make no difference. She fast as gazelle, strong as lion."

"Elizabeth used to run barefoot." Rourke smiled at the memory. "And swim. She shocked me one day by popping up to the surface with a conch shell. We were moored on the south shore. I had no idea anyone else was there, and then out of the water she came like a mermaid. Apparently she'd sailed that skiff of hers around the island and moored it out of sight in the mangroves." He laughed. "I started to scold her for taking such a dangerous chance, but she turned those wide blue eyes on me, and I couldn't."

"I remember. You take her back to boat."

"And made her promise not to sail or swim by herself again." Rourke chuckled. "I don't think she paid me the slightest attention."

"Dat's de way dey be."

"And there's nothing we can do about it."

Just as there was nothing he could do to shake the feeling that this salvage was going sour. Everything had gone wrong, starting with the pilot's poor judgment. If Rourke didn't know Poppinclerk was incompetent, he'd think the man had intentionally driven the ship onto the reef.

Or had he?

Rourke shook his head. What did the man stand to gain? Even if he conspired with the master to abscond with the salvage proceeds, he could never work in Key West again. Considering the unprofitable cargo, that risk made no sense. Unless the master had lied about the cargo.

Rourke's palms itched. He needed to know what was on that wreck.

He peeled off his coat and handed it to John. "I'm swimming across."

"No sir." John pressed the coat back into Rourke's hands. "You canna go dere. Dey see you, den dere be trouble."

Rourke growled against John's common sense. His mate was right. If the *Victory* was carrying something illicit, Rourke's unexpected appearance could trigger violence. He would face half a ship's complement alone. In his younger days, he'd bested three men but never ten. They'd ambush him, claim a misstep, and send his weighted body to the bottom to feed the crabs. He stood no chance. Moreover, Poppinclerk watched his every move from the quarterdeck of the *Windsprite*.

He slipped the coat back on and eyed the wreck. In the late afternoon sun, heat shimmered off the dark wood. Choppy seas slapped the hull. The *Windsprite* tugged on her anchors, eager to move.

"Soon," he muttered, casting another glance west.

The *Dinah Hale* had long since vanished over the horizon. Even the elongated mirage of her masts was gone. Soon Elizabeth would alight in Key West. Her father would greet her, taking her in his arms. Charles Benjamin would want the best for his only daughter. Rourke could not give her less than that.

The *Victory* promised the reward he'd wanted for so long.

Cross's peculiar behavior led Rourke to believe the cargo was of considerable value. Win a wrecker's fair portion in admiralty court, and he could set up as a merchant. Maybe then he would be good enough for Charles Benjamin's daughter.

A head appeared at the rail of the *Victory*, followed by another and another. One by one they crawled into the ship's boat, Captain Cross last.

What was going on? Rourke collapsed the spyglass and tucked it in his coat pocket before positioning himself at the head of the ladder. Whatever they'd found, he'd be the first to know.

Poppinclerk came alongside him. "Apparently your darkie was right."

Rourke didn't dignify the comment with a response.

The *Victory*'s crew pulled hard on the oars, sending the ship's boat skimming across the narrow distance between the vessels. With a bump, the boat pulled alongside the *Windsprite* and tied off. The master ascended first.

He glanced at Poppinclerk before addressing Rourke. "The salvage is yours."

"Stop!" the first mate cried as he scrambled onto the deck. "There's a thief on this ship." He pointed a finger first at Rourke and then at John. "One of you. If you don't return my property at once, I'll have you arrested the moment we reach port."

6

Father looked from Elizabeth to her great-aunt and back again, his expression a mixture of shock and dismay. She should have known he would come to the wharf at the first report of a wrecker's arrival.

"I realize this is a surprise," Elizabeth began.

"That is an understatement." His jaw worked. "I did not expect you."

Elizabeth hoped in vain that her aunt would not speak.

"What do you mean? Of course you expected us." Aunt Virginia mustered all the indignation of a woman who had suffered the worst of voyages. "You requested Elizabeth's return."

"I did no such thing."

"But Elizabeth said—" Aunt stopped mid-sentence.

"What *did* Elizabeth say?" Father turned his cross-examination on her.

"I—I—" Elizabeth tried to swallow, but her throat had gone dry as coral dust.

"I'm waiting." He tapped his walking stick on the dock to punctuate each word.

Elizabeth lowered her gaze, once more the child summoned to his study. Father always demanded the truth. Anything less than full disclosure warranted far worse punishment.

"I said—" It came out as a squeak. She tried again. "I told Aunt that you needed me." That much was true. Aunt had simply inferred that Father had asked for her return in his last letter.

"I do not recall saying that."

She hazarded a glance and was relieved to see bemusement had won out over anger.

"Perhaps not in words, but now that Mother—" She twisted the ribbon with the trunk key around her finger. "That is, now that you're alone, you must need someone to manage the house."

"Cook and Florie do admirably, as they have for years."

"And look after Charlie," she added with a bit less confidence.

"Your brother receives the best care."

"I didn't mean to imply . . ." Elizabeth could barely breathe. Fatigue had turned her limbs to stone and dulled her mind. All she wanted was to return to her room, bury her head in a pillow, and let the autumn breezes blow in the scent of the ocean and Mama's oleander. "I—" Unbidden tears stung her eyes. "I miss home." Her throat constricted. "I miss you, Papa."

His expression softened, but Father never displayed affection in public. "If you had written, I would have had Nathan ready with the carriage. Instead we must wait for the boy I hired to fetch him."

Elizabeth could scarce believe he accepted her unexpected arrival so easily. "I'm sorry, but the ship wrecked." It was a poor excuse but the best she could muster.

"Your appearance betrays that fact."

Elizabeth looked down at her salt-stained skirts. The tiny black bows had been torn off both sleeves and the bodice. The hem was soiled. Her hair felt like straw. Only Aunt Virginia wore a cap. None of them had a bonnet or parasol. They must look a sight. Indeed, several people had stopped to stare.

"Miss Dobbins." Father extended his arm to Aunt Virginia. "Shall we find a shaded spot?"

She readily accepted, and he ushered them off the dock and away from gawking bystanders.

Once they were situated in the shade of a gumbo-limbo tree, he turned to Aunt Virginia and asked, "Which ship did you take from Charleston?"

"Why, the *Victory*, of course."

He flinched ever so slightly. "Jonathan's schooner?"

"Naturally. Do you think he would send us on someone else's ship?"

"Of course not." His brow pinched under the brim of his top hat. "He will be grieved to hear of this misfortune." But his gaze and his voice had drifted far away.

"Indeed he will," Aunt said. "He has never had a ship wreck before."

The bystanders had followed them to the street, crowding close on their heels.

"Did you say a ship wrecked?" a man asked.

"How impertinent," Aunt scolded. "You should be ashamed of yourself, listening to a private conversation."

Instead of apologizing, the man gleefully called out, "Wreck ashore!"

The crowd hurried back to the docks, eager to see what salvaged cargo the *Dinah Hale* had brought in. They would be disappointed.

A wreck meant prized goods at an inexpensive price. Once the salvaged cargo was tallied and warehoused, the federal marshal would set an auction date and time. Then the goods would be sold piece by piece to the highest bidder until the salvage fee could be paid. Many a Key West home had been furnished with salvage. Many a lady wore jewelry sold at auction. From shoes to pianos to rum, wrecked ships brought excitement to the port.

"My word," Aunt exclaimed, "I've never seen such a to-do over misfortune."

Elizabeth smiled at her aunt's dismay. The carnival-like atmosphere of a shipwreck must appear curious to the uninitiated.

Father, his expression still grave, drew Aunt's attention toward town. "Welcome to Key West. You will find it quite unlike Charleston."

Aunt looked up and down the street with evident distaste. "I knew it could never compare, but I didn't imagine the island would be so . . . provincial."

Elizabeth stiffened at the affront. "I'm amazed at how the town has grown. I barely recognize any of the buildings."

Father swept his walking stick toward a trim building on two-foot-high piers. The scent of fresh-sawed lumber tickled her nose. "That's the new custom house. We have more warehouses now. Over there you may recognize Mrs. Mallory's boardinghouse."

Elizabeth frowned. "Even it looks different."

Nathan drove up with the carriage. That cut off any further sightseeing until Father had helped both Aunt and Elizabeth inside. Anabelle, who had followed at a respectful distance, looked away when Father glanced at her and then took her place on the driver's seat with Nathan.

"You repaired the carriage." Elizabeth ran her hand over the leather seat, marveling at how even the familiar was different.

With a flick of the reins, Nathan urged the chestnut mare forward.

"What happened to Patches?" Elizabeth asked. "He survived the storm."

"Died last year of old age." Father sat across from the ladies, facing the rear. "We were fortunate to get another. If not for your brother, I might have given up the carriage entirely."

Elizabeth's throat tightened at the reference to Charlie's inability to walk.

"Stop the carriage," Aunt Virginia cried out. "We can't leave without our trunks."

"Nathan will fetch them after bringing us to the house," Father said. "Don't worry. Nothing will happen to them. The marshal will have them brought into a secure area."

Aunt Virginia grumbled a little but was appeased by his assurances.

Elizabeth gawked at every corner and building they passed. The carriage turned onto Simonton Street.

"We're going this way?" Elizabeth frowned. "Did they rebuild the bridge over the tidal pond?"

"Unnecessary," Father replied. "The storm closed in the entrance. Property owners are filling the old pond, and the streets go across without bridges now."

On the day of the hurricane, the overflowing pond had slowed her progress to the harbor. No longer would it divide the town in two. Her Key West had changed. Gone was the debris from the storm. Roofs had been replaced and reshingled. New metal drainpipes gleamed in the late-day sun. Geiger trees blossomed bright orange against silvered verandas. Storefronts displayed china and parasols and every imaginable convenience. Key West might be small, but it was not provincial.

"It's a lot to take in," she murmured. "So much has changed."

"Poor dear." Aunt Virginia covered Elizabeth's thin hand

with her plump one. "You need to rest, and then tomorrow we will visit your mother's grave." Aunt leaned closer to Father as if sharing a confidence, though her voice did not lower. "I bear you no ill will. Given the heat and the primitive facilities, there was no time to post correspondence before interment."

Elizabeth shuddered at the thought of her gentle, graceful mother in a coffin beneath the earth. According to her friend Caroline, the cemetery had been relocated to high ground near where she and the other survivors had clung to trees waiting out the storm. Those bodies from the old cemetery that hadn't washed away were reburied there.

For once, Elizabeth was grateful for her aunt's chatter. It allowed her to examine the passing neighborhoods. So much had changed, yet traces of the past remained.

She gasped when they approached William Street. "When were those homes built?" She pointed to two unfamiliar houses.

Father grunted. "The Bahamians brought them over."

"Whole houses?" Elizabeth exclaimed. "How did they bring them from such a distance?"

"In pieces." Father clearly did not respect the ingenuity it took to bring an entire house hundreds of miles over the ocean. "Apparently they couldn't wait for good Florida pine to arrive from the mainland." The carriage rolled to a halt. "Here we are."

Elizabeth recognized her home at once. Though Mama's oleander was gone, the gumbo-limbo and wild tamarind still shaded the yard. In front, coconut palms rose on slender stems, their thatch giving modest relief from the sun. The same picket fence delineated the yard.

"It's exactly the same," Elizabeth said. "No one would ever know how badly it had been damaged."

"Your mother insisted I rebuild it that way." For a moment, Father looked lost in memory.

Elizabeth swallowed the lump in her throat. Mother had wanted it to stay the same. Her son had been crippled. Her daughter had gone to Charleston. So much had changed. This would not.

Father assisted Aunt Virginia and then Elizabeth out of the carriage. She drank in every shutter and spindle of her childhood home. Both stories boasted a veranda facing the street. Floor-length shuttered windows lined the ground floor. At this late hour, they'd been opened wide to allow the ocean breezes to whisk away the day's heat. Breathing deeply, she could almost smell Mama's oleanders.

"It's beautiful," she breathed.

"It's small," Aunt Virginia noted.

Cook met them at the door, wiping her flour-covered hands on her apron. "Is dat Miz Lizbeth?"

"There will be two more for supper," Father said. "Have Florie fetch my son."

Elizabeth's heart nearly stopped. Charlie. So soon.

"Yes, sir, Missa Benj'min." Cook hurried into the house as Nathan drove the carriage back to the harbor to fetch their trunks.

Father escorted Aunt Virginia up the five wooden steps to the front porch. The entire house was elevated so as to allow both excessive tides and cooling breezes to sweep underneath. Aunt huffed and complained on every one of those steps.

Elizabeth trailed them. Soon she would know how her brother felt toward her. She reached for Anabelle's hand, but her maid stepped away, her expression blank as stone.

Father turned back to Elizabeth. "Are you coming?" It was a command.

"Yes, Father." The pine planks creaked with each footstep.

Her salt-laden skirts forced her to tug them across the boards. Her stays let her draw only shallow breaths.

What would Charlie say?

"Your sister has returned," Father said, ushering her inside.

It took a moment for her eyes to adjust to the dimness of the interior hall. Before her sat a young man she barely recognized. His hair echoed Father's sturdy brown, with sparse sideburns extending to his jaw. Dressed in a fine linen suit, cravat tied at the neck, he looked every bit the proper young gentleman—except for the wheeled chair and withered legs.

"Charlie." Her voice trembled. "I've come home."

He turned to Father. "Take me to my room."

❧

Rourke struggled to rein in his temper at the mate's false accusation. "Search my ship for what you say you've lost. If you find it, it's not only yours but I'll pay half its value to compensate for the theft."

To Rourke's surprise, Captain Cross took his side. "See, Mr. Buetsch? No one took the brooch. Why would they?"

"A brooch?" Rourke echoed. "I would have noticed jewelry. What does it look like?"

"It bears my sweetheart's initial, a script *H*."

"I haven't seen it, but you can search this ship." Rourke spread wide his arms. "I know of no man aboard my vessel with a wife or fiancée whose name begins with the letter *H*."

"A man might not care about the initial when the piece is made of gold and rubies," the first mate countered.

That surprised Rourke. No mate aboard a merchant vessel made enough to afford the brooch he'd described. "Did you commission it, or is it an heirloom?"

Mr. Buetsch shuffled his feet. "No, I purchased it, but it's mine, and it's gone. How do I know you're going to search thoroughly?"

Cross stepped in before the mate's temper escalated. "With Captain O'Malley's permission, Mr. Poppinclerk will conduct the search."

Rourke didn't relish the thought of Poppinclerk rummaging through his cabin. "My mate will assist him."

Poppinclerk's grin faded, for John was much larger and stronger.

"Very well, then," Cross said. "We have a ship to salvage before she sinks any lower. Mr. Buetsch, ready the crew. Captain O'Malley, my men are at your disposal."

From what John had told Rourke, the ship had settled on an outcropping. A change of wind or wave direction could send it hurtling into the deep water that ran along the outside of the reef. If that happened, they would have to abandon the wreck, along with whatever the master had gone to find and the mate's prized brooch.

At least the ache and sweat of hard labor would shove all thoughts of Elizabeth Benjamin from his head. A wise man would forget her, but she had come back from Charleston more beautiful than the finest jewel. The time away had created a reserve in her that hadn't been there before, but the passion could not be gone. Elizabeth Benjamin had more spirit than any woman he'd ever met. No, he could not forget her. But could he win her hand? First he must win over Charles Benjamin. And for that, he needed a healthy stake to start a business ashore.

As the sun sank low in the sky, the breeze died. Rourke's men quickly rowed the boat across the gap between the ships. First Rourke would assess the state and quantity of cargo that could be salvaged, and then he would bring the *Windsprite* alongside for off-loading.

When the boat bumped against the wreck, Rourke scampered up the rope ladder that still dangled off the larboard side. Navigating the deck was just as tricky as during the storm. The slanted planking was still soaked and slippery as soap. Rourke used the same rescue line he'd strung earlier to keep his balance.

If the prior movement of the *Victory*'s crew was a good indicator, they had gone directly to the great cabin. Whatever they wanted was either inside it, on the deck below, or sitting on the bottom of the sea. With the chasm looming off the starboard side, it would have been easy to dispose of unwanted cargo. If that cargo had tumbled onto the reef, Rourke would find it. If it had fallen into the depths, no one would see it again.

"Don't you want to look in the holds?" the master called out to Rourke.

"Do you have all your personal effects?" Rourke countered.

Cross nodded. "Nothing's left in the cabins."

Rourke would get nowhere under the man's watch. "Good. Show the way."

After a deckhand from the *Victory* broke open the hatch cover, Rourke heard the splash of surging water. John had correctly stated the extent of the damage. Rourke swung the lantern over the hold. Unfortunately, the master hadn't exaggerated when he described the contents. Bolts of muslin sat atop bags of rice. The salt water had swelled the grain, causing the bags to split. Seawater lapped at the muslin.

Rourke groaned. The cloth could be salvaged, but it was a small percentage of the cargo. Unless he could discover what the master had tried to retrieve, this salvage would not set him up as a merchant.

❧

The trunks did not arrive until after Elizabeth had bathed away the salt and was nestled in her old dressing gown. Her trunk stayed in the cookhouse since everything inside was wet. Anabelle sent the salt-stained mourning gown downstairs with Florie to add to the laundry.

Elizabeth eyed the bed. "Since I don't have a proper gown, perhaps Cook will send supper to my room. I could sleep for days."

"You know your father won't stand for that." Anabelle swung open the doors of the wardrobe.

To Elizabeth's surprise, several of her old dresses hung inside. "I thought those were ruined. Why would my mother have them cleaned?"

"Because she's your mama." Anabelle riffled through the gowns until she found a deep blue dress. "This will do."

"It's a girl's dress."

"It's dark enough." Anabelle held it up to Elizabeth's tall frame. "A little short, but it will suffice until your mourning gowns can be cleaned."

Elizabeth kicked out the hem, which fell to her ankles. "I will look like a schoolgirl." A giggle rose to her lips. For a second she was a girl again, plotting all manner of schemes with her best friend. "Shall I wear the ruffled drawers?"

Anabelle frowned at the undignified suggestion. "You're grown now. And in mourning."

"And not allowed a moment's merriment." She sighed, holding out her arms so Anabelle could slip on a chemise and tie on the required petticoats, all of which were also too short. After Anabelle tugged on the gown, she held her breath while her maid buttoned the back.

Her gaze drifted toward the open side window, where the wild tamarind's seed pods rustled in the breeze. While the house had suffered under the storm, the tamarind still stood tall. Before the hurricane, she and Charlie would climb down its thick branches when the nights were too hot to sleep. Elizabeth had egged on Charlie, but Anabelle would never join them. Now none of them would think to do such a thing. Her brother couldn't.

She spread her fingers across her midsection, Charlie's cold rejection ringing in her ears. "He hates me."

Anabelle didn't ask who she meant. "He had no time to get used to the idea of your return."

That wasn't the reason, and both of them knew it. "Will he come to supper?"

"You will soon know." Anabelle closed the top button, nearly choking Elizabeth.

She tugged at the restrictive collar. "That's too tight. I can't breathe."

"You have grown in four years."

Elizabeth reached to the back of her neck and undid the button. "That's better."

Anabelle scowled. "The mistress of the house can't be seen with a button undone."

"The mistress of the house has a dress that is too short. At least we won't have any guests for supper since the family is in mourning."

"Hold still." Anabelle pulled a few strands of damp hair from the bun atop Elizabeth's head. "That covers the button. A cap would be even better."

"Thank goodness for the waterlogged trunk. I detest caps. They're useful only in cold climates. They are unbearable here."

"Sit." Anabelle plucked a pair of shoes from the wardrobe.

Elizabeth dug her toes into the rug. The wet slippers had blistered her feet. She couldn't bear the thought of donning shoes. "I suppose I must." She sat on her bed and subjected her sore feet to too-small shoes.

Anabelle had just finished when Aunt Virginia stormed into the room, radiant in her gray silk gown and pearls. She took one look at Elizabeth and shook her head.

"That gown will not do, not at all, though I suppose it can't be helped, considering everything in your trunk is ruined."

"But not in yours, apparently." Elizabeth recalled the mystery of the locked trunks. "I see your dress and pearls survived."

"Thankfully, yes. The small trunk was a ghastly mess, though. The stevedores must have thrown it about, for everything was a jumble inside."

"But everything was there?"

"Of course it was all there. Why wouldn't it be?"

"No reason." Elizabeth was glad that Aunt would not be able to call Rourke a thief. "I am simply grateful."

Aunt gave her a sharp look before proceeding to the door with a sweep of her voluminous skirts. "Your father wants to see you in his study before supper."

Elizabeth's nerves returned. She hoped he would explain her brother's cold reaction, but that was not his way. More likely he was angry over her rash decision to come home but hadn't wanted to scold her in public. He might also threaten to send her back on the first ship headed to Charleston. The possibilities flitted through her mind as she descended the staircase.

His study was located at the rear of the house across from the music room, into which Charlie had vanished. The door to that room was now closed, and she could hear no sound from inside. The study door was open, however, and Father stood behind his desk puzzling over a piece of paper. In exasperation, he tugged off the spectacles he wore for reading.

"Father?"

He looked up. "Elizabeth. Please come in. Have a seat."

He motioned for her to choose one of the twin chairs facing each other before the cold fireplace. That feature had always been an oddity, since temperatures seldom fell low enough to require heat. She had seen it lit only a handful of times.

Unlike the rest of the house, this room, shaded by the gumbo-limbo and sea grapes, had windows only on the side due to the housing over the cistern. The shelves of law books, the ponderous furnishings, and the partially closed shutters only added to the dim light.

As a child, Elizabeth had called this the throne room. The ornate mahogany chairs upholstered in burgundy velvet looked fit for a queen. She'd often crept into the room with Anabelle to play, only to be found by Mammy and shooed away. Once, Elizabeth had insisted Anabelle sit in the other chair and play princess rather than her usual lady-in-waiting. Mammy had swatted her daughter and scolded Elizabeth so thoroughly that neither of them dared enter the study again. Elizabeth could still remember her nurse's rebuke. "Yo' Daddy catch you bringing da help in here, he whup yo' behind."

She had never quite realized that Anabelle was considered help. True, Mammy was a servant and Anabelle's mother, but Anabelle had always been Elizabeth's friend. They played together and slept in the same room. Anabelle learned her letters just like Elizabeth. Until that moment, she hadn't grasped that Anabelle would one day leave the nursery to work in the cookhouse.

"One day" had arrived the next morning.

Afterward, Anabelle could play only after she finished her chores. Elizabeth's schoolwork extended to the entire day. She only saw her friend at night when Anabelle combed out Elizabeth's hair and slept on a cot at the foot of her bed. When nights were cold, Elizabeth would whisper for her friend to join her. Sometimes Anabelle came, but most times she refused. She would never say why.

Now the memories sifted over Elizabeth like raindrops. Above the fireplace, Mother's portrait overlooked the room. She had the same blonde hair and blue eyes as her daughter, but she'd been petite. Elizabeth had inherited her height from Father. Mother's gentle smile exuded a calm grace and dignity that Elizabeth hoped to emulate. She arranged her skirts in the same manner as in the portrait and folded her hands upon her lap. Then she waited.

Father set his spectacles on the desk and paced to the window. Instead of opening the slatted shutters wider to let in the breeze, he closed them. Even then he did not sit. Father seldom sat. His restless pacing had punctuated the nighttime hours for as long as she could remember. He would traverse the halls, hands behind his back and brow drawn. She'd learned many years ago never to interrupt.

He stopped at the chair opposite hers and rested his deeply veined hand on the back. Four years had changed him. His frame was thinner. Gray peppered his brown hair at the temples. His strong chin still poked from between the sideburns, but his jaw had developed jowls.

As an attorney, he never spoke in haste. Today was no different. He tapped his fingers on the chair back for some time before launching his opening volley. "I did not expect to see you arrive here in such a state."

A stranger might assume he meant her disheveled appearance, but she knew he referred to her marital status. Father had made his expectations quite clear over the years. She was not to return to Key West except as a bride.

Elizabeth fixed her gaze on the mantel clock. "When I learned of Mother's death, I had to return."

"By the time you received my letter, she'd been in the grave over a month. There was no need."

"But there is. You need me. You and Charlie."

He waved off the sentiment as if swatting at a mosquito. "As I told you, we are doing perfectly well. If I had need, I would have summoned you." He sat in the opposing chair, knees mere inches from hers. "You went to Charleston with but one objective—to marry well. It was your mother's dearest wish."

A knot formed in her throat. She'd never wanted to disappoint her mama, but marriage was so . . . final. She jutted out her chin. "I cannot marry without love."

"Love will come with time and better acquaintance. I understand you rejected suitors after a single interview."

"One or two. I knew at once that they were of questionable character."

"Questionable character?" He hopped to his feet. "How can you know a man's character? You are young and inexperienced. The wrong sort can mislead and take advantage of you."

"I believe I have good judgment."

His scathing look said otherwise. "I have sheltered you from the worst of society and placed you in the capable hands of your great-aunt."

Elizabeth kept silent on that last.

"You cannot realize that there are many who would pretend love merely to take advantage of your good name." He sighed.

"Perhaps I should have listened to your mother. She wanted you to know why it was so important that you marry well."

Elizabeth held her breath. No one had ever explained this.

"You are heir to a small fortune, Elizabeth."

She gasped. "Fortune? From where?"

His gray eyes softened. "With your mother's death, her inheritance passes to you. Do you understand now why you must be careful? Why you must trust my counsel?" He placed a protective hand on her shoulder. "I will guard you against fortune seekers."

Elizabeth struggled to grasp this startling news. "Mother had an inheritance?"

"Through your grandmother. The inheritance passes from mother to daughter, provided certain conditions are met."

"What conditions?"

"The heiress must marry a man approved by the family."

Elizabeth's spirits sank. Rourke would never meet with the family's approval. "Do you mean Grandmama, Aunt Virginia, and Uncle Jonathan? They are the only ones left on Mother's side."

"Correct. They make the decision."

She swallowed, but the knot would not leave. "Is that the only requirement?"

"It is." His cheek ticked, a sign that this conversation bothered him. "Surely you now understand why you needed to stay in Charleston. There is no one of sufficient quality in Key West."

Her emotions twisted and tumbled like a sheet in the wind. "There are many fine gentlemen here."

"No, Elizabeth. There are at most one or two. If you will not have them, you must return to Charleston."

"But you and Charlie are all the family I have. I couldn't bear to be parted from you."

He turned away, but not before she saw him blink back a
tear. "Do you know the risk you took coming here? You could
have drowned. You nearly did."

"If not for Captain O'Malley, I might have." This was her opportunity to demonstrate that he was one of the few in Key West
capable of meeting Father's expectations. "He braved the seas to
rescue both Aunt Virginia and me. The wreck was breaking up and
the waves were dragging me down, yet he brought me to safety."

Father stiffened. "I will not hear any talk of wreckers, do
you understand?"

"But he saved our lives."

"Lives you put in jeopardy through your rash actions." He
strode across the room, unstopped the decanter, and poured
brandy into a glass.

"But Papa, how could I stay in Charleston? How could I stay
when Mama is gone?"

"If you love her, you will obey her wishes." He lifted the
glass to his lips and drained it.

Elizabeth tried to hide her shock. She remembered him sipping brandy from time to time after supper, but she had never
seen him gulp an entire glassful before a meal.

His piercing gray eyes looked black in the dim light. "Tell
me why you turned down every suitor."

Elizabeth had not expected such direct examination. She
again tried to swallow the knot in her throat. "None were suitable." It was the response she had rehearsed in her mind the
entire voyage, yet it sounded pitiable when spoken aloud.

"Not suitable?" Father punctuated each word with disbelief.
"Society's elite are not suitable for the daughter of an attorney?
Your great-aunt tells me that many prominent men presented
themselves, yet you turned them all away. Do not presume to

think you can put off such men without repercussions. Thankfully Mr. Finch is a generous and forgiving man. He tells me that his affections have not changed."

Elizabeth could think of no response to this unwelcome news.

"You are fortunate," Father continued. "Most men would not risk rejection a second time. Mr. Finch is a man of uncommon courage. I expect you to treat him with all the courtesy that his position demands."

"Is he not employed as a clerk in your office?"

"I am not referring to his current employment," Father snapped. "Mr. Finch is the son of a highly respected plantation owner."

She had missed that bit of information somehow. "Why would an heir to a distinguished estate work as a clerk at a Key West law office?"

"As the youngest son, he does not stand to inherit. However, he is rising rapidly under my tutelage. Given his excellent academic record at law school, I expect to make him a partner soon." His gray eyes bored into her. "He would make a fine husband."

Shallow breaths would not still the pounding in her ears. "But I am in mourning."

"I am aware of that. However, Key West is not Charleston. Your great-aunt notwithstanding, few here care about convention. No one will look askance at a man under my employ calling at the house on occasion. I expect you to receive him, not run to your room. Do I make myself clear?"

Elizabeth choked back the panic churning up her throat. "Yes, sir."

She would obey the letter of Father's law, but she could not grant her heart to Percival Finch. Not when a man the caliber of Rourke O'Malley was within reach.

7

Three nights later Elizabeth sat at her vanity, waiting for her maid to appear. The day had been long and filled with the aggravations of taking on new responsibilities, but at least Percival Finch had yet to pay a call. That blessing would not last.

If only Rourke would return.

Restless, she crossed to the front window. She could see nothing between the posts of the upper-floor veranda and the coconut palms. Moreover, the restored room did not have a door or floor-length window to walk onto the balcony. She returned and flopped onto the bed.

Aunt's criticisms today had stung. Despite having no experience and little training, Elizabeth had waded into managing the household. She consulted with Cook each morning and asked Florie to clean specific areas that she noticed needed a little attention. Still, Aunt Virginia found fault with everything, from the way she addressed the staff to the poor level of housekeeping. Most of all she harped on Anabelle's insolence.

The entire matter had boiled over tonight when Cook served

fish instead of the chicken Aunt had requested. Cook had told Elizabeth that chicken couldn't be bought at any price, but Aunt Virginia refused to believe that was possible, instead attributing the fault to Anabelle since she had done the marketing. When Elizabeth leapt to her friend's defense, Aunt scolded her for almost an hour about the proper way to deal with servants.

"You must wield a firm hand," Aunt had insisted. "Threaten the whip and they'll stay in line."

Mother had never raised her voice, least of all had one of the servants whipped, and the household had suffered far less turmoil than Aunt had managed to stir up in a few days.

"If you don't take charge, the servants will rule the house," Aunt had insisted. "Show them you are mistress by starting with that maid of yours."

Anabelle had been with Elizabeth for as long as she could remember. There would be no whipping of servants in her house.

Hopefully Aunt Virginia would return to Charleston shortly, and the whole situation with Anabelle could be avoided.

Elizabeth sat up. Where was Anabelle? She should have been here the moment Elizabeth retired. Cook said she'd send her up, but that had been ages ago. She eyed the door. Going downstairs might wake Aunt and start a new round of criticism. She would wait.

She rubbed her forehead. Compared to her other problems, staff issues were minor. Her brother had not left his bedchamber in the old music room and refused to admit her. A parade of women called each day to express their condolences, taxing her patience. The threat of Mr. Finch hung over her daily. Whenever he did pay a call, she must give him greater consideration than she could muster. Worst of all, there had been no news from the salvage.

Where was Rourke?

She padded across the waxed pine floor to the side window and looked in the direction of the harbor. From here, she could see little but the neighboring houses and the yard below. She leaned over the sill but still could see nothing. Distant laughter mingled with the night breeze, but the street was empty. No blast of a steamboat horn or clanging of a bell. Even the turtle cannery was quiet at this hour.

Three days had passed without a sighting of the *Windsprite*. The *Joseph M* had brought in a load of raw muslin earlier that day, but her crew would not estimate when to expect the remainder of the fleet. The deckhand would only tell Anabelle that the salvage was proceeding without any accidents. The report brought Elizabeth relief, but worry returned with the freshening wind. Too many wreckers had met their end on a salvage operation.

Not Rourke, please not Rourke.

That afternoon, Caroline had brought new hope. "He sees no one," she had whispered to Elizabeth behind the cover of a silk fan.

Elizabeth knew that she referred to Rourke.

"All the ladies long for some glimmer of interest—a glance or smile—but he doesn't attend any social functions. Some say his heart was broken." Caroline's hazel eyes sparkled with laughter. "I cannot imagine who could have done such a thing."

The recollection of his strong arms and sea-green eyes made Elizabeth shiver. The years at sea had weathered his visage, to be sure, but she found his appearance nobler and more handsome. A man who could protect those he loved. A man of courage and honor. He struck such longing in her that she had to look away lest Aunt notice. Neither her aunt nor her father trusted wreckers, slipping them into the same category as pirates. If only Father truly knew Rourke, he would change his mind.

Moonlight silvered the roofs, and leaves rustled in the breeze. From the corner of her eye, Elizabeth caught movement below. A single dark figure glided noiselessly through the back gate, past the stables and cookhouse before heading toward the main house.

Anabelle. Her tall figure was unmistakable. Where had she gone at such an hour, well after the 9:30 Negro curfew? What could possibly tempt her to risk arrest and Father's displeasure?

As Elizabeth waited, her anger brewed. How could her maid put her in such a position? If Aunt Virginia found out that Anabelle had broken curfew, she would insist Elizabeth punish her. Why would she do this?

The bedroom door opened, and Anabelle slipped inside.

"Where were you?" Elizabeth demanded.

Anabelle glanced in the direction of Aunt Virginia's room, which was separated from Elizabeth's room by only a small reading room.

Elizabeth lowered her voice. "Don't deny you left. I saw you."

Anabelle lingered in the shadows, beyond the reach of the moonlight but not that of her mistress. "His sloop has not arrived."

Elizabeth drew in a shaky breath, the anger wiped away by the realization that Anabelle had risked arrest in order to bring her news of Rourke. "Oh, Anabelle." She raced to her friend and wrapped her arms around her. "You shouldn't have taken such a risk. If he had arrived, he would still be here in the morning." She squeezed her eyes shut to hold back tears, both for her shame at leaping to the wrong conclusion and for her gratitude that Anabelle would do this for her. "Thank you." She drew back. "But don't break curfew again. Promise?"

For a second, Anabelle said nothing. "I will not seek your

captain again after curfew." The light was just enough for Elizabeth to see her lips curve. "Unless you ask."

Elizabeth laughed. "You haven't grown up one bit. Remember how you used to help me sneak out late at night?"

"And tell you that you'd get a whipping if your daddy ever found out. Turn around." Anabelle began unfastening Elizabeth's clothes.

"He never did." Her thoughts drifted back to the harbor as Anabelle slipped off her gown. The appearance of the *Joseph M* today had raised her hopes. Often one wrecker's return signaled another was on its way. "What can be keeping them?"

Anabelle quickly unlaced the stays. "It takes time."

Elizabeth knew that, but knowing didn't ease her impatience. She nibbled at her lip as stays and petticoats fell away. "No news must be a good sign." She let Anabelle slip the nightgown over her head. She must content herself with the hope that Caroline's report had instilled. Rourke had waited for the woman he loved. That woman must be her. It had to be. "He will return to me. I'm sure of it."

"Perhaps." Anabelle turned away to hang the gown and undergarments. "But take care."

"What are you saying?" Elizabeth fought a rising tide of fear. "Did you hear something about Rourke? Is he betrothed?"

Anabelle closed the wardrobe doors and shook her head.

She sighed in relief. "Then what?"

"Your father does not favor him."

Elizabeth groaned. "He wants me to marry the dreary Mr. Finch."

"He wants what's best for his daughter."

She smiled at the bitterness in Anabelle's statement. Her friend knew that Rourke claimed Elizabeth's heart. "Tell me what to do. How can I change Father's mind?" According to her aunt, she shouldn't be asking advice of a servant, but Anabelle wasn't just a servant.

"Some men can't be changed."

"Mother could ask him for anything."

"Your mama was special." Anabelle's voice was thick with emotion. "So was mine. Now they're both gone."

Elizabeth drew in a breath, ashamed of her selfishness. "I'm sorry. I forgot." Mammy had been Elizabeth's nurse, an ever-present fixture in the household. Then one day she was gone. "Do you . . . miss her?"

"You know your mama is in heaven. I don't know where mine is."

"No one told you? I can't believe Mother wouldn't say."

"She's somewhere in Louisiana."

"I remember that day," Elizabeth said softly. "I cried and begged Father to tell me why."

"What did he say?"

Elizabeth remembered the moment with clarity. Mother and Father had sat her in Mother's bedroom late at night, after the servants were in their quarters. "He said that I didn't need a nurse any longer. They wouldn't tell me anything else. What did your mother tell you before she left?"

"My mama didn't tell me anything. You remember that. Mammy didn't say one word."

Rourke smiled with satisfaction when the stevedores in Key West began hauling the salvaged cargo from the holds of the *Windsprite*. His muscles ached, but the week of hard labor would soon pay off. He had loaded the most valuable cargo on his vessel. When John had hacked into the forward hold four days ago and discovered bale after bale of tobacco, all dry, their fortunes rose considerably. He wouldn't trust that to a Littlejohn ship.

Captain Cross scowled as the commission agent logged each bale. "I suppose you'll want a bigger cut now."

"Only what we agreed on." Despite the man's deliberate omission of the tobacco and his dragging out of the operation, Rourke would not go back on his word. A man's word was his honor.

The tobacco should fetch a handsome price at auction, more than enough to cover salvage costs and keep Rourke and his crew off the turtle grounds this year. He rubbed his hands, relishing the thought of time ashore. First he'd return to his rented room and order up a bath. Then a trip to the barber for a proper shave and haircut. Finally, he'd put on his Sunday best and call on Miss Benjamin. If her father put up a fuss, he would claim he'd come to see Charlie. Benjamin had never refused those visits. In any case, he would at least see Elizabeth, and she would know he had paid a call.

Tom said she'd asked about him on the trip to Key West. That was all the encouragement Rourke needed. Her father might disapprove, but he would also know the extent of Rourke's award by then. Since Rourke and the master had already reached an agreement, they could avoid wreckers' court. All that remained was the property auction. Key West streets crawled with well-off buyers from Kingston, New Orleans, Havana, and Europe. Yes, the cargo and ship's furnishings would fetch a fine price, perhaps enough to woo an attorney's daughter.

"Put her to anchor?" John asked after the last of the cargo had been unloaded.

Rourke could see the longing in his mate's eyes. He'd waited four years for his wife, only to see her vanish into the grasp of Charles Benjamin. "Aye. But I'll spend the night in town. I plan to pay a visit to a certain young lady."

John's look of frustration touched Rourke. He'd feel the same if their roles were reversed.

"I might suggest a stroll," he said. "Of course, her maid would need to accompany her."

John grinned. "Dat be de way of things."

"I find the shore lovely in the evening with the trade winds blowing in."

"Aye, Captain." John nodded. "Dat it be. Dat it be."

"You might be able to see us heading along the south shore toward the hospital."

"Dat I might."

"On the other hand, it looks like the seas are flattening. She might enjoy a row," Rourke added. "Bring the ship's boat around just in case."

"Yes, sir!" Whistling, John boarded the *Windsprite* to take her to anchor.

The agent brought the list of off-loaded cargo to Rourke for verification. After confirming the tally, he was done for the night. At the negotiated percentage, this could end up a profitable salvage.

"Thank you, Captain." The agent headed back to the custom house, where Cross likely waited for the same tally.

Rourke hefted his canvas bag and headed for Mrs. Mallory's boardinghouse, a reliably clean place that catered to seamen yet didn't stand for drunkenness or brawling. A warm bath and a hot meal sure sounded good. His stomach was rumbling already for her turtle soup and tuna steaks. From the first time he'd set foot on the island, the widow who ran the place had taken him under her wing, saying he was almost a Mallory with that last name of his. She kept his room spotless and baked his favorite lemon cake when he was in port. He played piano for the guests.

"Excuse me, Captain O'Malley." The town marshal, Clive Wright, stepped in front of him.

"What can I do for you?" Rourke spotted two deputies approaching from opposite sides. He'd seen law enforcement surround a man often enough to get nervous.

"I'm going to need to search your bag."

"My bag? It's just a change of clothing and a few personal items."

The marshal's thick mustache didn't move one bit. "I'm still gonna have to search it."

Rourke knew better than to fight over something so insignificant. He didn't have a thing of value in there. His grandmother's wedding ring was on a leather thong around his neck. He handed the bag to the town marshal. "Go ahead."

The man nodded to the deputy on Rourke's right. The man wasted no time opening the bag and pulling out every piece of clothing while Wright kept one hand near his revolver, as if Rourke would pull a knife on him.

"What's going on, Clive?" he asked.

Wright didn't soften. "I've had a complaint of theft."

"From that mate on the *Victory*, Mr. Buetsch? He claims someone took a brooch that he bought for his sweetheart, but they searched the *Windsprite* top to bottom and didn't find a thing. If you ask me, it's probably on the seafloor."

"That so?"

The deputy looked up. "Nothin' here."

"Good. Pack the bag and hand it to Captain O'Malley."

The deputy did as ordered.

When the man handed Rourke the bag, the town marshal let out his breath real slow. "I trust you won't leave the island. In cases involving foreigners, we sometimes have to lock up the suspect, but I've known you a long time, O'Malley. I'll take your word that you'll stay on the island until this complaint is resolved."

"You have it." Rourke extended his hand, and the town marshal shook. "I sure hope you find it."

"Me too." Marshal Wright hitched up his trousers. "Never easy to find things that disappear off a wreck." He stepped close. "Thought you might want to know that the master of that wreck filed a libel of salvage."

"What?" Rourke's temper flared. "We had an agreement."

"These things happen. The master changes his mind once he gets ashore, especially after a lawyer gets hold of him. Get yourself a good proctor and file your response. You can be sure Judge Marvin will sort it out."

Rourke tried to shake off a sense of foreboding. "Who is representing Captain Cross?"

"Charles Benjamin."

That news put an abrupt halt to Rourke's evening plans. Elizabeth's father would never let him in the house with a case pending.

8

"I do hope you will heed my advice," Aunt Virginia said as she heaped scrambled eggs and cured ham on her plate at breakfast.

Elizabeth pondered how one woman could eat so much. Even after a week ashore, Aunt still claimed the need to recover her strength. They were the only ones at the dining table. Father had gone to court early, and Charlie still hadn't poked his head out of his room.

"Are you listening?" Aunt said sharply.

"Of course." Elizabeth selected the smallest piece of ham and one spoonful of eggs. "You want me to heed your advice."

"Just so. You must take charge of the servants." Aunt grabbed two of the piping hot rolls that Cook sweetened with coconut milk and sugar cane syrup. "We can begin after breakfast with a review of the day's duties."

"Yes, Aunt." In the days that had passed since her aunt's last scolding, Elizabeth hadn't devised a way to deal with her dictates without injuring someone's pride. She certainly did not want to whip Anabelle or even rap her on the knuckles, but she could think of no alternative that would both satisfy her aunt and keep peace in the household. If not Anabelle, who else could she punish? Cook had been there too long. Florie was too young. Nathan? The big groom could bear physical punishment, but she feared touching their only male servant with Father gone from the house every day.

"I have waited patiently for six days," Aunt said between mouthfuls, "but you have done nothing to take control. You spend all your time flitting about town on this errand and that with nothing to show for it."

Elizabeth could not admit she kept watch for the *Windsprite*. Yet as of yesterday noon, the sloop had not arrived. The remainder of her days had been occupied with a review of "social betterment," as Aunt put it. Proper tea service, embroidery, and even piano lessons were again attempted, despite the utter lack of aptitude Elizabeth had already displayed in Charleston. By the time she had murdered three jigs and a sonata, even Aunt Virginia admitted defeat.

"Put the music away," she had advised, holding a handkerchief to her forehead, "before I perish of a headache and the neighbors pray to go deaf."

Elizabeth wished Aunt had never made Nathan roll the piano into the parlor. After yesterday's torture, she hoped her aunt would ask him to take it back to Charlie's room, the former music room, but she'd descended the stairs this morning to find it still in place.

"Are you listening, Elizabeth?" Aunt pulled her out of her thoughts. "You must tell Florie to polish the silver."

"But she just did it on Monday."

"That makes no matter. The silver must be polished and the furniture oiled." Aunt's cheeks glowed and her eyes sparkled.

Elizabeth groaned. Only one thing gave her aunt this much delight—matchmaking.

Aunt leaned as far forward as her girth would admit. "We are to have a distinguished guest for supper." She let that tantalizing morsel hang.

Rourke's name rose to Elizabeth's tongue, but she had the wisdom to keep it there. "We are in mourning. Wouldn't a supper guest be unwise?"

"Nonsense." Aunt settled back and lifted her teacup. "In such a provincial backwater, the rules might be eased, particularly when the caller is connected to the family."

"The family? There is no one else in Key West related to us. Has Uncle Jonathan journeyed here?"

"Of course not. I meant that he is connected in a broad sense." Aunt glanced around the room. "In addition to the silver, have Florie wash the crystal. I will accompany Cook to market. There will be no repeat of last week's debacle."

Elizabeth slowly breathed out. Aunt Virginia never left the house. Her departure would bring unexpected freedom. For perhaps an hour, she could do as she wished in her own home. The thought made her giddy.

Aunt leaned close again. "Are you not curious who our guest might be?"

"The judge, I suppose, or one of Father's attorney friends. You did say he is of some importance."

"Yes, he is important." Aunt sat back with a smug smile. "Enough so that your brother has promised to join us."

"He has?" The first tingle of nerves hit Elizabeth's stomach, and the ham no longer appealed. She pushed away the plate.

"Even your brother recognizes the significance of this visitor," Aunt said.

"Is it a doctor? Is it someone who can help Charlie?"

"A physician?" Aunt scoffed. "This guest is not coming for your brother's benefit, my dear, he is here for you."

Elizabeth's last hope vanished.

With a satisfied nod, Aunt declared, "Mr. Finch will join us."

❧

The attorney that Rourke had hired to serve as his proctor was taking too long to finish the deposition. The man was thorough, but by the time he finished, the opportunity to call on Elizabeth would be lost. Charles Benjamin would not stay away from home all day when court wasn't in session. Since Benjamin's office was open for business this morning, Rourke figured he had until noon. Time was slipping away.

Rourke eyed the late morning sun through the grimy window of the cramped office. William Winston, Esq., did business in a tiny room on Duval Street so full of books and papers and dust Rourke could barely turn around.

Winston's chair creaked when he leaned back and rubbed his forehead. "I've had enough experience with these cases to get a feel for how Judge Marvin will rule." He patted his stained serge waistcoat until he came up with a pince-nez. He placed it on his nose and pointed to something on the complaint that Captain Cross had filed. "This statement worries me. The master seems to be saying that you knew the pilot and had some prior agreement with him."

"I told you already that I know Mr. Poppinclerk. What master in Key West doesn't? The man parades himself about town in that gig of his, yet he couldn't navigate a pond."

Winston shook his head. "You can't say that. It's defamation. State only the facts."

"That is a fact."

"Perhaps I wasn't clear. Stick to what happened. Did you know he was piloting the, uh"—he checked his notes—"*Victory*?"

Rourke frowned. The man couldn't even remember the wreck's name? Maybe he should have waited until one of the top attorneys could see him. "Of course I didn't know Mr. Poppinclerk was the pilot. The first time I saw him was when he came across in the ship's boat. Captain Cross knows all this. He was there."

"That is not what he stated in his deposition." Winston set down the pince-nez and reached for his pipe.

"I don't care what Captain Cross said. I'm telling you the truth. You make it sound like Cross is saying I conspired with Poppinclerk to run the ship onto the reef."

"That's one way to read it." Winston slowly removed a pinch of tobacco from his tobacco jar and deposited it in the bowl of the pipe. Only after tamping it down did he continue. "It's our job to ensure your deposition makes it clear that you did not confer with the pilot prior to his taking on the *Victory*."

"How could I? We were on different ships."

Winston grunted. "You already said you know each other. Cross would say you met beforehand and agreed to wreck the next ship he piloted."

"That's ridiculous. I haven't talked to Mr. Poppinclerk in a month. I've been at sea."

"Hmm." Winston peered at his notes. "Apparently the pilot boarded the ship at Fort Dallas, where the *Victory* took on supplies. Did you see Mr. Poppinclerk there?"

"No, I've never been to Fort Dallas." The tiny port on the mainland was a mosquito-infested swamp from what Rourke had heard. "No reason to."

"You could have met before Mr. Poppinclerk arrived at Fort Dallas."

"I already told you I haven't spoken to him in a month." Rourke fidgeted in the chair, unaccustomed to sitting such a length of time and anxious to get this done. "When did he go there?"

Winston examined the complaint again. "It doesn't say."

"Then all we need to find out is if he left Key West while I was at sea. That would put an end to this talk of conspiracy over grounding the *Victory*. If Mr. Poppinclerk sailed that ship onto the reef, he did so on his own."

Winston drew his bushy brows together. "Do you have reason to believe Mr. Poppinclerk deliberately grounded the ship?"

Rourke would not leap that far. "If he wasn't generally known as a poor navigator and if not for the storm, I might have thought that. But no, I don't have any proof of wrongdoing."

"Hmm, then we'll keep a wide berth on that one. One more question. Had you ever seen Mr. Buetsch before arriving at the wrecked ship?"

"No. Never. Does this have to do with the brooch he said he lost? I never saw it. When he made the claim, I let him search my ship. Nothing was found. Mr. Wright's deputies didn't find anything in my belongings either."

"Good." Winston puffed on his pipe, wrapping the office in a mellow scent. He might not spend money on his attire, but he didn't scrimp on tobacco.

"From Havana?" Rourke asked, pointing to the tobacco jar.

"As a matter of fact, this is Carolina tobacco. I'm hoping the bales you brought in are similar quality." He set down the pipe. "They'll fetch a good price. That's probably why Cross is contesting your agreement. He doesn't want to lose his share."

"Maybe." But Rourke had a bad feeling about this. "He chose Charles Benjamin for his proctor rather than Mallory." They both knew that Stephen Mallory, son of the lady who ran the boardinghouse, had greater prestige thanks to his family's long-standing presence in Key West and his political connections.

Winston nodded. "Keeping it in the family, I understand. The *Victory* is owned by the late Mrs. Benjamin's brother."

Now Rourke knew the source of his foreboding. Benjamin always fought hard in court, but he would never give up when it involved family.

Winston looked him in the eye. "If this goes the way I think and a charge of collusion is leveled, you will need witnesses to corroborate your testimony. Choose the most respected men on your vessel—preferably United States citizens—and ensure they stay in town."

Rourke's mouth felt coated in sawdust. His mate was a Bahamian free black. The boatswain was a reformed drunkard. None of his men had the clout to counter the testimonies of Poppinclerk and the *Victory*'s officers. If Winston was right, Rourke stood to lose his wrecking license.

⌘

As soon as Aunt Virginia left for the market with Cook, Elizabeth settled on the shaded front veranda with a book of sonnets. The meeting with the staff had been painful, and she longed to escape to the far shore of the island where no one would tell her what to do. Since going anywhere unescorted was out of the question and Anabelle was busy oiling the furniture, Shakespeare would have to do. Yet she could not bring herself to read. Instead she leaned back on the rocker and closed her eyes with a deep sigh.

"Aunt Virginia isn't always right."

Charlie's voice startled her from near slumber. She looked around until she spotted his wheeled chair in the open parlor window. "I didn't know you were there."

His lips curved into a wry grin. "I heard your entire display of tyranny. Nathan couldn't very well push me back to my room when Aunt V demanded all the servants line up in the dining room."

"Oh, that." She sank a bit, embarrassed by the stern words she'd delivered.

He motioned to his wheelchair. "No matter how much I improve my strength, I can't move this chair by myself."

"I'm sorry." Elizabeth hopped up to assist. She should have considered his limitations, but she'd been consumed by her own troubles. In four years, nothing had changed. She needed to apologize. The words rose to her lips but would not come out.

"How would you know?" Charlie said. "Most people never see one of these contraptions, but it does serve its purpose." He pulled open the lower shutters, effectively turning the window into a door. "I believe I'd like a little fresh air."

She stepped into the parlor and grasped the handle she'd seen Nathan use the first day. "Do I just push?"

"Slowly. I don't want to go headfirst down the steps."

She was surprised by his attempt at humor. During the meals he had attended, he had spoken only to Father and Aunt Virginia. Each snub had decimated her resolve. Yet today he had initiated the conversation. This was her opportunity to set things right between them.

The chair was heavy. She struggled to push it over the threshold between the parlor and veranda. With extra effort, she maneuvered it near her rocking chair. "Is this all right or would you rather I wheel you elsewhere?"

"I would rather go to the harbor, board a ship, and sail the high seas."

Each word hit with the force of an ax splintering wood. It was her fault that he could do none of those things. He hadn't been able to play with other boys or go anywhere outside this house. Though she'd felt trapped here, he truly was.

"Charlie, I'm so—so—" She couldn't finish.

"Stop trying to be like her."

Elizabeth didn't have the courage to ask who he meant. Aunt Virginia or Mother? Both were true. "A lady must live up to certain expectations."

"That sounds like Aunt V. Why do you listen to her? You know things are different in Key West."

"You don't understand. Now that Mother is gone, I must take charge of the household."

He snorted derisively. "Who asked you to?"

Father's assertion that he and Charlie were doing well popped into her mind, but she could not believe she had overstepped her bounds. "A home needs a woman's influence."

He rolled his eyes. "Aunt V again."

"Perhaps she is right about this. Don't you miss having Mother around?"

His expression hardened. "You aren't Mother."

"I realize that, but I want to become like her."

"Then stop listening to Aunt V."

Elizabeth knew he was right. Aunt was nothing like Mother. One carried her authority with grace, the other wielded a sharp tongue and the threat of punishment. But it was difficult to admit failure to a younger brother. "I'm trying."

Charlie stared past her. "Call for Nathan to wheel me to my room."

120

The abrupt dismissal stung. "Why? I can do it."

"Because you have a visitor." He pointed to the street, where Rourke O'Malley drew near, an oleander blossom in his hand.

His hair was trimmed, his whiskers shaved, and he wore what must be his Sunday best—a tan-colored frock coat and dark trousers. His boots had been polished and a cravat was tied smartly atop a brilliant white shirt. Only the straw hat looked out of place. He doffed it with his free hand and bowed.

Elizabeth's hand flew to her hair. "Do I look all right? I should have had Anabelle curl my hair. I should be wearing a bonnet or at least a cap."

"Stop." Charlie grimaced. "You sound like a girl."

"I am a girl." Or a woman, rather. A woman of twenty, and a man was paying her a visit. Though she'd had a dozen and more gentlemen call at Aunt Virginia's house, none had sent her heart pounding and her insides fluttering like Rourke O'Malley.

"Good morning, Miss Benjamin." His gaze drifted to her brother. "Charlie."

To her surprise, her brother grinned at Rourke. "I was wondering when you'd get up the courage for another whuppin'."

"Whupping?" Elizabeth looked from Rourke to her brother and still didn't understand.

"Rourke plays chess with me," Charlie explained.

"I have yet to win." Rourke climbed the porch steps and handed her the flower. "I remember how much you liked your mother's oleanders."

Her eyes misted. "They were beautiful, but the storm destroyed them." She drew the fragrant bloom to her nose and savored the memory.

"I'm surprised she didn't replant them."

"Me too. I wish she had."

Charlie cleared his throat, turned from Rourke, and bellowed, "Nathan!"

Elizabeth heard the groom hurrying to the front of the house. He appeared momentarily, a blackened cotton rag in hand. "Beggin' yore pardon, Master Charles, I plumb fergot about fetchin' you."

"I'm afraid it's my fault," Elizabeth admitted. "Florie can handle the rest of the silver polishing. You see to Charlie's needs."

"Yes, miss."

Her brother gave her a look of grudging approval before bidding Rourke farewell.

"Do stay," she said, knowing that she needed a chaperone yet wanting to be alone with Rourke.

Charlie looked from Rourke to her with a smug grin. "I have to get back to my studies. Come back tomorrow, Captain, and I'll give you a thrashing fit for an admiral."

The bravado brought a smile to her lips. Her brother had changed so much that she barely knew him. The young Charlie had reveled in grand tales of adventure yet was timid out-of-doors. He hated the boat and refused to swim. He avoided confrontation. She would have thought the trauma he'd suffered would make him more timid. Instead, he spoke boldly and maintained a friendship with Rourke that Father could not like.

Rourke shook Charlie's hand. "You have a bargain, Master Charles, but you won't be the one giving the thrashing."

Charlie laughed. "We shall see."

Then Nathan wheeled him into the house, leaving Elizabeth alone with Rourke, a breach of propriety that Aunt would decry to Father if she ever found out. Perhaps sitting on the veranda in full public view was not the best idea.

"Would you care to sit in the parlor?" Elizabeth suggested.

"Your aunt is home?"

She shook her head. "She is at market with Cook."

"Then no, I must not stay. I simply wanted to know if you and your aunt have recovered."

"We have, thank you."

The air seemed to crackle between them, like lightning in a storm. Dangerous yet enticing. The rumbling awareness and flashes of excitement made her feel more alive than she'd been in years. Four years. She could not look away, could not breathe, could not run to safety. Perspiration trickled down her temple. She wished she'd brought a fan with her, but no breeze could whisk away the danger of the moment. Father might return for the midday meal. Aunt could return from market at any moment. Suddenly nervous, she lifted the oleander blossom to her nose.

"I wish I could smell these all the time."

"If you tuck it behind your ear, its scent will be close."

"What a fine idea." She managed a smile, though emotion made her fingers shake so that she couldn't manage to secure it.

"Let me help." He took the blossom and gently slipped it into her hair.

His touch sent prickles of delight racing all over her.

"Thank you," she breathed, hazarding a glance into those sea-green eyes.

He stood far too close. "It was my pleasure."

His pleasure. The stirring she felt at his words was not proper. "I will have Florie bring tea."

"Don't trouble yourself. I can't stay long." He twirled the straw hat between his hands. "You look . . . lovely."

She was wearing the everyday mourning gown without a bit of adornment. "Thank you." That was the polite thing to say, but she wanted to ask a thousand questions. Did he wonder why she'd left for Charleston so suddenly? Could she even explain it? Was she the woman who had broken his heart? Was that why he'd come here today? She wanted to ask every question that had crossed her mind over the last four years but couldn't manage to say a thing.

"Your aunt is well?" he inquired.

"I am perfectly fine," Aunt Virginia called out.

Elizabeth started. She had not been aware that anyone was near, least of all her aunt, who hurried toward the house at a prodigious rate. With each frenzied stride, she gasped for breath.

After Cook let them both in the gate, Aunt motioned her toward the cookhouse. "You, go on." Once Cook had left, Aunt turned on Elizabeth. "I was only gone a moment, and look what you've done."

Rourke descended the stairs and extended an arm to assist Aunt. "Good morning, ma'am. I'm glad to see you've recovered."

Though Aunt accepted his assistance, she withdrew her hand the moment she reached the top step. "I'm very sorry, Captain, but my niece has much to do and cannot entertain any visitors." She held out a hand. "Come, Elizabeth, you must prepare for tonight."

Rourke bowed and backed away. Then he gave Elizabeth the most wonderful smile. It spoke of love and a future and everything she had dreamed about for years. She watched him walk down the street, ignoring Aunt's fussing. He'd felt the connection between them. Without words, he had washed away the sins of the past and welcomed her into his future. His smile offered hope that turned storm clouds to sun.

"Come along, Elizabeth. We must prepare for Mr. Finch. Your father has great expectations for this evening."

In a single moment, Aunt snuffed out that hope.

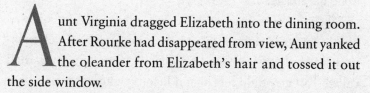

9

Aunt Virginia dragged Elizabeth into the dining room. After Rourke had disappeared from view, Aunt yanked the oleander from Elizabeth's hair and tossed it out the side window.

Elizabeth raced to the window in time to see Nathan accidentally step on it on his way to the front porch, broom in hand.

"Why did you do that?" she cried. "It was only a flower, and now it's ruined."

"You are in mourning and should not flaunt pink blossoms."

Elizabeth rounded to face her aunt. "You might as well have thrown me outside. That bloom reminded me of Mother. Oleanders were her favorite."

Aunt's expression softened a little. "Helen always was sentimental, but she would have wanted you to present the proper image, not accept flowers from a stranger."

"He is not a stranger."

"One meeting does not constitute an acquaintance. Now, let's get down to business."

Further protests would have fallen on deaf ears, so Elizabeth dreamed of Rourke while folding napkins. She envisioned him seated at the table when she arranged the place settings. The candles would cast his chiseled features in a warm glow. He would smile at her. She would blush and avert her gaze until Father wasn't looking.

"Nicely done." Aunt Virginia's rare compliment drew her from the daydreams. "Yes, this should impress Mr. Finch quite nicely."

Percival Finch. The silver and crystal would not touch Rourke's lips but those of Mr. Finch. Instead of garnering Rourke's smiles, she must suffer through those of Mr. Finch. The thought sat upon her like lead.

When Father returned early from the office and Aunt followed him to his study, Elizabeth retreated upstairs. That conversation did not bode well. Aunt would tell Father that Rourke had called. Father would reprimand Elizabeth and command her to give Mr. Finch her utmost attention.

She stared out the window, longing to run to the harbor like she had as a girl. On a night like tonight, she would have shinnied down the tamarind and escaped. Instead she must endure Mr. Finch.

"I think I shall go mad," she whispered.

The tamarind leaves rustled in response.

By the time the supper hour approached, Elizabeth decided not to encourage Mr. Finch in the slightest. She did not change from the everyday mourning dress she'd worn all day.

Aunt Virginia frowned when Elizabeth descended the stairs. "You could at least wear the crape mourning gown that you wore on our passage. Anything would be better than that plain old thing. Why, it has dust on the hem." She ordered Florie to brush the gown.

Elizabeth countermanded the order. "If this is an ordinary supper centering on business, then a finer gown would look out of place. You can return to the cookhouse, Florie."

"Yes, miss." The girl jerked into a little curtsey and hurried down the hallway.

Aunt Virginia was not done. "At least have that maid of yours curl your hair. And don a cap. You look more like a servant than mistress of the house. Anabelle!"

The murmur of male voices on the veranda announced Mr. Finch's arrival.

"It's too late," Aunt Virginia lamented.

Anabelle arrived with the dowdiest cap in Elizabeth's wardrobe and a quick grin for Elizabeth. "Dis be real purty, Miss Lizbeth."

Elizabeth stifled a chuckle. Anabelle was making sure she looked her worst. "Thank you, Anabelle."

Aunt shot her a warning glare, but it was too late to say anything, for Father and Mr. Finch entered the room.

Aunt brightened. "Mr. Finch, how wonderful to see you again."

"And you, Miss Dobbins." He removed his top hat and kissed Aunt Virginia's hand.

To Elizabeth's disgust, Aunt warbled with delight.

Their guest now turned his attention to Elizabeth. His dark gray suit was certainly elegant but impractical in this clime. She rather preferred Rourke's light-colored linen coat. And Rourke didn't have to keep mopping his forehead like Mr. Finch. When Mr. Finch unbuttoned his jacket, revealing a bright yellow waistcoat, Elizabeth nearly burst into laughter. With his sharp beak, the man appeared to emulate the bird with the same name. She had to feign a cough to hide her mirth.

Not so for Charlie, whose chuckle as Nathan wheeled him

from his room drew a startled look from Mr. Finch. Elizabeth turned her back to their guest to give her brother an affirming grin. The fact that his opinion of Mr. Finch matched hers buoyed her spirits.

"Miss Benjamin."

Elizabeth returned her attention to Mr. Finch, who was already bowed before her, hand extended. The thought of placing her hand in his turned her stomach, but Father watched with every expectation that she would behave properly. Childish impulses must be set aside. She dropped a limp hand before Mr. Finch. He took it in his clammy fingers and raised it to his lips. The press of his thin, dry lips made her shudder. If Mr. Finch noticed, he did not mention it.

From his superior height, he surveyed her with the keen eye of an auctioneer. "You are lovelier than I recall." He idly stroked the back of her hand with his thumb.

Elizabeth fought the urge to yank her hand away. While Father watched, she must display civility. However, a gentle, imperceptible tug would make her feelings known. "Thank you, Mr. Finch."

He released her hand. "Please, let us dispense with formalities. Since I work for your father, we are practically family. Do call me Percy." His nose twitched at the last, as if sniffing for her agreement.

"Hello, Percy," Charlie called out from beside her.

Mr. Finch frowned and jerked his head as if attempting to elude a pesky fly.

Elizabeth stifled a smile and inclined her head in the manner her mother had always used. She swept an arm toward the dining room. "Would you care to take your seat, Mr. Finch? I understand supper is ready."

Though she had carefully placed Finch next to her father

and across from Charlie, Aunt Virginia upset the entire order of things by dragging him to Elizabeth's side.

"You must sit here," Aunt insisted. "It has the best view."

In daylight, one set of windows opened onto the front veranda and street while the side window overlooked a tangle of buttonwood and mangrove beneath the wild tamarind, but the room had no view at this hour. Before the first course of turtle soup was served, darkness reigned.

Elizabeth concentrated on properly sipping the soup from her spoon, but Finch's nervous laughter and jerking head nearly drove her to distraction. Added to the yellow waistcoat, the sight was too much, and more than once she had to raise her napkin to her lips to smother a snort of laughter.

Charlie grinned and cocked his head to indicate he too found the man ridiculous.

Aunt Virginia glared at her.

Elizabeth coughed again before lowering the napkin. "Forgive me."

Mr. Finch leaned unbearably close. "Wine will ease the spasms." Without asking if she drank spirits, which she most certainly did not, Mr. Finch poured wine into her empty glass.

The only time Elizabeth had attempted wine, it made her cough and cough until Aunt Virginia sent her from the room with strict instructions never to attempt spirits again.

"Thank you, but tea will do." Elizabeth raised her teacup, took a sip, and smiled. "All better."

"Very well, then." Mr. Finch appropriated the wine and in short order downed both his glassful and hers, brightening his cheeks to a rosy hue.

"A toast," Charlie said, raising his glass of lemonade. "To my fair sister's return."

Father lifted his glass of wine and finished the toast. "May she prosper."

Elizabeth caught the hint of warning. Her hand shook as she lifted her teacup.

"Here, here," Finch called out before downing another glass of wine.

Elizabeth sipped at the tea, uncomfortable with the shift in attention.

Father must have considered the congratulatory toast finished, for he resumed discussion of the fort's construction. "I have heard rumblings that it will soon be named."

"Perhaps we might have a gathering in honor of the event," Mr. Finch said. "Perhaps a social or a tea. Wouldn't you like that, Miss Elizabeth?" Without waiting for her answer, he launched into a list of all the ladies who had invited him to tea. Elizabeth's thoughts drifted to Rourke. He would never attempt to prop himself up in her esteem by naming his conquests.

While Finch chirped on, she indulged the daydream of sailing Rourke's sloop across the straits. What was Harbour Island like? As far as she knew, his family still lived there. He had seven siblings, all younger, and a father who had taught him to sail and dive. The *Windsprite* had belonged to Rourke's father, but the elder O'Malley no longer wrecked. Rourke visited his family at least once a year. Many years ago she'd asked to go with him, but he had told her she must grow up first. Well, now she was fully grown.

"Isn't that right, Elizabeth?" Mr. Finch asked.

That jolted her from pleasant musings. She nodded and smiled, even though she had no idea what he'd said. Aunt's eyebrows had shot up at Mr. Finch's obvious breach of decorum by using her first name but eased back down when Father did not object.

"Do you expect Judge Marvin to hear that wrecking case on Monday?" Mr. Finch asked Father.

"Which case?" Charlie asked. "The one about Uncle Jonathan's ship?"

Elizabeth perked up. At last Finch had said something of interest. "Yes, is it about the *Victory*?" She had heard of no other recent wreck, but she'd only been here a week.

Aunt chimed in, "I do hope you will win the case for Jonathan."

Elizabeth's heart pounded. "Father, are you representing my uncle?"

"Of course he is," Aunt said.

That meant Father opposed Rourke. Elizabeth stared at the chicken that Florie set in front of her. Somehow Aunt Virginia had found poultry at the market, but that wasn't the change of events that caught her attention. The salvage was contested. That meant Rourke would face her father in court. Father never lost a case. This did not bode well for convincing Father that Rourke was a valid suitor.

⁕

"Must tell her de plan now."

John's plea wasn't the only reason Rourke strolled up Caroline Street in the weak light of a crescent moon. The morning's brief encounter with Elizabeth had whetted his appetite to spend more time with her. Something had changed in her, something that had quieted her youthful exuberance. He instinctively wanted to fix it and bring back the joyful girl he'd once known.

His mate's insistence that Rourke speak to Anabelle gave him an excuse. He could ask Anabelle to send her mistress out to speak with him.

Away from the harbor, the streets were empty except for a young couple who had eyes only for each other. He ducked into the alley that ran behind the Benjamin house. Anabelle might be inside at this hour—probably would be—but Rourke preferred waiting in the shadows here than with an anxious mate. John wanted to bring his wife to safety in the Bahamas, and Rourke had given his word to help. After the hours spent with Winston this morning, he knew it wouldn't be that easy. The salvage should have been a simple matter. A bilged ship usually met no resistance from the master. But not this time.

He waited behind the tangle of buttonwood and sea grape edging the Benjamin property. As with many of their neighbors, a tall picket fence surrounded the grounds. The rear gate, still open at this hour, could be locked at curfew, though few here did that. Immediately inside the gate stood the stable, which was quiet at this hour. The far end of the stable was set aside for slave quarters.

A woman hurried from the main house to the cookhouse. From her stature, it must be Anabelle. If he could get her alone, he could pass on the message. He crept to the side of the cookhouse and waited. And waited. It seemed she would never come out.

Finally she stepped out, carrying a large pan.

Rourke croaked the distinctive call of the egret.

She slowed her step as if waiting for more and then hurried forward.

Rourke followed, staying in the shadows.

She drifted toward him. "When?"

"Night of the Harvest Ball. Be at the gate an hour before midnight."

She nodded.

"If no one is there, go to the cemetery."

It was the perfect meeting place. With the fear of specters and disease running wild in the residents, no one would go there at that hour, when they thought swamp gasses lingered among the graves.

"Anabelle!" someone called from the back door of the house.

After giving Rourke a look of warning, Anabelle hurried toward the house and disappeared inside.

Disappointed that he would not see Elizabeth tonight, Rourke backed away, keeping to the shadows. When he rounded the stables, he noticed light streaming from the dining room windows. If the family was still eating at this hour, they must be entertaining. Elizabeth's aunt had said they needed to prepare something or other. Perhaps he might catch a glimpse of the lovely Elizabeth.

He walked around the block until he approached the front of the house. Earlier that day he had stood on the porch outside the dining room. Now the windows were opened wide to usher in the cooling breezes, and five sat at the table. Elizabeth's brother and aunt had their backs to him and effectively blocked his view of her.

Was she still wearing his oleander?

He slipped through the gate and circled around to the side of the house. Through that window he could see her sitting alongside that dandified clerk from her father's office. She was dressed in the same black gown she'd worn earlier. This supper must not be special. A black cap hid most of her golden hair, yet she still took his breath away. Her head was bowed, and she periodically raised a napkin to her lips. If she still wore the oleander bloom, it must be tucked in her cap on the opposite side.

The dandy gestured with his hands, his head bobbing as he talked.

Something the man said drew Elizabeth's attention. She turned her head and smiled at him.

She might as well have thrust a cutlass into Rourke's heart. Her smile encouraged the dandy, who looked at her with a proprietary gleam. Rourke instinctively balled his fists. Such a man might serve Charles Benjamin's plans, but he could never please a woman like Elizabeth.

The croak of an egret ripped his gaze from the window.

Anabelle was warning him.

He stepped back into the shadow of the buttonwoods. As he did, he noticed a spot of pink on the ground in the light cast from the window. The oleander bloom had been discarded and trampled.

⌘

Before Elizabeth could dig into the rich custard, Father rose.

"I am exhausted after a long day in court." He set his napkin on the table. "Please excuse me. Mr. Finch, I suggest taking in the cool evening breezes on the veranda. I'm sure Elizabeth will be glad to join you." His look was pointed. He expected her to entertain Percival Finch alone, or nearly alone, for Aunt Virginia was sure to lurk near an open window.

Elizabeth swallowed hard. "But I thought you had business with Mr. Finch."

Father waved off her concern. "Nothing that can't wait until morning." He bowed slightly. "Good evening, Mr. Finch. Nathan!"

The groom appeared.

"Please take Master Charles to his room."

"But I haven't finished dessert," Charlie protested.

Father's tone softened. "You may take it with you. I will follow. Perhaps we can discuss some of my current cases."

That mollified Charlie, though he cast Elizabeth a sympathetic look. Apparently their elders had conspired in this matter, for Aunt Virginia did not raise a single objection.

Though Finch dug into the custard with relish, Elizabeth stared at hers. How could she wriggle out of this? She picked at the custard, spooning off the rich caramel and nibbling at the pale interior. Father had made his intentions perfectly clear. She was expected to entertain Mr. Finch. When Aunt Virginia yawned and suggested they retire to the parlor, Finch seized the bait.

"Do let us." He hopped up to assist Aunt Virginia first.

Elizabeth would not wait for his return. Instead she pushed out her chair, drawing a scowl from her aunt.

"It is rather warm tonight." Finch offered Elizabeth his arm. "Your father's idea sounds splendid. Would you care to join us, Miss Dobbins?"

Naturally Aunt did not, instead retiring to the parlor with its floor-length windows opening on the veranda. Ah yes, Father's plan had worked to perfection thus far, but it could not proceed in the direction that Elizabeth suspected Finch would try to go.

"Would you care to rest, Miss Elizabeth?" The man gestured to the very chair she had sat in this morning before Rourke gave her the oleander.

"All I have done is rest. If I sit one minute more, I shall scream." She strode to the railing.

"What a fine sense of humor you have developed." Finch joined her. "I don't recall such wit in our encounters in Charleston. Where did you acquire it?"

The man's empty compliments did not impress her. "I found it the only means to endure the endless flatteries of would-be suitors." Society would consider that response rude. That was

Elizabeth's aim. If Mr. Finch found her repulsive, perhaps he would leave.

"How trying it must have been for you." He edged a little closer. "At least here you won't be subjected to such nonsense. From what I have seen, I am the only gentleman on this god-forsaken island suited to a woman of your stature."

Elizabeth stepped away. "I happen to love this island, Mr. Finch, and it has certainly not been forsaken by God. It is my home and always will be."

He looked momentarily shocked. "You cannot favorably compare this wilderness to the society of Charleston."

"I not only hold Key West in higher regard, but I pray I never see another city the rest of my life."

Finch's jaw dropped. Clearly he had not anticipated such frankness.

"My future is set," she said. "My brother and father need me. I shall dedicate my life to their care."

His lips twitched. "A noble sentiment, but your father and brother might not agree. Your father has confided his deep desire to see you married well."

Elizabeth spun away. How quickly he'd managed to bring the conversation back to the last topic she wished to address. "I intend to mourn my mother properly."

"Understandable."

"Six months of full mourning and another three of half-mourning. I can't imagine considering the joys of courtship for at least a year."

"A year?" he choked out. "But that is beyond reason, especially here."

She faced him so he might see her determination. "I care not for what others think. I have lost my dear mother. On this

I will not bend." She had to fight back the twinge of guilt, for she would indeed bend the rules for the right man.

"Naturally." He bowed slightly. "Forgive me for presuming otherwise. I can only account it to being dazzled by your beauty."

Elizabeth gagged on the fine words. More likely he was dazzled by the inheritance she would receive upon marrying. "Sir, I am wearing my everyday gown and took no great care with my toilette."

He caught her hand and clasped it in both of his. "Your beauty transcends all. It is such that I have thought of you often since leaving Charleston. Your father tells me you are disposed to consider my suit. In fact, he encourages it. If he is willing to dispense with the usual period of mourning, surely you can also."

After all she'd said, he would still pursue her?

Elizabeth yanked her hand from his grasp, turned from him, and gulped the somewhat cooler night air. "It is not possible."

"It is possible." He moved close again. "In fact, your father has already approved my suit. I will grant you the requisite period of mourning, but at the end—"

"No!" She broke from him and backed toward the window that opened into the parlor. "I cannot accept."

"But your father—"

"My father presumes too much. I made my feelings clear in Charleston. They have not changed."

Mr. Finch started for her.

She held up her hands. "Please, do not persist or I shall be forced to call for help. My aunt is in the parlor."

"Your aunt is asleep."

Startled, Elizabeth turned to see if that was indeed true, and in that moment of inattention, Mr. Finch took her in his arms.

"Elizabeth." His fetid breath made her recoil. "I adore you. I always have. Please make me the happiest man in Key West and marry me." His hands gripped her upper arms so tightly that they ached.

Elizabeth fought panic and gathered every ounce of regal courage she had. "Release me, sir. Such behavior is not worthy of a gentleman."

He did not let go. "A gentleman in love will stop at nothing to claim the object of his affection."

A chill ran through her. Would he dare to do the unspeakable?

She steeled her voice. "When the time of mourning has passed, I will only consider a Christian man with impeccable morals."

"You will need to search long and far to find such a man," he said. "This world does not reward the sort of perfection you demand."

"Rourke O'Malley is just such a man." Never had Elizabeth been so certain.

Finch laughed as he released her. "O'Malley? He's been charged with theft and conspiring to wreck the *Victory*."

Elizabeth reeled backward, landing with a thud against an open shutter. "Impossible."

"Not only possible but true. Statements from key witnesses have been filed, and Mr. Buetsch has pressed charges."

She wanted to slap the smirk from his lips. "It's a lie. The evidence will prove it."

"On the contrary. The evidence is irrefutable. I fear, Miss Benjamin, your model of perfection will soon be tarnished beyond repair. Perhaps then you will recognize the value of a true gentleman."

Elizabeth raised a shaking hand to her throat. "Leave me."

"As you wish." Finch bowed stiffly. "Good evening, Miss Benjamin."

Long after he had vanished into the darkness, Elizabeth still trembled. Collusion and conspiracy? Rourke? Never. Theft? Of what? She couldn't help but recall the mystery of their locked trunks. Had Aunt Virginia noticed something missing after assuring Elizabeth that all was there? Was this all because of a mistake? But Aunt had said nothing to her. She would have delighted in pointing out any defect in Rourke. No, it must be something else. Nothing had been amiss in her own trunk. Nothing had been lost at all, not even Aunt's pearls.

Elizabeth gasped.

The brooch! She'd forgotten to return it to the mate.

10

The crape mourning dress that Elizabeth had worn on the voyage hung precisely where Florie had put it after laundering and pressing. Elizabeth hadn't worn it since her arrival, favoring the more comfortable cotton gown.

She reached into the watch pocket.

The brooch wasn't there. Neither was Mother's miniature.

But they had been there before Florie laundered the dress. At least she'd had them aboard the *Dinah Hale*, when she'd locked her trunk. She supposed it was possible to lose them between the ship and home, but there was no hole in the pocket and she couldn't remember any unusual jostling.

That meant they were here somewhere. Elizabeth looked under the bed, wardrobe, and dressing table in case they had fallen out when Anabelle stripped off the dress.

Nothing, of course, but the room had been cleaned several times since then. Aunt Virginia would insist that one of the servants had stolen them, but that was preposterous. A Negro could never sell the brooch in Key West without raising alarms, and the miniature had only sentimental value. Still, if Florie had found them, she would have said something, wouldn't she? Either way, an unpleasant interview could not be avoided.

Anabelle slipped into the room. "Your father wishes to see you in his study."

"And I him."

Anabelle looked surprised, but Elizabeth didn't have time to explain. No doubt Aunt Virginia had only pretended to sleep while Mr. Finch was pressing his suit and had gone straight to Father when Elizabeth dismissed the man.

"Please send Florie here and tell Father to wait," Elizabeth commanded as she opened wide the wardrobe doors to check if the brooch had landed there.

"He will not be pleased," Anabelle said.

Elizabeth squared her shoulders. "That can't be helped. Send Florie."

Anabelle dipped into a brief curtsey, the mode of acknowledgment expected at Aunt Virginia's house. "Yes, miss. At once."

Anabelle's stiff, almost contentious formality struck a raw note, but Elizabeth had too much on her mind to delve into the reasons at the moment. Theft was serious. Father would turn the servants' quarters inside out looking for the pieces. When they were found, the thief would be whipped. Elizabeth cringed at the memory of the strap against flesh that she'd witnessed in Charleston. She hoped Florie had an answer.

Mr. Finch presented an even greater problem, for she doubted he would accept her refusal, not with Father pushing him forward. She rubbed her forehead, which had begun to ache. Why would he be so persistent? Father must have promised him Mother's inheritance, but that was intended for her, not for a man she did not love.

After thoroughly checking the wardrobe, she crossed to the

side window for fresh air. The wild tamarind's fine leaves, born on arching fronds, waved in the slight breeze. She could still reach the limb she'd crawled down as a girl. Back then she'd run to the harbor to see Rourke. Lamplight revealed the ground far below. Could she make that climb today?

"Miss?"

Florie had arrived. Elizabeth gathered her nerve and faced the girl.

Florie cast her gaze down. Her fingers worked the hem of her apron. "You ask fo' me?"

Several years younger than Elizabeth, Florie had worked in the cookhouse from a tender age. Unlike Anabelle, Florie was dark as night with a shorter and sturdier frame. Her stride bore none of the elegance of Anabelle's, and she did everything with a marked deference that Anabelle had never displayed.

"Miss?" Florie asked again, a bit more anxiously.

Elizabeth took a deep breath. She did not want to accuse but to extend grace like her mother had. She smiled to ease Florie's discomfort. "I fear I may have lost my mother's miniature and a golden brooch. I had tucked them in the watch pocket of the dress I wore on the voyage here, but now I can't find them. Did you happen to see either of them when you did the laundering?"

"Yes, miss. I seen dem. I puts dem in dere." She pointed to Elizabeth's keepsake chest.

Relief rushed in like the tide. "I never thought to look there. Thank you, Florie. I'm sorry I brought you up here for nothing."

The girl looked surprised. Something akin to respect flickered across her face before she curtseyed and departed. Perhaps Elizabeth could become like her mother after all.

She opened the small rosewood chest. After depositing her trunk key into it upon arrival, she hadn't looked inside once.

As Florie indicated, the brooch sat atop the bits of pearly shell she'd collected as a child and alongside the miniature. She fingered the brooch. It was heavy for its size, perhaps made of gold. Bits of glass or rubies spelled out the letter *H*. Interesting. The mate's name was Mr. Buetsch, if she remembered correctly. Perhaps it belonged to his mother's family. Regardless, this brooch must be returned to him so the charges would be dropped against Rourke.

Father could do that.

She descended the steps and knocked on the study door.

"Come in." Father sounded tired.

Elizabeth cracked the door. "It's me."

"Elizabeth." He closed the folio on his desk and rose to greet her. "Please sit."

She shook her head. "I wanted to ask a favor."

He rounded the desk to lead her to one of the twin chairs. "I understand tonight did not go well. Mr. Finch is perhaps a bit too eager, but I believe his affections are genuine."

"It doesn't have anything to do with Mr. Finch."

His eyebrows jerked upward. "Then what is troubling you?"

"This brooch." Elizabeth opened her hand to reveal the golden pin. "I found it in our cabin on the *Victory* and forgot to return it."

Father took the brooch and examined it in the light of the oil lamp. "You found it lying about the cabin, you say?"

"Not exactly. I was looking for footing after the ship grounded and pulled out the bottom desk drawer to use as a step. The brooch was on the floor under the drawer."

"I see." He turned it over and over, appearing deep in thought. "It bears your mother's initial."

The melancholy in his voice brought a lump to her throat,

but she could not let emotion deter her, not when she could clear Rourke's name. "I believe Mr. Buetsch gave up his cabin to us. This must belong to him. Could you please return it?"

"Dear, honest Elizabeth. You always think of others before yourself. That is how I know you will make the right choice concerning Mr. Finch." He closed his fingers around the brooch. "I'm not certain if Mr. Buetsch is still here."

"Mr. Finch led me to believe he was."

Father frowned. "Percival mentioned the man? Perhaps he saw him about town."

This did not fit with Mr. Finch's account. Surely Father would know that Rourke had been charged with theft. Unless Mr. Finch was lying. She could believe that, but he'd had a look of earnestness about him, as if eager to pass along information that he believed would dispel her interest in Rourke.

"You still look troubled," Father said.

Elizabeth could not speak ill of Mr. Finch. Father would never believe his clerk capable of deceit. Yet Rourke's innocence must be assured. "Please locate Mr. Buetsch and show him the brooch."

"Certainly." Father pocketed the piece. "Though I suspect it's only a trinket of glass and polished brass."

"But Mr. Finch said Captain O'Malley has been accused of theft. I thought perhaps it concerned this brooch."

He laughed and encircled her shoulders with his arm. "Dear Elizabeth. Don't fret over what happens in court. I will take care of everything."

She breathed a bit easier. "Thank you. I cannot believe any ill of Captain O'Malley. He saved my life. He saved all our lives."

"Many men worked to bring you home." He tweaked her chin. "I'm glad to have you here, sunshine."

"You are?" Elizabeth warmed in the glow of his seldom-bestowed smile. Father had not called her by that pet name in years.

"Of course. You're my only daughter. If I sometimes seem gruff or demanding, it's only because I want the best for you. Always remember that." He enveloped her in an embrace.

Elizabeth soaked up the familiar scents of wool and pipe tobacco. She had finally come home.

Rourke did not care to cross paths with Charles Benjamin just yet. When he saw the man headed toward him, his first instinct was to turn around. This part of town did not lie on the route between Benjamin's home and either his office or the courthouse. The man must have business to attend to, and judging from the way he'd homed in on Rourke, that business was with him.

"Captain O'Malley." Benjamin planted himself in front of Rourke.

"Mr. Benjamin." Rourke nodded curtly, wishing he'd worn his Sunday clothes rather than sailors' garb. "I'm headed to my ship."

"A fine sloop she is, fastest in the Florida Straits, I've heard."

Rourke's guard went up. Benjamin did not give compliments. "That she is."

"How long does the crossing to Harbour Island take?"

"Depends on the wind, sir." Rourke hedged, uncertain where this discussion was headed. "With a stiff breeze off her forward quarter, she'll make the crossing in two or three days. Why?"

"Curiosity."

The man's smile did not ease the worry gnawing at Rourke's

gut. Did Benjamin know Rourke's plan? Had Anabelle told her mistress? Before the other night, Rourke would have trusted Elizabeth. Now he couldn't be sure. Hadn't he seen her entertaining that clerk of her father's, a fact she'd failed to mention mere hours before?

"You make the trip what, once or twice a year?" Benjamin asked.

"Yes. Why?"

"I simply wondered when you last saw your family."

Benjamin's placid smile could not hide his fangs. Rourke had no doubt the attorney was deftly leading him into a snare. Unfortunately, he couldn't figure out how. "My visits are not public record."

If Benjamin caught the legal reference, he didn't say so. "Of course." He stepped aside. "Since I'm headed to the harbor, why don't I join you?"

All sorts of warnings fired off in Rourke's head, but he couldn't think of a way to shake the man. He settled for setting a brisk pace. If Benjamin wanted to follow, he'd have to keep up.

"Don't you usually return home this time of year?" Benjamin asked, slightly out of breath.

Rourke began to perspire. Did the man know of his plans? Anabelle should know that no one could be trusted, but she had been close to Elizabeth all her life. If she had talked, then the escape was off.

"No firm plans."

"How unfortunate. Your mother must miss you."

What was the man getting at if not warning Rourke that he knew of the plan to whisk Anabelle to freedom? "I'm sure she does, but my younger brothers and sisters are keeping her busy."

"Hmm. Many siblings?"

"Seven." Since when did Charles Benjamin care about his family? He hazarded a glance. Benjamin looked genuinely interested. Maybe Rourke was reading too much into this. Maybe Benjamin now considered him a viable suitor for Elizabeth.

"Seven must be a lot to handle. Do I remember correctly that your father died?"

The tension winched up a few turns. His father's death had been a desperately low point in Rourke's life. He'd nearly given up wrecking. "Last year."

"I'm sure your mother could use extra help . . . and income."

Benjamin was rubbing salt in the wound, and Rourke had had enough. "What are you getting at?"

Benjamin's smile could freeze a red-hot coal. "I see you prefer plain talk."

"I do."

"Very well, then. I'll make myself clear. I propose an . . . exchange, shall we say. The case against you will not go well. Once Mr. Buetsch and Mr. Poppinclerk add their testimonies, Judge Marvin will have little choice but to terminate your license."

"That's your opinion," Rourke said through clenched teeth.

Benjamin slipped papers from his valise and handed them to Rourke. "The depositions have already been taken. I only need to hand them to Judge Marvin. The choice is yours."

Rourke scanned the mate's and pilot's testimonies. Lies. All lies, but sworn before a witness. "Captain Littlejohn can deny some of this."

Benjamin slid yet another deposition from his case. "As you can see, not a soul on the *Victory* will testify on your behalf. Neither will any of Captain Littlejohn's crew." He paused to let the conclusion sink in.

Rourke spotted the same falsehoods in Littlejohn's testimony.

Benjamin must have bribed everyone to lie. Standing against that, Rourke had only a colored man, a loyal crew that most considered derelicts, and the newcomer Worthington. No judge would weigh those testimonies against the ones Benjamin had accumulated and rule in Rourke's favor.

Rourke handed back the depositions. "Why don't you give these to the judge and be done with it?"

"I'm not cruel, Captain. I would never deny a man his living. Moreover, you have been kind to my son."

Rourke set his jaw. "I'm listening."

"I'm glad to see you're a reasonable man. It's quite simple. You can stay to face the inevitable consequences, or you can exchange that verdict for one highly palatable task."

"Which is?" Rourke wasn't sure he wanted to know.

"Visit your mother. Help her at home. Ensure she is faring well, and confine your wrecking to Bahamian waters."

"You know as well as I that far fewer ships wreck on the Bahama Bank than in Florida waters. I'll never be able to provide for my family from Bahamian waters alone."

"There are always turtling and fishing."

"A man can't live off turtling and fishing. He certainly can't support a large family." That was why Rourke brought much of his earnings to his mother on his annual visits. His father had barely eked out an existence. His brothers tried to provide. Fish was plentiful, but without Rourke's money, they could not afford clothing, candles, or repairs to the boat. No, he couldn't resort to fishing.

"I'm not asking you to stay there forever," Benjamin added.

Something turned over inside Rourke. "How long?"

That viperous smile returned. "One year. That's all. Is one year too much to ask of a loving, responsible son?"

One year? Rourke struggled to steady his breathing. In one year, Elizabeth could be married. Probably would be if her attentions to Benjamin's clerk last night were any indication. Still, if her father was willing to bargain, then she must harbor some affection for Rourke. Hope trickled in.

"When must I leave?"

Benjamin licked his lips. "As soon as possible."

Rourke calculated the days until the Harvest Ball. He couldn't pick the exact date in case of adverse weather. He must give enough leeway for a second attempt. "I will need two weeks to prepare the ship and round up a new crew. Most won't want to stay in the Bahamas a full year."

"Understood." Benjamin nodded. "You're doing the right thing."

The right thing? What did Charles Benjamin know about doing right? He twisted the law to suit his client. He used fear to lord over his servants. Selling Anabelle's mother had been a warning. Both John and Anabelle knew it. Rourke had just one chance to save her. Fail, and Benjamin would tear them apart forever.

Rourke despised such men. As a youth he'd been hot-tempered and prone to settle disputes with his fists. The Lord had changed him. At this moment, though, Rourke wanted to lash out at Charles Benjamin.

He must not.

Breathe deep. One. Two. Three. Lord Jesus, help me turn the other cheek. Help me to do unto others as I would have them do unto me.

How could he turn his cheek on injustice? Though John bore the scars of slavery, Anabelle was still bound to a master, when she ought to be bound to her husband.

Rourke unclenched his fists. If he pursued Elizabeth, Anabelle would remain Benjamin's property. His promise to John would be broken. He must agree to Benjamin's proposition.

He would not, however, shake the man's hand. Charles Benjamin must take him at his word.

"I accept."

A simple nod sealed the agreement.

11

Elizabeth cradled the miniature of her mother in her palm, restless and unable to sleep after yet another unsatisfying day. At breakfast, Aunt Virginia had insisted they go through Mother's bedroom and pack away her belongings. Elizabeth could not bear to see the room where her mother had died so recently. She certainly didn't want to hide away every trace of her mama. She had dug in her heels until Aunt relented.

Later that morning, the wife of the Army detachment's commander paid a visit and happened to run her gloved finger across a tabletop. Aunt Virginia was mortified that the woman's glove had turned black. Elizabeth had explained that the dark coral dust was in the air and couldn't be avoided, but Aunt refused to believe her. Instead, Elizabeth received another scolding over her lax treatment of the servants. She'd been forced to punish Florie by making her scrub the privies, a duty that Nathan ordinarily handled.

Tonight, Anabelle had been unusually silent while preparing Elizabeth for bed.

"Are you angry over my treatment of Florie?" Elizabeth had finally asked.

"No, miss." The curt answer revealed Anabelle's true feelings.

"I must maintain order." Elizabeth hated that her words sounded like her aunt's, but it was the only explanation she could give. "As mistress of the house, I am responsible to ensure the household runs smoothly."

"Yes, miss."

Anabelle could not have delivered a more stinging rebuke. The chasm between them widened, and not another word had been spoken until she curtseyed and left.

Now the silence wrapped around Elizabeth like a blanket. She set the miniature in her keepsake chest and returned to the window. The quiet ought to bring peace, but the most vexing thought of all wove through Elizabeth. Rourke had not paid another call. Though his first visit had been cut short by her aunt's return, she thought it had gone well. He had acted as if he too felt the connection between them. He'd even remembered how much she loved her mama's oleanders. Anger rose at the memory of her aunt tossing the bloom out the window.

Her family might disapprove of Rourke, but he was not one to let other people's objections keep him away. He apparently visited Charlie often, though he had not kept his promise to return the following day. What had kept him away?

She nibbled her lower lip.

The claim of theft ought to have been dropped now that Father had Mr. Buetsch's brooch, but the salvage award still hadn't been settled. At least there had been no mention of it in the newspapers. Rourke should still be in port.

A younger Elizabeth would have gone to him. She crossed to the window. A sliver of moon hung above the neighboring house, casting its faint light on the empty street below. No laughter or conversation. No rattle of carriage wheels or snort of a horse. Not even a footstep or the whistling of a merry tune. Nothing.

Elizabeth reached out to the rustling tamarind leaves. An old black seedpod clung to the branch. She pulled it off and cracked open the dried pod, spilling the seeds into the palm of her hand. Key West had recovered from the dreadful hurricane, but her family had not. Like the seedpods, they clung to the security of the past. Could she let go and seek fresh soil?

She cast the seeds out the window.

Movement drew her eye toward the back of the house, beside the stables. Someone or something lurked in the shadows. An animal or an intruder? The hairs rose on her arms. Perhaps it was nothing more than one of the servants attending to necessary business, but what if it was a man, like Mr. Finch? That prospect thundered in her ears.

She blew out her candle and found a clear view of the stable and gate. She searched the shadows for another sign of movement. For a long while, nothing happened. She'd begun to think the first movement had been a figment of her imagination when the bushes rustled again, this time near the gate. The shadow identified it as a person in a long, voluminous cloak.

Elizabeth gripped the window frame and leaned out a little farther. Who would be leaving at this hour and in such a manner? Father would not dart about in the dark. Charlie couldn't leave. Aunt Virginia was snoring down the hall. That left either a servant or an unwelcome visitor.

She waited, safely screened by the tamarind branches. Soon the person must step into the weak moonlight. Then she might see who it was.

153

The fitful breeze rustled the leaves, and a cloud scudded across the crescent moon. At that moment, the person darted out of the shadows.

Though the darkness obscured any features, enough light remained to silhouette the figure for an instant. The long skirt betrayed her gender. Elizabeth peered into the darkness, trying to make out who it was. Only the faint outline of a hunched figure could be discerned.

The cloud departed, and the yard illuminated just as the woman touched the latch on the gate. Soon she would be gone, and Elizabeth would not know who it was. Somehow she must get the woman to turn her face. She dare not shout, but she still held the empty seedpod. If she threw it against something, it might startle the woman. She looked around and spotted the drainpipe that funneled rainwater into the cistern. Of course.

She flung the pod with all her might. It rattled off the metal pipe and dropped to the ground. The sound was enough to startle the woman. She stood tall and looked back. Elizabeth gasped.

Anabelle!

Where would she be going at this hour, well after curfew, when Elizabeth had specifically asked her not to do that again? If Aunt saw her . . . Elizabeth shivered. Thank goodness Aunt Virginia was still snoring. Father might spot her, though, and that could not come to any good.

Elizabeth must stop her. She threw on the old dark blue gown since it didn't require corseting. Her nightgown could serve as chemise and petticoat. With her kid shoes in hand, she slipped into the hallway. No light filtered from beneath the door to Father's bedroom, nor did light cast the stairway in a soft glow. Father must either be asleep or be closed inside his office.

She crept down the stairs by touch alone, taking care to avoid the creaky spots. Still, a lower tread groaned under her weight. She halted and listened. Not a sound. Since the staircase emptied into the hallway, she only had to pass Charlie's room and Father's study. Both rooms were dark. The rear door stood wide open to let the cool night air flow through the house.

Once outside, she tugged on her shoes. Crossing the yard took mere moments, but she'd lost a lot of time. The crescent moon was higher now, giving her a little more light. She whisked past the stable and found the gate resting against its latch. By the time she hurried through and checked the alley in both directions, Anabelle was gone.

Which way did she go? Elizabeth thought quickly. If Anabelle was visiting a Negro friend, she was most likely headed toward Africa Town, the area past the Marine Hospital where the colored people lived. Elizabeth headed in that direction at a brisk pace. At Eaton Street, she again looked in both directions.

No Anabelle. Not one soul could be seen.

She was about to give up when two blocks ahead she saw the woman dart out of a small building and turn onto Duval Street heading toward the wharves. Why would she go west? Africa Town was in the opposite direction.

Elizabeth soon traversed the two blocks to the building that Anabelle had exited. Four years ago, a grogshop occupied this spot. Today, piano music drifted out the door, but these tunes were not the jigs and chanteys of a saloon. Instead, the pianist played a hymn, "Blest Be the Tie That Binds."

She paused, drawn by this favorite tune. The pianist expertly moved across the keys, allowing the bass notes to counterpoint the higher octaves. Who would be playing at such an hour?

A look would only take a moment. The door was open. She

could identify the pianist without losing more than half a block to Anabelle.

One little step into what had appeared to be utter darkness revealed a chapel with chairs lined up on either side. At the front, against the right-hand wall, stood an upright piano with a single candle flickering atop it. No music rested on the music shelf. The lighting would have been too poor to read the notes in any case. The pianist played from memory and with such abandon that he did not appear to have seen or heard her.

Elizabeth could not move, enthralled. The beloved melody had drawn her in, but it was the man at the piano who held her there. Every phrase flowed from his fingers. Every note wrapped around her like a cool breeze, gently ensnaring her. Each line led to another. She did not want to leave. She could not leave.

Rourke had never told her he played.

⌒↟⌒

Someone had entered the chapel. Rourke heard the soft movement, the light steps. A boy or a woman, he judged, too small to cause trouble. He closed his eyes and concentrated on the music. Though his fingers stayed the course, his mind soon drifted. Whoever this person was, he or she had just missed Anabelle. God's doing, no doubt. Even a woman or boy might tell tales that would bring condemnation on both Anabelle and him. The fact that this person remained silent meant that none of their conversation had been overheard.

Rather than stop at the end of the hymn, he moved straight into another and another. Still the person did not move or speak. The longer he played, the greater the chance that Anabelle would safely reach her husband aboard the *Windsprite*.

Rourke had cleared the way for their meeting, but it had in-

156

volved too many players for his comfort. He did not yet know if Benjamin's groom could be trusted. He'd appealed to the man's sense of justice as well as the love of a husband for his wife. Though Nathan was not married to his love in the way that whites defined the institution, they had lived as husband and wife for many a year. In every way but law they were a family, with a daughter to show for it. Such a man should understand a husband's desperate longing for his wife.

What if Nathan didn't? What if the footsteps Rourke had heard enter the chapel belonged to the man's daughter? She could betray Anabelle to her master. Charles Benjamin would ensure Anabelle never had another chance to escape. He had sold her mother to a Louisiana planter. The daughter could easily follow. Anabelle could disappear into a place where neither Rourke nor John could ever find her.

At all costs, Benjamin must not discover this plot.

The hymns rose as prayers—for strength, for standing upon God's promises. Rourke would play through the night if it would guarantee Anabelle's safety.

By the fourth hymn, a familiar scent tickled his nose. Jasmine. Elizabeth.

His fingers stilled, the last note dropping into the darkness like a raindrop into a cistern. Could it be her? Or were his senses mistaken? No word had been spoken. Another person might use that scent. On the other hand, enough time had passed for Anabelle to have reached the *Windsprite*.

Drawn like a moth to flame, he turned.

There she stood, in a dress too short and too plain. Her honey-eyed hair flowed over her shoulders in loose waves. The dying candle bronzed the curves of her face. Her eyes were closed, her face tilted up as if drinking in heaven's glow.

He held his breath and wished the moment would not end.

Then her lips parted, her face turned to him, and she opened those blue eyes. "You stopped playing."

Her words reverberated in the empty room, soft and low and deeply felt, almost reverent.

He could not rip his gaze from her. "I reached the end."

Still she did not move. "You play so beautifully. I did not know. How long?"

"Many years. The boardinghouse has a piano."

"I've never known a sailor to play."

"Many do."

"Hymns?"

"No." He could not tell her that they played in grogshops for a drink or a strumpet's attention. A woman like Elizabeth should never know the darker side of life. Her father was right to protect her. Rourke must too.

"A pity," she breathed. "They are so . . . peaceful."

Peace. That was what he'd seen in her expression a moment ago and what had been missing from it the other night at supper with Finch. "You aren't at peace?"

"How can I be?"

She looked at the piano with such longing that he wanted to play the song that would bring back her contentment. Unfortunately, a song would only soothe for a short while. Elizabeth needed to heal. He understood such grief, for he had endured it also. "You miss your mother."

"How can I not?"

Though he knew no words could soothe, he said them anyway. "She was a good woman."

Elizabeth averted her gaze. "I want to be like her, filled with grace and compassion, but I make such a blunder of things." She swiped at her face.

He had no idea what was bringing the tears to her eyes. He only knew that he wanted to wipe those tears away, and that was dangerous thinking. "You're very much like her. You have grace and compassion."

"But not peace," she said with a hint of desperation. "Never peace."

"God grants peace."

"Does He? That is not my experience."

Rourke had suffered his own shortage of peace lately. Did that mean he'd strayed? Surely bringing a slave to freedom counted as righteous in God's estimation. Yet with Elizabeth standing before him fragile as a newly opened bloom, he recognized why peace evaded him. Desire. For all his plans to do what was right, he still wanted to love her, to hold her, to make her his wife. He would throw away every ounce of righteousness for that one taste of desire. Yet that was wrong. Love considers first the beloved. No wonder he knew no peace.

Elizabeth gazed at the chapel's rude altar, perhaps unaware that the poor, the sick, and the enslaved worshiped here. "I know little peace of late."

She had echoed the words of his heart and unwittingly confirmed what he must do. Love cannot live in tainted soil.

She stared ahead, not at him. "Why would she get yellow fever after all these years? Newcomers catch it. They're the ones who die. Not someone who has lived here for years. Not my mother."

Her anguish knifed through Rourke. "It can afflict anyone."

Instead of consoling, his words brought tears. She pressed her sleeve against her eyes. Though she sobbed in silence, the shudder of her shoulders betrayed her heartache. He could not sit at a piano when the woman he adored suffered.

The jasmine scent grew stronger the nearer he came.

"I'm sorry," he whispered, but words were inadequate.

She shook her head.

"She was a fine woman," he tried again, blundering badly. He stood within reach, longing to touch her, yet fearing the repercussions if he did. "She loved the Lord and is with Him now."

"How do you know?" She lifted a tearstained face torn with anguish. "How can you be certain?"

He couldn't, of course. None but God knew a person's heart. Yet he'd seen signs. "She helped the less fortunate. She visited the sick at the hospital."

Her coral lips curved into a perfect oval. "Is that enough?"

It wasn't. Only faith in Jesus Christ could guarantee salvation. "Our Lord is enough."

She collapsed again into wracking sobs, and this time he could not restrain himself. He wrapped his arms around her. She fell against him, the jasmine enveloping him so completely that he lost all sense of time. He wanted to stand there forever. He held her, rubbing her back gently as if she were a child. In some ways she was.

"It will get better with time." At least it had for him. Occasionally the aching loss still rolled over him, but it struck less frequently now. Perhaps the time had finally come to share the pain of that loss. "I still miss my father, but I don't think of him every day anymore."

"Your father?" The candlelight flickered in her eyes. "I didn't know he passed on."

"Last year." His throat constricted. He couldn't say the rest, not even to Elizabeth. "It was a difficult year, but it gets better."

"I hope you're right." She wrapped her arms around his neck, and the shock of her touch nearly cost the last of his control.

Drawn from painful memories to the much more pleasurable present, he traced a finger down her temple and around her ear. "It will."

Her head lifted from his shoulder, and a pocket of cold came between them. "In time and with effort and dedication."

She will obey her father's wishes.

The thought startled him. This Elizabeth was not the carefree girl of four years ago. This Elizabeth clung to the strictures of society. He had waited for her for four years. Would she wait a year for him? His heart hoped she would, but his head—and all the evidence he'd seen thus far—said she wouldn't.

The moon had transited enough to now stream through the doorway, turning her to marble. Cold, hard stone.

He removed her hands from his neck and stepped away.

She reached for him like a child to a parent. "Don't let go."

"I must." He could not trust himself to explain further.

"But don't you understand? I-I-I care for you. Don't you . . . ?"

Her desperation broke his heart. She could not know the emotions that warred inside him, how much he wanted to confirm her dearest hopes. He had waited four years to do so, but Anabelle's life was in his hands. He could not promise Elizabeth anything, nor could he tell her why.

"I must leave." He backed away.

The last fragment of hope died in her eyes. She staggered back, tears pooling, yet the old Elizabeth reappeared in the stiffened shoulders and jutted chin. "I understand." Her voice wavered. "I understand perfectly. You don't care."

He could not look in her eyes. Agreeing would be the kindest thing to do. It would sting for the moment but eventually heal over. It would also be a lie. "I must go."

When she discovered that he had sailed away and would not

return for a full year, her anger would flash and her affection would wither.

A sob hiccuped out of her.

He turned from her before he changed his mind.

Her footsteps raced away as the candle sputtered and died.

12

Rourke hadn't answered her. He hadn't insisted he loved her or even cared for her. No, he'd let her stand there raw and vulnerable. Then he'd looked away before firing the final volley. He had to leave, as if being near her was intolerable. He'd even turned his back on her.

Elizabeth carried that pain home with her. She woke up to it—and to a raging dispute in the pantry between Aunt Virginia and Anabelle.

She could not face her aunt this morning, not when she knew Anabelle had broken curfew and left the house after midnight. It was getting more and more difficult to defend her friend.

Elizabeth still ached from Rourke's rejection. She could not bear to see another soul, so she escaped to the only room no one would think to search—her mother's bedchamber. She turned the knob, and tightness gripped her chest. What would she find inside? Often the bedding, the clothes, and even the furnishings of a yellow fever victim were burned. Was it all gone? Were the miniature and the portrait in Father's study the only things that remained of her mother?

She took a deep breath and pushed open the door.

Time seemed to have stood still inside the room. Her mother's brushes lay on her dressing table exactly where she must have left them. The bristles were even turned up—so they would stay stiff, Mother had always claimed. Elizabeth stepped into the room and closed the door behind her. A gentle breeze tickled her cheeks. The air smelled antiseptic, of vinegar and lime. She wandered to the dressing table where a saucer was filled with water mixed with chloride of lime. She'd seen this used near coffins and in sickrooms to purify the air. She drew the stopper from the bottle of rose water. The fragrance brought a trace of her mother near, as if she had whispered past and floated out the open windows.

Open windows. That meant Florie kept the room clean. Mother's favorite quilt, appliquéd with oleander blooms, topped the bed. The piles of pillows were plumped and freshly covered with crisp linens. Mama's Bible lay open on her writing table, which had been pulled beside the bed.

Elizabeth glanced at the page. Psalms. The twenty-third.

Mother knew she would not live. Yet nothing in the room spoke defeat. The light cotton curtains billowed in the breeze. A vase of brilliant orange-red Turk's Caps graced her writing desk. The blotter stood ready beneath the open Bible. Ink pot and pens waited in the upper right corner. A blue satin gown hung at the ready, as if she expected to go to a soiree the next day.

Elizabeth let the tears well in her eyes. "I miss you, Mama."

The breeze carried her whisper around the room and out into the shimmering blue sky.

"Why?" A sob escaped. "How could you die? You were here too long to let yellow fever take you. Did you give up? Was it because I disappointed you?" She pressed her wadded handkerchief to her face. It wiped away the tears but not the questions. "Didn't you know that I would need you? Why did you have to go?"

She sank onto the edge of the bed. A teardrop splashed against the blotter. She swiped at it, but it had already soaked in, marring the pristine surface. Mother was so careful in her writing. She never left an ink blot or misspelled a word. This blotter appeared unused, yet Elizabeth had received a letter from her dated a week before she perished. Had Mother kept her letters?

Elizabeth pulled open the smaller drawer. Extra pens and nibs were neatly arranged beside two bottles of ink. The larger drawer contained the letterhead, embossed with "Mrs. Charles Benjamin" and a floral flourish. It also contained letters received. Elizabeth's letters sat in front, tied by a bright blue silk ribbon. Her most recent letter had been written nearly six months ago, three months before Mother's death. If Elizabeth had been a good daughter, she would have written each day.

She slammed the drawer shut and drew in a shaky breath. Maybe she shouldn't have looked through the desk. Memories only intensified the pain.

Oh, to hear her mother's voice again, to know what she was thinking. She had encouraged Elizabeth to keep a diary, advice that Elizabeth had not followed. Surely if Mother advocated writing, she would have kept one herself. Then where could it be? There wasn't one in the writing desk. The dressing table drawer contained pins and combs and paste jewelry.

Her gaze landed on the washstand. Though the pitcher and basin waited atop the little table, it also had a drawer, generally used for soap and creams. Elizabeth pulled it open but found only the usual toilette articles. She sank to the floor. No diary. Nothing at all written in her mama's hand. That seemed odd. For a woman who loved to write, who sent Elizabeth several letters each week, surely there would be something of her writing in the room.

Unless someone had removed it.

Elizabeth's stomach turned. Who and why? If they hadn't burned the curtains and bedding, they wouldn't burn her diary. Then where was it? Had Father found and kept it?

Her head ached and her feet were going numb. She unfolded her legs. Mother and Father did not display emotion in public or before their children. She could not remember Father holding Mother or comforting her beyond handing her a handkerchief and telling her to gather herself. But a calm public face could hide deep passions. Perhaps losing her had hit Father particularly hard. He might need to hold on to Mother's words.

"Elizabeth!" Aunt Virginia called up the stairs.

Under no circumstances did Elizabeth want her aunt in this room. She rose, but her feet were still tingling. They gave way, and she grabbed at the washstand for support. Her fingers caught the drawer handle just before she landed on her backside. Her momentum pulled the drawer out, spilling its contents.

"What's going on?" Aunt Virginia called out from much nearer.

"Nothing," Elizabeth yelled as she stuffed the contents back into the drawer. "I'll be with you in a minute."

She knew Aunt Virginia wouldn't settle for that, so she shoved the drawer back into the stand. It wouldn't close. She tried again, assuming she hadn't gotten it aligned properly. Still it wouldn't close. Over and over she tried with the same result. Something was jamming the back of the opening. She pulled out the drawer and verified that the contents were all in place. That being the case, she stuck her hand into the opening and felt around. Her fingers settled on something stuck in the back of the opening. By wiggling and tugging, she was able to remove a small book covered in black leather. A glance at the first page confirmed this belonged to her mother.

The missing diary had been found.

"Where are you?" Aunt Virginia huffed from the hallway, clearly out of breath from climbing the stairs.

Elizabeth slid the drawer back into place and tucked the diary in the pocket of her dressing gown. Whatever Mother had written must wait for now. How the diary had gotten jammed behind the drawer was a mystery, but she was glad she'd found it.

"Elizabeth?" Aunt Virginia sounded perturbed.

After padding across the rug, Elizabeth smoothed the quilt and eyed the adjoining door into Father's room. He would be gone to work by now. She tiptoed across the room and slipped through the door. In seconds she darted into the hallway behind Aunt Virginia, who was standing in the doorway to Elizabeth's room.

"You were looking for me?"

Aunt Virginia jumped. "Goodness! You startled me."

"I'm sorry. What happened?"

Thankfully Aunt Virginia launched into a tirade over Anabelle's insolence and neglected to ask why Elizabeth had been in her father's room. Elizabeth tried to listen, but the entire time she longed to read the little diary secreted in her pocket.

◦━◉━◦

Town Marshal Wright ambled up the dock as if he had no purpose in mind, but his path led directly to Rourke. What had happened now?

"Load the rest of the supplies into the boat," Rourke said to John.

His mate grinned. "Got company, I see."

Rourke stretched his stiff back. Lowering supplies into the

ship's boat at low tide gave him a backache these days. Yet another sign that he needed to get out of the business.

"Good news, Marshal?" he called out when Wright got within earshot.

The man didn't reveal his reason for the visit until he stood eye to eye with Rourke. "Marshal Maloney tells me the auction date has been set for the salvage from the *Victory*."

"It has?" Rourke wondered why the federal marshal hadn't informed him directly.

"Seems the plaintiffs removed their objections." Wright's dark eyes harbored misgivings. "Mighty peculiar, if you ask me. Once a man goes to the bother of hiring a lawyer, seems he'd want to follow through."

"It would seem so."

Wright grunted, clearly not satisfied with the outcome of the case. He glanced over the edge of the wharf at Rourke's loaded boat. "Looks like you're planning to head out."

"Only after you tell me I'm free to leave. Did Mr. Buetsch find his brooch?"

"No. Claims he doesn't care anymore what happened to it." Wright eyed the ship's boat and then the *Windsprite* at anchor in the far reaches of the harbor. "Mighty odd. Put up a fuss, press charges, and then claim not to care." He shook his head. "I'd put down a day's wages that it's in someone's hands."

"Yes, sir." Rourke knew better than to argue with an ornery lawman.

"On the other hand, can't rightly hold a man for theft when there's no evidence."

So Benjamin had done his job. Probably talked Buetsch into recanting his charges. That ought to feel good, but the dropping of charges meant Rourke had to sail for home. Soon. With the night of the escape ten days away, he'd have to either come up with a good reason to hang around the harbor or slip away to one of the hidden coves nearby.

"Thank you, Marshal." He tipped a finger to his hat in acknowledgment.

"Don't think I'll forget," the lawman blustered. "I've got my eyes on you, O'Malley, and on the pawnbrokers and jewelers. If I see anything resembling that brooch, I'll come looking for you." Seemingly satisfied with that threat, he moved on.

Rourke's name hadn't been cleared. If anything, it had been muddied.

"Good news fo' de master," John sang out from the boat. "Good news fo' de mate. God be happy."

"God might be happy, but we have work to do." Rourke scrambled into the boat. "Let's head out. I need to speak to the crew."

Only the most loyal would stay with him for an unprofitable year in Bahamian waters. That could leave him very shorthanded for the crossing, but Rourke would not lie to his men. They must be made aware of his downturn in fortune. However, he couldn't tell them the whole story quite yet. The less they knew of his plan to bring along an unexpected and illegal passenger, the safer they and his plan would be.

Still, as the boat pulled away from the wharf, a terrible emptiness settled in. He had waited four years for Elizabeth. Could she wait just one?

⁓✦⁓

Elizabeth could not read the diary during the day. After speaking in private with Anabelle about her nighttime excursion, she had to endure Aunt Virginia hovering over her every move. When Caroline and her mother paid a visit, Elizabeth was glad to leave the older women in the parlor to discuss the new ladies' temperance league while she and her friend withdrew to the veranda.

"Thank you." Elizabeth sighed as she and Caroline enjoyed the breezes. "I couldn't bear another minute of supervision. I do wish you had called sooner. We haven't had much chance to talk."

"It has only been a couple weeks. You have much to do to get properly settled." The petite woman leaned forward to squeeze Elizabeth's hand. "Things will return to normal in time."

Elizabeth shook her head. "What is normal? Everything has changed." A lump formed in her throat at the thought of Mother's diary. Maybe reading her mama's words would bring back her soft voice and gentle advice. "I miss her."

Caroline didn't need to ask who Elizabeth meant. "Of course you do. The next time I visit, we will bring flowers for your mother's grave."

Elizabeth swiped away a tear. "I seem to be a basketful of emotions these days." This time she squeezed Caroline's hand. Though plain and undistinguished in society's terms, Caroline Brown had always been her dearest friend after Anabelle. "Thank you for your consideration. I would like to do that. Perhaps we might continue the walk into town." Her mind drifted toward the harbor, but her ears noted Aunt's strident voice through the parlor windows. "Today wouldn't do."

Caroline leaned close and shielded her face with her fan. "His ship is still here."

Elizabeth felt an uncontrollable thrill despite the finality of his words last night, but it was not something she could admit, even to Caroline. "I presume you don't mean Mr. Finch."

Caroline laughed. "Certainly not. Someone far more interesting." She wiggled her eyebrows. "The girls are plotting ways to claim a dance."

"A dance?"

"At the Harvest Ball a week from Saturday."

"Harvest Ball?" Aunt Virginia screeched from inside the parlor. "A ball is just the thing to lift everyone's spirits." She bent close to Mrs. Brown to share a confidence.

"This is horrible," Elizabeth groaned. "Now I shall be pestered day and night."

Caroline laughed. "You will find it charming. One of the ladies from New England suggested it last year. Apparently the Northerners celebrate the harvest with a feast and dancing. All the ladies agreed to try it last October, and it ended up quite the success."

"In spite of the fact that we don't have a harvest?" Many came to Key West from New England, bringing with them customs that didn't always fit.

"Do you think that minor irregularity would stop the planning of a grand ball? Why, the ladies can talk of nothing else, and since they are collecting donations for the benefit of the Marine Hospital, they have managed to drag their husbands on board."

"And their daughters."

"Naturally." Caroline smiled coyly. "Lavinia Dawson had a new dress made just for the occasion from imported French silk, and Sophronia Bell's gown is said to have taken forty yards of satin to construct."

"Forty yards!" Elizabeth couldn't imagine such an unwieldy gown. "How will she move about?"

"Carefully."

"It will trail behind her like a wake."

Caroline laughed. "That could create quite a spectacle on the dance floor. Can't you see the dancers tripping and falling over her dress?"

"Especially since Sophronia is a tiny little thing. How will she manage such a gown?"

"I understand she is wearing an enormous dress improver." She sighed. "The price of vanity."

Elizabeth had to laugh. If ever there was a woman without a drop of vanity, it was Caroline. "A very big price."

"I doubt she will be able to reach to the edge of her gown. Why, her dance partners will have to be very tall or have very long arms."

"Like—" She halted, unable to say Rourke's name but knowing Caroline understood. "His arms would be long enough."

"Yes, but his heart is already taken."

Elizabeth felt a blush heat her cheeks despite last night's rejection. "I believe you are mistaken."

"Not at all. When a man waits four years to pay a call on a lady, that lady can be certain his affections are sincere."

Elizabeth wasn't nearly as confident as her friend. Since the topic only brought discomfort, she changed course. "What are you wearing?"

"My gown from last year is perfectly serviceable. You, however, need something new and beautiful."

"I'm in mourning. I won't be attending."

"But you must. Everyone with any social standing at all will be there, including many widows. Dancing might be frowned upon, but there is no reason you cannot dine and converse. I shall be glad for your company."

If only it was that simple. Elizabeth couldn't abide the thought of seeing Rourke take the hand of another woman, even for a single dance.

By the time Caroline had covered every aspect of the ball and its preparations, Elizabeth was exhausted. She had never particularly cared for these events designed to showcase young ladies with the aim of securing a match. She would rather walk along the shore with a gentleman and engage in intelligent conversation. Even casting a fishing line in the water would be better than sitting around hoping the right man would get up the nerve to ask for a dance.

"I believe I will read a book."

If Aunt Virginia hadn't interrupted at that exact moment, Caroline might have rebuked her again. As it was, Mrs. Brown wished to call on another friend, and they bid farewell after Caroline promised to call again to firm up plans for the ball.

A ball! The hope that event might have raised two days ago wilted under the memory of Rourke's scorn. She had laid her soul bare, and he had stomped on it. No, she would not go to any ball that might include Rourke O'Malley on the guest list.

By the time she could retreat to her bedroom for the night, Elizabeth was exhausted. Once Anabelle had finished preparing her for bed, she settled into the chair and pulled her mother's diary from her keepsake chest. Even in the candlelight, Mother's strong hand was clear.

The first entries, written soon after her marriage and arrival in Key West, bubbled with excitement over this "odd, rustic place." From the colors of the sea to the tidy little houses, Helen Dobbins Benjamin noted every detail with wondering eyes. But soon that changed. A petulant entry just a week later noted the "exceeding ill manners" of the local population and the utter lack of society. The need for a minister and a schoolteacher had the women protesting to their husbands. Complaints about the sparse variety of the diet soon followed. "Fish and turtle every day, but not a fresh vegetable to be found."

Elizabeth had heard the same sentiments from newcomers

all her life. Before her years in Charleston, she hadn't understood the complaints. Did they not have every variety of fish in the sea? Many kept hens. Their eggs and the eggs of turtles were plentiful. A few of the more agrarian minded grew sweet potatoes, squash, and melon in the small amount of soil they could scrape together. Some had planted the coconut palm and banana tree with great success. Limes and sapodillas also came in from the other keys. Any given ship might bring the necessities like flour, lard, sugar, and molasses.

Then she went to Charleston. Fresh beans and peas, not dried. Peaches so sweet and juicy that she ate until her stomach ached. Fresh beef and pork, such a rarity in Key West, were common table fare. She had reveled in the variety. No wonder her mother had been shocked by the limited selection in Key West.

Though that disappointment was understandable, the next entry sent a shudder through Elizabeth.

How distressed Mama and Papa would be to learn what I must endure in this wilderness. The match they promoted bears little resemblance to the reality I face. I cannot return home, of course. As Mama would say, life is filled with trials and disappointments. We must do our best with what we have been given.

I have no confidante here, no special friend. The few women of self-proclaimed quality would gleefully shout my difficulties from the street corner if they knew of them. On these pages alone can I lament. If not for this diary, I would go mad.

Charles shows much less affection than during courtship. Having caught the prize, he is content to observe from afar or parade me before others, all the while maintaining the perverse habits of bachelorhood. Surely this is not the kind of union God intended.

Perverse habits? Father? He held honor and propriety in the highest regard. She did not recognize the man Mother described. True, he did not display affection in public, but he had always asked a special blessing for Mother when saying grace and had kissed Charlie and her good night. He had deferred to Mother in all household matters, and she had turned to him for every decision that extended beyond the house. Elizabeth had always viewed their marriage as perfectly matched.

She reread the words.

The match they promoted.

If Mother had been unhappy following her parents' counsel, why would she set Elizabeth on the same course? It made no sense, unless things had changed between them later or Mother had been mistaken about the most shocking of accusations, that Father had maintained perverse habits. She must have meant smoking a pipe or drinking brandy. That might have shocked her when they were first married, since Grandpapa had not indulged in either.

Elizabeth read on, hoping to learn more. Instead, the next entries detailed the common travails of everyday life, from a problem servant to a lack of sugar or stormy weather. None of them addressed her mother's feelings.

She leafed ahead to find more of the same. The words blurred, and her eyelids threatened to drift shut until the entry in October of that year when there was a frightening incident that cost a man his life. Mother's fear was palpable.

Though Commodore Porter claims to have eradicated the pirates, I cannot but wonder if one of their kind has returned. Others think it's a Negro gone mad. Charles scoffs at such fears, insisting the guilty party will be found and brought to justice. That is so like him! But he is at court most days, leaving me here with the servants and a rifle I cannot work. How I wish I had never come to this place! I fear for the child I am carrying.

Elizabeth calculated the years and months. She must have been that unborn child.

She turned the page, but the next entry was dated weeks later and made no mention of a fugitive. In fact, it mentioned only the birth of a slave baby and Mother's long vigil with the baby's unnamed mother. She leafed ahead and saw no further mention of either pirates or justice.

As the candle sputtered out, she closed the diary and crawled into bed.

Shadowy pirates tormented her dreams that night. Again aboard ship, she fought them off with nothing but a belaying pin. In the way of dreams, their flashing swords could not smash her wooden pin, though they drove her closer and closer to the rail and the black water below. When she could not hold them off any longer, she awoke. They retreated from her memory, no more substantial than the heavy clouds threatening rain.

She threw off the bed sheet, and something thudded to the planked floor. Mother's diary! After tugging the bedclothes onto the feather mattress, she found the diary underneath the bed. By kneeling, she could reach it with her fingertips and drag it close enough to grab.

All the answers lay inside.

Elizabeth crawled back onto the bed, where she could shove the diary beneath the covers if anyone walked into the room. A servant would knock first, but Aunt Virginia would barge in unannounced.

After locating the spot where she'd left off last night, Elizabeth continued forward. The entries detailed such commonplace occurrences that her attention waned. Surely something more interesting had occurred than the arrival of fine cotton lawn. Yet day after day, the diary read like a list for the mercantile.

She set the diary down and rubbed her eyes. Soon Anabelle would arrive to dress her. After that, the day would not allow for another look at the diary until nightfall. She heard Father close his door across the hall. He always left the house early and did not expect her at breakfast. Aunt Virginia was another matter. She would rise within the half hour. Elizabeth could read a little longer before hiding the book where no one would find it.

She picked up the diary again and turned the page.

I wish that woman had never come.

The words leapt off the page. Unlike Mother's usual sprawling style, this writing was cramped. Each stroke of a letter wobbled. Her anguish speckled the page with scribbled-out words.

How could I have trusted him? Do vows mean nothing? I have heard of such things but never expected to find it in my own house. How I regret my ungracious comments to others, implying that the wife is somehow to blame for a husband's wandering. Now I have felt that dagger pierce my own heart, and those careless words will be flung at me.

What can I do? No one here would understand, even if I dared to speak. My parents stop their ears to any complaint. I have nowhere to turn, no course to follow but one. Such matters must be hushed up, swept out with the dust. A virtuous woman must endure. She must hold her head high and pretend nothing has happened while the world laughs at her.

The entry ended with a watery splotch. Elizabeth rubbed a finger over the puckered paper. A hot tear had fallen there. In despair, Mother had cried out in the only way open to her.

Her words slashed open the memories of Elizabeth's own fears and failures. Charlie. Rourke. Only she was the one who had broken faith. An older sister was supposed to care for her little brother. A true friend did not let someone take the blame for her.

A knock sounded on the door. "You ready fo' me, miss?" It was Florie, not Anabelle.

For a second, Elizabeth wondered why, but she wasn't ready for either of them. She must read more.

"Not yet," she called out. "Come back in fifteen minutes." That ought not raise alarms.

"Yes, miss."

Elizabeth turned back to the diary.

What should I do? How can I raise my child alongside such a travesty? How can I stay silent with the proof of my husband's unfaithfulness before me?

13

Rourke must secure Elizabeth's promise to wait if he hoped to have a chance at her hand in a year. That night in the chapel he had wanted to kiss her. Instead he'd deliberately shattered her heart. Under such circumstances, few women would agree to see him, least of all wait a full year for his return. He must offer her hope, and that could only be accomplished in person. Somehow he must wiggle past the imposing figure of her great-aunt and her watchdog of a father.

After ensuring Charles Benjamin was in his office, Rourke left the harbor in search of Elizabeth. According to Anabelle, the day's marketing took place between ten and eleven in the morning. Occasionally Aunt Virginia joined the family's cook. He hoped that was the case today.

He angled past the grocer on Duval and spotted the Benjamins' cook but not Elizabeth's aunt. That would make his task more difficult, but he hadn't time to waste. With the salvage libel dropped, Rourke stood to collect a handsome amount if the cargo sold for a good price at auction this afternoon. Once that was over and the amount due paid to him, Charles

Benjamin would expect the *Windsprite* to set sail. Though Rourke had claimed to need two weeks, the chandlers would readily reveal that he was fully supplied and crewed. That was all Benjamin needed to press him to leave. Rourke must see Elizabeth now.

"I wondered when you would show." Poppinclerk stepped from the shadows beside a grogshop.

Rourke skirted around him. "I'm busy."

"So it seems." Though far shorter, Poppinclerk managed to match his stride. "I see the *Windsprite* is fitting out for a long voyage."

"Every wrecker prepares for weeks at sea," Rourke snapped. After reading the incompetent pilot's lies in his deposition, he wanted nothing to do with the man.

"Of course he does. I did so myself in times past."

Rourke growled at the man's reference to his wrecking career, as if it had lasted two years instead of two months. At the first opportunity and doubtless after a great deal of money changed hands, Poppinclerk took up piloting the vessels of unsuspecting masters.

Poppinclerk either did not hear Rourke's irritation or chose to ignore it. "In your case, I hear you have a different destination in mind."

"My destination is none of your concern."

"Forgive me if I'm wrong, but I heard that you were sailing for Harbour Island. It must have been a rumor. You know how quickly rumors race along the wharves. Why, I once heard that I'd perished at sea—and the man divulging this bit of information was standing right beside me."

"In the grogshop?"

Poppinclerk brushed the reference to his drinking habits away as easily as the gnat that landed on his coat sleeve. "You seem to think I'm your enemy."

"You lied in your statement to the court."

"Now, now. That's such a harsh word for a simple difference of perspective."

Rourke halted. "Difference of perspective? You said I led you onto the reef, when in fact your incompetence drove it aground."

Poppinclerk had the gall to look affronted. "I saw a light and thought your vessel was safely outside the reef."

"That is why you're a menace to every vessel you board," Rourke muttered as he hurried on, hoping to shake the man.

Poppinclerk caught up. "In the spirit of camaraderie, I'm going to ignore that statement. In fact, I sought you today because I want to do you a favor."

That startled Rourke into stopping again. "What favor?"

Poppinclerk was breathing so heavily that he could not speak for some moments. After glancing about, as if afraid someone would overhear, he whispered, "Your enemy knows."

Rourke had no patience for cryptic warnings. "Speak plainly. What enemy? Knows what?"

"Who opposes you in wreckers' court?"

Charles Benjamin. There could be no doubt. "What of him?"

"He knows your plans."

Rourke's blood ran cold.

"What plans?" he snapped. The man couldn't possibly know that he intended to spirit Anabelle away from her master.

Poppinclerk's malevolent grin confirmed Rourke's worst fears. "No need for secrets between old friends. We both want the same end."

Poppinclerk wouldn't care about a slave. Unless it made him money.

181

"What end is that?" Rourke asked.

"Our fair share."

"That is settled now that the libel has been dropped."

"I'm not talking about a wrecking award. I have information of value to you, information that will give you what you want most."

Elizabeth. The man must be talking about her, not Anabelle. How could Poppinclerk know anything that would make her his? Did he have proof of some scandal lurking in Benjamin's past? Rourke shook his head. Though tempting, such information would only divide father from daughter and the bearer of the news from the hearer. A strong and honest marriage could not be built on division.

"If you expect me to give you a cent for this supposed information, you're mistaken." Rourke headed back toward the harbor. He could not walk to Elizabeth's house now.

Naturally Poppinclerk joined him, though he did not comment on the change of direction. "I'm trying to help you," he panted. "A gift."

Poppinclerk gave nothing away. His recent antics showed he would do anything for a price. No doubt he expected substantial payment for the kind of information that could destroy a family. Rourke wouldn't grant him the satisfaction.

"I don't need your kind of gift."

"You will soon regret that decision." Poppinclerk straightened his coat. "Your enemy has not played his last card."

Benjamin must have guessed Rourke's plan or thought he would steal away his daughter. Dread shivered down Rourke's spine. For a moment he was tempted to accept Poppinclerk's offer, but he would not deal with a cheat and scoundrel.

He walked away, certain of what he must do next. Instead of

finding excuses to stay in Key West, he must leave. After collecting his share from the sale of the wreck's cargo, he would set sail as if heading for home. That might convince Benjamin that Rourke had no intention of spiriting away Elizabeth. However, Anabelle might fear he'd abandoned her, especially when she heard that he had headed for Harbour Island.

Somehow he had to get a message to her. He couldn't do it himself. Benjamin would be looking for him. No, he had to send someone else.

The *Windsprite* bobbed on her anchor. The ship's boat inched toward the wharf with Tom Worthington at the oars. Tom had brought Anabelle to Key West aboard the *Dinah Hale*. She would recognize him, and no one in the house would think twice of him inquiring after their welfare.

Rourke would send Tom. The lad could even deliver a second message to Elizabeth, one that Rourke hoped would bring her back to his side.

⁂

Caroline called on Elizabeth the following day, creating a welcome diversion from the sickening knowledge that she had an illegitimate sibling. She hadn't been able to look Father in the eye at supper last night, a fact that he noticed. When he asked what was ailing her, she complained of a headache, though it was only partly true. Every part of her ached from the knowledge. This morning she'd hidden the diary beneath the shells in her rosewood box and vowed never to open it again.

Now Elizabeth embraced her friend. "I'm so glad to see you, more than you can imagine." For a moment she toyed with the idea of telling Caroline what she'd read but dismissed it just as quickly. That was not the sort of thing shared outside the family. "I wish my mother was still here."

Caroline, donned in a sensible straw bonnet and a rust and cream striped gown, pointed to her basket of flowers. "That's why we are visiting her grave."

"I'm sorry, but I'd rather not." The cold marble had given her chills when she visited with Aunt. "Mother isn't there. I do appreciate your efforts, though. Can you forgive me?"

"Of course." Caroline squeezed her hand. "The flowers will look just as nice in a vase."

After Elizabeth left the blooms in Anabelle's hands, Caroline suggested they walk to the shops.

Aunt Virginia sailed into the foyer, making no attempt to hide that she had been eavesdropping. "A walk is out of the question. It threatens rain."

"Then we shall duck inside if a shower approaches." Elizabeth had to get away from this house before she said or did something that would rend the fragile peace.

Caroline added unbeatable ammunition. "I would so like Lizzie's help picking out gloves for the ball."

"The ball!" Aunt brightened at once. "Why didn't you say so? Naturally you must go. Elizabeth, you could stand a new pair too." She smiled coyly. "And when you return, I hope to have a little surprise for the two of you."

Though Caroline dutifully begged to know what that might be, Aunt refused to divulge the secret, other than that it too pertained to the ball.

"The entire town is abuzz," Caroline said when they finally strolled down the street.

Indeed it was busy. Servants carried baskets, some atop their heads. Bells clanged, and workmen called out. The roll of wagon wheels, the smell of fish, and the crunch of gravel tickled the senses. Women scurried here and there, many with children in tow. Men drove wagons laden with barrels or crates. Elizabeth searched the faces of those near her age, both hoping to see a resemblance and terrified that she would.

Caroline stopped in front of the first shop window. "All everyone talks about is the ball."

"Not as much as Aunt Virginia." Elizabeth heaved a sigh and pretended interest in the shoes on display. "I have done nothing but walk with a book atop my head, practice sitting properly, and engage in meaningless conversation. If you hadn't paid a visit, I should have gone mad."

Caroline laughed as they moved on. "I suppose now we shall be forced to at least look at gloves. I saw some lovely lace ones in the Greene Mercantile."

"If they fit, I will put them on Father's account, and then we may do something more pleasurable. Unless, of course, you want them."

"You know what I think of such extravagances. I'm surprised your aunt believed me."

"I'm surprised you're even going to the ball."

Caroline inclined her head. "Mother quite rightly pointed out that the scions of society will be in attendance. What better place to promote the league?"

"The temperance league? At a ball?"

"I'll admit it is a bit of a stretch."

"Spirits will doubtless be served."

Caroline jutted out her pointed chin. Though lovely in every way that mattered, the brunette would be considered plain by most. "Jesus ate with sinners. I am simply following His example."

Elizabeth let that idea settle. "You are more courageous than I could ever be. Why, it's like Daniel stepping into the lions' den."

Caroline laughed. "These lions prefer to use their claws, I fear, but as a minister's daughter, I am granted a little leeway by most. They might listen more keenly, however, if you joined me."

"I couldn't. Father would object." His preference for brandy had grown over the years, not diminished. "Besides, if not for Aunt Virginia's insistence, I wouldn't even attend."

"I thought you hoped to see a certain someone."

Elizabeth felt her cheeks heat despite knowing Rourke had refused her. Would this embarrassing attraction never end? "I do not."

Caroline heaved a sigh. "What a relief. I was afraid you would be disappointed." She stopped in front of a window display of parasols and bonnets.

"In what?" Elizabeth choked when she noticed her friend's flushed cheeks. "Are you . . . that is, do you . . . or rather, has a gentleman caught your attention?"

Caroline stared at her as if she were mad. "What an odd thing to say. Of course not. This is about your certain someone. I heard—" She abruptly stopped.

"What did you hear?"

Caroline shook her head.

Elizabeth grabbed her arm. "Why won't you tell me?"

"Good afternoon, sir." Caroline looked past Elizabeth. "I don't believe we are acquainted."

Elizabeth whirled around. "Tom!"

Caroline's eyebrows shot up.

"Mr. Worthington," Elizabeth corrected herself. "A fine day, isn't it?"

Tom, dressed the same as he had been on the voyage to Key West, looked to the sky. "Rain's coming, I fear."

His eyes darted toward Caroline, and Elizabeth realized she'd forgotten to make introductions. After that was done to everyone's satisfaction, she asked if he was looking for her.

"Indeed I was, miss. I paid a call at your house and spoke to your aunt. She said you had walked into town to look at gloves." Most men Tom's age would wrinkle their noses at the mention of shopping for any part of a woman's wardrobe. Tom managed to say it without edging away. He dug into his jacket pocket. "I have a letter for you, Miss Benjamin." He handed her a square of folded paper sealed with wax.

"For me?" She did not recognize the hand. "Who is it from?"

"An admirer." Tom looked toward the harbor. "I need to be on my way. Mr. John will have my head if I'm late."

"Thank you," she called out as Tom hurried away into the crowd.

"He works on the *Windsprite*?" Caroline asked after he was gone.

"Yes."

"Curious. The rumor I heard was about that ship. Apparently they're about to set sail for Harbour Island."

The news knifed through Elizabeth. "Are you certain?"

"Perhaps that letter will tell you more."

Elizabeth ripped open the seal and unfolded the single sheet of paper. The first two lines confirmed what Caroline had heard. "He is . . ." She choked out a shaky breath. "He is returning home." Her hand trembled at the next. "They might be gone a long time, as much as a year." Tears stung her eyes. He was leaving her the way she'd left him—fit punishment for her sins.

"Is that all? No explanation?"

Elizabeth shook her head and tried to blink away the tears enough to read the final words.

I was a coward that night, dearest Elizabeth. I should have admitted my feelings. Please forgive me. You are always in my thoughts. Though your kind regard is undeserved, I dare to hope you will wait.

Your ever faithful servant,
Rourke

Those were not the words of a man who despised her. Quite the contrary. Hope returned with such a surge that she threw her arms around Caroline. "He loves me. I knew it. He loves me."

"Yet he is leaving?" Caroline asked after Elizabeth had composed herself.

"There must be difficulty at home. It's the only explanation." Caroline looked unconvinced.

"What?" Elizabeth prodded. "You don't think that's possible?"

"It's possible," Caroline said slowly, "though hardly something to keep secret."

"Rourke is a private man. He wouldn't share his difficulties with anyone."

Though Caroline still looked doubtful, she acquiesced. "Then you will wait, even if it's a year?"

Though Elizabeth nodded, she knew how difficult that would be. "I will convince Father. Somehow."

❧

When Elizabeth returned home, Aunt Virginia informed her that Mr. Finch would join them for supper. In one statement, she deflated Elizabeth's excitement and pinpointed the problem that awaited her. How could she possibly push away Mr. Finch for an entire year?

"I will dine in my room," she stated.

"You most certainly will not," Aunt said. "The lady of the house must serve as a gracious hostess even when plagued by headache or fatigue. Your mother always did."

The mention of Mother shamed Elizabeth. Mother would not dwell upon disappointment. She would not run headlong through the streets, as Elizabeth had longed to do when first reading Rourke's letter. She would accept life's blows and move forward with grace.

That meant suffering through Percival Finch with his canary-yellow waistcoats, cloying compliments, and clinging fingers.

Aunt Virginia clucked her tongue. "Where did you and Miss Brown go? Your skirts are caked with dirt. Why, they're as filthy as your maid's. I'm beginning to think she is going all over town when she is supposed to be here. Yesterday she showed up at cockcrow with her eyes heavy and her skirts damp. Nathan insists he didn't see her all night. Cook and Florie claim they were asleep. No one seems to know where that girl of yours spent the night. Unless she stayed in your room. You know that's unwise. I told you over and over how quickly a darkie will turn on you."

Elizabeth's heart sank. She had spoken to Anabelle about the late-night forays and asked her not to leave again after curfew. Why would she continue to do so? Now Aunt had begun to suspect. "I will speak to her."

"You must discipline her."

Though the thought made her ill, Elizabeth nodded.

Seemingly satisfied, Aunt Virginia returned to the business

at hand. "We haven't much time before supper. You certainly can't wear that gown. No amount of beating will get the dust from it."

She headed for the staircase. "I'll have Anabelle dress me in the crape."

"You will do no such thing. That was my big surprise, which apparently you and Miss Brown completely forgot." Aunt pouted. "I can never be your mother, but I'm trying to do my best by you."

Elizabeth's heart softened. Aunt had truly looked forward to revealing her big surprise. After all the excitement surrounding Rourke, Elizabeth had completely forgotten about her aunt. "I'm sorry."

"Oh, it's quite all right to forget your poor old great-aunt." Aunt dabbed at her misty eyes. "Never mind that I took the liberty of finding a gown for you the moment I learned of the ball. It wasn't easy, mind you. The seamstresses here are dreadful, and there was almost no time to have something made, but Providence smiled on me, dear Elizabeth. Mrs. Evanston happened to have the perfect gown on hand. Apparently the girl who ordered it changed her mind. Though she's a bit shorter than you, Mrs. Evanston assured me she could make the alterations."

Elizabeth blinked. "I have not agreed to attend."

"Of course you will attend. Moreover, Mrs. Evanston was kind enough to await your return. Run along upstairs now. We will have the fitting in the reading room."

"You kept her here until my return?"

"Naturally." Aunt Virginia's note of triumph rang through the house. "She was only too happy to wait for the daughter of Key West's most prominent attorney."

Elizabeth was too tired to argue. She obediently followed

Aunt upstairs. The reading room had been transformed into a
fitting room with sheer drapes covering the windows. A woman
of perhaps forty years of age stood beside a dressmaker's form
bearing a stunning steel-blue silk gown.

"It's blue," Elizabeth cried. "I can't wear blue."

"It's gray," Aunt Virginia countered. "Isn't it, Mrs. Evanston?"

The woman, clearly already under Aunt Virginia's control,
nodded agreeably. "It will look especially fine on someone of
your stature and complexion. We will refashion the existing skirt
by adding a flounced underskirt of this lovely matching silk."

The shimmering creation was a ball gown fit for the finest
dance in Charleston. In no way did it reflect that Elizabeth was
in mourning.

"It's not appropriate," she whispered to her aunt.

"Nonsense."

"It has red rosettes on the skirt and bodice."

Aunt waved away Elizabeth's concern. "A tiny splash of color."

"I'm in mourning."

"Your father informed me that such customs are not observed
here. In fact, he insisted you have something a little less harsh
for the ball." She pinched Elizabeth's cheek as if she were a
young girl. "You need to get the color back in your cheeks."

"But Mother died less than three months ago."

Mrs. Evanston looked sympathetic, but she was fully in her
patron's employ. This was clearly an attempt to pretty up Elizabeth for courtship, but neither her aunt nor Mrs. Evanston
could know that they'd selected the exact shade she'd worn the
day she'd hoped to win over Rourke O'Malley. The day of the
hurricane. The day her brother lost the use of his legs.

She closed her eyes against the sudden rush of pain.

Four years ago, chasing after Rourke had wrought disaster. She had proceeded to Charleston as planned rather than fight to stay. This time he was leaving. Miles upon miles of turquoise sea would lie between them. Gone for as long as a year, he'd written. Gone at the very time she needed someone to stand by her side.

Now she stood alone, unable to hear the music, while the world danced around her.

14

Mr. Finch proved as insufferable as Elizabeth had expected. His eyes gleamed when she entered the foyer, even though she was covered from head to toe in black crape thanks to the alterations required on the ball gown.

"How lovely you are, Miss Elizabeth." He bowed, revealing a bottle-green waistcoat beneath his unbuttoned tailcoat.

Overdressed yet again. The very sight of him disgusted her. His touch made her skin crawl. She extended a limp hand and allowed him to lead her into the dining room.

During supper, she nodded and murmured unintelligible responses to his comments without hearing a thing he was saying. Mr. Finch could not compare to Rourke any more than a vulture could pretend to be a magnificent frigate bird. The latter soared high on the breezes, dipping to earth to snatch up a fish or to mate. When would Rourke alight again? Soon, she hoped. A year was far too long to wait when she now knew he loved her.

Despite Caroline's misgivings, the only explanation for such a long and indefinite absence was a family crisis. If his mother was ill, he might not return for a very long time. All of his seven siblings were younger than him. Some must still be at home. With his father gone, he would have to take on responsibility for the family. Just like her.

She glanced at her brother, who shot back an accusatory glare, as if she were to blame for Mr. Finch's presence. Did Rourke's brothers and sisters give him the same fits Charlie gave her? Yet Rourke got along famously with her brother. And Father did not object to those visits. Apparently his disapproval of Rourke extended only to her.

Mr. Finch looked at her as if he'd asked a question.

She nodded and smiled again.

Charlie scowled.

Father grinned and clapped his hands. "Good. It's settled then. Shall we say seven o'clock? We will want to arrive early with such an announcement to make."

"Announcement?" Elizabeth asked, but neither of them appeared to hear her.

"Excellent." Father's pleasure rumbled forth with the addition of a raised wineglass. "I have looked forward to this day for years. We will take my carriage."

The air squeezed out of her lungs. "The carriage?" What had she just agreed to?

Mr. Finch gave her a doting smile. "You wouldn't want your lovely gown to get dusty, would you? The hall is a goodly distance from here."

"The hall." Elizabeth quickly pieced together that she had just agreed to attend the Harvest Ball with Mr. Finch.

"Dearest Elizabeth." Finch laughed. "Where else would a ball take place but at the hall? There isn't another room large enough."

"Nor is there a better place to announce your engagement," Father added.

Engagement? Panic rose like a storm tide. When had she agreed to an engagement? One of those polite nods must have been mistaken for agreement. "You misunderstand."

"Not to fret, my dear." Finch smiled. "We all make mistakes from time to time."

"Mistake. Yes, that's it. This is all a big mistake." The blood pounded in her ears. What had she done to make him think she would ever approve his suit? Had she not refused him out-right twice already? "I can't. I won't." She pushed back from the table.

"Elizabeth." Father's gray eyes pinned her in place. "This is what we agreed upon."

No, it wasn't. This was what Father and Mr. Finch agreed upon. Not her. She could not abandon Rourke for a pale sub-stitute, even if she must wait a year.

"No," she croaked.

The men ignored her words. The air thickened. She could not breathe, could not think, could not hear. Her hands shook. She had to leave. Now.

She rose.

"Are you all right, dearest?" Mr. Finch hopped to his feet and took her arm.

His hovering presence and heavy perfume only made her feel worse.

"I-I can't." She pulled her arm from his grasp and ran from the room. How, she did not know. She could not feel her limbs. Her ears buzzed. The furniture blurred as if underwater. She grabbed the staircase railing. Her room. She must get to the safety of her room.

"Elizabeth?" Finch's voice shot through her like a bolt of lightning. "Dearest?"

"No," she gasped, struggling to gather her wits. "No. I'm not. I can't."

"Take her to the parlor," Father instructed, his disdain at her feminine weakness evident.

Finch reached for her.

She pulled away. If only she could climb the stairs, but she could not summon the strength to lift a foot.

"Come with me," Finch demanded, this time tugging on her arm.

His grasping recalled the last time, when he had gripped her arms so tightly that they'd bruised. If she hadn't insisted upon strict Christian morals, he would have forced a kiss upon her. His lips had been so close that she'd reeled from his fetid breath. She could not do this. She could not. The eddy was swallowing her. Soon she would be lost, and she hadn't the strength to fight. Her lips formed words, but nothing came out.

Then she felt a tug on her skirt.

"I want to talk to my sister," Charlie said. "She's coming with me."

To her shock, Finch stepped away. Father acquiesced. Aunt Virginia stayed silent. In that moment, Elizabeth saw who ruled the house. Her brother, who had seemed so weak, was in truth the strongest of them all.

"Wheel me to my room, Lizzie."

Elizabeth gratefully obeyed.

⤝✦⤞

After sailing east-northeast until well past sundown, Rourke doubled back and nestled the *Windsprite* into a quiet mangrove cut within rowing distance of Key West. The waxing half moon offered enough light for Worthington to find the vessel, yet as the hours passed without one sign of the lad, Rourke regretted sending the least experienced of his crew on such an important mission. He should have been here by now.

Rourke paced the deck. At every about-face, he pulled out the spyglass and scanned the moonlit channel entrance.

"He come," John said. "He see de mast."

That was true. No nearby cove could completely hide a vessel the size of the *Windsprite*. Rourke had expected John to be the only crew member to make the crossing with him, yet all had remained. Good men. Loyal men. Men who deserved to know the full truth. If Worthington returned.

"He should have been here by now. If Benjamin catches him prowling about, there's no telling what he'll do."

"Tom not tell secrets."

Rourke wished he could believe that. Charles Benjamin had a way of forcing information out of a grown man, not to mention someone Tom's age. Whether by threat or enticements, Benjamin could pry open the deepest recesses of a man's heart.

"God will be with him," Rourke said, mostly to convince himself. "He has to be."

Surely God would aid a man acting in righteousness. The Bible was filled with examples. He had directed Gideon into battle against the Midianites. He had protected David from King Saul's jealous wrath. Rourke's small act would not change a nation, but it would save two precious souls. He hoped that would be enough to attract God's protection.

The moon sat atop the mangroves now. Not a breath of breeze rustled the leaves. Soon the moon would slip behind the trees, casting their cove in darkness. Rourke took one last look at the channel mouth.

Nothing.

No boat. No splash of oars. No croak of an egret, their agreed-upon signal.

Rourke collapsed the spyglass and stuck it in his coat pocket. "God be with you, Tom Worthington."

As if in response, the splash of oars sounded across the still waters.

Rourke motioned for John to stand still. He held his breath, every muscle taut.

There it was again. Splash. Splash. Splash. The regular rhythm could only belong to a strong and experienced rower.

He listened for the egret call but heard only silence. Even the splashing had stopped.

Was it Worthington or had the young crewman been intercepted? If the latter, the *Windsprite* was trapped. The cut had only one way out. Rourke should have known better than to choose a cut over a channel, but he'd thought the unconventional choice would throw off the curious or the vengeful.

He might have thought wrong. Rourke instinctively reached for his cutlass. It would do him no good against firepower, but he might stand a chance in hand-to-hand combat.

The whites of John's eyes vanished when Rourke shuttered the lantern. His chief mate crouched behind the deckhouse, also with cutlass in hand.

Rourke did not move a muscle. Every sense was trained on the entrance to the channel, where the splashing sound drew closer.

Soon they would know if they'd been betrayed. Rourke tightened his grip and lifted the blade.

Kaw-roak.

The deep croak of the great egret sounded across the water.

Worthington. Rourke relaxed. John, however, stayed crouched behind the deckhouse. This could still prove a trap. Rourke raised the cutlass again.

By now, the mangroves cast the *Windsprite* in complete darkness. The moonlight spread a silver veil across the sea outside the channel entrance. A foe would cling to the shadows. Worthington would push into the light to announce his presence. Unless he'd been followed.

Again came the call of the egret. Rourke echoed it this time. The splashing increased in frequency, and soon a dinghy bearing a single man popped into the light outside the channel mouth.

Tom. Rourke set down his cutlass and hurried to the ship's side to help the lad aboard. As the boat drew near, he whistled and drew an answering whistle.

"Hey-ho," Worthington called out. "One to board."

Even John dropped his cutlass.

"You weren't seen or followed?" Rourke asked as he opened the shutter on the lantern.

"Nay, Captain." Worthington scurried up the rope ladder. "No one saw me leave town or the island."

"De message?" John asked eagerly. "She get it?"

Even in the dim light of the lantern, Rourke could see Tom's shoulders droop.

"I couldn't get to her. I waited, like you said, until the servants retired to quarters, but Anabelle never went near the gate. I waited until the last light went out in the house and the servants' quarters got quiet. That's why I was late. It took a long time for their guest to leave."

"Guest?" Rourke asked.

"Red-faced man with a pointed nose and a green waistcoat. He didn't leave Miss Elizabeth's side."

Finch. Charles Benjamin had wasted no time setting the man on Elizabeth. "Did she respond to his attentions?"

Tom shrugged. "She looked at her plate mostly, though she didn't eat much. She left the table first, and they all went somewhere I couldn't see."

That did not bode well.

"But she didn't join him on the porch when he left," Tom added.

Rourke clung to that shred of hope, foolish though it was. How could he expect Elizabeth to fend off a full year of pressure from her father and Finch? "Were you able to get the letter to her?"

Worthington brightened. "Aye, Captain. Saw her in town with her friend Miss Brown earlier in the day and gave it to her then."

Rourke breathed in with relief. Maybe there was hope after all. "Did she open it?"

"I didn't stay. I figured she wouldn't read it until she was alone."

"You're probably right." He wished he could have known if his few words had given her hope.

"How we reach Anabelle?" John's voice trembled.

Rourke chastised himself for dwelling on Elizabeth when greater troubles lay ahead. "Anabelle is shrewd. She knows where to go. She'll be there as planned. We have to believe that."

John's worried expression eased slightly.

Not Tom's. "There might be a problem with that. The back gate is locked, and I thought I saw a man lurking in the alley behind the house."

"A man?" Rourke did not like the sound of that. "Did you recognize him?"

"Not in the dark. He wasn't very big, though. I could have taken him down, but he took off before I got close. Since you wanted me to talk to Anabelle, I figured I'd better not chase after him."

"A small man shouldn't be a problem," Rourke mused.

"No, Captain, but that fence is. If the back gate's locked, I'd guess the one between the backyard and front is too. That fence is tall. No one is going to climb over it, especially a woman."

Rourke ran a hand through his hair, smoothing it off his forehead. Their task had just gotten a lot more difficult. "Then we'll have to find a way to get her out."

Poppinclerk's offer of help came to mind. He'd claimed to have information that would give Rourke what he wanted most. Maybe he knew who was guarding the back gate. Maybe he had a key to enter the Benjamin property. On the other hand, Rourke's first instincts might be right, and Poppinclerk would walk him straight into a trap.

❦

By the time Elizabeth shut the door to her brother's room, she had regained her senses. No one could force her to marry. If Mr. Finch had the audacity to announce an engagement, she would counter with a denial. She must.

"Where would you like me to wheel your chair?" she asked Charlie.

"To the desk."

Now that she had been admitted to Charlie's domain, she took a good look around. A large desk dominated the front half of the room, while bookshelves lined the wall.

"It looks just like Father's study," she said. "I had no idea you were so interested in your studies."

"There's not much else to do when confined to a room."

The truth stung. "I-I'm sorry."

"It's a fact."

This was neither the timid boy of years ago nor the young man who had joked with Rourke. Charles Benjamin II wielded power, even over Father. If not for the withered legs hidden beneath a blanket, his brilliant blue eyes and engaging wit would have captured many a girl's heart. But the legs made all the difference, and he knew it. Sarcasm tinged his replies, as if he dared her to fight. She could not, for he was stuck in this state because of her mistakes.

The rest of the room served as his bedchamber. A chair and small table sat beside his bed. A pair of crutches leaned against the wall.

"Crutches? You can walk?"

"One of Father's ideas." His frown carried into his voice. "He wants to make me whole, but nothing can do that."

Elizabeth shivered and wrapped her arms around her midsection. "I'm sorry." How many times must she say it before it made any difference?

"You should be. Why would you agree to marry that fool?"

It took her a moment to grasp what he'd just said. "Mr. Finch."

"Of course Mr. Finch. I've never seen a more pompous idiot, and yet you agreed to marry him."

"I didn't. At least not knowingly. I wasn't paying the slightest attention. He must have thought I was nodding in agreement, but I wasn't."

"As I thought." A faint smile curled his lips. "Hold the chair still." He lifted himself onto the desk chair, then opened one of the dozen volumes stacked on the expansive desk. "I don't like Percival Finch."

"Neither do I."

He lifted his head. "Then why entertain him at all?"

"Father insists."

"And you obey everything Father says."

"You tried the crutches, didn't you?"

Charlie ignored the jab. "I'm not the one getting married."

"Maybe you can get away with flaunting Father's commands, but daughters are expected to obey and to marry."

"Then you would marry a bore just to please him?"

It didn't sound so noble put that way. "Not to please him."

"Then why?"

She couldn't mention the inheritance, for Charlie could claim no share of it. Neither would she allow security to dictate her future. "I will not marry such a man."

He grinned. "Then you still like Rourke?"

The bald question sent heat rushing to her cheeks. She did. Oh, how she did, but he was gone. He had left her alone to fend off the pressure to marry her father's choice of suitor. Just like Mother. The similarity hurt. "How I feel doesn't matter."

"That sounds like Father speaking."

She turned away.

"Avoiding the truth won't make it disappear," he said.

"Rourke is leaving. Perhaps you did not hear. He is returning home for as much as a year."

That silenced him. She felt his hurt. Rourke was the only person who visited Charlie, his sole friend. Elizabeth had received a note from Rourke. Apparently Charlie had gotten no word.

"I thought you would know," she whispered.

He shook his head, putting on a brave front. "What Captain O'Malley does is none of my concern." He turned the page of his book, pretending to study, but his eyes did not move.

"I'm sorry. If I hadn't dragged you to the harbor that day, your life would be normal."

Charlie stared down at the book, his curly locks hiding his expression.

"I'm sorry." Each word took enormous effort. "I-I know you'll never forgive me. I accept that. It's my fault. I wish I could change things, but I can't. I'm sorry."

Still the bowed head. Still the silence.

Elizabeth backed away, sick at heart. If he would not accept her apology, what could ever bring them together again?

The answer came in an instant. "I will wait for Rourke."

Charlie finally looked up. "Do what you want, Lizzie. You always have."

The truth of the accusation struck harder than the tallest wave. Her selfish desire had cost Charlie the use of his legs. Then she had let Rourke take the blame. Now they were both lost to her. A sob rose up her throat. She could not let it out. She could not let Charlie know how deeply the guilt hurt. Blinded by conscience, she yanked open the door and ran.

15

Elizabeth pored over the diary, looking for something that could mend her relationship with Charlie. The next entries consumed the weeks leading to her birth. Her mother had turned her anguish into busyness. She oversaw every detail of the new nursery, made baby clothing, and followed every directive of the midwife.

Still, the question lingered. Who was the other child? Finally, a month before Elizabeth was born, Mother wrote just one line in the diary.

I asked Charles, and he did not deny it.

Elizabeth clutched the diary to her chest and wept. She had a half sibling. Mother had married her parents' choice only to discover her husband loved someone else. Such pain. How her mother must have hurt during what should have been a joyous time.

Who was this illegitimate child? The offspring of a newcomer, certainly. Mother had lamented the woman's arrival in town. She must also have become a friend of the family, someone who brought her baby to the house often enough that Mother couldn't imagine raising Elizabeth with the other child so near. The association had been close enough that Mother could not even write her name in her private diary. In such a small town, everyone knew each other.

Maybe the baby had died. Mother had never hinted at another child. Elizabeth knew it was wrong to wish for anyone's death, but she couldn't suppress the hope.

She read on, seeking the answer.

The diary bounced between notes of commonplace occurrences to prayers for strength to deal with "the situation." Then came a conspicuous break in the dates. From March until May of 1830, Mother wrote nothing. Elizabeth had been born on the first day of spring.

Mother had always called Elizabeth her "little light of hope" because of her birth date. The dark days of winter were gone. Spring had arrived. In Mother's native South Carolina, that meant the planting of crops and the hope for a good growing season. Here in Key West, it meant the return of abundant fishing as the waters warmed.

Elizabeth's birth also seemed to usher in new confidence for Helen Benjamin. In the first entry after the gap, she wrote:

What a treasure this perfect baby girl is. Charles wanted a son, of course, but God has blessed me with a daughter, as if an answer to my pain. A son would have pleased Charles, but beautiful Lizzie's smile wipes away every fear and jealousy of the past months. No other girl can compare.

Father had wanted a son.

Most men did, but seeing it written in ink turned conjecture to cruel knowledge. No wonder he had doted on Charlie growing up. The accident must have destroyed his plans. If he knew Elizabeth had dragged Charlie into that disaster, he would never forgive her.

Father had wanted a son. But he got a daughter. Two daughters, if she read her mother's entry correctly. What had happened to that other baby girl?

Mother's joy overflowed onto the page as she recorded every little thing that Elizabeth did. That joy even washed away the anger and grief over Father's mistress.

How can I harbor anger with her, when she must feel the same as I? A perfect girl, beautiful in every way, is a blessing from God, regardless of the sin that led to her existence. I must forgive. Indeed forgiveness has already soothed my heart. I cannot explain such a change except as God's grace. If He has forgiven me, shall I not also forgive others? So I have, and with that I see now that grace has granted me an advantage. As I have been forgiven and blessed with this child, so shall she. These precious children will be raised alike, neither one better than the other. I will ensure it.

Elizabeth turned the page, eager to read what Mother had done, but she was met with just one line:

It is done.

Then the diary ended. Not a single word after that. No explanation. No names. Nothing.

Elizabeth slammed the book shut. "How could you?" she cried out.

A night breeze whispered through the tamarind leaves. Somewhere a shutter banged. Father paced the hallway beneath her room. Aunt Virginia snored and then coughed. The familiar sounds could not soothe. This diary had turned everything upside down. Instead of fighting for her daughter, Mother had given the illegitimate girl the same benefits as Elizabeth. How could she?

⌒⋒⌒

Approaching Poppinclerk was a last resort. As the days passed, Rourke puzzled out another way to get Anabelle out of the Benjamin house the night of the ball. John wanted to sneak her out, but Rourke preferred to act. Drive an ax through the fence and pull her out, except that would only put a bullet in his back or clap his legs in irons. No, he needed another idea.

So he gathered the men. It was time his crew knew the whole plan—and the risks. Someone might see a solution that he couldn't.

It took precious few minutes to detail their mission and the obstacles they faced.

"I don't want a one of you to accept blame if we're caught," Rourke said, even though his men all appeared eager to whisk away John's wife. "As far as you know, we're heading to Briland to fish. Nothing more. Understand?"

John caught the flaw in his attempt to shield the crew. "Der be no women fishin' on de *Windsprite*."

Anabelle. Rourke scrubbed his whiskers. "We might have to disguise her as a man." At the rumble of protest, he added, "Only as a last resort. Once we reach Briland, you can sign on to another ship or fish with me. I won't hold it against a man for wanting to return to Key West. Any questions?"

"How long we settin' here?" asked Rander, a cantankerous deckhand with a soft heart.

208

"Five more days."

Five short days before the pendulum swung to either freedom or death. Somehow he had to devise a way to spring Anabelle from Benjamin's trap. A rat would gnaw off its leg to get free. Barracuda and sharks could bite their way off a hook and line. The crafty lobster hid deep in the jagged reef. None of those offered a solution, but something tickled at Rourke's memory. As a girl, Elizabeth had sneaked out of the house. He'd seen her once, crawling through that large wild tamarind like a monkey. Anabelle was no girl, but she was strong. That tree extended over the fence into the neighbor's yard. Perhaps she could climb out that way. Then they'd rendezvous at the appointed location.

He spelled out the idea to his men. All but John seconded it.

"How she get to Miz Lizbeth's room dat late? Massa lock dem in de back."

John had found a flaw in his plan, but Rourke didn't want to admit it. "Do you have a better idea?"

John's head drooped.

"I do," Tom Worthington said.

All heads turned toward him.

"It's the night of the ball, correct?" Tom looked around the assembled group. "She could go there with Miss Benjamin and slip away while everyone else is busy."

Few ladies brought their maids to such a function—at least in Key West—but maybe Anabelle could convince Elizabeth. It would also be difficult to disappear from a ball, but Anabelle had managed to reach his ship a half dozen times without being seen.

Rourke had to admit it was the best option they had. "It's worth trying. Tom, you're going to have to play messenger again. I'm going to write a note describing both ways to get out of the house. Can you get it to her?"

Tom nodded. "If I can get near."

"Stay in town until you do."

"What if they don't let her out of the house?" Tom asked. "Mr. Benjamin must suspect something if he's locking the gate."

"Don't she go to market?" Rander asked.

Rourke could have blessed the pock-faced sailor with a kiss on each cheek. "That's the answer. Try to catch her at market."

"In the daytime?" Tom sounded skeptical. "Someone will see me."

"True." Rourke rubbed his chin. This could go badly wrong, and Tom was smart to consider options. "If you think anyone is following you, don't come back to the ship. We will have to trust you finished the job."

"Aye, aye, Captain."

"Good." Rourke clapped him on the shoulder. "I know you won't fail us."

⌘

The following days brought no relief from the twin torments of Mother's diary and the pending engagement announcement. Elizabeth could resolve the latter by talking to Father, but he seemed to be avoiding her. He took supper in his office. The door was always closed. When she knocked, he either did not answer or asked her to come back later.

That left the diary. What had happened to the other daughter? Twenty years of silence shrouded the answer. She might have died or left Key West. She might still live here. Who would know? Who could Elizabeth ask? Certainly not Father. Aunt Virginia wouldn't know. Despite her proclaimed closeness to Mother, this was not something that Elizabeth's mother would have shared with anyone. None of the current servants had been here at that time. Nathan and Cook arrived shortly before Charlie was born. Florie came along soon after. Only Mother's maid and Mammy had served the household, but both were gone now. Mother's maid died of fever when Elizabeth was little, and Mammy left the summer before the hurricane. Anabelle was born two months after Elizabeth. There was no one to ask.

By evening, her head ached so fiercely that she begged Aunt Virginia to excuse her early from their reading in the parlor.

"You do look rather out of sorts." Aunt Virginia lifted a handkerchief to her nose. "I hope there isn't another of those dreadful yellow fever plagues coming around."

For an instant, Elizabeth was tempted to claim the onset of fever. It would keep even Mr. Finch away, but it wasn't true. She felt none of the aches associated with tropical fevers. A little hint wouldn't hurt, though. "I hope not, but it's prudent to take precautions."

"Especially with the Harvest Ball nearly here." Aunt Virginia shooed her away, handkerchief still covering her nose. "You must be in the best of health by then."

Only after Elizabeth shut her bedroom door did her headache begin to ease. The layers upon layers of petticoats along with the crinoline felt like lead. She stripped off the dress and as much of the underpinnings as possible and then lay on the bed staring at the plastered ceiling.

A knock on the door signaled Anabelle's arrival. "Miss?" One eyebrow lifted at the sight of her partially undressed mistress.

"It's too hot." Elizabeth rolled onto her stomach. "Get this dreadful corset off me."

Anabelle closed the door. "I thank God every day that I don't have to wear that contraption."

As she loosened the stays, the air came back into Elizabeth's lungs. "When Aunt Virginia leaves, I'm forgoing it also."

"Do you think Mr. Finch will look favorably on his future wife shunning proper attire?"

Elizabeth winced at the words *future wife*. "Aside from the fact that I have no intention of marrying Mr. Finch, I don't think I shall ever be a proper wife."

"Oh?"

"I despise shoes and hats and corsets and all of this frippery." Elizabeth tossed the pile of petticoats off the bed. "Teas and visits bore me to tears. The thought of spending the rest of my days managing a household is insufferable. I want to do things. Go places. See strange and marvelous sights."

"And how would you pay for this gallivanting about? Your father wouldn't support such goings-on."

"I could write articles for the newspaper."

"I doubt Mr. Finch would want his wife to stoop to working," Anabelle said as she untied the crinoline. "In my experience, husbands make all the decisions."

Perhaps that was what terrified her. "Like Father."

"Like your father." Anabelle hung up the underpinnings. "Do you want a nightgown, Miss Lizzie?"

The airy cotton chemise felt wonderful, but it was even better to hear Anabelle use her nickname. Elizabeth was transported back to when they'd giggled under the covers late into the night.

She scooted over and patted the bed. "Why don't we pretend we're girls again? I'll tell you a secret, and you can tell me one."

Anabelle looked at Elizabeth as if she wasn't quite sure she should trust her. She glanced at the closed door. "Your aunt will wonder where I am."

"You're with me. I'm mistress of the house now, and I want

you here tonight." It felt good to take charge, to finally do what she wanted, not what everyone else said she should do. "I want to talk with you."

"Very well." Anabelle sat stiffly on the edge of the bed. "What do you want to discuss?"

Elizabeth had to laugh. "Goodness, you're acting like you're afraid of me. What happened to the old Anabelle?"

"She grew up."

Elizabeth hugged her knees to her chin. How glorious it felt to go back in time! One day soon she'd have to step forward into the dismal future, but she deserved just one night as a girl, didn't she? "I'm sorry. For everything."

Anabelle didn't ask what she meant. "You didn't have a choice."

"I suppose not." Elizabeth examined her soft, pale hands, so different from Anabelle's lean, callused fingers. Instead of inheriting Mother's long, graceful hands, Elizabeth had gotten Father's. Who else walked this earth with Father's features? Mammy was the only one still alive who might have known.

"Your mother," she began.

Anabelle jerked as if shot. "My mother is gone."

"I'm sorry. It must hurt to not be able to see your mother. Maybe one day I'll take you to her."

Anabelle laughed harshly. "Your husband would never allow it."

"I am not marrying Mr. Finch, even if it means I never marry."

"Your father won't stand for that."

"My father will learn to accept it." Elizabeth bit her lip. Anabelle had distracted her from the question she was dying to ask. "I wanted to ask about your mother. Mammy lived here before I was born."

Anabelle gave her an odd look.

Elizabeth pressed on. "Did she ever mention another baby?" She hesitated, unsure how to say this. "An illegitimate baby?"

Anabelle's gaze bored through her, unreadable. "No."

Elizabeth slumped against the pillows. "Then there's no one who knows."

"God knows all."

The simple truth caught her by surprise. "He might be the only one."

"Sometimes that's best." Then Anabelle squeezed her hand, like a friend commiserating with her, not a servant. "I'm sorry."

"Oh, Anabelle," Elizabeth cried, throwing her arms around the woman she'd called friend for so many years. "I missed you."

After stiffening at first, Anabelle hugged her back.

Elizabeth swiped at a tear. "I'm sorry for getting so emotional. So many things have gone awry lately."

"You miss him."

"Him?" Elizabeth echoed, though she knew full well who Anabelle meant.

"I heard a rumor that he is gone, but I don't believe it."

A clot formed in Elizabeth's throat. She couldn't bear to speak his words aloud, so she retrieved Rourke's letter from her rosewood box and handed it to Anabelle. Her friend slowly opened the paper and then read the lines. She clutched a hand to her waist and rocked forward, eyes closed as if in pain.

Elizabeth held on to her. "Are you all right?"

Anabelle grimaced. "A spasm is all." After a moment, she sat up, somewhat paler. "Then the rumor is true."

Elizabeth nodded.

Anabelle squeezed her eyes shut again, and the letter drifted to the floor.

16

Elizabeth took Anabelle with her to the final dress fitting the next morning. Surprisingly, Aunt Virginia didn't put up a fuss. Apparently anything that related to the fast-approaching event went above scrutiny. Elizabeth was simply glad to leave the house. She still needed to tell Father that she would not marry Mr. Finch, and he was still avoiding her.

Anabelle said little, which was to be expected, but her brow was pinched with worry beneath the plain straw hat. Elizabeth had forgone her oppressive bonnet for a wide-brimmed straw hat decorated with a broad dark blue ribbon. Though its cheerfulness opposed both her mood and her mourning gown, she couldn't bear to don the heavy black bonnet again.

The sun sparkled off the windows. The white sand shimmered. Many people crowded the streets. Since they must pass the harbor, Elizabeth instinctively checked the numerous vessels anchored and moored. The *Windsprite* was not among them.

One year. One full year. Would he miss her? She imagined Rourke striding across the deck barefoot, his hair a bit too long and his face clean-shaven in opposition to the dictates of fashion. Rourke was his own man, sure of his place. Such a man would wait one more year. So would she.

The scents of salt and fish permeated the air. The bustle of stevedores and the crunch of wagon wheels mingled with the ringing of bells and the slap of halyards against masts. This was home. This was where she belonged, not caged inside a lovely house.

"He is not here," Anabelle murmured.

"No, but all he loves is here."

"Mrs. Evanston will be waiting."

"I suppose I must," Elizabeth said with a sigh, "even though I would rather be out on the sea."

"Yes, miss."

Anabelle's sudden formality drew her attention. A claret-colored gig with green wheels drew to a stop beside them.

"Miss Benjamin?"

Elizabeth had to tilt her head to see who had called her name. "Captain Poppinclerk."

He secured the reins and hopped down from the high seat. "May I escort you somewhere? My carriage is at your disposal."

She eyed the high seat. "No, thank you. I prefer to walk."

The pilot looked surprised. "Extraordinary. Most ladies would leap at the chance to ride in style."

"I do not leap, Captain, nor do I prefer the jolting of a carriage to a leisurely stroll."

Mr. Poppinclerk bowed. "My error. Perhaps you would enjoy company on your stroll."

To Elizabeth's consternation, Anabelle slipped away.

Elizabeth attempted the aloof disinterest practiced by many of the ladies she had known in Charleston. "I fear I have an appointment with Mrs. Evanston and have no time for a stroll."

"Ah, Mrs. Evanston is the finest seamstress in Key West. I suspect she is making you an evening gown for the coming ball."

Elizabeth looked for Anabelle, who had disappeared. "My aunt believes I need one."

"A lady as beautiful as you deserves many new gowns."

His flattery was even worse than that of Mr. Finch. "I am in mourning, Mr. Poppinclerk, and have not yet decided to attend."

"But you must. The Harvest Ball is the event of the season. Everyone of note will be there. If you were not in attendance, Key West would miss its brightest flower."

Elizabeth strained this way and that looking for Anabelle. This man's platitudes sickened her. Why did every man treat her with such obvious artifice? Every man except Rourke. She smiled at the thought of him.

"Ah, you agree," Poppinclerk said. "I, for one, am very glad. Perhaps you will save me a dance?"

Startled, Elizabeth looked at him and finally saw Anabelle. Her maid stood across the street talking to . . . impossible. She took a step to her right in order to see past Mr. Poppinclerk's horse.

"Dear Miss Benjamin, I hope I have not offended you." Mr. Poppinclerk followed her as she tried to get a view.

"Not at all. I'm simply looking for my maid. We must hurry to my appointment."

"Of course." He bowed in front of her, blocking her path. "Then may I assume you will save me a dance?"

"Of course," she murmured in order to get rid of the man.

"Excellent. Good day, Miss Benjamin." He bowed yet again and returned to his gig.

Thank goodness. Elizabeth walked a little farther until she

could get a better view. A big wagon from the wharves blocked the street for a moment, but after it passed, Anabelle's companion came into view. She clapped a hand to her mouth.

What was Tom Worthington doing in town? He should be on the *Windsprite* headed for the Bahamas. Did that mean Rourke had returned?

She started to cross the street, but Mr. Poppinclerk drove past in his gig. After he shouted another greeting, the street finally cleared enough for her to see Tom talking to Anabelle. He handed her maid something. She nodded, and he turned toward the harbor.

"Tom," Elizabeth called out, waving her hand.

Both Tom and Anabelle started. His eyes widened. She dropped something small and square and white that she hastily scooped up and shoved in her apron pocket.

Elizabeth hurried across the street. "Tom, I did not expect to see you here. I thought Captain O'Malley left for the Bahamas."

"Yes, miss." He looked pale. "He said any of the crew that didn't want to go could stay and look for another berth."

Elizabeth sucked back the disappointment. "Then he is gone, truly gone."

"Yes, miss." Tom touched a finger to his hat. "I ought to be getting along now, if you don't mind."

"Not at all."

He hurried off, perhaps a bit too eagerly.

"I wonder what that was all about." As she looked to Anabelle, she remembered the exchange between the two of them. "I saw him hand you something. It looked like a note."

"No, miss." Anabelle pulled a folded handkerchief from her apron pocket.

"Oh, I see." But she didn't. Not entirely. Anabelle didn't lack for handkerchiefs. Why would she ask for one from Tom? And why did both of them look so guilty?

"We'd best be going to Mrs. Evanston's," Anabelle said, her face taking on that impassive expression that meant she would say no more.

Elizabeth would go to her appointment, but this matter was not forgotten, not at all.

⤙⤚

The rest of the day Elizabeth worked through what she'd seen on the street that morning. Tom wouldn't leave Rourke. He had spoken so reverently of him on the *Dinah Hale* and had been so eager to return. This morning, when Elizabeth asked if Rourke was truly gone, he hadn't been able to look her in the eye. No, something was afoot.

As for Anabelle, that was not a handkerchief that had fallen to the ground. Elizabeth tested how a folded handkerchief fell. Then she compared it to a falling note. Tom had definitely given her a note. Maybe he had told Anabelle where the *Windsprite* went. Since Aunt Virginia had interrupted the fitting and hovered over Anabelle's mending, Elizabeth had had no opportunity to speak with her maid until bedtime.

"If you don't hold still, I'll never get this nightgown on," Anabelle chided.

Elizabeth stopped pacing long enough for Anabelle to slip the gown over her head. Her maid was acting differently tonight. The regal posture and firm speech were replaced by an averted gaze and rounded shoulders.

Oh yes. Something was going on.

When Anabelle took up the hairbrush, Elizabeth held out her hand. "I can do that."

Anabelle hesitated. "It's easier for me to brush out your hair."

"I need to do things for myself. You might not always be with me."

Anabelle jumped and dropped the brush. Before Elizabeth could question her, her maid dropped to her hands and knees. "I'm sorry, miss. Your mama gave you this brush. Thank God it didn't break. I would deserve a whuppin' if it broke." She stood and began brushing.

Elizabeth pulled away. "Why did you jump just then?"

Anabelle trembled, a hand pressing to her midsection. "Are you going to send me away like my mama?"

"Of course not. Why would you think that?" But it did explain Anabelle's reaction. Elizabeth softened her tone. "Did Father or Aunt Virginia say something to you?"

Anabelle bowed her head. "What makes you say that?"

"Because I know my father and great-aunt." Elizabeth blew out a sigh. Handling servants was much more difficult than it looked. "How did my mother do it?"

"Do what?"

"Manage the household."

Anabelle was silent for some moments. "Your mama knew God's grace."

"What do you mean?"

"She cared about people."

"But then why send me to Charleston? Why promote a man I don't like? Why send Mammy away?" Elizabeth caught her breath. Mammy wasn't just her nurse, she was Anabelle's mother. "Why did she leave?"

Bitterness stole across Anabelle's face. "She didn't leave. She was sold."

"Why?" Was that her fault too? Had Elizabeth's mistakes sent Mammy away?

"Some things it's best not to know."

A chill shivered up Elizabeth's spine. "It was my fault."

Anabelle's lip curled with disgust. "It wasn't your fault. It's the way it is."

"She must have told you why. She must have said something."

Anabelle wouldn't look her in the eye. "One night Cook woke me up saying my mama was going away."

Elizabeth could not imagine watching her mother being taken away by force. "Did you see her before she left? Did you get to talk?"

"She told me enough."

The bitterness in Anabelle's voice should have warned Elizabeth, but she had to try again. Mammy was the only one who'd been around at the time of the illegitimate baby. "And she never told you about . . . about . . . another baby?"

Anabelle neither nodded nor shook her head. "Your mama would have known."

"I know. She kept a diary. I found it in her room and I read it." Elizabeth reached into the rosewood chest and fumbled retrieving the volume. "She wrote it all in here, but she never gave names. Do you know who?" She held out the diary to Anabelle.

She didn't take it. "Forget the past. Look to your future."

Rourke was her future. If Anabelle wouldn't talk about what happened years ago, she might help Elizabeth move forward. She took a shaky breath. "You know where to find him, don't you?"

"Find who?"

"You know who. He hasn't left for home yet, has he?"

Anabelle looked away. "I don't know where he is."

Elizabeth wouldn't let this go so easily. Her entire future

depended on finding Rourke. Under no circumstances could she marry Mr. Finch. Rourke was her escape. "Tom must know. I saw him talking to you. Where is he staying? Tell me." She grabbed Anabelle's shoulders. "Tell me."

"What good will it do? Your father locks the gates at night."

Elizabeth drew in her breath. "Why would he do that?"

"Why do you think?"

"He thinks I will run off? But that makes no sense. I can go out the front door anytime."

"Can you?"

Elizabeth knew the truth of Anabelle's question. No doubt Father in his nighttime pacing would hear her open the door, but she could not give up this opportunity. "I will find a way. Tell me where Tom is staying."

Anabelle stared into her eyes. "I will tell you if you take me with you to the Harvest Ball."

"To the ball? Why?" Of all the things that Anabelle might request, this made no sense. "How on earth would I explain that?"

"Many ladies will bring a maid to ensure they look their best throughout the evening."

Elizabeth doubted that, but it was a simple thing to grant, especially since she had no intention of attending. "All right."

"Do you promise upon your mama's grave?"

That made the request more serious and even more perplexing. "Why do you want to go to a ball? You would only sit outside with the other servants."

Her maid's gaze dipped. "I want to see it."

"Why?"

"Please." Anabelle wrapped her arms around her midsection and rocked, her expression so desperate that Elizabeth feared

222

she would do herself harm if not granted this request. "It's not much to ask of someone who grew up as your friend."

Pain closed Elizabeth's throat at the memory of what they had once shared. It was little price to pay for a chance to find Rourke. "I promise upon my mother's grave. Now where is Tom?"

Anabelle drew a shaky breath. "Mrs. Mallory's boarding-house, but he is likely already gone."

That was enough. Elizabeth's mind whirled with a daring plan. She would call on the boardinghouse and pry the location of the *Windsprite* from Tom. Then . . . She eyed the tamarind. She hadn't shinnied down it since she was a girl. It was time to give it a try.

17

When Tom didn't return by the third night, Rourke assumed that the young man either had failed to reach Anabelle or had been discovered. Both left him in an awkward position with the planned escape just two days away. Rourke gripped the rail. He was a man of action. All this sitting and waiting, each day risking detection, was driving him mad. He needed to do something, anything.

"I'm going ashore," he told John.

"How you go ta shore seein' as Master Tom has de boat?"

As usual, his mate's logic couldn't be questioned, but it didn't improve Rourke's temper. "I can't just sit here swatting at mosquitoes."

"Don't see dat you got much choice."

John was right, but Rourke couldn't sit still when every crewman's future was at stake. This had to succeed. John knew that as well as anyone.

"How can you be so calm? If I were you, I'd be swimming for shore."

John grinned. "We do our part. De rest in God's hands."

Simple enough to say. Tough to believe. "Your faith is stronger than mine."

"God bring my Anabelle home in His time. He bring Miz Lizbeth home in His time."

That was what kept Rourke awake at night. Four years of uncertainty had been difficult. He couldn't wait another four years. "I'm no Jacob, working seven years only to have her father hold her back and ask for seven more."

John guffawed and slapped his thigh. "Dat be you, aw right. But remember, in de end, Jacob get his Rachel."

Rourke shook his head. "I have my doubts."

"She wait."

Even if she did, Rourke might never be able to return. If Charles Benjamin discovered Rourke had helped Anabelle escape, he could never again set foot on Key West soil. To do so meant prison.

So he waited.

Aside from the rustle of mangrove leaves, nighttime brought relative quiet. Few animals inhabited the smaller islands. Most had no source of fresh water. Those living creatures that could exist in the harsh environment were small and relatively quiet. Crabs, lizards, and snakes might be on the move, but no human would hear them. Occasionally a school of small fish skittered across the surface, racing to escape sharks or barracuda.

A whistle rang through the air. Startled, Rourke glanced up to where the lookout had been perched since nightfall. He crossed to the mast and waited for Rander to climb down.

"Tom or trouble?" Rourke asked the moment the man's feet hit the deck.

"Dunno. Skiff looks 'bout the right size, but if it's him, he's hurt. He stops ta rest every couple strokes."

"Stand by to haul anchor at my command." Rourke rushed to the bow where he could get a first look at the incoming boat. If this wasn't Tom, if it was a traitor, he would give the signal. The tide was still strong enough to carry them through the narrow opening without the assistance of sail. He trained his gaze on that opening and motioned for the men to be silent.

Dark mangroves lined each side of the cut and limited his view to dead ahead, but he could hear the erratic splash of oars. Instead of a regular pull, each shallow dip came at a different pace. Either Tom was wounded, as the lookout had surmised, or they were about to face an uninvited guest.

Rourke motioned for each man to arm himself. John held out his hand for the key to the gun locker. Rourke reached for it but reconsidered. In the darkness, gunfire could do more harm than good. One jumpy crewman could fire early and set off a cascade of bullets.

He waved off the request. They would use blades.

Rourke listened for the egret croak but heard only the erratic splashing. This could not be Tom unless the lad was too badly injured to call out. Rourke wrapped his fingers around the hilt of his cutlass. If this was a foe, he intended to win the confrontation.

The bow of a skiff slid past the edge of the mangroves. Rourke motioned for his men to line both gunwales. Until he knew which side the boat would approach, he had to prepare for both. The lookout had seen just one man at the oars. Rourke's crew of nine could take a single man handily.

The next pull of the oars brought the boat squarely into the channel. Even in the moonlight, he recognized his ship's boat. Tom? No, the stature of the rower wasn't right. Too small. The oars drooped.

"Ahoy, the *Windsprite*." The weak, high-pitched call from the skiff did not belong to Tom. It sounded like a young boy.

Why would a boy seek them out? Unless . . . Would Tom have sent him? If so, wouldn't he have given the boy the signal?

Confused, Rourke lowered his weapon and pulled out his spyglass.

The boy in the boat stood. He appeared to be wearing some sort of cloak, judging from the shape. Rourke could not make out a face, but he could see that the boy was alone.

The boy lifted his hands to his mouth as the boat wobbled unsteadily. "Rourke?"

He hesitated. The voice sounded familiar. Moreover, the boy knew him by name. Maybe Tom had hired a local lad to bring a message. Someone Rourke knew. Or it could be a trap. Poppinclerk's warning sprang to mind.

John tapped him on the shoulder. He wanted to know what to do.

Rourke wasn't sure. He motioned for John to wait and peered into the spyglass again.

At that moment, the lad lost his balance. Arms flailed, and a high-pitched screech rent the night air. The hood fell off, and in the last instant before the rower plunged into the water, the moonlight revealed long, golden hair.

Elizabeth!

Rourke threw aside the spyglass and dove over the ship's side.

⚬✦⚬

"What are you doing here?" Rourke squatted in front of her, his eyes blazing in the glow of the lantern.

Elizabeth pulled the wool blanket tight around her shoulders. Seawater from her skirts pooled on the deck of the *Windsprite*, and the cooler night air made her shiver, but she hadn't felt this alive in four years. "I rowed the skiff across. It wasn't terribly difficult. Walking to where it was hidden was far worse."

"I didn't ask how. I asked why."

He was being unreasonable. "I want to go with you." She'd told him this a dozen times, but he refused to believe her.

"Don't you know how dangerous this little adventure was? You could have been hurt. You might have drowned."

"I wasn't and I didn't."

Rourke rocked to his feet and paced a short distance away before pivoting back to face her. "How did you find us? Tell me that. Only one person in Key West knows where we're anchored."

"Tom."

"Tom told you? I'll make him pay."

"You will do no such thing." She jutted out her chin. "I found him, not the other way around, and he refused to say a thing for the longest time. I forced it out of him."

"You? Forced it from him? How? Did you hold a pistol to his head?"

"Don't be ridiculous. Common sense and persuasion go much farther than violence."

Rourke growled. "What common sense and persuasion?"

She tugged the blanket a little tighter. "I needed to see you. He needed to get a message to you. Our purposes matched."

"Not good enough." He walked away from her again, clearly incensed.

"He told me not to let anyone see me. I was very careful, even though I have no idea why you insist on all this secrecy. I promise not to tell a soul. Moreover, if you take me with you, it will be impossible for me to tell anyone."

"Not possible." He stalked back toward her. "How did you even know Tom was in town?"

"I saw him talking to Anabelle."

He growled again. "Then she knows you're here too."

"She knows I wanted to see Tom. That's all."

"Where is she?"

"Safe at home. Where else? I can't bring a maid with me."

This time, Rourke's Negro mate muttered something unintelligible.

Rourke shot the man a warning glare before returning his attention to her. "What was the message Tom asked you to bring to me?"

Elizabeth closed her eyes and pictured the words she had memorized. "He said to tell you that all is done as directed and the man in the alley is Mr. Poppinclerk. What does that mean?"

Rourke ran a crooked finger below his lower lip, back and forth, deep in thought. "It means exactly what he said. Now that you've relayed the message, we need to get you home."

The man took stubbornness to a new height. "Like I told you, I can't go home." Why wouldn't he believe her? "I love you, not Mr. Finch. If I go home, Father will announce that we are engaged. I could never marry him."

"Then don't. No one can force you to marry."

She shuddered at the memory of Mr. Finch's attempted kiss. How far would he go to claim her? Something had led Mother to marry Father even though she did not love him. She had assumed Mother obeyed Grandmama and Grandpapa. What if that wasn't the only reason?

Rourke knelt before her again and gently lifted her chin. "Look at me, Elizabeth. You are a strong woman. Remember

229

that. No one can force you to do something you do not want to do."

He knew what she faced, and yet he would not help. Elizabeth choked back tears. "For an entire year?"

"Perhaps." He smoothed a lock of hair from her forehead, and she leaned into the caress.

She had to make him understand. "I can't live without you."

"You managed for four years. You can last a little longer."

"I shouldn't have left without word last time. I've changed. I would never do that again."

"I know."

"Then why not take me with you? Is it because I let you take the blame for what happened to Charlie?" She knew what she must do, but it was so difficult. "I shouldn't have. I never should have. It was my fault. I'm sorry."

He touched her cheek. "Look at me, Elizabeth."

"I can't." How could she look him in the eye? He would see her guilt, her shame, the cowardice buried deep inside.

He lifted her chin and caught her gaze. "There is nothing to forgive."

"Yes, there is." A terrible trembling began in her limbs. How weak, how frail, how flawed she was.

"No." He stroked her jaw, not in anger but with tenderness. "We all make mistakes. All of us. Myself included. I could regale you for hours, but the Lord washed those mistakes away when He died on the cross. I only had to accept that act of love. That's what love is. It thinks first of the other person. It forgets itself. It does right even when it hurts."

She had heard all this many times before.

"If He can forgive my mistakes," he continued, "I can certainly forgive anything you have done."

She sucked in her breath. "Anything? Even four years of silence?"

He smiled. "It was a long time but hardly silent. Your brother told me a great deal."

"My brother? How did Charlie know . . . oh, from my letters to our mother."

"He loves you. He needs you."

She shook her head. "Then why does he push me away one moment and act like a friend the next?"

"He's a boy. A boy trying to become a man. Wanting to be strong and afraid to ask for your love in case it makes you think he's weak."

Elizabeth had never considered that. "I came home to take care of him."

"He doesn't need a nursemaid." Rourke settled beside her on the hatch cover. "He needs a sister."

She squeezed her eyes shut. In her desperation to claim Rourke, she had cast aside her brother. "You must think me very selfish."

"No." He clasped her hand. "Very passionate. Very determined. Very certain of what you want. But you must realize that a future cannot be founded on broken hearts and deception. I won't take you anywhere without your father's blessing." He kissed her forehead. "I'm sorry."

Elizabeth had thought her heart broken before, but this ached far worse. A sob escaped. "Father will never agree."

"Never is a long time."

She would not cry. She would not. She bit her lip to stop the powerful swell of emotion. "Will you return?"

He brushed a finger across her cheek, sending shivers all the way to her toes. "God willing, dear Elizabeth."

She let her lids drift shut, hoping either that he would kiss her or that she would awake and find this a dream.

Instead he pulled her to her feet. "Let's get you home."

❦

Rourke hated hurting her. When she closed her eyes and those perfect lips parted, it took all his will not to kiss her. Her disappointment nearly changed his mind. She loved him. She was willing to give up everything, even her family, to be with him. He had dreamed of hearing such a declaration, but now it was impossible.

She didn't know about the plan. Based on what she'd said, she didn't know John and Anabelle were married, least of all that he planned to bring her to freedom in the Bahamas. Taking Elizabeth instead of Anabelle to Briland wasn't just selfish, it broke a solemn promise and locked a soul in bondage.

Rourke dug the oars into the still water, now calm at slack tide, and reached the mouth of the cut in just four strokes. The boat glided silently onto the ocean. To the north and east lay his homeland. A favorable wind would bring them into the Gulf Stream and out of Florida waters in a few short hours. An unfavorable wind could keep them bottled up in the Keys. That was a problem.

He lifted the oars.

Elizabeth, sitting in the bow, eyed him. "What is it?"

He motioned for her to be quiet, not from necessity but because he needed time to think. What would he do if the *Windsprite* was becalmed? He hadn't provided that option to Anabelle. In fact, he hadn't considered the wind at all. What kind of captain forgot to take into account the wind?

He pulled once on the oars.

Even if he did manage to weigh anchor and slip away from the island undetected, if the wind failed, the harbor's new steam tug could easily catch him. Rourke had to get word to Anabelle. Elizabeth was the obvious choice, but she knew nothing of the planned escape. He was not going to tell her now. First, she might not approve of losing her maid. Second, it made her an accomplice. No, he would have to get word to Tom, who would then tell Anabelle.

"Where are you going?" she whispered loudly.

Rourke shook himself from his thoughts and discovered the boat had drifted east when he needed to row west. He plunged the oars into the water and gave three strong strokes.

Unfortunately, he couldn't get word to Tom. He couldn't risk being seen.

"Something is wrong," Elizabeth said again.

"No, I'm fine."

He rowed a few more strokes. Elizabeth could bring a message to Tom, who would then find Anabelle, but that was ridiculous. She could go straight to Anabelle. He just had to make the message vague enough that Elizabeth wouldn't figure out its true meaning.

"The oars blistered my hands," she said. "Are they hurting yours?"

He shook his head. "I have a little more experience rowing than you do."

"I used to row Charlie's skiff."

"That was Charlie's boat? I always thought it was yours."

"Father gave it to him, but he was scared to use it because he couldn't swim."

"How did you learn? I always figured Charlie showed you."

She grinned. "I watched you and learned how."

"Don't let your father hear about that. It'll be another strike against me."

"I promise." She inched toward him a little. "You looked a million miles away just then, like you were riding on the stars."

He smiled at the image she painted. Elizabeth was like a freshening breeze, promising a fine adventure ahead. "I was thinking that I needed to get a message back to Tom."

"I'll do it." She leaned toward him. "And I'll be discreet."

"I know you will, but it would be better if you sent Anabelle. People might already be talking about you showing up at the boardinghouse."

"No one saw me. It was after dark, and Tom happened to be on the veranda."

"How fortunate, but you can't rely on that happening again. No one will think twice of a servant bringing a message. You may write it in a note if you wish."

The moonlight shimmered off her wide, eager eyes. "Tell me what you want me to write."

Rourke stopped rowing. Better he say this where he could see that no one was around to hear. "Tell him to proceed if the wind is favorable."

"And if it's not?"

"The first day it is." Tom had the experience to understand that message, but Rourke hoped it never got that far. Would Anabelle know a fair wind from a foul one? The voyage to Charleston and back ought to have taught her that much. If not, she would at least get the note to Tom. "And make sure he knows that he is to get everyone ready."

"Everyone? You have more crew in town?"

He hadn't anticipated that reaction. "One or two more." If he counted Anabelle as crew.

"All right. Let me repeat the message. Proceed if the wind is favorable. If not, wait until it is, and get the crew ready."

"Close enough." Tom would know what to do with that. "Also make sure he gets it tomorrow. All right?"

"I will," she promised.

Rourke resumed rowing, this time at a steady pace. "Keep quiet now. We're approaching the island."

She nodded and slid forward to the bow. With her right hand, she grasped the painter, ready to leap ashore and tie off. With her left, she held the gunwale. Elizabeth Benjamin knew boats.

He chuckled inwardly at the memory of her misstep years ago that had landed her in the water instead of on the *Windsprite*'s deck. She had popped to the surface like a drowned rat, sputtering mad and saying he'd pushed the skiff away at the last minute. She'd been even angrier that he had the audacity to laugh. He had adored her like a kid sister then, but the years flew past, and she'd become a young woman. Still impulsive and adventurous, but very much a woman. His affection for her had blossomed into romance. Then she left. Those years in Charleston had shrouded her finer qualities so thoroughly that he hadn't spotted them until tonight. The night he had to say goodbye.

As Rourke lifted the oars and let the boat drift ashore on the island of Key West, he wondered how he would endure the separation. A year might as well be forever if Benjamin announced Elizabeth's engagement to Finch.

She tied the painter to an overhanging mangrove with a triple half hitch and hopped ashore before he had a chance to assist her. Then she stuck out her hand to assist him. That was the Elizabeth he loved. That was the one he would miss.

They walked in silence past the salt ponds, quiet at this hour. The salt-growing process had begun for the year, and the ponds were flooded. Paths ran between the rectangular ponds, which were sealed off with gates. He chose the path next to the mangroves. Something rustled in the underbrush.

She squeezed his arm. "Don't leave me."

"Is this the same woman who earlier tonight ran through this very spot alone?"

"I didn't think I'd have to go back."

The sorrow in her voice brought a lump to his throat. "I'll stay with you until we reach the cemetery. You should be able to get home safely from there."

She didn't say anything, though she clung close to his side. How perfectly she fit, as if she had always belonged there. Rourke placed an arm around her waist. When they crossed the first street, he breathed out in relief. Soon she would be safe.

At the cemetery, she slowed and halted. "I don't want to let you go."

Rourke couldn't answer at first. He didn't want to leave her either, but he must, preferably without sending her into tears. He held her hands. "I'm relying on you to complete your mission."

The military-style command was meant to stiffen his resolve. It made her laugh.

"Of course." She squeezed his hands in return. "I will wait for you. No matter how long it takes."

The hint of desperation nearly undid him. He pulled her hand to his lips and kissed it.

She cupped his chin in that delicate palm. "I love you, Rourke O'Malley. I always will."

Emotion battled sense. He wanted to give her hope, but with no certainty he would ever be able to return, to declare love now would be cruelly selfish. "You are the finest woman I have ever known, Elizabeth. You have had my heart for years."

A sob wrenched from her. "Such a sorry pair we are, your Romeo to my Juliet."

He knew enough Shakespeare to understand her reference—and to fear it. "Promise me you won't do something foolish."

"Promise me you will return."

That he could not do. Except she hadn't asked when. She hadn't demanded a time. He couldn't have given one if she had. Maybe she realized that. He pulled the leather thong from around his neck and removed his grandmother's ring.

He pressed the ring into her hand. "This belonged to my grandmother. Take it as a pledge."

She turned the ring over and over in the moonlight. "It's beautiful."

He lifted her chin. "Not as beautiful as you." Then he kissed her, slow and soft and filled with the promise of what he hoped would be one day. She responded gently at first and then with the same hunger she'd once had for sailing. She clung to him, held on with all her strength, clearly afraid to part.

But part they must.

He held her one last time. Kissed her forehead. Drank in the jasmine scent and the taste of salt. He ran a finger across cheeks soft as a lapping wave, marveled at eyes bright as stars. A bell rang in the distance. Much as he wanted to stay here the rest of the night, he must let her go.

"Godspeed." He pushed her toward home before he lost the will. Then he walked away, not daring to look back.

"Godspeed, my love," she echoed.

18

The kiss warmed Elizabeth all the way home. It followed her when she slipped through an open window undetected. It nestled with her beneath the bedsheets and welcomed her into the new day. It confirmed what Rourke could not say in words. He loved her. He would return for her.

She lay against the bolster and pillows, letting the sunlight dance across her face. Her body ached with fatigue, but the memory of last night wiped away any sleepiness. He had pledged his love and honor. She pressed his ring to her lips. It fit her third finger perfectly, as if it had been made for her rather than his grandmother. Though she could not wear it publicly, this pledge gave her the strength to face as much as a year apart. *Please, Lord, make it less.*

She turned the silver ring, examining its intricate pattern. It looked very old. It must be an heirloom, passed down from generation to generation. A man would only give such a ring to the woman he intended to marry.

A knock sounded on the door. "Miss?" Anabelle was already here.

Elizabeth twisted the ring from her finger. "Please come back in ten minutes."

After Anabelle's footsteps faded away, Elizabeth flitted across the room to her dressing table and opened the rosewood box. The ribbon she had used for her trunk key would work. She removed the key and threaded the ring onto it. Then she slipped the ribbon over her head and beneath her chemise. Until Rourke put this ring on her finger before witnesses, she would wear it secretly near her heart.

Secret. Oh dear, she had promised Rourke to get a secret message to Tom today. She must hurry.

Elizabeth kept paper, pen, and ink in the reading room. When she was growing up, this space had been a nursery and then a room for play and studies.

One day she and Rourke would have children. How they would laugh and play together. They would all learn to sail—boys and girls alike. Swim also. The gossips could blather all they wanted about how unseemly it was for a girl to swim. But a child of the sea must know such things.

Another knock sounded on her bedroom door.

"One moment," Elizabeth called out as she gathered up the necessary writing implements.

Though Rourke suggested she send the note through Anabelle, Elizabeth would not give up the chance to talk to Tom. He might be able to tell her what Rourke had not—why he'd been called home.

Anabelle stuck her head in the room. "Are you ready for me, miss?"

"Not yet. I have a note to write. Come back in another ten minutes."

Anabelle frowned but acquiesced.

Alone again, Elizabeth settled at her dressing table and dipped the pen in ink. What had Rourke wanted her to write? She searched her sleep-muddled mind. Oh yes, something about when they were sailing. The wind. That was it. She scratched out the note.

Captain O'Malley wants you to proceed at the first favorable wind. Otherwise wait.

There was something else. What was it? She searched her memory. Ah yes. The crew.

Prepare everyone.

She folded the note and wrote Tom's name on the outside. All it needed was a seal. She rose to fetch the sealing wax when Aunt Virginia's strident voice rose from the floor below.

"It's gone, I tell you."

Aunt must be in the dining room, which was situated directly under Elizabeth's bedroom.

"I didn't lose it," Aunt Virginia declared. "Someone stole it."

Not the string of pearls. Elizabeth hoped Aunt hadn't misplaced her pearls or the entire household would be turned upside down looking for them.

Father's reply was so muted that she could not make out a single word. Doubtless he knew that voices carried. He also didn't rattle easily, even though Aunt Virginia could discombobulate the most placid soul.

"Impossible," Aunt cried. "My trunks were locked. I made sure of it by giving my keys to Captain Poppinclerk as soon as I reached safety. I was not going to let those pirates and darkies near my belongings. They would have stolen everything."

That explained how Aunt's trunks had gotten locked.

"Someone in this house must have stolen it," Aunt continued. "If you ask me, it was that maid of your daughter's. I don't trust her."

Elizabeth gritted her teeth. Any number of people had entered this house. Aside from the servants, dozens of callers had passed through, as had Mr. Finch. True, only the servants had been granted access to Aunt's bedroom, but it was still possible that someone had wandered upstairs unchecked. Yet in Aunt's eyes, Anabelle was automatically guilty. Elizabeth could not understand why Aunt hated Anabelle so much. It made no sense. Anabelle had shown the utmost deference in Charleston. She obeyed every order, yet Aunt still treated her with contempt.

Elizabeth glanced to the closed door. Had Anabelle heard this latest tirade?

"In my opinion"—Aunt gathered steam and volume—"that girl thinks she's above her station and needs to be brought into line. I've told Elizabeth to discipline her time and again, but she refuses. At most she gives the girl a slap on the hand. If nothing is done, the hens will be running the henhouse. You must step in. Do what must be done, like you did with her mother. The missing document gives you the perfect reason."

The scrape of a chair indicated the conversation was over, but it left Elizabeth both puzzled and disturbed. Mammy had been sent away. Surely Father wouldn't sell Anabelle simply because Elizabeth had refused to punish her. Moreover, Aunt said the fuss was all over some missing document. What document? Was she referring to the inheritance? But that made no sense. Father had informed her of the inheritance when they first arrived. He had said nothing about needing a document.

The sound of a door clicking shut roused her from her

thoughts. She turned to see Anabelle standing with her back against the door, eyes wide and countenance pale. Her hand trembled where it rested on the doorknob. She had heard.

"Don't let him sell me," Anabelle whispered.

Elizabeth had never seen her friend more terrified and unsure. "He wouldn't do that."

Anabelle's lips pursed and then quivered. "Help me. Please."

"Father won't send you away," Elizabeth repeated, this time taking Anabelle by the shoulders. "I won't let him."

Anabelle averted her eyes, gulped, and then looked straight at Elizabeth. "Perhaps you can save me, but—" She drew in a rasping breath, clearly struggling over what she wanted to say.

"But what? What's wrong? You can tell me."

Anabelle shook. Her lips worked. Tears gathered in the corners of her eyes and slipped down her cheeks. "I might be with child."

The revelation shot through Elizabeth with the speed and pain of an arrow. "How is this possible?"

What man could Anabelle have known? The only Negro male in the household was Nathan, and he had been with Cook for as long as she could remember. Aunt's only male servant was aged. None served aboard the *Victory*. Her head spun as horrible thoughts wiggled into her mind. No, impossible. She would not believe ill of her friend.

Then she remembered Anabelle's nighttime outings. She must have gone to meet someone.

"Who is it?" she hissed.

Anabelle drew back, her expression hard. "Does it matter? A slave's baby will be sold once it's weaned." Despair curled around every word.

"Not always," she offered weakly. "Father kept Florie."

"Your mama did."

Elizabeth recalled her last conversation with Anabelle. "That's why you wanted to go to the ball, isn't it? To see him."

Anabelle said nothing.

Elizabeth would not accept silence. "What did you think you would do? Escape with him? There's nowhere to go. Even if you could get to the next key, the hounds would find you." She ignored the fact that she had made that journey without being detected. "Well, what were you planning to do?"

"Tell him," Anabelle said softly. "Like you would tell the man you love."

Her words shivered down Elizabeth's spine. What if she were in Anabelle's place? She would do anything to tell Rourke. For all her righteous indignation that Anabelle would get herself with child, the fact was that these things happened. Mother's diary had spelled that out often enough. Perhaps she might persuade Father to purchase the father of Anabelle's child if it came to that. They had not been home a full month. If this man lived in town, Anabelle could not be certain yet that she was with child. This might all work out on its own.

"I will do what I can," Elizabeth promised.

⊱❦⊰

After Anabelle dressed her, Elizabeth tucked the note for Tom into the watch pocket of her dress and headed downstairs to see Father. First she would ensure he had no intention of sending Anabelle away, then she would deliver the message to Tom.

Fortunately, Father had not yet left for court. She knocked on the open door of his study.

Upon seeing her, he gathered up the papers he'd been reading and put them in his valise. "What is troubling you, sunshine? I must leave for the office."

She smiled at the nickname, but her request was not trifling. "Aunt Virginia might not realize my bedroom is directly above the dining room."

He closed the door behind her. "Likely not, or she would lower her voice." He returned to his desk. "Did something she said concern you?"

"My aunt has an unfounded dislike of Anabelle. Though she does nothing wrong, Aunt insists I punish her. I see no reason to do so."

Father heaved a sigh. He looked exhausted, as if he hadn't slept well in days. "Don't worry what your aunt thinks."

"I knew you would understand. You know how close Anabelle and I were growing up."

His brow hitched. "It's never wise to befriend the servants. Remember that you are their mistress. Too much familiarity leads to disrespect."

"But Mother treated them with kindness and garnered their respect."

"Your mother had unique capabilities born from her good breeding."

"And I don't?" The implication stung.

He smiled, but it looked forced. "You are your mother's daughter, true. Yet you would do better to avoid getting too involved in the servants' personal lives."

Her mouth grew dry. Had he heard Anabelle? Did he know the awful situation she found herself in? If so, then the question Elizabeth must ask would not seem peculiar.

"You would not sell her, then?" She held her breath.

His gaze narrowed. "What has your aunt said that led you to think that?"

Aunt Virginia offered a convenient scapegoat, but placing the blame on her would not be the truth. "You sent Mammy away."

"You no longer needed a nurse."

"But Charlie did."

Father's expression grew grave. "You are asking about things that are not your concern."

She would not give up that easily. "If I am to manage the servants, I must know when a servant needs to go."

He nodded slowly. "There are many reasons, but the chief one is usually financial. It costs a great deal to house and feed servants."

"Then there is no need to sell Anabelle?"

"You ask a difficult question." He sighed. "I did not want to worry you, but if our circumstances grow any more severe, I might need to sell a great deal of my property."

A chill swept over her. "But Anabelle is more than a servant. She's a member of our household."

"In hard times, servants must be let go. So too horses and carriages and fancy ball gowns."

She blanched. "Are we in hard times?"

"Rebuilding the house cost a great deal. Your brother's care is costly. He requires the regular attention of physicians as well as medicines for the pain. I have searched the country to find something that will give him a measure of independence. The wheeled chair is the best I've found thus far, but I will not stop until I find something that he can operate without assistance. In short, our savings are depleted."

"Everything?" Elizabeth could barely draw a breath. "Why didn't you tell me?"

"A girl your age should be dreaming of beaus and balls, not suffer the burdens that her father ought to bear."

Tears stung her eyelids. She had misjudged him so badly.

Perhaps she had even misread the diary. Her father was simply trying to do the best he could with what he had.

"But I do want to help." She grasped his hand. "That's why I came home. I don't need a new ball gown. I will ask Mrs. Evanston to find another buyer."

"No, my dear. That is the one thing you need most of all. Don't you see? You are my shining hope. Your marriage will not only bring healing and hope to this family, but it will secure your brother's future."

"My marriage?" The words sank into the pit of her stomach. He could not know of Rourke's pledge and the ring that had secured it. He was referring to Mr. Finch.

"That's why I told you about the inheritance. Your great-aunt has approved Mr. Finch. The inheritance will be released when you marry him. Then you will truly be able to help your brother."

Her head spun. "Me? It all rests upon me?"

"Your engagement announcement at the ball is the first step. I'm so proud of you."

The noose tightened around her neck. How could she find a way out?

Father patted her hand. "You alone can keep our family together."

Family included Anabelle. Father would agree to anything if she did as he wished. She looked her father in the eye. "Will you give me Anabelle?"

"Give her to you? As a wedding gift?"

"As a pledge." She would not be forced down that road. "And I wish to bring her with me to the ball."

A dark cloud rolled over his countenance. "There is no reason for a maid to go to a ball."

"I need her assistance. After all, a woman about to announce her engagement must look her very best." She did not name her betrothed.

His displeasure did not ease. Instead, he watched her, assessing the veracity of her statement. She pasted on a hopeful expression despite the pounding in her ears. He thrummed his fingers on the desktop, beating out the ramifications of his decision.

At last he stopped. "No, Elizabeth. The ball is no place for Anabelle."

"But—"

He lifted a hand. "No debate. That is my final decision."

Since Mrs. Evanston delivered the gown that morning, Elizabeth could not leave the house until late afternoon. Even then, she had to bring Anabelle along, ostensibly on an errand to locate shoes suitable for her ball gown. The shoes were easy to find. She'd seen them when surveying shop windows with Caroline. Speaking with Tom would not be so easy.

To maintain propriety, she must send Anabelle to the boardinghouse and have her bring Tom to a public place where Elizabeth could meet him seemingly by chance.

She waited near the custom house. Though the streets were crowded, Elizabeth had the distinct feeling that someone was watching her. She looked around but saw no one suspicious. It must be nerves. Rourke had stressed the importance of this message. She could not fail him.

"Miss Benjamin. Fancy meeting you here." Tom appeared from behind and stopped at her elbow.

Elizabeth slipped the note from her watch pocket. "From your captain."

"Hush." His gaze drifted left and right before he slipped the note into his jacket pocket. "Is that all?"

Elizabeth withdrew from her bag the letter she had penned after speaking with her father that morning. "Please give this to him before tomorrow evening."

"I can't promise to see him."

"Please try. It's vital. Tell him that I will be at the ball."

Tom took the sealed letter and secreted it in the same pocket. His gaze darted left and right again. "With your maid?"

It was her turn to be puzzled. "How did you know about that? Did Anabelle tell you?"

Instead of answering, he offered his arm. "Would you care to walk, Miss Benjamin?"

She sensed he wanted to say something that he couldn't reveal in such a busy, public place. "I would enjoy a brief stroll, Mr. Worthington."

They walked into the less busy residential area between the harbor and the hospital. Anabelle followed a short distance behind.

Tom spoke only when they were alone. "Did you notice anyone following you?"

A shiver raced down her spine. "I had a peculiar feeling that I was being watched, but I didn't see anyone."

His frown deepened. "Return home and tell no one that you saw me."

"Why? What do you suspect?"

"Probably nothing. Just jumpy from waiting." His laugh rang false.

Further questioning got her nowhere. He returned her to the custom house before bidding farewell. She left feeling that everything was unraveling at precisely the wrong time, and she had no idea how to stop it.

19

Elizabeth had to believe Rourke would come for her. Her instructions had been very specific. During the break between dancing and supper, she would excuse herself to use the necessary and slip away into the night. She would meet him at the little chapel where he had played piano. From there they would hurry to the *Windsprite* and set sail for his homeland.

It had all made perfect sense when she wrote the letter, but as she considered what she might bring with her, problems cropped up. First, she would be wearing dainty slippers, not sturdy shoes. The path to the eastern end of the island was treacherous. Slippers offered little protection. Her feet would be bleeding and bruised by the time she reached the ship, but it was a cost worth paying. Second, she could not carry anything with her but the tiniest bag, sufficient for handkerchief and smelling salts and not much else.

She fingered the few coins in her keepsake chest. They would not purchase much, if anything, in the Bahamas. Her mother's miniature might fetch a price, but she could not sell it. At least it would fit in the bag. Mama's Bible would not. Neither would her diary. She would leave them with Charlie.

Her brother. A pang of guilt ripped through her, making this plan seem terribly selfish. What had Rourke said? That Charlie needed a sister?

Her hand trembled. Would Rourke again refuse to take her with him? Was this plan of hers founded in selfish desperation and cowardice? Father was counting on her to save the family from financial ruin. All she had to do was marry a man she despised.

Anabelle rapped on the door and entered. "Sorry, miss. Your aunt insisted I assist her to bed first."

"She did?" Elizabeth pulled herself from her gloomy thoughts. Aunt Virginia never wanted Anabelle's assistance, even on the voyage from Charleston. "How peculiar. Is Florie ill?"

Anabelle shook her head. "She warned that my days here are numbered."

"What?" The tightness in her throat turned to anger. "How dare she. You are my maid, not hers. Mine."

Anabelle removed Elizabeth's cap. "I believe, in fact, that I belong to your father."

"For now, but I asked him to give you to me." As soon as she said the words, she remembered the terms of that agreement. She had asked for Anabelle as a pledge. He had offered her as a wedding gift.

"He agreed?" Anabelle plucked out the hairpins as she unwound Elizabeth's coiled hair.

Elizabeth swallowed hard. "Not outright, but I did ask to bring you with me to the ball."

Anabelle's fingers stilled. "What did he say?"

There was no way to cushion the news. "No."

The hairpins fell to the floor.

"Forgive me," Anabelle murmured, dropping to her knees.

"We will find another way to arrange a meeting with your love," Elizabeth said, ignoring the fact that after tomorrow night she would be gone. "Perhaps tomorrow morning."

"No." Anabelle's cry came out in a strangled sob. "The ball is my only chance." She swiped at the spilled hairpins and scattered them again.

Elizabeth dropped to the floor beside her and gathered the pins. "Why?"

Anabelle lifted red-rimmed eyes. "He will be gone."

"Sold?"

Anabelle shook her head. "He is free."

"Then . . . I don't understand. Why would he leave?"

"He leaves for home. Harbour Island."

"The same as . . ." Elizabeth sat back as she made the connection. Rourke had an entire crew, including a Negro chief mate. He was the one who had rescued Anabelle. First. Ahead of the whites. Despite Aunt Virginia's protests. Moreover, Rourke had approved it. Aboard the *Windsprite*, Anabelle had watched the man's every move. "John?"

Anabelle straightened at the sound of his name, finger to her lips before she whispered, "My husband."

Elizabeth drew in her breath. "How? When?"

Again her maid motioned for quiet. "Before the storm four years ago."

Elizabeth reeled. "Four years?" Anabelle had kept this secret from her for four years. "Why didn't you tell me?"

"What would you have done?"

"Come home sooner."

Anabelle shook her head, and Elizabeth knew she was right.

Returning early could never have happened. Aside from not having the fare for passage, she hadn't had the will to defy her parents' wishes.

"I must go to the ball," Anabelle whispered.

Elizabeth gathered her scattered thoughts. If John was leaving tomorrow night, that meant Rourke was leaving also. It was her only chance. Thank goodness she'd sent the letter to him through Tom. He would come for her. She was sure of it. But could she risk bringing Anabelle? Two women racing through the dark streets would be twice as difficult to disguise. Moreover, Father had forbidden Anabelle's attendance.

"I don't know how. Father refused."

Anabelle grasped Elizabeth's shoulders. "You must convince him."

Elizabeth pulled away from her crushing grip. "How? His mind is set."

"I must go." Anabelle rocked, arms wrapped around her midsection. "Don't you see? If I can't meet up with him, I will never see him again. My baby will be taken away." She grabbed Elizabeth again. "Please, help me."

Agitated, Elizabeth slipped from Anabelle's grasp and rose to her feet. "I can't." She backed to the window. "Please don't ask such a thing. I can't."

Anabelle collapsed face-first on the floor. Her shoulders heaved from suppressed sobs.

"I'm sorry. I'm sorry." Though Elizabeth felt for Anabelle, she couldn't give up the man she loved. "If there was any other way . . ."

Anabelle raised a tear-streaked face. "You will not help a friend?"

Elizabeth felt ill. "It has nothing to do with our friendship."

"Doesn't it?" Anabelle said bitterly. "Would you do more for a sister?"

"Of course, but I don't have a sister." Elizabeth caught herself. She did have a half sister. One whose identity only her late mother and Mammy knew. Unless . . . She stared at Anabelle. "You know, don't you? That's why Mammy was sent away. She knew about the baby, and she told you."

"Of course she knows. The mother always knows."

"Mother?" Elizabeth jerked back. "Mammy was the mother?"

"She is my mother, sister."

⌘

The Lord blessed the chosen day with a brisk wind from the southeast. Though the sun had not yet crested the horizon, Rourke paced the deck, anxious to begin. Time had moved slower than a sea slug the last week. It would stand still today.

He had heard nothing from Tom, but then he hadn't expected to. Rourke assumed Elizabeth had given his message to Anabelle, who would then inform Tom. The lad would bring Anabelle to the meeting spot tonight. Rourke would converge from the east, and together they would bring Anabelle to the *Windsprite* and freedom.

Any number of things could go wrong. Elizabeth might have forgotten to give Anabelle the message. She might not bring Anabelle to the ball. Tom might get waylaid en route. They might have to help Anabelle out of the gated yard. The salt company's manager might pick tonight to reflood the ponds.

He scrubbed his whiskers.

"No worry." John brought a steaming cup of coffee and a handful of hardtack.

253

Rourke took the coffee but declined the biscuits. "I'm not hungry."

"You eat." John shoved the biscuits at him. "Need strength."

For John's sake, Rourke nibbled at one. It was stale. No weevils yet, at least none he could see in the pre-dawn light. He dunked the biscuit in the coffee. Better but still unpalatable. It took another gulp of coffee to wash it down. "Fish would taste better."

"We catch some, soon as de light touches de water."

Rourke's mate appeared relaxed, even jovial. "How can you be so cheerful when everything is at stake?"

John snatched at the air and held it tight. "God hold us. God see us home."

Rourke hoped his mate's faith paid off.

⚜

Elizabeth could not stop shaking. Sleep was impossible. Instead she lived over and over the terrible moment when Anabelle claimed to be her sister. Elizabeth had stared, unwilling to believe. To think some unknown woman walked the world as her half sister was bad enough, but Anabelle?

"You're lying," she had cried.

Anabelle stood tall, unbending. She neither insisted nor denied her claim.

"You're younger than me. The illegitimate baby was older."

"I am older," Anabelle said quietly. "My mama told me never to tell a soul."

"Lies, lies," Elizabeth sobbed. She pressed a pillow to her mouth lest the sound send Aunt and Father running to her rescue.

For the truth stood before her. From their unusual height to

254

similar noses, chins, and short fingers, they were alike. Yet how could this be? Her father and Mammy?

Elizabeth's stomach churned. "Leave me."

Anabelle had gone, but her departure didn't take away the pain. If anything, it grew worse. Her father and Mammy? Father would never have done such a thing, and Mother would never have allowed it under her roof.

Yet Mother's diary confirmed it. Every word now made sense. Mother's distress at her new husband's "perversions." The agony over another woman. Elizabeth had assumed—had wanted to assume—that the mistress was another settler. She did not want to believe her father could have an unholy alliance with a slave. Yet Mother's insistence that the girl be raised with the same benefits as her own daughter spoke the truth. Anabelle had learned to read and write, unusual among slaves. Elizabeth squeezed her eyes shut to stop the tears.

Mammy was beautiful, with exotic almond eyes and the same regal bearing as Anabelle. Her scolding over Elizabeth and Anabelle playing on the throne chairs now made sense, as did Anabelle's banishment to the cookhouse.

In the wee hours, when the world stood still and thoughts tormented, Elizabeth knew.

It was not only possible, it was fact.

She hadn't truly prayed since the hurricane. Oh, she had cast off those quick pleas in times of desperation, but her heart hadn't turned to God. No, she could stand on her own. Faith was for the weak and hopeless.

Anabelle's revelation had left her weak and hopeless.

"Why?" she cried out to God. Over and over through the long night.

The pages of Mother's Bible had yielded familiar stories

but no answers. What would she do? What could she do? As much as she wanted to claim Anabelle was lying, the proof stood before her. From Anabelle's features to Mother's words to every little reaction of her parents through the years. Every single thing validated the fact that Anabelle was her half sister.

Friend was one thing. But sister?

Elizabeth buried her face in the pillow again to drown the sobs. How could she accept this? Why had Mother insisted Anabelle be raised as her equal? How could she even think such a thing? They weren't and never would be equals. Elizabeth could inherit her mother's family fortune. She was an heiress. She was legitimate.

Even worse, Mother forgave Father. How could she? How could she keep his mistress and illegitimate daughter under the same roof? Elizabeth pounded the bolster, the pillows, the mattress. Mother's reasons had gone to the grave with her.

Did Charlie know? He and Mother had spent many hours together during his recovery. Perhaps he already knew the terrible truth. Did everyone but her know?

She shoved the Bible away and it crashed to the floor. Mother's Bible! Horrified, she flew off the bed and found it lying askew on the floor, pages torn from the binding.

"No, no," she sobbed as she attempted to replace the pages. Did everything she touched fall to pieces?

Paul's epistle to the Galatians had been torn completely loose at the third chapter. As she pressed it back in place, her eye was drawn to the words directly above her fingers.

There is neither bond nor free, there is neither male nor female, for ye are all one in Christ Jesus.

The words knifed deep into her heart. Bond. Slave. She had seen Anabelle as lesser, but the apostle Paul clearly stated that they were equals. That was what Mother had meant. That was why she had insisted on raising them side by side, why she made Father promise to do so. In spite of the terrible betrayal she must have felt, in the depth of despair she extended grace.

Elizabeth sobbed, ashamed.

Forgive me, Lord. Forgive me.

She pressed her forehead to the mattress and wept.

This time the tears cleansed, and by the time dawn graced the horizon with its glorious oranges and pinks, she knew what she must do.

∽✣∾

Rourke dropped a blanket and cutlass into the ship's boat. The weapon was for Tom. Rourke would go unarmed.

John gripped his shoulder. "I go."

"I know you want to do this, old friend, but a white man stands a better chance bringing your wife through town."

Rourke's argument had a sliver of truth at the core, but his real reason centered on something far less noble than ensuring Anabelle's safety. He must settle things with Elizabeth. Since their last meeting, he had gone over her plea hundreds of times. She had come to him from desperation, and he had turned her away with a shallow promise and a cry for duty. He wasn't fool enough to think she would be able to outwit her father for an entire year. Charles Benjamin would use every manipulation available to bend her to his will.

Tonight Rourke must face the man, armed only with the truth and reliance on God.

He clapped John on the shoulder. "You are in command. Once Anabelle is aboard, leave."

"I wait for my captain."

"No. Leave at once. Set sail for Andros Island. Get your wife to freedom first before going home to Briland."

"No, sir. Dis not good."

"It is good, and it's right." Rourke pulled a paper from his coat. "If I do not return, this gives you ownership of the *Windsprite*." As much as it hurt to give up the sloop that had seen him through good times and bad, he would not see it fall into Benjamin's hands. "The wording might be simple, but any court should accept it."

John looked with wonder at the paper. "Why you do dis?"

"Because you're my friend."

For a second, John's shoulders trembled before he cleared his throat and lifted his head. "No one ever do such thing fo' ole John."

Rourke cleared his throat to cover the welling emotions. "It's about time, then." Before he lost control, he swung his legs over the bulwark and descended the ladder to the ship's boat.

From below, his sloop loomed tall, her sleek hull faster than any other wrecker out of Key West. He ran his hand along the smooth Madeira planking. He had grown up on the *Windsprite*. His father had bought her as a derelict and rebuilt her from the keel up. Every plank had been crafted with love. Until now, giving her away would have felt like betraying his pa, but at that moment he knew that his father would approve. Pa, who had rescued John from a cruel master, was doubtless smiling down on him today.

Rourke gazed into the endless blue sky. If tonight went wrong, this might be his last glimpse of the sun.

⌒⟊⟊⌒

Father leaned back in his desk chair, apparently no longer concerned that Elizabeth had interrupted his reading. A smile slowly curved his lips. "I'm glad you came to your senses."

Elizabeth clung to the back of the nearest throne chair for support. This had taken every ounce of courage she could muster. "After a great deal of prayer."

"Whatever brought you to this conclusion, I am glad for it." He approached her, arms outstretched.

Elizabeth saw Anabelle in her father's every feature. Why hadn't she noticed before? Because she hadn't wanted to see the truth. She hadn't wanted to believe her father capable of such a thing. She could not believe he had loved Mammy, yet the alternative was far more horrific.

Neither his embrace nor his words comforted her. "You will be a happy woman."

"If happiness is measured by pleasing others."

"I am pleased." He patted her back and returned to the desk. Pulling open the top drawer, he withdrew a small object. "I had intended to give you this after the announcement of your engagement, but I believe now is an appropriate time."

"B-but—" Elizabeth sputtered. She had not yet stated her terms, and he had already leapt to the conclusion he desired.

He didn't seem to notice her consternation, instead extending his hand with a smile. "Here, my dear. A token of my delight."

Since she did not move to take his offering, he opened his hand to reveal the brooch that she had found aboard the *Victory*.

"But that belongs to Mr. Buetsch." She stared at him. "I asked you to return it."

"Mr. Buetsch no longer owns it. When I saw that it bore your mother's first initial, I asked if he would sell it to me. He assured me he had no sentimental attachment to it. He bought it from a Saint Augustine curio shop. He gave me a good price, and I purchased it." He pressed the brooch into her hand. "Take it in memory of your mother. She would be very proud of you."

Elizabeth felt faint. Everything Father said and did turned the screws that much tighter. She would never escape the cage, just like her mother. Her only consolation was that she could help her sister, if she could summon the courage. *Lord, give me strength.*

She took a breath and straightened her back. Courage didn't flood in, but the posture did create the impression of confidence. "I do have one condition. I cannot accept Mr. Finch without it."

His expression darkened. "What is that?"

Her confidence faltered. She looked toward the fireplace and the portrait of her mother. "I'm certain my mother would approve."

"Go on."

She took another deep breath and plunged in. "Give me Anabelle."

He flinched ever so slightly, but she saw it.

Seizing the opportunity, she pressed harder. "Mother was the one who insisted I take Anabelle with me to Charleston. She has been my maid for my entire life. I trust you wouldn't send me away without that small comfort."

His hesitation was small but noticeable. "Why insist upon that? It's trivial. I will give her to you as a wedding gift."

"I need that assurance now."

"Need?" He stalked to the desk and pivoted to glare at her. The tactic might work in a courtroom, but Elizabeth was no defendant or witness. "Isn't my word sufficient?"

"Your word is your honor, Papa. That's why I'm asking for your word. I wish to bring Anabelle to the ball with me." She held her breath. This was the test. If he truly loved her, he would agree.

"Is that all?" His expression eased. "Bring Anabelle if you

must." He smiled. "I know that your word is your honor also. We shall announce your engagement tonight."

She had done the right thing. That ought to make her feel better. Instead her insides churned even worse. What had Rourke said, that love did what was right even when it hurt? He didn't say the pain would keep increasing.

She stumbled from the study, the brooch clasped tightly in her hand.

"Why did you do it?" Charlie had somehow managed to move his wheelchair to the door of his room.

"You were listening."

"It's impossible not to hear." His face contorted, cheeks blotched with red. "How could you? How could you betray him?"

She took a shuddering breath. "You don't understand."

"Don't treat me like a child. I understand perfectly, but I don't believe it." He slammed a fist against the arm of his wheelchair. "I never thought my sister would sell her soul to a cheat and a charlatan."

20

Charlie's words stung. The cheat and charlatan was not their father. No, Charlie meant Mr. Finch. Elizabeth agonized through late afternoon, but she could think of no other way to help Anabelle. Rourke said love required sacrifice. She wished the cost was not so high. The thought of marrying Mr. Finch made her ill.

Finally, with the approaching darkness came an idea. She would seek help from the only person who agreed with her estimation of Finch.

She knocked on Charlie's door. "May I enter?"

"I don't have anything to say to you."

Elizabeth glanced at the study door. It was open, and Father was not inside. "I need your help."

"Why?"

She didn't trust that Father wasn't pacing nearby. "May I come in to explain?"

She took his grunt as assent and stepped in, taking care to close the door behind her.

Charlie sat at his desk, curls tousled and lips turned down. "I didn't give you permission."

She hurried to his side. "I can't speak above a whisper in case Father is listening."

That piqued his interest. He set down his pen and straightened his spine. "Father left the house half an hour ago. I suspect he went to inform Mr. Finch that he is engaged."

Elizabeth pressed a hand to her midsection. "That's why I need your advice. How can I be rid of him?"

Charlie's brow ticked upward. "Isn't it a little late for that?"

She couldn't explain why she'd taken such a drastic step. If Charlie didn't know that Anabelle was their half sibling, she couldn't add that distress to his already shattered life.

She drew in a deep breath. "I don't intend to go through with the engagement, but I must make Father believe I will until tonight."

"I knew it! I knew you couldn't abandon Rourke."

"I won't. I can't." She sank onto the chair beside his desk. "But how do I rid myself of Mr. Finch before it is too late?"

"Refuse him."

"I have refused him three times already. He will not listen. Father will not listen. I can't understand why they are so determined."

"Your inheritance."

Elizabeth stared. "You know about that?"

"I've known for years. Mother told me. Grandmama refused to settle it upon her and insisted it go to you instead."

"If I marry the right man," Elizabeth said dully. "But I don't understand. I thought Grandmama approved of Father. Mother said—" Too late she realized she'd betrayed knowledge that Charlie could not know since he hadn't seen the diary. "Mother always led me to believe that Grandmama and Grandpapa were pleased she married Father."

Charlie shrugged, apparently not noticing her slip of the tongue. "The point is that Mr. Finch is desperate to get his hands on your inheritance. Have you told Father this?"

"Not in so many words. I don't think it would matter. Father is set on this match." She couldn't divulge that he expected her to rescue the family, since that largely meant helping Charlie. Her brother would never approve.

"That's odd," Charlie mused. "Usually Father sniffs out a man's motives from the first conversation, yet he can't see a thing wrong with Finch."

Elizabeth's pulse quickened. "You're right. He appears to have a blind spot concerning Mr. Finch."

"The question is why."

"I don't know."

"Mr. Finch might be blackmailing him."

Elizabeth couldn't believe her brother would think such a thing, least of all say it.

"The question is over what," Charlie said.

Her thoughts drifted to the conversation she had overheard in the dining room. "Aunt Virginia told Father that someone stole a document from her trunks."

"That must be it. I wonder what it was."

"I don't know. She was very upset, though, and blamed Anabelle." She puzzled through the events that had bewildered her at the time. "She said Mr. Poppinclerk locked her trunks the moment we arrived on the *Windsprite*, so the paper must have been taken from here."

"Finch."

Elizabeth shook her head. "I've considered that, but he was

always surrounded by our family when he visited. When could he have slipped upstairs to search her trunks?"

"Maybe it was Mr. Poppinclerk, then."

"What did he stand to gain?"

"We can't know until we learn what was in the document," Charlie wisely pointed out.

Elizabeth sighed with frustration. "None of this helps me figure out a way to get rid of Mr. Finch."

"It would if we knew he had stolen the document, especially if it had anything to do with your inheritance."

"I don't think so." Elizabeth thought back. "Father told me about the inheritance the night I arrived. Mr. Finch wouldn't have had any opportunity to take the papers before then. Oh, this is all so confusing."

Charlie grinned. "It's like chess. To beat your opponent, you need to consider all the possible moves and what will happen for each one much farther into the game. We're considering all the possibilities."

"But none of them tell me what to do."

"To best a man, you need to know his tendencies and his desires. What are Finch's tendencies? Where does he spend his time and with whom?"

Elizabeth stared. "How do you come up with this?"

Charlie grinned. "You probably don't know where he goes and whom he counts as a friend."

She shook her head.

"Neither do I, so let's concentrate on his desires. What does he want?"

"Money. Status. To marry me."

"All of which come back to money. Now, let's consider how we can use that against him."

The answer was so obvious that Elizabeth couldn't believe she hadn't thought of it sooner. "Take away the reward, and he will lose interest." She sprang to her feet and wrapped her arms around her brother. "Oh, thank you, Charlie."

He squirmed out of her embrace, but his high color told her he was secretly pleased.

Now all that remained was to convince Aunt Virginia.

Before dressing for the ball, Elizabeth approached her great-aunt. After frank discussion and a great deal of persuasion, Aunt Virginia agreed to her plan, though she would not sign over the inheritance until they learned how Mr. Finch reacted. Since Aunt now had business to address, she claimed a headache too severe to attend the evening's festivities.

By the time the carriage arrived in front of the house, all had been set in place. Though the night was fair and overly warm, even with the persistent southeast breeze, Elizabeth donned her black silk mantle. The blue-gray ball gown would be too visible in the light of the full moon.

Father frowned when she walked into the foyer. "A wrap in this heat?"

"I wanted to wear something black out of respect for Mother."

"Humph. At least you're no longer using that as an excuse not to marry."

He assisted her into the carriage but was less enthusiastic when she insisted Anabelle ride beside her rather than on the driver's seat with Nathan. Anabelle's presence forced Mr. Finch to sit across from Elizabeth, where she must endure his smug satisfaction but was free from his groping hands.

He also could not refrain from commenting on her mantle.

"Do you expect a sudden chill? Surely the night air is not too cool."

"One can never be too prepared. The winds might change."

"Then allow me to carry it for you. I would not want you to feel the slightest discomfort."

Elizabeth offered her thanks but demurred. She wanted every possible layer between them.

Anabelle kept her gaze averted, but Elizabeth couldn't help wondering if the two men facing her saw the resemblance between them. If so, they said nothing. She breathed deeply. This course she had set in motion was the right one. Now all she needed was a moment alone with Mr. Finch.

The carriage slowed.

Father tapped his walking stick on the roof. "What's the delay?"

Nathan leaned over and yelled down, "Line of carriages, sir."

Father frowned. "I had hoped to make the announcement at once, before the orchestra strikes up and the dancing begins."

"There will be time enough." Elizabeth clutched her bag, feeling both Mother's miniature and the gold brooch beneath the beaded silk. If all worked and she was able to leave with Rourke, that brooch could bring a handsome price to help them start wedded life. "Perhaps Mr. Finch might regale us with stories of growing up on a plantation. Cotton, was it?"

"Tobacco."

"Ah, tobacco. Then you must partake of it?"

"Snuff, on occasion."

That explained the foul odor when he had attempted to kiss her. Though her stomach churned, she must play the part of the eager fiancée. "Did your father always raise tobacco?"

Mr. Finch gave her a searching look. "Why all the questions?"

"Isn't it common practice for a couple planning marriage to converse about their lives?" She had certainly talked to Rourke over the years. She knew he had three brothers and four sisters, all younger, and that his father had fished like his father before him. His mother not only kept the house but taught Bible stories to wee ones at their church. The stories of Rourke and his brothers taking the boat out at night to fish for sharks had thrilled her. His tales of diving wrecks terrified her. Within the past year his father had died. They shared similar loss.

Mr. Finch, however, had never mentioned his mother. She knew only that his father was a planter. Even now, he looked out the window rather than answer directly. "This is hardly the place, Elizabeth."

"Agreed." Father tapped his stick on the roof again. "I'm getting out. Maybe I can get those carriages ahead of us to move aside."

Nathan hopped down from the driver's seat and opened the door seconds before Father burst through it. Father was not a patient man, particularly when it came to small talk.

Elizabeth watched the door close, hardly able to believe her good fortune. The moment she needed had been handed to her by Father's impatience. Now she must broach the matter in a way that seemed natural.

When Mr. Finch's gaze returned to her, she offered a smile. "I'm glad for this moment alone."

He glanced at Anabelle. "We are hardly alone."

"My maid will always be with me. Did I tell you that Father has given me Anabelle as an engagement gift?" Out of the corner of her eye, Elizabeth saw Anabelle's fingers twitch. "Isn't that wonderful?"

Mr. Finch did not look pleased. "I'm only a legal clerk. My salary isn't sufficient to support a houseful of servants."

Elizabeth pouted. "But I can't do housework, and Anabelle is a lady's maid. We must hire a staff as soon as we marry. Or perhaps your father might send us some of his servants from the plantation."

He blanched, just as she suspected he would, and avoided eye contact. Mr. Finch was hiding something, and she intended to find out what it was.

She batted her eyes, playing the part of the most spoiled belle she could imagine. "Surely on such a large plantation he can spare one or two slaves."

He looked out the window. "Why aren't we moving yet?"

Since he looked ready to bolt after Father, she threw out another bone. "Father hinted to me that he might make you a partner."

Mr. Finch's head snapped back. "He did?" His lips curled into an insufferably smug smile.

Though it galled her to play the role, this was her moment of opportunity. "Yes, indeed." She threw a twittering giggle in for good measure. "How fortunate since Mother's family has given the inheritance I was to receive to another member of the family."

All color drained from his face. "Surely you are mistaken. Your father indicated that they approved me—that is, your decision to accept my proposal."

Aha! So Mr. Finch knew of the inheritance all along, just as Charlie suspected.

She inched that smile a little higher, playing the role of the addle-brained fiancée. "At first they did, but my great-aunt informed me tonight of their change of heart."

His gaze narrowed. "Impossible."

"You may ask her yourself."

"Where is she?" He scowled at Anabelle. "I expected her to join us."

"A headache."

He smirked. "How convenient. I couldn't help but notice you waited until your father left to tell me this. Could it be, dear Elizabeth, that your ardor is not as great as you would have me believe?"

Elizabeth hoped her momentary panic didn't show. Charlie and Aunt Virginia had given her enough to work with. She must put it together in a way that convinced Mr. Finch he stood to gain nothing through this alliance.

"How can you question my affection now," she whined, "after I agreed to marry you? I'm simply expressing my appreciation for the depth of your love. Many men would walk away from a woman with no dowry or prospects."

His eyes darted this way and that, attempting to verify the truth of her statements. "Your father is well-off."

"Alas, he is not." She dabbed at her eyes. "All his savings are gone, spent on my brother's care. Poor Charlie! We will, of course, take him in. He will need a woman's care, and Father is too busy at the office to spend time with him."

"Your brother is nearly grown." Mr. Finch stopped trying to hide his exasperation.

"He is crippled."

"But not our responsibility." He was beginning to look panicked.

"But he is. He would not be crippled if I hadn't insisted we walk to the harbor that day. I will carry that responsibility the rest of my life."

The inner battle played out on his face. "That is why the inheritance would help—to care for your brother. Surely your mother's family understands that. It's all the more reason to settle the money on you."

They understood Charlie's needs completely, though not in the way Mr. Finch anticipated.

Elizabeth took a deep breath. Sometimes a chess move had an uncertain outcome. Her information was sketchy, based only on what she and Charlie had surmised and Aunt had confirmed. Lacking proof of Finch's involvement meant she must send forward her rook with no backing.

She forced a smile, as if apologizing for what she must tell him. "Apparently there was some silly little matter pertaining to a document that went missing. Let me see . . . Aunt told me, but I have no mind for business. It had to do with shipping." She scrunched her brow as if struggling to remember. "Ah! A bill of sale, I believe she said. For Father. He owned a share of the *Victory*, you see."

Elizabeth didn't mention the ethical conflict of interest. Father, who always adhered to a strict code of ethics, should not have represented the owners in admiralty court once charges of collusion had been leveled at Rourke. In the past, he had railed against any attorney who didn't withdraw from a case when he had a vested interest, yet he had done just that. As angry as that made her, she must concentrate on the task at hand.

Without breaking her smile, she added, "Apparently Aunt brought the document with her from Charleston, but it disappeared from her possession."

The smirk never left his face. "It probably fell overboard when the ship wrecked."

"Oh no." This was where her information got sketchy. "You

see, her trunk was latched, and the document was secured inside a pouch. When she examined the pouch later, the other papers were inside but not that one."

"Then she misplaced it."

Elizabeth shook her head and leveled the part that was pure conjecture. "That does not explain how it ended up in your room at the boardinghouse."

They must have guessed right, for Mr. Finch turned gray as weathered cypress. "How? What? You looked through my belongings?"

"Now, now. All is well. Aunt Virginia and I plan to give it to Father after the ball."

Finch swallowed, his eyes darting from one side to the other. "Why won't this carriage move?" He reached for the door handle.

"But Percy, surely you don't want to leave me." She clung to his arm like a lovelorn girl. "What is a little matter like a lost inheritance compared to love?"

He tossed her aside. "Vixen." He shoved open the door and jumped out. Turning back for a moment, he snarled, "Congratulations. You got what you want. May you suffer for it." Then he slammed the door shut.

Through the carriage window Elizabeth watched him sprint away. To her puzzlement, Mr. Finch did not head for his boardinghouse but for the harbor.

"Good riddance," Anabelle said as the carriage jolted forward.

Elizabeth pressed the side of her face against the curtained interior, exhausted. "I hope you're right. He could still cause trouble."

The most dangerous part was yet to come.

❦

Father was not pleased to discover Mr. Finch gone.

"He ran off all of a sudden," Elizabeth said, "as if he had forgotten something."

Though Anabelle nodded, she could tell that her father did not quite believe her explanation.

He checked his pocket watch. "I hope he doesn't take long. Nearly everyone is here. The band is tuning. Soon the dancing will begin, and we would then have to wait for supper to make the announcement."

Thankfully Father did not consider making an engagement announcement without the prospective groom in attendance, perhaps because no one in town had any inkling they were courting. Oh, they must have known he had called at the house. The neighbors would have spread that all over town. However, courting was another matter, especially since she was still in mourning.

Elizabeth placed a gloved hand on her father's arm. "Then you will be able to dance with me, Papa."

At the endearment, his worried expression eased, at least for a moment. "I would like that, sunshine."

She beamed up at him, content to limit this ball to the two of them—at least until she slipped away to join Anabelle. With Mr. Finch gone, she had only Captain Poppinclerk to avoid. The tension between him and Rourke had been evident on the *Windsprite*. She didn't trust any man that Rourke disliked.

"Shall we join the guests?" Father motioned toward the entrance, where seemingly the whole of Key West society had gathered.

First Elizabeth unhooked the mantle.

Anabelle finished removing the garment. "If that's all, miss."

Elizabeth nodded, and Anabelle drifted away to join the other servants.

"How lovely you are, my dear." Father's eyes misted as he looked at her.

Her heart ached to know if he did indeed love her despite his sins and hers. Financial desperation and love for her brother had driven him to ask her for a tremendous sacrifice. He must have lost a great deal in the sinking of the *Victory*. On the other hand, he had dealt cruelly with Mammy and broke Mother's heart. He risked censure to vilify Rourke in court. He would not even consider her feelings for Rourke.

The hall soon filled to overflowing. She and Father hadn't gotten far inside the door when Justice Marvin drew him into a conversation about some matter of admiralty law. Elizabeth attempted to listen for a while before drifting farther into the room. Ladies stood in groups conversing or seeking a particular gentleman. Elizabeth looked for Caroline but couldn't spot her petite friend among all the guests.

The musicians, situated at the far end, struck up a lively tune, and couples moved into position for an old-fashioned cotillion. That opened up the edges of the room so she could spot Caroline, who was standing with her mother and several women from the church. So much had happened since Elizabeth had last seen her friend, and even more would take place tonight. Though she didn't dare tell Caroline that she would be leaving for Harbour Island, she could at least share a few moments with her.

A gentleman began calling the dance figures. As the dancers glided and swirled, Elizabeth wove through the guests to reach her friend, who was dressed in a rather plain ochre-colored cotton gown that did nothing for her complexion.

"You look beautiful," Caroline said, "as always. Your aunt chose the perfect color to highlight your eyes."

Would Rourke say the same? Would he remember that this was the exact color of the dress she'd worn on that fateful day four years ago? Would her appearance dazzle him so much that he would forget his misgivings and whisk her away? She hoped so.

"Too bad a certain someone has left port," Caroline whispered behind her fan.

Elizabeth blushed and had to hide behind her own fan. "It's already quite hot in here."

"Indeed."

She conversed with her friend through cotillions and waltzes, brushing aside all requests to dance. Father's discussion with the judge had grown to a small circle of attorneys. To her relief, Mr. Finch did not reappear. Based on the way he'd run from the carriage, she must have guessed correctly that the missing bill of sale was in his room. If he went there and found it, he might return to the dance. She had originally planned to slip away during the break between dancing and supper when the large number of guests milling about would disguise her absence, but that might be too late. She turned to Caroline to excuse herself and was interrupted by an obnoxious woman who had paid a condolence call when Elizabeth had first arrived. The woman's name eluded her.

"Miss Elizabeth Benjamin. I see you are out of mourning already," the woman sniffed.

Elizabeth offered a smile, though she was anxious to leave. "Only for tonight. My aunt insisted this gray would be appropriate."

The woman lifted her glass and peered at Elizabeth's dress. "Gray? Looks more like blue in this light."

"Perhaps so." Elizabeth curtseyed. "Please excuse me."

She slipped away as the dancers left the floor. Groups congregated in front of her no matter which direction she attempted. Frustrated, she backtracked and found her path blocked by Captain Poppinclerk, dressed in a green frock coat, striped waistcoat, and silk cravat.

"Please excuse me." She stepped to the side.

He followed. "I believe you owe me a dance, Miss Benjamin. The orchestra is striking up a waltz. Shall we?"

"I fear I must decline."

"Now, now, Miss Benjamin, the floor is clearing just for us." He swiped a hand toward the center of the room and a familiar figure.

Elizabeth gasped.

Mr. Finch had returned.

❧

No one waited at the cemetery. Rourke had walked the perimeter three times, leaving no shadow unchecked. Only the rustling of the leaves and rush of the wind disturbed the silence. He stood in the shadow of a gumbo-limbo tree and drummed his fingers on its peeling bark. The constellation Pegasus pranced high in the sky. Soon the full moon would rise high enough to illuminate the entire graveyard.

Tom and Anabelle should have been here by now. Their absence meant something had gone wrong. Rourke itched to act. This infernal waiting was driving him mad, but if he left and they were simply delayed, he might miss them entirely. On the other hand, they might be caught and need assistance. If so, where would they be? He had no idea if Anabelle had convinced Elizabeth to take her to the ball or if she was trapped at the house. To find her, he would have to comb the town, where hundreds of people could recognize him.

Rourke slapped a hand against the tree trunk in frustration. The cemetery was a safe meeting place. No one came here at night. If Tom could get to Anabelle, he would bring her here. Rourke had to be patient. He had to trust that others would do their jobs. That was the tough part. It had always been difficult. Even today, leaving the *Windsprite* in John's hands had gutted him. His mate had earned his trust over the years, but Rourke still struggled to let go.

Lord, help me to trust.

In the eerie quiet of the graveyard, he thought he heard a whisper. *I am.*

Rourke shook his head. It must have been the wind. God might have spoken to Moses, but not to a Bahamian wrecker. Yet as he pondered the whisper, his restlessness eased. God was, is, and always would be. He knew all of time and every thought in a man's heart. Somehow, no matter what happened tonight, God would be with him.

The wind still rustled through the trees. No one else walked the graveyard. Nothing appeared to have changed, yet everything had. Clarity and strength came from God, not from a man's struggle.

He closed his eyes and imagined Elizabeth sweeping across the dance floor, her honeyed hair afire in the lamplight. She turned to him, her eyes begging for the life he longed to share. But he stood outside, dressed in sailors' garb, unfit to step into the ballroom. Her father swept her away, cradling her like a tender bloom too easily torn by the winds of life. For all her talk, Elizabeth Benjamin had not been raised for the harsh realities faced by a sailor's wife. Cooking, cleaning, and hunger were strangers to her. She might know death but not fortitude. It was wrong of him to encourage her hopes, especially when it could cost two precious lives their freedom.

A croak sounded.

He should have discouraged her from the start by revealing the stark truth. Life as his wife would be little better than that of her father's servants. They would know freedom but not security. She deserved better.

Again the croak. Closer this time. An egret.

Tom! He must have Anabelle.

Rourke's pulse pounded. This was the dangerous part. If anyone had recognized them walking through town, they were all at risk for aiding a fugitive. Curfew had long passed. No excuses could be made. Benjamin would leap at the chance to press charges. Rourke must wait until he was absolutely certain no one had followed Tom and Anabelle.

Keeping to the shadows, he scanned the cemetery. At first he saw nothing. Then a mangrove branch bobbed thirty paces to the east. That must be a signal. Tom would know not to step into the open.

Rourke waited for a cloud to cross in front of the moon and then slipped back to the thicket of swamp cabbage and mangrove that edged the cemetery. Grasping a branch, he shook it in exactly the same manner, followed by an egret call.

Soon the lithe figure of his newest crew member darted out of the mangroves and skirted the edge of the cemetery. Anabelle did not follow.

21

I must use the necessary," Elizabeth blurted out, no longer concerned for propriety.

Mr. Finch was headed directly toward her. She could delay no longer. Gathering her skirts, she ran through the crowd, weaving around startled guests. The stays made it difficult to draw a breath, but panic drove her on. She escaped through the rear door, emerging into the gathering of carriage drivers, footmen, and maids. Their singing and laughter halted the moment she appeared.

"Miss." A tall black footman stood to let her pass.

"Anabelle," she whispered. Between the moonlight and a few lanterns, she ought to be able to spot her, but could not. "My maid."

"Sorry, miss." The footman stepped back.

The servants parted like the Red Sea, assuming she needed to relieve herself as she had told Mr. Poppinclerk. Oh dear, what if he followed? She glanced back. No one at the door yet, but either he or Mr. Finch could appear at any moment.

She must proceed to the necessary.

The footman extended a hand to assist her down the steps.

"Thank you," she said before making her way across the yard. Coarse sand found its way into her slippers, but she didn't dare stop to remove it. Only when she reached the shadow of the outbuilding did she hazard a glance back. The servants had gathered into groups again, though they spoke quietly.

She must find Anabelle. Had she gone on without her? Elizabeth could cross the island on her own, but Anabelle had her mantle. Without the dark covering, she would stand out in the moonlight.

She tested the door in case anyone was watching. It was bolted. In use. She shrank away.

"Sister." The whisper came from the shadows behind the outbuilding.

Elizabeth's pulse raced. Anabelle had waited. When a cloud blotted out the moonlight, she slipped into the shadows between buildings. A strong hand grabbed her wrist and pulled her toward the back fence.

"Ana—"

Her maid touched a finger to her lips.

Silence. Of course.

Anabelle helped Elizabeth into the mantle. If anyone stopped them on the streets, Elizabeth would tell them they were visiting a sick friend. Likely no one would notice a Negro maid in the presence of her mistress.

"Finch returned," Elizabeth whispered once they had left the area.

That news worried Anabelle, judging by her expression, though she only stated their destination. "My friend lives on Thomas."

Africa Town. It made perfect sense to meet there since Anabelle would blend in, but the thought of entering that part of town at night made Elizabeth nervous.

Elizabeth grasped her arm. "I suggested the chapel on Eaton."

Anabelle shook her head and repeated that her friend lived on Thomas. "They expect us there."

That made no sense unless Anabelle had somehow made other arrangements. Elizabeth wavered. What if she was walking into a trap?

"Hurry," Anabelle whispered, pointing to the hall. "Soon they come."

Finch would follow. Elizabeth's heart pounded. She no longer held control but must place her trust in her half sister. *Lord, protect me.*

She gathered her nerve and followed Anabelle. They moved quickly through the streets, turning right after a block. Then down an alley. Then left onto a path. Within minutes, Elizabeth was dizzy from the exertion.

"Stop," Elizabeth gasped. "I can't breathe."

Anabelle glared but paused in the shadow of a darkened building.

"Why this route?" Elizabeth managed once she'd calmed the dizziness. She couldn't even see Anabelle in the inky shadow.

"Hush," Anabelle hissed, pulling her into the blackness. Her breath tickled Elizabeth's ear. "We're being followed."

Hope succumbed to fear. "Finch."

"Don't look. They will know we suspect."

"They?"

"I thought I saw two men."

Mr. Finch and Mr. Poppinclerk. It had to be. Or Father and Mr. Finch. Or the town marshal and a deputy. Her head spun.

"We must elude them," Anabelle whispered.

281

"How?"

"Follow me." She headed down a dark alley between two houses.

Elizabeth had no choice but to follow. Her sister was fleeter afoot, though, and unencumbered by the weight of crinoline, bustle, petticoats, and corset.

Anabelle darted between buildings as if she hadn't been gone four years. She seemed to know every path and shortcut on the island. Around prickly bougainvillea. Under gumbo-limbo trees. Past jasmine with its overpowering perfume. Between buildings so close together that the women had to gather their skirts to squeeze through. Still Anabelle raced on.

Elizabeth gasped for breath as she tried to keep up. The back of her gown was drenched beneath the mantle. Her heart pounded. Stones bruised her slippered feet. She stumbled behind a grogshop roaring with laughter and scrambled to her feet before anyone noticed her.

Something darted in front of her. She shrieked, sending Anabelle into the blackness to their left. Having lost track of her sister, Elizabeth stumbled ahead, searching the shadows. She wasn't familiar with this part of town. Her forays since returning had kept her close to home.

A light blinked high overhead. The lighthouse. Anabelle must have led her in that direction, but Elizabeth still wasn't certain where she was. The moonlight revealed shacks and what appeared to be rubble or rocks. The lighthouse's beam cast an eerie brightness on tangled mangroves. For the first time tonight, Elizabeth was truly afraid. Paralyzed, she waited.

Nothing moved.

No sound.

"Anabelle," Elizabeth whispered.

She had no idea where they were.

A hand grabbed her arm.

Elizabeth yelped.

Another hand pressed to her mouth.

"Hush!" Anabelle hissed. "They are almost upon us."

⌘

Rourke met Tom halfway. "Where is she?"

Tom gulped for breath. "Poppinclerk has them in his sights."

"Them?"

"Anabelle and Miss Benjamin."

Rourke groaned. "Why is Elizabeth involved? That only complicates matters."

Tom hesitated. "She gave me a letter for you, but I didn't have a chance to deliver it since Poppinclerk watched me day and night." He cleared his throat. "I shouldn't have read it since it was addressed to you, but I was worried it had to do with our plans, that Anabelle was sending word through Miss Benjamin."

Rourke bit back a twinge of irritation that Tom might have read something deeply personal. "Understandable."

"She loves you, you know."

He couldn't think about that. "What did it say?"

"That she wanted to join you tonight. She planned to leave the ball and wanted you to meet her at the little chapel on Eaton Street."

"With Anabelle?"

"She didn't mention Anabelle," Tom said. "That's what worried me. I don't think she knows what we planned for tonight."

"But you said they're together and that Poppinclerk is following them. What are you doing here? Poppinclerk will have seized them by now."

283

Tom shook his head. "I don't think he wants to catch them. Even though Anabelle and Miss Benjamin zigzagged all over the island, he could've stopped them a couple times. Then Finch joined him. If you ask me, they want to see where the ladies are headed."

Rourke was getting a very bad feeling. "They're looking for me." He didn't care to spell out what that meant. A sharp lad like Tom had probably figured it out already. That was why he came here.

"Aiding a fugitive," Tom said. "You would lose the *Windsprite*."

Not any longer. The sloop belonged to John now. Rourke wouldn't lose the ship, but he would lose far worse, for Charles Benjamin would tighten the noose until he strangled any hope of gaining Elizabeth's hand.

"Forget that." Rourke slipped into command. "We have two women to rescue. Where did you leave them?"

"I lost them when they ducked into a dark lane near the lighthouse. Only a few blocks from here. Their pursuers walked right past. When the men turned around, grumbling that they'd lost them, I figured I could fetch the ladies, but they weren't there."

"That means they're between here and there."

"My thought exactly. That's why I headed this way, but I didn't see them."

"Where did they go?" Rourke growled. "We can't help them if we don't know where they are."

"Anabelle doubled back a few times," Tom offered. "Maybe she did that again."

"That means they could be anywhere. I can't sit here when they might be in danger." Rourke knew that setting foot in town increased his chance of being discovered, but Tom's arrival had already jeopardized that. Nevertheless, Tom still stood the better chance of getting Anabelle to the boat. "Take my cutlass." He handed over the weapon. "If we are discovered, the men will follow me. Lead the women in a different direction. Now, let's head toward the lighthouse. While we're still in the graveyard, tell me everything that happened tonight."

They set off at a brisk pace.

Tom kept his voice low. "I was watching for Anabelle like we'd planned. She arrived with Miss Benjamin in the carriage."

"What did you say?" Rourke stopped him. "Anabelle was *inside* the carriage?"

"Ye-es. Is that unusual?"

"Very unusual. Charles Benjamin never allows servants to ride with the family. Who else was in the carriage?"

"Mr. Benjamin, but he got out while they were waiting in line outside the hall. Then a little later Mr. Finch left in a hurry."

"So Finch was with them." That didn't surprise him. Benjamin had been promoting Finch to Elizabeth since her arrival, but a hasty departure meant something had gone wrong with that plan. "How did he look when he left the carriage? Pleased or worried?"

"Worried. He headed straight for the harbor."

"The harbor?" Rourke started walking again. He could think better when afoot. "Why on earth would he go there?"

"I don't know, but about an hour later he came back to the hall and went inside."

"Hmm." Finch's actions suggested he went to meet someone. Since Tom said he later joined Poppinclerk, Rourke suspected that was who he'd met at the harbor. "Still no Anabelle?"

Tom shook his head. "She stayed in the backyard with the other servants until Miss Benjamin joined her. Then they left together."

That sounded as if the two women had planned all along to travel together. Something had happened to drive them into the surprising alliance, something that had also prompted Finch and Poppinclerk to ally. "Charles Benjamin?"

"Never left the hall."

They had reached the edge of the cemetery. Rourke motioned for quiet, but his mind still raced. If Benjamin hadn't followed his daughter or Mr. Finch, he'd either left the work to others or knew nothing of what was happening tonight. Rourke couldn't believe the latter. That meant Charles Benjamin was keeping his hands clean until the very last moment, when success was assured.

He and Tom hurried down the empty, sparsely settled streets. Before long, homes would press into this area. Already several had been built on the quieter southern side of the island, but the dense hammocks and mangrove thickets still hung on here and there. The number of buildings increased as they neared the lighthouse.

Suddenly Tom stopped and whipped around, knocking Rourke off balance. While Tom took off at a run, Rourke tumbled back into a pitch-black gap between two shacks. He stepped on uneven ground and fell. The back of his head struck the building.

"Rourke," a sweet feminine voice gasped.

He must be dreaming. Tom couldn't have pushed him into the exact hiding spot of the two ladies.

"Rourke." Elizabeth urged him to turn from the beckoning dark waters.

He shook his head and clarity returned. One fact was clear. Tom had not only disappeared, but he'd taken the cutlass with him. It was now up to Rourke to save the ladies—without the benefit of a weapon.

Elizabeth dropped to her knees, finally able to breathe. "Rourke." She felt around in the dark until she found his slumped form.

"They're gone," Anabelle whispered.

Hiding in this cramped and filthy space hadn't eased her pounding heart, especially when Captain Poppinclerk and Mr. Finch showed up, prowling the street and poking into every building. Sooner or later, she and Anabelle would be discovered.

Then Rourke and Tom had arrived. Mr. Finch and Captain Poppinclerk slipped into the shadows at the very next building. Elizabeth wanted to warn Rourke, but Anabelle wouldn't let her.

All seemed lost, and then Tom shoved Rourke, sending him into the tiny space that she and Anabelle occupied. He hit the ground hard.

"Mr. Rourke is hurt," Anabelle whispered.

"I'm all right," he groaned, "just a little woozy."

"Let me get my handkerchief." Elizabeth rummaged in her bag, but the handkerchief had gotten tangled in the brooch. She pulled the whole lot out and unraveled the mess.

"I'm not bleeding," he insisted. "Give me a second to gather my wits."

Elizabeth wrapped her fingers around the brooch. They must run again. The distance to Rourke's boat was far. Too far. Anabelle was the stronger sister. She could make it. Moreover, Mr. Finch didn't care about a slave. He wanted Elizabeth. If he caught them, he would let Anabelle go. Her sister had a chance at happiness, though life would be a struggle in a new land.

Elizabeth handed the brooch to Anabelle. "Take this."

"No," her sister whispered.

She closed Anabelle's fingers around the brooch. "For your family. Have Rourke help you sell it once you get there."

Meanwhile, Rourke had risen to his feet. "We need to get out of here. The men will be back as soon as they realize Tom is leading them on a wild goose chase."

They stepped out of the cramped space, staying in the shadows.

Rourke looked at both of them, but his gaze lingered on her.

Elizabeth pressed together her dusty lips, ashamed that her first thought had been to wonder if he liked her dress. "Which way do we go?"

"Toward the cemetery." Rourke had not stopped gazing at her. Now he touched her shoulder with the gentleness of a man in love. "Are you able to run?"

Her feet were so bruised that every step hurt. The stays limited her breath. Mr. Finch and Mr. Poppinclerk could return at any moment. "Go. Get Anabelle to safety. I will keep up as best I can."

"I cannot leave you."

"You must." She swallowed her fear. If Mr. Finch found her, what would he do? Such thoughts would paralyze her if she let them. "Anabelle must get to the ship."

Rourke nodded. Taking Anabelle's hand, he headed up the street at full stride. Elizabeth hurried after them, but her clothing hindered every move. Petticoats tangled between her legs. Stones bit the arches of her feet. Perspiration rolled into her eyes, blurring her vision. She struggled for every breath. If only she could rid herself of these constraints, but all she could do was unhook the mantle. That gave minimal relief.

At the next corner, Rourke and Anabelle waited.

His eyes drifted to the lovely gown with the rosette at her

throat and a bodice that revealed her small waist. "You're beautiful."

How often she had longed to hear those words, but not now, not with so much at stake. Anabelle quivered with anxiety.

Elizabeth could not risk her sister's future. "Hurry."

Rourke extended a hand. "I will carry you."

"No. I will only slow you down. I see the cemetery ahead. I will follow."

Anabelle took off at a run. After a moment's hesitation, Rourke followed the woman who had been Elizabeth's friend and maid for so many years. He caught her within a few strides. Though Elizabeth ran until her throat ached, she could not catch them. By the end of the next block, she had fallen farther behind. The cemetery lay ahead. She knew the way to the ship from there, past the salt ponds and through the hammocks. But the route was long, and she was losing both ground and strength.

By the time she reached the cemetery, her limbs had turned to lead. Each step took enormous effort, like slogging through water. Her knees wobbled. Spots danced before her eyes. The years of idleness in Charleston had taken their toll. She could not go on.

Rourke waited beside a gumbo-limbo while Anabelle paced at the edge of the mangrove thickets.

"Hurry," Elizabeth gasped, unable to draw enough air to rejuvenate her limbs.

Rourke held out his hand. "I will not leave without you."

"You must." She turned at the sound of carriage wheels crunching over the gravel. "Father." Even in the moonlight, she recognized their carriage.

He took her by the shoulders. Desperation danced in his eyes. "I will carry you."

She wanted it. Oh, how she wanted it. To be with him always, to truly live. But if she agreed, then they would all fail. Rourke would be arrested, and Anabelle and her baby would be sold.

She pressed her fingers to his lips. "Love does right even when it hurts."

His hands shook. "I will never see you again."

She squeezed her eyes shut against that truth. Aiding a fugitive slave brought terrible penalties. If he managed to escape, he would not be able to return. To do so meant prison and destitution.

"I know." She drew a shaky breath and pushed him away. "Save my sister."

Instead of letting go, he stared into her eyes. "Your sister?"

The carriage was drawing near. She could see Mr. Finch at the reins.

"Go!" She wrenched from his arms.

He held on until her fingers slipped from his.

She could not watch him go. His ring burned against her throat, symbol of what might have been. Tears burned her lids as she stumbled toward Father's carriage. Romeo to her Juliet. Separated forever.

Father stepped from the carriage.

Elizabeth dropped to her knees. *Please help me, Lord.*

22

Rourke saw Elizabeth drop to her knees, and it took all his will not to run to her. He wanted to take her in his arms and shield her from the pain to come, but he could not. She had given her happiness for another. Her sister. His mind reeled. Anabelle was her sister. Though his blood raged against a man who would do such a thing, he could not let Elizabeth's sacrifice be in vain.

How he loved the woman she had become. The impulsive child had been tempered with a depth of character he had not imagined possible. This Elizabeth could endure trials. This Elizabeth had the grace and compassion to overcome. Yet he must leave her, almost certainly never to return.

"Father!" she cried, rising to her feet. "Papa. Papa." She ran to the man and threw her arms around his neck.

At the same moment, a thick cloud blotted out the moon. Rourke knew that was his chance, but he could not rip his gaze from the scene unfolding in front of him.

Anabelle tugged on his arm. "Go."

The short command broke the hold that Elizabeth had on

him. For her sake, he must leave. Tom had not returned. He was probably in Poppinclerk's clutches. Only Rourke knew where the ship's boat was hidden. Only he could get Anabelle to the *Windsprite*. Benjamin might still follow. They were not safe yet.

He grabbed Anabelle's hand and ran for the cover of the mangroves. She easily matched his stride. He led her down the narrow path toward the salt ponds. They had little time to outpace Finch and Benjamin.

He let go of Anabelle. "Run!"

The command wasn't necessary. Anabelle proved fleet of foot and silent as the night.

By the time they reached the salt ponds, his lungs burned.

Anabelle still ran. If she panted, he could not hear it over the pounding of his heart.

They had to run single file beside the ponds, where salt water was baked off in dry months until only glistening salt remained. During this rainy season, the holding ponds were wet. One wrong step and an ankle would turn or a leg break.

He followed her, amazed at her speed and fortitude. More than fear drove her on. Her husband awaited her aboard the *Windsprite*. Rourke hoped his mate had the sloop ready to sail.

Rourke dared a look back, and what he saw pushed him forward faster. Lights bobbed in the trees at the other end of the salt ponds. The men were following. If Rourke didn't get Anabelle away from the open ponds and into the trees, they would be discovered. Soon. The pursuers had almost reached the first of the hundred-foot-long containment ponds. Ahead of him stretched the last pond.

They wouldn't make it.

Rourke couldn't grab Anabelle or she'd trip and fall. He couldn't shout or the men would hear him. He searched for an avenue of escape and noticed that the overhanging branches on the far end of the ponds created just enough shadow to shield them until they reached the trail to the boat.

Summoning every ounce of strength, he powered ahead and steered Anabelle toward the trees. *One more minute, Lord.* That was all they needed to get to safety.

Voices shouted across the ponds. The men had arrived, and they'd seen them.

"Follow me," Rourke gasped. "A little farther."

The shadows loomed ahead, but their pursuers would see which direction he'd gone. There wasn't time to mislead or throw them off. He had to get Anabelle into the boat and pull away from shore. Only then would they stand a chance.

His mind raced over the possibilities. Benjamin and Finch wouldn't have a boat here. They would have to return to town to get a boat under way, but Poppinclerk hadn't come to the cemetery. If Tom didn't have the worthless pilot tied up, Poppinclerk could bring a steam tug out of the harbor and intercept the *Windsprite* before Rourke got away from the island.

Help us, Lord.

He raced along the mangroves, looking for the trail that would lead them to the boat. He could hear the angry slap of the ocean, but he couldn't find the path.

Please, Lord.

It should be near. He caught his foot on a mangrove root and went flying—right onto the path to the boat. Unfortunately, the crash echoed across the ponds.

Time was running out.

He scrambled to his feet and plunged onto the narrow path, trusting Anabelle to follow. Love could drive a person beyond her endurance. Rourke had to count on that.

When they emerged at the ship's boat, she said, "Now we go home."

"Now we row." Rourke struggled to untie the painter, wishing he had the cutlass so he could sever it. "In this choppy sea, it'll take longer than I'd like."

Anabelle stepped into the boat and took a seat.

The knot finally loosed. Rourke pushed off and hopped in. The boat glided out, but the wind and seas pushed it right back into the mangroves. Rourke grabbed the oars and put his back into each stroke. Soon they pulled away from shore, but if Benjamin had a ship lying in wait, all that effort would be for naught.

The seas fought them. The waves fought them. The race across the island had sapped his strength. Facing backward, Rourke saw the lights drawing near, but he couldn't see the *Windsprite*. His stroke faltered.

"She planned to join us," Anabelle said.

Rourke didn't need further encouragement, but Anabelle provided it.

"She will wait."

He rowed with renewed vigor.

⌒⌒⌒

Father brought Elizabeth home when Captain Poppinclerk arrived. After a brief discussion, the ship's pilot and Mr. Finch left to hunt down Rourke. Father drove the carriage. That left Elizabeth alone inside. She spent the short drive on her knees praying that Rourke and Anabelle would reach safety.

Once home, Father escorted her into his study and closed the door. "Sit."

No "please." No smile. No leniency. He was furious.

Elizabeth hadn't the strength to stand anyway. Rourke and Anabelle were now in God's hands. She sank into the chair farthest from Father's desk.

He stood behind the other, unblinking gaze fixed on her. "Why?" When she didn't answer, he clarified. "Why would you send away your maid?"

At least he had acknowledged that Anabelle no longer belonged to him. Nor did she belong to Elizabeth. "She is not mine."

"Of course she's yours. What is wrong with you, Lizzie? Have you lost your mind?"

The rebuke gave her strength. "On the contrary. I have found it."

He scowled, crossed to the decanter of brandy, and poured a glass.

"Now is no time to drink spirits, Father."

He whipped around. "Do you think to tell me what I can and cannot do?"

"I can't tell you anything. Neither could Mother."

He stiffened. "Leave your mother out of this. Tonight's debacle is entirely about your willful defiance." He downed the brandy in a single gulp. "Mr. Finch informed me that you insinuated you would get no inheritance. I told him it was another attempt on your part to dissuade him from marrying you."

"I did not insinuate. I stated a fact."

His face flushed red. "You lied."

In the past, such an accusation would have sent her into a cowering panic. Tonight she felt only calm. "No, sir, I did not lie. I told the truth. I discussed the matter with Aunt Virginia and arranged to have the inheritance distributed to another more deserving person."

"What?" His hand shook. "Do you know what you have done?"

"I know exactly what I have done. How could I take money for a dowry when my brother needs it? Aunt Virginia agreed. Late this afternoon she hired an attorney to draw up the paperwork."

Father's jaw literally dropped open, and all the fire went out of him. "Your brother?"

"Yes, Charlie."

He dropped into the other chair, shoulders slumped, and rubbed his forehead. "You gave your inheritance to Charlie?"

She nodded. "Aunt Virginia will verify it."

He blinked, once or twice at first and then more rapidly. His Adam's apple bobbed above the loosened cravat. "Perhaps I misjudged you." His voice came out ragged. "I thought you were defying me."

"Most of the time I was. I could never marry Mr. Finch, not after he tried to take liberties with me."

His head shot up, the old fire rekindled. "He did what?"

She almost regretted saying that. "He forced himself upon me."

"How?"

"He attempted a kiss I neither wanted nor encouraged."

"Oh." Father waved a hand. "Is that all?"

"That is quite enough. It proves he does not love me, though I can't imagine why he insisted on marrying a woman who despised him."

"You would grow to love him."

"Like Mother grew to love you?" she snapped.

"Precisely."

She didn't. The words were on the tip of Elizabeth's tongue, but she couldn't bring herself to say them, for they were spiteful, hurting, and the diary had ended years ago. Rourke's admonition came to mind again. *Love does right even when it hurts.*

"You know I love Rourke O'Malley."

Father's face twisted with distaste. "He is not good enough for you."

"He loves me. He waited four years for me. He is a good and honest Christian man."

"He is a barefoot Bahamian wrecker with no future."

This argument was old. She knew every point. "Many wreckers came here from the Bahamas. Some have made a goodly fortune."

"Not Mr. O'Malley. He still sails his father's sloop."

"The fastest ship in the fleet."

"And the oldest. He will never earn enough to give you a life of comfort."

She would not give up. "Love is comfort enough."

"You will think differently when your hands are raw from cooking and cleaning all day, when the parade of babies has worn you out, and your husband is gone for months at a time. This is not the life you have been raised to lead. You don't even know how to cook or clean."

"I'll learn."

Father poked again and again until it hurt. "Will you learn to do without food and clothing and shoes? Will you die in childbirth because he can't afford to hire a physician?"

"Yes, yes, I would do all that," she cried, hating the bits of truth in what he said.

"Enough, Elizabeth. I will not see my only daughter throw her life away."

"I'm not your only daughter." The words struck with the force of a tidal wave.

He stiffened. "What did you say?"

Though her heart pounded and her breath grew short, she could not deny the truth now. "I know about Anabelle."

His hand trembled until he fisted it. "What about your maid?"

She took a deep breath. "Anabelle is not my maid. She is my sister. My half sister."

All the color drained from his face. "Whatever she told you, it's a lie."

Elizabeth felt eerily calm. "She didn't have to tell me a thing. Mother spelled it out in her diary."

That clearly surprised him. "Her what?"

"She kept a diary." She rose. "Mother's words shocked me, but once I looked, really looked, the truth became obvious. Anabelle and I share your nose and chin and hands."

"Coincidence."

"So too our stature. Moreover, Anabelle's skin is light."

"Stop!"

She could not. "Mother made you promise to treat her exactly the same as me. That's why you let her grow up as my friend, why she learned to read and write, why she slept in my room."

"You know nothing of what happened."

"I know what Mother wrote, how disappointed she was, how her heart broke when she discovered what you had done."

He rose. "Silence!"

Though he towered over her, she could not stop. Once begun, the words must run their course. "I love my sister and want the best for her and her baby. Yes, she is married. She has been for four years. It's time she lived with her husband."

"That decision was not yours to make."

"Wasn't it? You gave her to me."

"Upon your wedding, which you have done everything to ruin. Anabelle is still my property."

"She's your daughter." Elizabeth would not back down. "The truth cannot be hidden. The harder you try to smother it, the more it wiggles free. Now even Charlie knows." She had left the diary and Mother's Bible with him before leaving tonight for what she had expected would be her farewell voyage.

"Charlie? You told Charlie?" The veins bulged on his forehead. His cheek ticked, but she ignored the warning.

"I gave him the diary."

The blow snapped her head around and spun her backwards. She slammed against the wall. Pain shot down her spine and robbed the strength from her legs. She slid to the floor and into darkness.

23

Shadowy images and muffled sounds drifted in and out of Elizabeth's consciousness. Whether dream or reality she did not know. Heaviness pressed upon her. Even her eyes could not open. Pain knifed marrow from bone and soul from body. Death beckoned, promising the peace that life could not bring.

Rourke.

His name tugged her back toward the pain.

She looked for him in this land of shadows, but he was always just beyond sight. She tried to call to him. Her mouth moved. Her lips opened, but no sound came out.

Rourke.

There he was, just above her. He grasped for her hand, but she slipped away, falling, falling. She clung to the last bit of canvas. The abyss beckoned. The black ocean tugged. He called out for her, stretched forth his arm. She could see his hand, could nearly reach his fingers, but the distance was too great.

Don't leave me.

He looked back. Just once. Then he was gone.

Forever. Somehow she knew that he would never return. That

knowledge weighed upon her. The pain and emptiness were too much to endure.

She let go. The waters closed over her, yet she gasped for breath.

A murmur of voices broke through the shadows, pulling her back from the depths.

A woman's frantic cry. "Will she end up like her brother?"

A man's hushed reply. "It's too early to know."

Though the murmuring continued, she slipped away again, this time to the shore. Her toes dug into the narrow fringe of glistening white sand. The turquoise sea stretched before her, endless as the sky. If only she could get to the other side. Then she would find Rourke. He'd been here, nearly within her grasp moments before, but now he was gone. She searched the horizon for his ship. She called out his name. She reached out her arms and wept for their emptiness.

"Lizzie, my Lizzie," a man wept. "Can you ever forgive me? Please open your eyes. Please give me a chance to beg your forgiveness. The fault is all mine. I was wrong, so wrong, in so many ways." Sobs muffled his words until the last. "Please, God, don't make her suffer for my sins."

Not Rourke.

Father. His agony pleaded with her, yet she recoiled. Ran. As fast as she could along the shore, where the glassy waves lapped against her toes.

Again she looked for Rourke. Again she reached out.

Return to me.

Yet the horizon remained empty.

❦

With a shudder, Elizabeth awoke. Her eyelids flew open, and she immediately closed them against the blinding light.

"Good afternoon, Lizzie."

"Charlie?" His name rasped against her dry throat.

"At least you know who I am. I don't suppose you're ready to play chess, though."

She cautiously opened her eyes a fraction. "Bright." And closed them again.

"I'm sorry."

She heard a thumping sound, then sensed diminished light. This time she lifted her eyelids a bit at a time.

"I wanted to study," he said. Again that thumping sound. "Seeing as you've been sleeping for four days now, I saw no reason to keep the room dark."

"Four days?"

"The doctor didn't know if you'd ever wake up."

She let her lids close, but the turquoise sea was gone. Only the pain remained. Her head hurt. The tiniest movement sapped her strength. Her throat was parched. She forced her eyelids open again. "Water?"

"Even better." Charlie appeared at the bedside, towering over her. The thumping stopped. "Cook sent up a pot of tea twenty minutes ago. Earl Grey. Your favorite." He lowered himself into a bedside chair and set aside crutches.

"You can walk," she gasped.

He looked abashed. "I've been practicing for weeks. Months, actually. Father had one of the Army engineers at the fort make the leg braces and crutches in August, but they take some getting used to. I took a lot of spills before I got it right."

"But . . . the wheelchair?"

He lowered his gaze. "I didn't want to fall in front of people. Father helped me practice at night, and Rourke would help when he came to play chess."

At the mention of Rourke's name, her throat constricted.

Charlie continued. "Once you arrived, I told Father I couldn't learn to use them. It was easier to stay in my room." He gave her a sheepish look. "I might have been a little angry at you too. I wanted to make you feel awful for what happened."

"I am sorry."

"It's not really your fault. Rourke tried to make me see that, but I didn't understand until I saw how courageous you were."

"Me?" She rubbed her throat.

"Sorry." He poured tea into a teacup. "By helping Anabelle to freedom. That's when I realized you weren't totally selfish."

"But I was."

"When it mattered, you acted unselfishly. I figured if you could do that, I could accept that I'm crippled and stop worrying what people say." He held out the cup. "Here."

She winced at his words. He had to accept so much, and no matter what Rourke said, it was her fault. She attempted to take the teacup from him, but the handle slipped from her fingers, and the brown liquid spilled all over the coverlet. "I'm sorry." Tears rose. "I made a mess of everything."

He blotted at the spill with a cloth. "My fault. I should have known better. Here, let me hold the cup for you."

With great care and patience he eased the liquid to her lips, asking after every sip if she wanted more.

Elizabeth marveled at his gentle spirit. "You're a lot like Mother."

"I miss her. Father spent time with me every day, but it wasn't the same. And now he's gone."

"Gone?" Memories tumbled through her head. Anger darkening his expression. Fury. The blow. She touched a hand to her cheek. It didn't hurt.

"It's healing," Charlie confirmed, "but it's a nasty green and purple color."

She did not care how she looked. Rourke would never return. And he wasn't the only one missing. "What do you mean that Father is gone?" Anger rose again. Before she had recovered, he left. "Where did he go? To fetch Mr. Finch?"

"He left on business."

"What business? That doesn't make sense. Attorneys don't need to travel."

Charlie shrugged. "He didn't say, just that it was urgent."

She squeezed her eyelids shut. He had gone after Mr. Finch. Or Rourke. Her eyes flew open. "Rourke? Was he caught?"

"No. They should be at Harbour Island by now."

Elizabeth breathed out, both relieved and devastated. "He will never return."

Charlie squeezed her hand. "You have to hope."

But she knew the cost of Anabelle's freedom. Rourke had to pay. She had to pay.

"Tom Worthington stopped by after Father left," Charlie said. "He told me everything that happened, what you did to help our half sister."

"So you do know about Anabelle."

"You left me Mother's diary. Of course I know. It wasn't difficult to figure out, and Father confirmed it."

"He did?" That did not sound like Father.

"There's no reason to keep it secret now."

Anger warred with relief. No more secrets, but it had cost her everything. "Do you hate him?"

A frown creased his brow. "He was always good to me. I suppose I was angry with him at first, but Mother found a way to forgive him, so I figure I should too."

That was too simple. Elizabeth could not set aside so easily the pain his actions had caused. "I can't. He destroyed everything I loved."

"Everything? You're alive. You still have your family."

Her conscience pricked. "I do love you, Charlie." But everything else was gone. Rourke. Anabelle. The loving father she'd thought she had. Elizabeth squeezed her eyes shut against the pain.

"He loves you," Charlie said.

He might mean Father, but she chose to believe he was referring to Rourke. Father had struck her when she didn't bend to his will. That was not love. *Love does right even when it hurts.* Father had not done right. Not at all. He had run off while she hovered between life and death. Didn't he even have the courage to face her?

"Charles Benjamin the Second!" That burst of matronly energy could only belong to Aunt Virginia. "You were supposed to ring for me the moment your sister awakened. That's why I left the bell here."

She bustled into the room and proceeded to demonstrate, making Elizabeth cover her ears.

"Now, how are you, dear?" Aunt rounded the bed and tugged at the coverlet until she noticed the tea stain. "What did you do, Charles? Spill the entire pot on your sister? Call for Florie to clean up this mess, and have her bring up some hot broth for your sister. Go on now." She waved him away.

Charlie gave Elizabeth an apologetic look and picked up his crutches.

"You ought to have bell pulls in every room to summon the servants," Aunt stated. "When your father returns, I'll see he installs them."

Charlie rolled his eyes, which in the past would have made

Elizabeth laugh, but the thought of facing Father soured any amusement.

Even before Charlie had made his way from the room, Aunt fluffed the pillows and resituated the bolster so Elizabeth sat more comfortably.

"Now, dear, do you feel well enough to hear what has gone on the last few days?"

Elizabeth leaned her head back. Whether or not she wanted to hear, Aunt would tell her.

As expected, Aunt did not wait for her answer. "You will be relieved to hear that Mr. Finch has left the island. Bound for New Orleans, I understand. He took the first packet Sunday morning, before your father could find him."

As she suspected, Father intended to change Finch's mind.

Aunt did not notice her discomfort. "That was fortunate for both men. If your father had found him, he would have wrung his neck. I told him that we discovered Mr. Finch had taken your father's copy of the bill of sale. Before you'd danced your first cotillion, I'd talked the boardinghouse owner into checking Mr. Finch's room. It was in the wardrobe. The man didn't even have the intelligence to hide it."

Elizabeth had no difficulty believing that. Finch's ambitions outweighed his sense.

Aunt sighed. "I fear, dearest Elizabeth, that Mr. Finch was using that bill of sale to blackmail your father."

"He said that?"

"Your father admitted everything. Apparently that bill was his only proof of ownership other than writing to Charleston, since the ship's papers were lost in the wreck. Apparently he violated some sort of rule about conflicting interests, and Mr. Finch took advantage. He needed your inheritance, you see.

Inquiries revealed that he owed a tremendous sum around town, especially at the gaming tables."

"Then Finch really did take the papers from your trunk."

"Not quite as directly as that. Since I gave my keys to Captain Poppinclerk, I suspect he was the one who rummaged through my trunk and found the papers. He then must have given—or sold—them to Mr. Finch."

"But why?"

Aunt harrumphed. "Something about carrying a grudge against your father for driving him out of the wrecking business by getting his license revoked. He must have figured Mr. Finch would use the papers to sully your father's reputation. No doubt he would have, given the opportunity."

Elizabeth's head ached trying to understand it all. "It doesn't matter much anymore, does it? He is gone."

"Praise God for that blessing. If you hadn't come to me with that idea to test Mr. Finch, we might have made a terrible mistake. I have sent a letter to Jonathan to investigate the man's background more thoroughly."

"But I thought you had. Father always touted his pedigree."

"I'm ashamed to admit we took Mr. Finch at his word." She sighed. "I am humiliated by how he deceived us. He might have taken the family for a great deal of money."

Elizabeth recalled her father's assertions of financial distress. "I fear that even with Mr. Finch gone, we are destitute."

Aunt Virginia jerked back. "Destitute? Whatever would make you say that?"

"Other than Charlie, of course. He has Mother's inheritance." She rubbed her aching temple. "A few days ago, Father told me his savings were gone. That's why he insisted I marry Mr. Finch. We needed the inheritance for Charlie's care."

"My dear." Aunt chuckled. "I suspect at the time he was reeling from the loss of the *Victory* and under duress from Mr. Finch's blackmail threats. The auction of the ship's cargo paid off all debts, and now that proof of ownership has been confirmed, the insurers will reimburse the balance. Your father is certainly not destitute."

It was all too much to take in. Her head was aching.

Florie arrived with the broth, which Aunt Virginia would doubtless ladle down her throat. Elizabeth closed her eyes, exhausted. The family might be returning to normal, but she had never felt more lost.

⌘

Recovery came slowly. Though Elizabeth was out of bed and moving around the house within a few days, she could not summon the strength to look ahead. Father's absence gave her time to heal. It also gave her time to think. Would he return alone? With Mr. Finch out of the picture, she could think of only one reason Father would leave before she'd awoken. He intended to catch Rourke and bring him back to face prosecution.

"How long did Father say he would be gone?" she asked at breakfast on a windy late October morning.

Aunt set down her teacup and looked to Charlie. "He told me it could take weeks. Did he say differently to you?"

Charlie shook his head. "Just not to worry."

Elizabeth gnawed on her lip. That sounded like Father would not rest until he convinced the Bahamian government to release Rourke and Anabelle into his custody. "Did he say where he went?"

Charlie shook his head.

Aunt must have seen her expression. "Something is worrying you."

Elizabeth couldn't express her fears, for Aunt Virginia didn't approve of Rourke either.

"It's only natural that you have the jitters," Aunt continued, "considering what happened, but he is your father. You forgive and move on."

Elizabeth could not forgive him. Not now. Perhaps not ever.

"Aunt is right," Charlie said between mouthfuls.

She rose, unable to listen to this anymore. "Excuse me. I am no longer hungry."

Upstairs, she paced her room. She needed to find out where Father had gone. With Mr. Finch gone, no one remained in Father's office. He must have sailed or taken a steamer. Perhaps one of the shipping agents would know which ship he had taken and its route. She grabbed a straw hat and hurried back downstairs.

"Where are you going?" Aunt called out from the dining room.

"To the harbor. I need the fresh air."

Charlie pulled himself to his feet and hobbled from the table into the foyer. "I'd like to show you something first. It's in my room."

Though Elizabeth would rather leave, her brother might know more than he was willing to acknowledge in front of Aunt Virginia. She followed him down the hall and into his room.

"Please close the door," he said as he lowered himself into the chair behind his desk. Books still covered the desktop. Many were open, and his notes covered the pages. He set his crutches to the side.

"You take your studies seriously."

"The law is a serious pursuit."

"Is there something in those books that you wanted to show me?"

"No." He opened a drawer and pulled out a chart. It looked vaguely familiar.

"Our pirate treasure map?" As children they had taken a nautical chart of the area and plotted the most likely hiding places of buried pirate treasure.

"Yes and no." He motioned to the other chair in the room. "Join me."

She pulled the chair beside him and sat down.

He spread out the chart. "We are here." He pointed to Key West. "This is Briland, or Harbour Island." He pointed far to the right. "I've been thinking that they might not have gone there." He pointed to a much closer island. "Andros would be quicker to reach."

"Maybe they did at first, but Rourke would go on to Harbour Island. That's where his mother and brothers and sisters live." A lump formed in her throat. She traced the route with her fingertip. "It's a long distance. Do you think Father went after Rourke? If the winds calmed, a steamer might catch the *Windsprite* before they reached safety."

"I considered that," Charlie admitted. "That's why I suspect Rourke headed for Andros Island. He would have had a short run with the brisk southeast winds."

"Did any steamers leave port?"

Charlie ducked his head. "Father took a steamer, but he didn't leave until the night before you awoke. Three days had passed. Rourke could have gotten all the way to Briland in that time."

Elizabeth breathed out with relief.

"Besides, he's not back," he added. "If he had caught up to Rourke, they would be back by now. Rourke and Anabelle must be safe."

That made sense, but she still had a feeling that they were

missing something. One unaccounted thread could unravel everything. She ran through the people involved. Mr. Finch had left for New Orleans. Father could not have reached Rourke in time. That left just one. "Captain Poppinclerk! Where is he?"

Charlie looked surprised. "I'm not sure. Why?"

"Aunt Virginia believes he is the one who took the papers from her trunk. If he left port . . ."

His eyes widened. "You think he would chase Rourke all the way to Harbour Island? Why? What could he hope to gain?"

"I don't know, but I have a terrible feeling about this."

"There's only one thing to do, then."

She looked up, startled by his certainty. "What could we possibly do?"

"Find Rourke."

She drew in her breath at the bold proposition. "How?"

He grinned. "Mother's inheritance ought to go to something worthwhile, don't you think?"

She shook her head. "It's for your future. Your security."

"I have enough security. Aunt Virginia might be a little overbearing, but even before you decided to give me Mother's inheritance, she promised to pay for law school. Mother meant her inheritance for you. Use it. Find him."

Elizabeth couldn't hold back the tears. "How did you manage to grow up so wise and honorable and generous in such a short number of years?"

"I had great examples."

"Mother." Her compassion and grace far surpassed what Elizabeth could muster.

"And Rourke."

24

I t didn't take long for Elizabeth to spot the holes in Charlie's idea. She could not travel by ship unescorted, and there was no one to travel with her. Caroline would not do. Not only was she unmarried and Elizabeth's age, but she could not return unescorted, which is precisely what she would have to do.

Since Rourke was a fugitive from the law, Elizabeth must remain on Harbour Island. Though Father had promised to give Anabelle to her, he had not yet done so. Therefore, Rourke had helped a slave escape to freedom. He would go to jail if he set foot in Key West or any state in the union.

Aunt Virginia certainly wouldn't go with her. She despised wreckers in general and still thought Rourke more a pirate than a suitor. Elizabeth had no choice but to trust that God would reveal an opportunity.

Until then, she intended to discover where Captain Poppinclerk was located. Though Charlie dismissed her fears, she could not rest until she knew his whereabouts. That very afternoon she walked to the harbor to make inquiries of the shipping agents. The short distance proved taxing, even with the cool breeze.

As she neared the harbor, she heard the growl of machinery and shouts of workmen. A new warehouse was under construction. The coral rock foundation was already in place, and workmen were raising heavy beams with ropes and cranes. Elizabeth tilted back her head to watch.

"Best stay out of the way, Miss Benjamin."

Elizabeth looked for the source of that warning and spotted a familiar figure. "Mr. Worthington. You are still here?"

He bowed. "At your service."

"I expected you to rejoin Captain O'Malley at the first opportunity."

"I shall, but no ships are headed that way."

She caught her breath. Perhaps this was the opportunity she sought. A young bachelor might not be considered a respectable escort, but she trusted Tom. He would see her safely to Harbour Island. Moreover, he would not need to return.

He peered at her with an odd expression. "Is the sun too hot, miss? You look peaked. Let's step into the shade."

Her cheeks must have flushed at the thought of seeing Rourke.

Tom was well-mannered and respectful. He would do, if she could convince him. No doubt he would balk at the impropriety of a young man escorting a young lady on a sea voyage, but he might do it if he thought Rourke would approve.

He started for the shade and then, seeing she did not follow, came back and offered his arm. "Pardon, miss. I should have waited."

She gave him an encouraging smile. "The fault is mine. I was lost in thought."

They walked across the street and into the shade of gumbo-limbo and mahogany trees.

"You're thinking of the captain, aren't you?" he asked softly.

How could she deny it? Yet her throat constricted at the thought.

"He's safe," Tom said. "You can be sure of that."

Elizabeth let out the breath she didn't realize she'd been holding. "Do you have information? Have you learned something?"

Like her brother, Tom insisted Rourke would have been brought back by now if he'd been caught.

The thought of capture made her dizzy.

"Are you all right, miss?"

She shook her head to clear it. "I'm simply anxious."

"Don't be. The captain had a solid beam reach and clear sailing. I reckon he made the crossing in record time."

She knew he was trying to ease her fears, but when one died down, another popped to life. "What if Captain Poppinclerk went after him?"

Tom laughed. "He didn't go anywhere, thanks to a sharp cutlass."

She gasped. "You killed him?"

"Naw, he got so scared he ran off like a rat in floodwaters and tripped over his own feet. He's been nursing a broken nose well out of sight of the ladies."

Under other circumstances, the description would have amused her, but she must be certain that he had not pursued Rourke. "Then he is still indisposed?"

"Very much so."

That quieted another fear but not all of them. Until she saw Rourke with her own eyes, she could never find peace. That meant making the crossing to Harbour Island.

"I wonder," she began softly, "if I might ask a favor."

"Anything, Miss Benjamin."

She squared her shoulders. Charlie was right. Everything was settled here. She was ready to step into the future she had long wanted. "I'm looking for passage to Harbour Island."

He stared at her. "You what?"

"Passage." This time her voice squeaked. "To Harbour Island in the Bahamas. Within the week if possible." Surely Father wouldn't return by then.

"Why are you asking me?"

This was the moment of truth. "Because I need someone I trust to escort me there."

"Me?" He looked flabbergasted. "Now, miss, that's kind of you, but there's one big problem with that idea."

She couldn't let him dismiss the request. "Please understand that I don't intend to return. No one here will know you are my escort. I promise."

"That's not the problem." He looked toward the harbor. "You see, there's not a single ship heading that way. Not this week and not the next."

Just like that, her plan deflated.

⌘

Days turned into weeks without word of a ship heading to Harbour Island. Neither did her father write or return. To Elizabeth, it felt as if the two men in her life had vanished. Yet only one would return, and not the one she wanted to see. When Father returned, all hope of reaching Rourke would disappear. Each day brought that inevitability closer.

By late November, she went through the motions each day, content to let Aunt Virginia run the household. Sometimes she played chess with Charlie, always losing, until he claimed she wasn't even trying. Every day she walked to the harbor and checked the name of each ship. Then she spoke to the shipping agents. When the sun dipped low, she returned home disappointed.

Nothing could salve the ache in her heart.

"You must occupy yourself," Aunt Virginia insisted. "Embroider, sew, do charity work, help your friend with the temperance league."

Aunt meant well, but Elizabeth could muster no enthusiasm for any of the ordinary pursuits. She attended a temperance meeting with Caroline, but her mind drifted far away to Bahamian shores and she heard none of the speech. Sewing met a similar fate with just four uneven stitches by the afternoon's end.

"Then practice piano," Aunt insisted. "This lovely instrument hasn't seen a moment's use. Practice will perfect your playing."

Elizabeth could not bear to touch the keyboard, lest her awkward attempts ruin the memory of Rourke's beautiful playing. That night in the chapel, he had touched her soul. When the organist played "Blest Be the Tie That Binds" at Sunday worship, tears had rolled down her cheeks. The tune still echoed in her mind.

"Well," her aunt grumbled, "you can't go on like this. A young woman your age has her entire life ahead of her. You must look to the future."

"My future is with Rourke O'Malley."

Aunt's sharp look told Elizabeth that she had voiced that thought aloud. She bowed her head and waited for the inevitable reproach.

None came.

Instead, Elizabeth heard only the clicking of Aunt's knitting needles. She dared a peek. The woman was frowning. At Elizabeth's glance, she stopped knitting.

"Do you think Captain O'Malley would want you to pine after him to such an extent that you waste your days?"

Deep inside she knew her aunt was right. Rourke would not want her to mourn. Love not only meant doing what was right, but it also meant hoping against all odds. She had tried, truly she had, but she could not find the strength.

She stood. "Please excuse me. I wish to lie down."

Elizabeth did not wait for her aunt's response. When she reached the hall, she saw Florie heading upstairs to clean. Cook was working in the dining room. Charlie's tutor was drilling him in mathematics. That left nowhere for her to retreat except Father's study. She hesitated but a moment. It was better than Aunt Virginia's constant advice.

The study door was unlocked. She slipped into the cool darkness. The smells of pipe tobacco and musty books hung in the close air. She opened the windows and pushed open the louvered shutters. After drawing a deep breath, she looked around the scene of their last argument. The chairs were in order. No blood marked the spot where her head had struck. The desktop was empty except for blotter, pen, and inkwell—and one small volume. Inching closer, she recognized her mother's diary lying open in the center of the blotter.

Her hands fisted. How could Charlie give it to him? Mother's words were sacred, private. She would have accepted her children reading them, but not Father. Never Father. After all he had done to Mother, to know that he'd read her anguish punched the air from Elizabeth's lungs.

She started to close the diary when she noticed that he had written in it. How could he? She dipped the pen in the inkwell, intending to scratch out the sacrilege he had scrawled beneath Mother's words of forgiveness.

I am not worthy.

The words burned like an iron against flesh. Did he truly think that four little words could erase all the pain he had caused? It was not enough. It would never be enough. She scratched the pen along the paper, but the nib was dry. There was no ink in the well.

"Are you sure you want to do that?"

She looked up to see Charlie propped in the doorway. "I thought you were working with your tutor."

"We're done. I wondered how long it would take you to come in here."

"You knew about this?" She shook the diary. "You knew he wrote in Mother's diary and didn't blot it out?"

"Words can never really be erased. We will always know."

He was right. She sank into the desk chair. Above the fireplace, the portrait of her gentle mother looked down upon them. How much she had endured at Father's hands. How much they all had. "It doesn't get rid of his guilt. He hurt her. He hurt us. Nothing can change that."

"I suppose you're right," Charlie said slowly, "but if there aren't any second chances, then we're all doomed. We all make mistakes. We all hurt each other."

She knew he was right, but she couldn't admit it, for that meant revisiting her own guilt.

"Mother forgave him," Charlie whispered.

Elizabeth rose and gave the diary to her brother. "It took time."

"What if we don't have time?" he asked as she whisked past him.

❧

As a girl, Elizabeth would run to the south shore of the island whenever something upset her. There she had talked to God and listened for His whispers in her heart.

Today she made her way to that same shore. Like in her dream, the turquoise seas stretched out endlessly before her. The breeze tugged at her skirt. Waves lapped the shore. Unlike that dream, white sails and the black smoke of steamships punctuated the horizon. Gleaming white coral sand rimmed the shore.

Holy ground.

Just like the verse from Exodus. *Put off thy shoes from off thy feet, for the place whereon thou standest is holy ground.*

Such things happened thousands of years ago, but here? Today? On Key West? To a woman who had turned her back on God, blaming Him when the blame lay squarely on her shoulders? God might have whispered to her as a child, but no more.

Yet the verse would not leave her. The sand shone like the sun, pure and white.

In her dream she had walked barefoot. What would it hurt to do so now? She sat on the grass and removed her shoes. Only then did she step onto the sand. It burned against the soles of her feet. The physical pain felt better than what she had endured of late. Father's betrayal. Anabelle's secret. Rourke's departure, his fingers slipping from her hand. She touched his ring where it rested against her throat. What good was a pledge that could never be fulfilled?

"Why?" she cried to the sky and the screeching gulls. "Why must I be separated forever from the man I love? Why would my own father do such horrible things? What can take away this pain?"

Heat. It purified. Laundry must boil. Drinking water must boil. This heat burning her feet would scorch away the guilt and the anger and the despair. She stood until the heat brought tears to her eyes, but no peace came.

Everyone insisted she must forgive in order to continue.

Mother forgave Father. Rourke forgave her. So did Charlie. That was what he had been trying to tell her.

Forgive us our debts, as we forgive our debtors.

She had repeated the Lord's Prayer every Sunday yet never grasped the significance—and difficulty—of those words. To be forgiven, we must forgive.

To receive forgiveness, she must forgive. Not some things. Not just those who treated her well. Everyone. Even Father.

Her limbs trembled at the enormity of the task. She sank to her knees and looked up into the endless blue sky. "I am not able."

I am not worthy, Father had written.

Neither was she. Charlie, Rourke, and even Anabelle had forgiven her when she did not deserve it. All had suffered for her actions.

"I am not worthy," she choked out. It hurt, yet it also healed.

Those first words led to more and more. There, on sacred ground, she poured out her heart to her one true Father. Her hurts and resentments, her transgressions, her selfish desires. All of it.

He listened. He did not turn His face. He did not run from her the way she had run from Him. She prayed until there was nothing left inside but silence. Even then she continued to kneel. The wind whispered. Gulls called out. As the warmth soaked through her skirts and into her knees, she knew what she must do. The answer came not with the whisper of a breeze but with the roar of a gale.

She took a deep, rattling breath. "Papa, I forgive you." The words tasted bitter as salt water.

She tried again. "I forgive you, Papa."

How many times must she say this until it didn't hurt? The

320

Bible said seven times seventy. Four hundred and ninety. She would perish first.

Nevertheless, she said it again. "Father, I forgive you." Over and over until the words blurred and her throat dried. Only then, deep, deep inside, did something resembling peace take root. She couldn't explain it, but the anger was gone.

She dropped to the ground, exhausted, and lay there looking up at the wide blue sky. Like a frigate bird, Rourke had soared beyond her grasp. Maybe one day he would return, silent on the breeze.

She drew a breath and sat up. It was time to go home. She began putting on her shoes when a schooner caught her attention as it sailed toward the harbor. It must have approached from her left, yet she had not seen it until now. The ship's sails were filled, and she maintained a swift speed, faster even than the *Windsprite*. Her rakish lines reminded Elizabeth of the ships built in the Bahamas.

The Bahamas! Perhaps it would return there. Perhaps she could go to Rourke after all.

She tugged on her shoes and hurried toward town. A gust of wind blew the straw hat from her head. She reached for it, but it flew off into the ocean. By the time she passed the lighthouse, her hair had fallen from its pins. She didn't stop to fix it. At the ship's rate of speed, it would reach the harbor well before she did. She must speak to the captain before he left the ship. She must get passage to Harbour Island.

Little did she care that her hair flowed loose and her hem gathered dust. Her prayers had been answered. She would go to Rourke.

She reached the edge of the harbor at the very moment the new schooner came about to head alongside a wharf. Some crew members lowered sail while others readied the mooring lines. Two men stood at the helm. One wore an uncharacteristic gentleman's dark suit and top hat. The other, tall and dark and barefoot, looked very much like . . .

Impossible!

She danced along the docks, trying to get a better look. Could it be? He sported a dark blue coat that she'd never seen before. He even wore a black cocked hat like a naval officer. No, it couldn't be. She must be mistaken.

Still, she waited, breath bated, hoping against hope that her eyes were not deceiving her.

At last the ship turned enough so she could see him.

Rourke! He had returned.

He spotted her, and a smile stretched across his face. Then the man in the suit turned to face her.

Father.

Her spirits plummeted. The only reason Father would be with Rourke on a new ship was to bring him to justice.

"No!" The cry wrenched from her. She clung to a dock post, shaking.

Then her father lifted his hat in a salute. He clapped Rourke on the back and swept his arms in an encompassing circle.

What on earth? Rourke did not act like a man condemned. No, he smiled and appeared completely at ease talking to her father. To all appearances, they had reconciled, though how that had been accomplished and why they were on a strange new vessel mystified her. Nothing in her father's prior actions would ever lead her to believe such a thing possible. Nothing except those scrawled words: *I am not worthy.*

Could a man change that much in a matter of weeks? Elizabeth struggled against doubt.

The schooner slipped into its berth. The crew moored the ship with expertise. Several of the men looked familiar from the *Windsprite*. None of this made sense.

The crew extended the gangway, and only one man disembarked. Father. He walked straight toward her.

She stepped back, fearing what he would say yet knowing she could not avoid it. That was part of forgiveness.

He stopped before her. "Dear Elizabeth." He cleared his throat and looked at the ship, as if drawing courage from someone aboard.

She followed his gaze and saw Rourke directing the opening of the hatches from his perch on the quarterdeck. He looked her way and nodded.

"Elizabeth." Her father mopped his brow. "I did you great harm. Unforgivable." His shoulders shook. "I don't expect you to forgive me. I don't ask it. I thought I was preserving your future, giving you safety and comfort. I forgot what was most important."

She could not find words to meet this uncharacteristic and painful admission.

He managed a weak smile. "I can never repair all the damage, but I will do what I can. Your mother—God bless her soul—deserved better. There are no excuses for my behavior. She showed compassion, but I was too proud to admit I needed it."

Elizabeth recalled his scrawled words, but this time they were tempered by the whispers of her heart. "None of us is worthy."

He looked up, startled.

"I failed people too. Mother. Charlie. Captain O'Malley. Even you." That was hardest to admit.

"No, child. Not once did you fail me. You were open and honest and caring." He swiped at his eyes. "You put your brother and Anabelle before yourself."

Her fingertips tingled with a new fear. "Where is she?"

Father pointed to the mouth of the harbor. "With her husband."

The *Windsprite* was slipping into the harbor.

"No, Father, you cannot force her to return. You promised you'd give her to me. Well, I want her to be free. Promise you'll emancipate her."

"Hush, hush. It's already done."

"It is?"

He nodded. "Her husband is captain of the *Windsprite* now, and they have decided to settle here in Key West."

"But if he's captain of the *Windsprite*, what is Rour—Captain O'Malley to do?"

Sometime during the conversation, Rourke had joined them. "Command this schooner when I'm not ashore."

She looked from the schooner to the *Windsprite* to her father and at last to Rourke. "But how? How did you get another ship, and why is my father with you?"

"That's why I went to Harbour Island, to make a business proposition," Father said.

"Charlie said you left on business, but I still don't understand."

Rourke took over. "I've wanted to leave wrecking for some time now. I had saved a good sum, and the award from the *Victory* added to it, but I still needed a bit more to build a warehouse and set up a shipping operation. That's where your father stepped in."

Her jaw dropped. "You're partners?"

Father shook his head. "I'm only an investor. My share of the settlement for the *Victory* provided just the amount Captain O'Malley needed to purchase this schooner and build a warehouse."

She looked at Rourke. "You're the one building the new warehouse?"

He laughed. "Actually, your father hired the work crew and set things in motion." He pointed toward shore. "Did you notice the sign?"

She squinted into the sun. Beneath the peak of the roof, large letters had been painted on the wall of the second story. "O'Malley. Then it truly is yours."

"That's my understanding."

"But why, Father? You never liked Rourke. What changed your mind?"

Her father looked uncomfortable. "Now, that's not quite right. Rourke was a good friend to your brother the last few years. I just had difficulty seeing him as a son-in-law."

"I see." For all his change of heart, that had not changed.

"Look at me, Lizzie." Father lifted her chin. "I did this because he loves you and you love him. You do, don't you?"

She had never thought to hear such words from her father. "But you refused to listen to me whenever I brought up his name."

"I was a fool." Father cleared his throat again. "We, uh, came to an understanding."

"Understanding?" She realized she was echoing what he said, but this was so surprising she could not find words.

Rourke took her hand, and before she even knew what was happening, he dropped to one knee. "Miss Elizabeth Benjamin. Last month I promised to return to you. On that day I also gave you my grandmother's wedding ring as a pledge for the future."

She touched her throat. The ring had become a part of her these past weeks, but she had not dared to believe this could happen. "Are you—?"

Rourke grinned. "I believe I'm supposed to take the lead on this."

Her cheeks heated, and not from the sun.

He gave her a little wink of encouragement, and the twinkle in his eye sent her insides fluttering in the most wonderful way.

"Miss Elizabeth Benjamin, will you consent to marry me following a proper courtship?"

"Yes! Oh yes." He might have had more to say, but she would not wait one second in case he or Father changed their minds. "But must it be proper? Might we hurry it a bit?"

Rourke looked shocked, but her father chuckled.

She drew another breath. "Wait until Anabelle hears. And Caroline and Charlie and, oh, Aunt Virginia."

"Will you at least give me time to put the ring on your finger?" Rourke said with what she hoped was exaggerated exasperation.

"Of course." She pulled the ribbon from around her neck and handed it to him.

He held the ring and snapped the ribbon.

"In a hurry, Captain?" her father said.

"I have waited four years." Rourke slipped the ring on her finger. "I can't wait a day longer."

He swept her into his arms right there on the docks, despite her tangled hair and dusty skirts. He gazed deep into her eyes, and then he kissed her with such passion and promise that it erased every heartache of the last four years. Hope unfurled far inside and blossomed outward until she could not bear the joy.

"Ahem." Father loudly cleared his throat. "We are in public."

Elizabeth reluctantly broke the kiss, but she would not leave Rourke's arms. "I'm never letting you out of my sight again."

"Never?" But Rourke's stern question was paired with a grin. "Do you propose to take the helm when I head to sea?"

She laughed. "Perhaps I shall."

"She's a lot to handle."

Elizabeth wasn't sure if he meant her or the ship.

He must have read her mind, for he laughed and then turned her around. "But she has a good name."

She blinked back tears as she breathed it aloud. *"Redemption."*

"Fitting, don't you think?"

She swallowed the lump in her throat, for in that instant she knew without a doubt that her place was not aboard a working ship. "I belong here, with my family."

Rourke brushed aside her hair and kissed the nape of her neck. "I'm glad to hear that, because I intend to spend most of my time ashore now."

"You do?"

"It would make it easier for you to keep me in sight every moment of the day," he teased.

She protested, but he kissed her again, and the protest died. Those sea-green eyes shone with the promise of a lifetime.

"How can I be away from you a single moment?" he whispered.

Her heart filled to overflowing.

"I do have one more thing to show you." He guided her along the docks and pointed up at the warehouse. "I noticed that someone took the liberty of adding a little more to that sign."

She'd thought her heart would burst before.

"Wonderful, isn't it?" He beamed with pride.

"O'Malley and Sons?" Though the idea of children underfoot delighted her, he—and Father—had to learn not to act so hastily. "Aren't you two putting the cart before the horse?"

"Maybe," Rourke admitted without the slightest hint of regret, "but I can't imagine anything sweeter. Should I have the painters change it?"

Elizabeth leaned against the man who would soon be her husband. "No, don't. I rather like the ring of it. Unless, of course, we only have daughters, then I do expect a change."

Rourke let loose the most wonderful laugh she had ever heard, while high overhead, a magnificent frigate bird soared against the sun, its mate at its side.

Acknowledgments

First and foremost, all glory and honor belong to the Lord my God, Author of all things. With Him all things are possible.

My deepest gratitude to my critique partners, Jenna Mindel and Kathleen Irene Paterka, whose support, encouragement, and creative energy pulled me through the doubts and dead ends. Love you!

To my editor, Andrea Doering, and the whole fabulous team at Revell—thank you!

Thanks also go out to my agent, Nalini Akolekar, who believed in this project from the start.

I owe a debt of gratitude to those researchers who have compiled histories and resources on the Florida Keys. Also to the wonderful Florida History Department in the Monroe County Public Library in Key West, which houses the records from the "wreckers' court" among its extensive historical collections.

My deepest appreciation to all the readers and encouragers. Your support means so very much to me. May God bless you richly.

Keep Reading for a Sneak Peek of
Book 2 in the

KEYS

— OF —

PROMISE

Series

1

Nantucket Island
April 20, 1852

"What will you do now?" The gentle nudge came from Mrs. Franklin hours after Prosperity Jones had laid her mother to rest in the church graveyard.

They sat on sturdy wooden chairs in the only home Prosperity could recall, while neighbors bustled about preparing a meal for those who condoled with her. She had attempted to help, but they had shooed her away from the kitchen. Stripped of the ability to do something useful, she battled a barrage of conflicting thoughts and feelings that ultimately came back to Mrs. Franklin's question.

What would she do?

That question had never been broached until now. Prosperity always knew what she must do. As a child she had tended house for her oft-ailing mother. The year that fire had swept through town and the sea claimed her father's life, she added nursing and managing their meager funds to her duties.

Nearly six years later, Ma breathed her last, ushering in

overpowering loneliness. Prosperity's entire family was gone. No more could she turn to Pa for counsel or weep on Ma's shoulder. She had been set adrift on a vast ocean.

What would she do?

At some point she must have donned the black cotton mourning gown. Somehow burial had been arranged and the funeral carried out. Even now, mere hours afterward, disjointed memories ricocheted through her mind: the deep grave carved into the cold earth, hymns so familiar they flowed by without notice, mourners weeping uncontrollably while she could not muster a tear. Well-meaning statements about God's will drifted past like dandelion fluff on a breeze.

After tossing a handful of dirt on the plain pine coffin, she would have preferred to climb the dunes and gaze across the sea at the endless horizon, as she had for months after her father's whaling ship disappeared. Instead, she had returned home with the neighbors who now buzzed about like a hive of bees. Only Mrs. Franklin's inquiry had managed to break through the fog.

What *would* she do?

Before Ma's passing, Prosperity had whiled away countless hours dreaming of her future.

David.

She touched the locket at her throat. He had given it to her after she agreed to marry him. It would one day contain tiny portraits of the children they hoped to have. Now it held a lock of his sandy blond hair. That was all she had to remember him by, for more than two years ago the Army had sent him to faraway Key West, and he would not return for six more years. What would she do until then?

"Are you all right, dear?" Mrs. Franklin asked.

Prosperity knit her fingers together and nodded.

She was spared further questions by Mrs. Newton, who chased two boys from the kitchen with a scolding that they must wait until dinner was served.

Mrs. Franklin chuckled. "I think he nabbed a biscuit off the tray. That was my Donnie back in the day."

Her voice blended into the drone of the half dozen women gathered in the tiny parlor. Outside on the porch, the men clustered together, supposedly to keep the children in the yard. Their guffaws punctuated the knowing whispers and pitying glances of the women sitting on the chairs loaned by generous neighbors. Aunt Florence held court in the opposite corner, informing all who would listen that she'd known her sister would die and was amazed she'd hung on so long in this dreadful, drafty shack.

True, the rough slabwood walls held no charm and retained little of the stove's heat. A scarred table occupied the center of the room, topped with a vase of daffodils, shadbush, and white violets brought by one of the ladies. Little else graced the room, for Prosperity had been forced to sell every item of value in the years following her father's death. Nothing frivolous or beautiful remained. Even the cold gray of late April refused a ray of sunlight.

"There is nothing left here," she breathed.

Mrs. Franklin, a kindly soul, clasped her hands with the warmth of a dear friend. "You must find the strength to go on. Your mother would have wanted it."

"I know."

Yet it was easier to say than to do. Once the condolers left, she would be alone with nothing but memories, a few personal items, and David's letters. Those had brought comfort in the most difficult days. He had pledged a life together. David Latham never broke a promise.

"He will return," Mrs. Franklin stated with a knowing nod.

"How did you know I was thinking of Mr. Latham?"

Mrs. Franklin sighed, her gaze far off. "A woman gets a certain look when she recalls the man she loves." She patted Prosperity's hand. "Never fear. You only need write, and your lieutenant will come back from that wilderness."

"Key West." It might as well be Tahiti, for both lay beyond reach. Ship passage, even in third class, cost far more than she could save.

"Wherever it is, your young man will set sail for home the moment he receives your letter. Mark my words, he will not hesitate."

Prosperity wasn't as certain. David had stressed that his tour of duty would last eight years. Even now she could recall how worry had pinched his brow that day. Eager to brush it away, she had promised to wait. A rare smile had flickered across his lips, and she had been pleased. She had not accounted for this day.

"I doubt the Army will grant leave," Prosperity murmured.

"Nonsense. You must write. He will find a way to return to you. Then you can decide together what to do."

That was the fanciful talk of a woman seeking to comfort. The Army would not grant David leave because his fiancée's mother had passed away. No, she must find her own way. She couldn't stay in this house. That much was unavoidable. She could not afford to pay the overdue rent, least of all continue the lease of an entire house on her own. Mother's rainy day jar had been emptied long ago. There were no secret bank accounts, no accounts at all. John and Olivia Jones had left this world as poor as they'd come into it.

Mrs. Franklin, short and portly and pink-cheeked beneath her white lace cap, must have been chattering for some time, but just one statement caught Prosperity's attention. "You can stay with us if your relations can't take you in. Mr. Franklin would dearly enjoy your delicious currant cakes each morning."

Prosperity mustered a smile, though she could not manage the emotion to go with it. Her parents were gone, and life on Nantucket Island was slipping away.

"You are very generous," she said, though living with the Franklins was out of the question. No Jones accepted charity.

"Only until your young man returns for you, of course."

Prosperity nodded, unable to speak over the knot in her throat. Two years had passed since David offered for her. Each morning and night she recalled his handsome visage. The cornflower-blue eyes and curly hair the color of sand brought a smile to her lips. How stiff he'd seemed when she first met him. She had laughed at his formal bow, and he had acted affronted, but in time she'd grown to appreciate his careful ways. Nothing was out of place. No possibility had gone unconsidered.

He was a product of his demanding father and austere upbringing, so serious of temperament that she'd made silly faces at him to induce a laugh. Oh, how he resisted. First, the corner of his mouth would tick up a fraction. Then he would force a frown. Will would battle emotion until, in the end, a deep guffaw would burst out. Only then would the corners of his eyes crinkle and pleasure fill his gaze.

If only she could see that again. If only she could hear his voice and feel how the very air shimmered when he walked into a room. Then she would know all was well. She could endure any hardship. Alas, her David was beyond reach, and she had only memories to lean upon.

Over time his features had grown dim. Was that tiny mole above the right corner of his mouth or the left? Did his brows sweep high in an arc or duck low? Did the spectacles he used for reading leave the same red marks on the bridge of his nose? Had he succeeded in taming the tuft of frizz at the peak of his brow?

She closed her eyes and tried to recall.

The shifting shapes of memory faded like a dream in morning's light.

"He will return. You must believe it." Mrs. Franklin's voice dragged Prosperity back to the painful present.

Until he returned . . . Her breath caught at the daunting prospect. Alone. Impoverished. Without a home.

"He will." Mrs. Franklin patted her hand for emphasis. "He is a gentleman."

A man of honor. Yes, David was that. He never failed to write each Sunday. The letters might arrive late or all in one batch, as was the case right now. She had not received a letter in nearly a month, but tomorrow might be the day. Until then she treasured each written word, reading the letters over and over until his sentences wove into the fabric of her days. He was saving all he could. He would marry once he had saved enough. If that came sooner rather than later, he might send for her. No woman on Nantucket or Key West could compare to her in beauty and intellect. He kept her portrait on the desk in his quarters.

He was an ever-true, unshakable mark. To this she could cling.

At her side, Mrs. Franklin rose, pulling Prosperity from her thoughts.

Aunt Florence approached with a swish of her flounced skirts. "I'd like to speak to my niece."

Mrs. Franklin offered her condolences to Aunt Florence and trundled to the kitchen.

Prosperity rose, aware that her future might depend on good relations with her last living blood relative, who had made the voyage to Nantucket Island from Boston with her husband. "Please have a seat, Aunt Florence."

How different Aunt was from her sister! While sunlight and love had creased Ma's face into a starburst, Aunt's face was pinched, her lips pressed into a white line. Thin and bony, Aunt wore a silk mourning gown that rustled as she moved. Its fine black-on-black striping took Prosperity's breath away. Never would she touch, least of all wear, such a gown.

Aunt Florence looked down her nose at the chair. "Given the option, I prefer to stand. After the grueling journey, I cannot endure another hard bench."

Prosperity swallowed. "I hope your accommodations were comfortable. Dumfrey Hotel is the finest on the island."

"It was barely habitable, but better than this," Aunt sniffed with a caustic glance at Prosperity's home. "My sister chose unwisely. I trust you have done better. Livvy wrote that you are engaged to marry an Army engineer." She never once looked directly at Prosperity. "It's certainly better than a whaler, though a true gentleman would have married and brought you with him."

"He is a true gentleman."

Aunt didn't seem to notice that she had spoken. "I fear that your uncle and I must return to Boston at once. Harold can't be away from the bank for long." She opened the clasp on her elegant silk bag and pulled out a small ivory envelope that must have cost dearly at a stationer. "We want you to have this."

With trembling hand, Prosperity took the fat envelope. What on earth could it be? She'd met Florence just once before, on her aunt's brief visit to the island when Prosperity was a child.

Perhaps it was a note of condolence or one of Ma's letters to her sister.

"Thank you," she whispered, her throat dry.

"Do understand that we can't take you in." Aunt Florence's cold smile revealed perfectly white teeth. "Harry and his family visit often, and of course Amelia is still at home. Between friends and family, there isn't a week that we don't use every bed in the house."

Prosperity averted her gaze. "I understand." Her last living relative was deserting her.

Aunt waved a hand toward the envelope. "Use this to make your way in the world. Livvy wrote that you are quite capable of caring for yourself, but we wanted to give you this assistance until you can secure a position as a governess or housekeeper."

Prosperity stiffened. She was the daughter of a whaler. Her fiancé was an engineer. Her future did not depend on going into service. Mrs. Franklin was right. David would help. And Prosperity would turn the other cheek on the affront.

Swallowing her pride, she managed to speak. "Do thank Uncle Harold for me."

"You can thank him yourself. We must leave now in order to catch the boat to the city. You may escort me to the carriage."

Prosperity could not regret Aunt's early departure. For her mother's sake, she expressed sorrow as she led her aunt to the door. Behind her, the women carried the food to the table. The moment Prosperity escorted her aunt off the porch, the men and children rushed inside, leaving Prosperity alone in front of the house with her aunt and uncle.

He tipped a hand to his beaver. "Miss Jones."

"Uncle Harold."

"I fear we must leave."

She nodded. "It can't be helped."

"Indeed."

"We will be late for the boat," Aunt Florence said.

He helped his wife into the hired carriage. Before climbing in himself, he turned back to Prosperity.

"Be a good girl, now." He too did not meet Prosperity's gaze. "That little sum should help you make a start of things." He cleared his throat, muttered something unintelligible, and then entered the carriage. With a final apologetic glance, he closed the door.

After the carriage rolled from view, Prosperity broke the seal on the envelope. A single sheet of paper, unmarked, cradled a number of large bills. She could not count the sum now, in the street, but it appeared enough to settle accounts and pay for room and board until David learned of her circumstances. A letter would take weeks or even a month or more to arrive. Then the same time for his reply to return. By then . . .

Prosperity pressed the envelope to her midsection, overcome by the speed with which the world was closing in upon her.

Help me, Lord. Show me Thy path and the way Thou wouldst have me walk.

The simple prayer calmed her.

"She's gone, is she?" Mrs. Franklin joined her in the yard. "Good riddance, if you ask me. Livvy deserved better from her sister, but there's no sense fussing over what can't be changed. Come, dear, let's go inside and have a bite to eat." She took Prosperity's arm. "There will be plenty of time to consider your future tomorrow."

Prosperity did not move, for the answer to her prayer struck with perfect clarity. Why wait for letters to wend their way south and then north again?

341

"I will go to Key West."

Mrs. Franklin's jaw dropped. "You cannot be serious."

"I am not only serious, I am certain."

"But my dear, you are letting your emotions speak. You have suffered a great loss and are not thinking clearly. Give yourself time to grieve. By the time your young man returns, you will be in a much better state of mind."

"I am perfectly sane. In fact, my thoughts have never been clearer."

"Naturally you want to see your fiancé, but do be practical. Even if you could afford such a voyage, someone must travel with you."

Prosperity clutched the envelope. "I shall travel alone."

"Alone? You cannot. Sea travel is neither comfortable nor safe. I speak from experience, dear. Mr. Franklin and I have traveled to Charleston in the past. It's not a voyage to be taken without great care. A woman alone?" She shuddered. "Your reputation and quite likely your person would suffer."

"It does not matter. David awaits me."

"You cannot mean that." Mrs. Franklin's voice rose with every word, her expression earnest. "I will account your rash decision to grief, but even if you will not guard your reputation, you must consider the uncertainty of the seas. Your father was a seasoned sailor, yet the sea claimed his life. The risk is too great. Better your fiancé return to you."

"He cannot. He would never leave his post."

"Then wait. You are welcome at our house."

Though Mrs. Franklin's concerns chipped at Prosperity's confidence, she would not be swayed. When weighed against servitude or destitution, the risk was small, for if she succeeded, her beloved awaited.

Prosperity squared her shoulders. "I am sailing for Key West, and you cannot persuade me otherwise."

⁓

Key West
That Night

Lt. David Latham's hand trembled. A drop of ink splotched onto the white paper.

"Not again." His muttered frustration echoed off the walls of the small but adequate quarters.

Already the sheet of paper was a tangle of scratched-out beginnings and blotted ink drops. Once he got the wording right, he would begin anew with a fresh sheet of stationery, but two hours of wrangling had produced only the date. In thirty minutes, even that would be incorrect.

Ordinarily he handled any difficulty with calm precision. An engineer in the United States Army Corps must rely on logical analysis to conquer frequent setbacks. This one, however, was both personal and painfully unexpected. It drove a spike into the heart of his carefully drawn future.

It made this letter far from ordinary.

He returned the pen to its holder and flexed his fingers. To his right, the window opened onto a star-filled sky barren of suggestions.

How to begin? Every letter required a salutation, but no combination of words worked. His usual address bespoke an affection that would gladden his beloved's heart. What cruelty when a paragraph later he must crush that joy. On the other hand, formal address would send her into a panic before he'd cushioned the blow with careful reasoning.

343

No, this was a delicate affair.

He laughed bitterly.

Affair was too kind a word. *Debacle* fit much better, especially when he could not recall a single moment of the slip into temptation that led to this painful decision. To counter his disbelief, she had brought forth witnesses. The result could not be denied. He was responsible.

Oh, Prosperity, dear Prosperity, what have I done to you?

He ran a finger over the daguerreotype that he had commissioned immediately after she agreed to marry him. The frozen image could not capture the glow of compassion in her gold-flecked hazel eyes. The interminable wait without moving a muscle resulted in too severe an expression. Despite the hardships Prosperity had endured, she brought joy and light to the darkest day. Her plain gown and cap in this picture reflected her present lowly estate. He had planned to one day clothe her in the fine gowns she deserved.

That hope was gone, whisked away in a single night of shameful revelry.

He kneaded his throbbing temples. Why couldn't he remember? He had no recollection of Aileen Carlyle beyond some playful jesting when she brought the rum to the table he and his soldier friends occupied. The first toasts led to more and more until he awoke the next morning in the soldiers' barracks with a splitting headache and no idea how he'd gotten there. After a stern reprimand, the incident seemed over until Miss Carlyle approached him two weeks ago with news that chilled his bones.

Why hadn't he turned away at the grogshop door? Why had he even gone there? He never drank spirits, but the men had insisted, and he had been flattered by their attention. He'd let camaraderie draw him into temptation.

Why such a terrible price?

How many times he had prayed for God to relieve him of this burden. How often he had dropped to his knees pleading for a miracle that would absolve him, but this sin could not be whisked out the door.

The fruit of his error grew, and honor dictated he must set matters to rights. That entailed breaking the unwelcome news to his fiancée. Such a thing ought to be handled in person, but she dwelt nearly fourteen hundred miles north of this tropical island outpost. A letter was his only means of communication. Delivery would take weeks, perhaps a month if weather delayed the ship. By the time she received this . . .

He heaved a sigh.

It would be done.

Irrevocable in the sight of God.

Thus he must write the painful letter, and a letter began with a salutation. He drew a clean sheet of paper from the desk drawer.

As an engineer working on the construction of the new fort, named in honor of the late President Zachary Taylor, he would move to larger quarters sufficient for a family after the wedding.

The event that had once filled him with anticipation now churned up dread. He had always envisioned a proper ceremony back home on Nantucket Island. His parents and brothers, cousins and uncles would witness the joyous uniting of kindred spirits in their family church. He had promised to wed as soon as he finished his tour of duty in Key West. Though this meant years apart, the income he earned here would build a solid financial foundation to start a family. The reasoning had made perfect sense at the time, and she had gazed up at him with complete trust.

Oh that he had tossed reason to the wind and married her at once.

He raked fingers through his tangled locks. Nothing could be done now to alter the plans. Fate—or rather, despicable conduct—dictated his future. He would wed sooner rather than later, and not to the woman he adored.

She gazed at him sweetly from the daguerreotype. Despite the loss and hardship she'd endured, hope shone in her eyes. That hope had been rooted in his promise.

He slammed the image facedown on his desk. How could he look her in the eye?

She trusted him, and he had betrayed that trust. He must break her heart. Dear, gentle Prosperity deserved the best after all she had suffered, not another loss.

Unable to bear not seeing her, he lifted the image once more. He traced the curve of her cheeks to the dimpled chin. If he closed his eyes, he could still hear her resonant voice, surprisingly deep for one so small. He could still feel the softness of her hair, a lock of which was buried deep in his trunk. He could still smell the freshness of the sea upon her, as if she'd just climbed the dunes to look for her father's lost whaling ship.

"You deserve better," he whispered.

The cricket he'd not managed to evict from his room answered with a shrill taunt.

He ought to destroy the daguerreotype. That part of his life was over. But he could not bear to lose this last link to her, so he tore apart the frame and removed the silvered plate. He tucked the image between the pages of his Bible. Then he closed the volume and slid it into the bottom desk drawer beneath his engineering manuals and the Army regulations that ordered his days.

The time for regret was over. A man accepted his responsibilities, no matter how distasteful.

He picked up the pen, his hand steadier.

Dearest Prosperity, he scrawled, forgoing the initial "my." She was dearest to him still, though he could no longer claim her affection.

> *I cannot ask your forgiveness, nor do I deserve it. Though I am tempted to soften the blow, your honest, practical nature would not wish me to couch what I must tell you in false cheer. Thus I will be straightforward, trusting that your affections have so sufficiently dimmed over the two years of our separation that this news will not inflict great suffering.*
>
> *I fear that I must break our engagement.*

The trembling began again, so violently that he had to set down the pen. Driven by torment, he sprang to his feet and paced to the darkened window. Yanking off his spectacles, he stared into the night. In the distance, a few lanterns dotted anchored vessels. Nearer, lamps brightened the commander's windows and glowed dimly at one end of the soldiers' barracks. Soon they would be put out, leaving only the moon and the stars to light the post.

No light could illuminate David's soul. Such sooty blackness could never be scrubbed clean. She was better off without him, but he was lost without her.

Despair welled again. Once more he pushed it down. Honor dictated but one course. Lives would be wrecked no matter which path he took, but only one protected the innocent.

Once again he sat at his desk and picked up the pen. He

could not profess what was in his heart, that he loved her still, that he would love her until the day he died. That would be cruel. No, this letter must sever their bond in a single stroke, break every connecting sinew, and leave not even a ray of hope. Only then could the wound heal. Only then could his beloved let go of the future they had planned together and turn her gaze toward another.

He dipped the nib in ink and touched it to paper. The words did not come easily. His unsteady hand bore witness. He scratched it out as best he could.

I will marry tomorrow.

Award-winning author **Christine Johnson** fell in love with the beautiful Florida Keys during her first visit in 1985. Since then, she has spent more and more time there each year, reading about the history and exploring the islands. Born on the shores of Lake Michigan, she has always been drawn to the water. From sailing trips on the Great Lakes with her husband to her years as a docent aboard a 1908 passenger ship, she gravitates to all things nautical.

Her historical romances have garnered the Laurel Wreath and the Winter Rose award, among others. She is a member of American Christian Fiction Writers, Romance Writers of America, and the Faith, Hope, and Love chapter of Romance Writers of America. After many years as a librarian, she is thrilled to write full-time now. Thank you, hubby!

These days she splits her time between Michigan and Florida with her ship captain husband. When not writing, she loves to kayak and explore God's beautiful creation. You can connect with her through her website at http://christineelizabethjohn son.com, on Facebook at http://www.facebook.com/Christine JohnsonAuthor, or on Twitter @ChristineJWrite.

Christine Johnson

WHERE ADVENTURE LEADS HOME

ChristineElizabethJohnson.com

 Christine Johnson Author

 ChristineJWrite